Ryan Bartelmay graduated from the University of Iowa in 1998, where he was a member of the Undergraduate Writer's Workshop, and then went on to Columbia University to receive an MFA in fiction writing in 2005. He lives in Chicago with his wife, daughter and two cats.

ONWARD TOWARD

What we're

GOING TOWARD

Ryan BARTELMAY

corsair

CORSAIR

First published in the United States of America in 2013 by Ig Publishing.

First published in Great Britain in 2014 by Corsair.

1 3 5 7 9 10 8 6 4 2

A CIP catalogue record for this book
is available from the British Library.

ISBN: 978-1-4721-1534-8 (trade paperback)
ISBN: 978-1-4721-1535-5 (ebook)

Printed and bound in Great Britain by CPI Group (UK) Ltd, Croydon, CR0 4YY

To my girls, Rene and Vivian

"Any idiot can face a crisis; it's day-to-day living that wears you out."

—Anton Chekhov

One

Chic Waldbeeser & Diane von Schmidt

September 1950

On the Trailways bus bound for Florida, Diane wouldn't hold Chic's hand, wouldn't even look at it sitting on his knee like a dead fish. She pretended to sleep. Then she didn't and glared straight ahead at the derby hat of the man in front of them. This wasn't like her. For the last month, she had been chattering like a psychotic woodpecker about their honeymoon—*they were going to do this, they were going to do that, this and that, and this and that, and this*—and here they were, and she was grinding her teeth loud enough he could hear it.

At a bathroom break in Kentucky, he asked her if she wanted a NuGrape or some Nibs. She huffed and stared out the bus window. Inside the filling station, he bought a bottle of Coca-Cola from the vending machine and stood at the filling station's screen door watching a few navy guys taunt a yip-yip dog with a stick. His mind flashed to Lijy, his brother's wife. He wondered what she was doing right now. What was that back rub about at the reception?

The old man behind the pay counter said, "That Truman shouldn't even be in Washington. My vote would have been for Wallace. That is, if I could get someone to watch the store so I could vote."

Chic took a pull off his soda.

"Couldn't though. My son doesn't wanna have anything to do with it. And my wife, she spends all day at the sewing machine."

"They're gonna hurt that dog," Chic said.

"Nah. That dog's fine. Seen it get hit by a truck, get back

up and keep barking. We're all like that dog. We all just keep barking."

Chic dug a dime from his pocket. He was gonna get himself some Korn Kurls.

"Hey, where's that bus headed?"

"Florida. Then, I don't know. Back I guess."

"You know if I was going to Florida, I'd go to Gatorland. I hear they got albino alligators."

"I don't think my wife would like that."

"You got a wife?"

"Yes sir." Chic set his dime on the counter.

"I'd find me a way to get to Gatorland. Don't be letting your wife not let you see an albino alligator."

"You seen it?"

"Heard about it."

Back on the road, Chic stuffed Korn Kurls in his mouth. He was thinking about that albino alligator. He'd never seen anything albino. There was a kid in his grade school class, a kid whose name he couldn't remember, who had real blond hair and everyone said he was an albino, but he wasn't. Albinos had pink eyes and that kid had blue eyes. Then that kid moved away. Whatever happened to him? He probably went to high school somewhere, probably got married, probably got a job.

"Can't believe you sometimes, Chic Waldbeeser."

He looked at his new wife, her anger so obvious he could hear it whirling like a drill.

"You haven't said anything to me in . . . " He looked at his watch. ". . . twelve hours. Now you tell me you can't believe me. What's wrong with you?"

She cocked herself away from him and stared out the window. The bus passed a billboard that read, "Drive carefully. The life you save may be your own."

He knew he had to do some fancy footwork. He dangled a Korn Kurl in front of her. "Want one? They're good."

She rested her head on the window and pretended to be asleep.

Chic ate the Kurl. He tried nudging her with his elbow a couple of times. He tried poking her arm with his index finger. After about a minute, she opened her eyes and said: "Will you please stop that."

"Why are you mad?"

"You should know." She closed her eyes.

He poked her arm—once, twice, three times, four times.

"If you don't stop that, I'm going to scream."

He finished his Korn Kurls and checked out the other passengers in the bus. The navy guys were sitting in the back talking in low whispers. A peanut sailed from the back of the bus and clinked off the woman in the seat opposite Chic. Chic turned around and saw the navy guys giggling. One held a hand over his mouth. The woman wiped her arm. She'd gotten on the bus at Carbondale, Illinois and Chic had heard her tell the driver she was going to visit her "Nana" in Pensacola. He looked over at Diane to see if she was awake. Her eyes were closed.

Chic never had a girlfriend in high school. Every time he approached a girl he froze up and his tongue felt like a sponge. He was not an unattractive boy with his flattop haircut, cuffed Levi's, and starched white t-shirt, but the confused look on his face made him appear like he was a few steps behind the herd. His shoes were always untied. After walking into a room he wasn't quite sure where to go, so he just stood there, causing a bottleneck in the doorway. Teachers and other adults liked him, though. He smiled a lot, kept his fingernails trimmed, said "please" and "thank you" and called women "ma'am." In November, at a Middleville football game, while he sat in the bleachers, Diane approached him and told him that he, Chic Waldbeeser, was going to take her to the Dairy Queen after the game. He was sitting with a bunch of guys who weren't even really worth mentioning, guys just about like him, guys who all stopped talking and craned their necks to look up at Diane. Everyone knew Diane von Schmidt. Her father was a math teacher, but she didn't act like a math teacher's daughter. She wore high-heeled shoes to the school dances. She'd gone steady with Randy Rugaard for two years, and in gym class, he bragged that she was a real "Sheba." And by that he meant she was a tomcat. And by that he meant that she pretty much wore him out.

After ice cream, sitting in the front seat of Chic's mother's Plymouth four-door sedan, Diane stuck her mouth on Chic's and gave him a big lip-to-lip smooch-a-roo. She pulled away and giggled, wiped her mouth. Then she asked, "What do you want more than anything in the whole wide world?" Her voice was full of the type of confidence that made Chic shaky.

"A big dog," Chic said.

"No. I mean in life."

He thought about this. A big dog would make things a little better. Big dogs made happy families, and for the past ten years, his family life had been in shambles. When he was eight, his father went outside behind the barn and sat down in the snow and, no kidding here, froze himself to death. Diane knew about this. Everyone did. And they all looked at Chic a little bit out of the corner of their eyes as a result. He pretty much didn't let himself think about it all that much. He just thought about having his own family someday, and that big dog. That seemed to be the way to handle things like this—keep marching forward and don't look over your shoulder. That's what his mother had done. The day after his father's funeral she was riding around in Tom Mc-Neeley's Dodge Fore-Point pickup. What did he—Chic Wald-beeser—want more than anything? That was easy if he let himself think about it, but he pushed it to the back of his mind, way back where the spiderwebs grew and there was the constant sound of a dripping faucet. But since she asked, since she was Diane von Schmidt, daughter of a math teacher, a real Sheba, he was going to tell her. "I want a normal family," he whispered.

"Excuse me?"

"A normal family. A normal life."

About a year later, Diane's father shelled out for a big wedding. Blessed Sacrament, the Catholic church in Middleville, Ilinois was stuffed full of Diane's aunts, uncles, cousins, second cousins, and third cousins. Chic's mother sent a fruit basket and card that said she couldn't make it. She was down in Florida learning how to play tennis. She had moved down there with Tom McNeeley the day after Chic graduated from high school. The lone invitee on the Waldbeeser side was Mr. Kenneth Waxman, a friend of Chic's father; Mr. Waxman was squeezed off on the far side of the church next to Diane's third cousin Mary Lou from Junction City, Kansas, and her seven children.

An elderly uncle on the von Schmidt side, a longtime resident of Middleville, leaned over to his wife and said, "Now, what exactly did the Waldbeeser father do?"

His wife said, "Committed suicide, maybe ten years ago."

"Yeah, yeah . . . I know that. What did he do, *do*, I mean."

She shrugged. "Worked at the cannery probably."

Chic's brother, Buddy, stood at the altar next to Chic with the ring in his pocket. He'd recently returned from out East or West, or someplace, whereever it was. He wasn't too forthcoming. When he returned, just in time for Chic's high school graduation, he had a wife, an Indian woman, who, because she was Indian and dressed in a sari and wore flip-flop shoes that showed her toes, caused the townsfolk to whisper. Buddy was a long boy, tall and lean like a two-by-four. In a crowded room, his was the only face you'd see, but that's where the metaphor for head and shoulders above the crowd stopped. He had gotten mostly Cs in high school. He was shy. At the reception, he got lit up on the spiked punch and, during his best man speech, slurred his words and blabbered on about his father and his father's father and his father's father's father from Germany, Bascom Waldbeeser, who had founded Middleville with his wife Kiki, and their son, Bascom Jr., after the couple came north from New Orleans.

The people seated on folding chairs looked at each other. Every Middlevillian knew R.S. Archerbach and his sons had founded Middleville and started the cannery in 1880-something. There was a book, *Middleville, Illinois: Our Town, Our Lives, Our Story,* put together by Mrs. Ruth Van Eatton, an English teacher at the high school. The book had black and white photographs of the Archerbach family and other first Middleville families and the pumpkin cannery (which is now a National Historic Landmark) on Main Street circa 1884 and the railroad stop on Jefferson and First Street that connected Middleville with Peoria, twenty miles to the north. Diane leaned over and asked Chic why his brother was claiming the Waldbeeser family was responsible for the cannery. Chic shrugged, pretending not to know what his brother was up to, but he knew. This was what their grandfather had told them when they were young, a fairy tale meant to give Buddy and Chic incentive to pull themselves up by the bootstraps and to go forth into the world and chase down their destinies. Or, at least, that's how Chic interpreted the story.

After fifteen minutes, a ten-year-old second cousin switched off the lights, and the entire reception hall went black. Aunts and other women gasped. Someone whispered, "Thank god."

When the lights came back on, Buddy was in the middle of the dance floor, wavering a little bit, drunk. He held up his glass. "Congrajewl . . ." He burped. "Congrajewlations."

Diane's father guided him out a side door to the parking lot, and someone started the jukebox, Patti Page singing "All My Love."

With the reception getting back to normal and people grabbing the hands of their loved ones and dragging them to the dance floor, Chic found himself standing behind Lijy, Buddy's wife. She was picking lint off the front of her sari. The whole reception, Chic had noticed Diane's aunts and uncles nudging each other and whispering about her. Other than pictures in books, she was the first Indian anyone in Middleville had ever seen.

On Main Street, when she went into Witzig's, the department store across from the Dairy Queen, Buick Roadmasters literally screeched to a stop and eight-year old kids in backseats rolled down their windows and pointed. Standing there on the fringe of the dance floor, Chic pressed in, getting close enough that he could smell her hair. It smelled odd but good—earthy and spicy, musky maybe. She reminded Chic of a doll.

She turned around and cleared her throat.

Chic immediately noticed the bulge of her breasts under the sari. He hadn't noticed them before, but there they were—about the size of grapefruits. "I was . . ." He quickly looked at his wing-tips and tightly closed his eyes. She'd seen him; she'd seen him staring at her breasts. "Sorry," he whispered.

She wasn't even paying attention to him. She was looking through him, beyond him, to where Buddy had disappeared through the side door to the parking lot. Chic glanced over his shoulder, and there was Buddy, coming back into the reception, Diane's father behind him. Buddy was wiping his mouth with a hanky and his tie was loosened. He was pale, like he'd just vomited.

"Do you want a back rub?" Lijy asked.

Chic wide-eyed her.

"Did you hear me?"

Was she serious? He scanned the reception. On the dance floor, Diane was doing some sort of high knee thing while a guy played an accordion. Family members had made a circle around her and were clapping along. Lijy grabbed his forearm and led him to an empty table and told him to take off his tuxedo coat and sit down in the chair. Then she laid her hands on him. They were cold, but she did this trick where she rubbed them together, then shoved them back up his shirt and squeezed his shoulders, and it felt good—better than good.

Chic didn't know this because he was too busy nearly drooling, but while Lijy rubbed and kneaded and massaged his back, she kept a sharp eye on Buddy, who hadn't even noticed that she had dragged his brother, the groom of the gosh dang wedding, to an empty table and was giving him a back massage. She watched Buddy stumble up to the punch table, where some woman ladled him a glass of punch. In one swift motion, he downed the punch and held out his glass for another.

"This is your ansa phalak," she whispered into Chic's ear. She moved her hands to the middle of his back. "The vrihati. Your parshva sandhi. Your katika tarunam." She hoped Buddy would turn around. She willed him to turn around.

Chic thought about Diane looking over, but then that thought floated out of his mind because the back rub felt so good; it just felt so good. "Keep doing that," he whispered. "Right there."

But then Lijy stopped and brushed past him, leaving him sitting in the chair with his shirt untucked and his tuxedo jacket tossed on the table. He saw Buddy going out the side door to the parking lot; Lijy followed after him.

Chic was exhausted in the motel room after the bus ride to Pensacola. Plus, Diane still wasn't talking to him. After they brushed their teeth and tucked themselves into bed, he lay in the dark thinking. The entire wedding day he had fended off the jokes from Diane's uncles and cousins about the honeymoon. And now here they were, and she was mad, and he was nervous. Her back was to him. He nudged up behind her and threw his arm around her. This would do it. This was it. Only a matter of time now. He waited. Her hair didn't smell like Lijy's; it smelled like bus and cigarette smoke. He nuzzled closer, spooning her. He counted to ten. Then he counted to twenty. The motel room's window was open and the drapes billowed in the ocean breeze.

Diane opened her eyes and looked at his hand on the mattress. He still had his watch on. She rolled out from under his arm and went into the bathroom, closing and locking the door.

This was it. She had gone into the bathroom to freshen up, to get ready, to maybe put on something more appropriate, to turn into the real Sheba that Randy had told him about. Chic slid off his boxers and lay there in the dark with a steaming erection. Then he felt weird lying naked on a motel bed and put his boxers back on. He listened to Diane in the bathroom. He couldn't hear much. Maybe she was putting on some perfume and was going to—any minute—throw open the door and strut into the room and hop on him and get this honeymoon rolling.

The Seashell Inn, a pink stucco motor lodge, sat behind Jack's Hamburger Shack. Jack's was a drive-through with a bevy of waitresses hustling hamburgers, hot dogs, and French fries to tourists' cars. Below their motel window was Jack's back screen door, which led to the kitchen. Two cooks were standing outside the screen door smoking cigarettes and talking about going to a place called Mo's Cantina after they cleaned up the kitchen.

After twenty minutes, Diane hadn't come out of the bathroom, and there was no sign that she was going to.

"Diane?"

She didn't answer.

"Honey."

She still didn't answer.

Chic stared at the ceiling, thinking about Lijy. He imagined her in the bathroom pulling a brush through her long black hair.

"Honey, did you see something at the reception?"

She didn't answer.

"I can explain that."

The sink was turned on, then it went off.

"It's not what you think."

When Chic woke up the next morning, Diane still hadn't come out. Chic got up and knocked on the bathroom door, but Diane didn't answer him. He imagined her sitting on the toilet. He knocked again. "Honey."

Nothing.

Fine. Be that way. Be mad. It was just a back rub, a lousy back rub, and besides, he had apologized. Besides that: it only lasted like two minutes. He threw open the drapes and let the Florida sunshine flood the room. He wasn't going to let this ruin his honeymoon.

In the motel lobby, he ate a complimentary orange, then he walked down the Pensacola Beach pier. He had all this fenced-in sexual energy—his honeymoon, the back rub—all of it bouncing around inside him like a pinball. He felt like a rocket on the launchpad smoking and fuming. He had a headache. The entire morning his left testicle throbbed, or actually, throbbed wasn't the right description. It felt heavy, a boulder testicle swaying back and forth while he walked down the boardwalk. He knew what he needed to do. He ducked into the penny arcade and found the bathroom back by the Skeeball. He stepped into a stall and locked the door behind him. He unzipped himself and, standing over the toilet, masturbated quickly, thinking about Lijy, thinking about her hands on his back and her grapefruit-size breasts, thinking about Diane, too, and what Randy Rugaard had said about her.

That afternoon, Chic went tourist. He walked up and down the boardwalk with purpose. He was pretty much strutting, although he felt a little shy and found it difficult to look anyone in the eye. After all, he'd masturbated in a public bathroom. But, physically, he felt great. Better than great. The best. Wonderful. Relieved. He checked out the casino and the souvenir stands. He ate a stick of cotton candy. He bought a guayabera shirt and rolled up his khakis and walked along the water so that his feet got wet. He didn't like wet sand squishing between his toes, so he went back to the boardwalk. He ate lunch at a place called the Katy Hooper and drank a Spearman's Straight Eight Beer. There were posters on the wall advertising an upcoming Friday night boxing match between Bruno Schneider and Jimmy Dixon. In a rack of tourist brochures, Chic spotted a brochure for Gatorland and grabbed it and stuck it in his back pocket.

When he returned to the Seashell Inn, Diane was still in the bathroom. Chic flopped on the bed and unfolded the Gatorland brochure. There was an albino alligator. He heard Diane wring out a washcloth. He suddenly felt guilty for what he'd done in the penny arcade's bathroom. He told himself any other guy would have done just what he did. What if someone saw him? That would be embarrassing. No one saw him. He'd checked for feet under the other stalls. He was fine. It was over. He had to do it. He unbuttoned his new guayabera shirt and let air from the open window breeze over his bare chest. He heard the dull, incomprehensible muttering voices of the drive-through patrons outside Jack's Hamburger Shack. He wondered what was going on back in Middleville. He thought about his job at the pumpkin cannery. Mr. Meyers, his boss, hadn't wanted him to take such a long time off.

Chic looked at the closed bathroom door. "People only go on honeymoons once, you know."

He waited for an answer.

"I said, people only go on honeymoons once."

Secretly he hoped she'd unlock the bathroom door and burst into the room and get into an argument with him. He'd tell her about the penny arcade bathroom. He'd tell her he thought about Lijy while he was doing it.

In the end, she didn't burst into the room, and he folded up the brochure and set it on the nightstand.

"I'm not going to wait around for you all day," he said. "I'm going to the pool."

The pool was behind the Seashell Inn, adjacent to the parking lot. It was a tiny, egg-shaped thing with a shallow and deep end and a slide. Three kids, who all looked to be siblings, slid down the slide and made a whole lot of unnecessary noise. Chic just wanted some peace and quiet, wanted to soak in the pool and figure out how he could cheer Diane up. It was only a stupid back rub. Sure, Lijy was an attractive woman, and he was attracted to her—who wouldn't be—but she was his brother's wife, *his brother's wife*. Not that his brother deserved a woman like that. He didn't. His brother was a strange guy. He had pretty much abandoned Chic as soon as he had graduated from high school, leaving Chic to fend for himself, to watch his mother and Tom McNeeley seal their relationship with pot roast dinners and long talks, with giggling on the porch. Not to mention that Buddy was always leaving Lijy in that big house they lived in on the "new side" of Middleville to go off and do whatever the heck he did with those gold coins he collected. If Lijy were his wife, Chic would sit next to her on the couch and put his arm around her and never let go. But he and Buddy were different. For one, there were the gold coins. Buddy had suitcases full of them. The gold coin thing had begun when their grandfather, Bascom Jr., the same guy who made up the story about their family founding Middleville, gave them each an 1899 Double Eagle. Buddy carried that coin with him everywhere he went. He took it out at random times, like at recess while all the other kids were playing tetherball. Chic bought a stick of gum with his, chewed that stick for about twenty minutes, then spit the wad on the sidewalk and forgot all about the stupid gold coin. On Sunday afternoons when they were kids, their grandfather lugged over his personal collection, which he kept in steel military ammunition boxes. While he and Buddy held the coins under the magnifying glass, their grandfather told Buddy (and Chic but Chic wasn't picking through the coins with them) his elaborate story about his father's father, their great-grandfather, Bascom, being responsible for founding Middleville. According to the story, Junior's Pumpkins—the pride of Middleville—were named Junior's Pumpkins because of him, Bascom Jr., their grandfather. He was the Junior. Chic remembered his brother staring at his grandfather as he told him this, his mouth a little agape, a look of amazement on his face. They both believed him, of course. Buddy was eight, Chic was five. Because of the story, Buddy always talked about their grandfather—Grandpa *this* and Grandpa *that*. Not to mention, whenever they went to Stafford's, the grocery store, with their mother, Buddy would run off to the canned food aisle and stand there admiring the rows and rows of Junior's Pumpkins. Buddy was the older brother. He should know better. But, apparently, he believed it, or at least, he wanted to believe it. Buddy had always been the kinda guy that wanted something. But he had something. Didn't he know that he had something? If he didn't look out, he was going to lose what he had. And he, Chic Waldbeeser, had something, too, and he wasn't about to lose what he had.

Later that afternoon, Diane waltzed into the pool area wearing a massive sun hat with a brim so large it cast a dark shadow over her entire face. Chic was soaking in the shallow end and watched her position a recliner sun chair. Her back was to him, and when she slipped off her robe, her shoulders were white as Elmer's glue, and she wore one of those swimsuits like the girls on the beach, with a skirt that covered her upper legs. She futzed around with the chair, and finally, when she got it where she wanted it, she sat down and started to read a book.

Chic climbed out of the water and slopped over to her, blocking her sun and dripping on her legs. She put her book down and squinted up at him.

"I'm sorry."

"I saw you, Chic. You and that . . . your brother's wife, the Indian woman."

"I said I'm sorry."

It hadn't registered until now, but she was hurt. He could see it in the way her lip quivered. This was a different Diane, not the woman who knew what she wanted and didn't stop until she got it. Chic had fallen hard for that woman and her confidence, but this woman wasn't confident. She looked like she was about to burst into tears. He sat down and touched her leg.

"What she was doing was an Indian custom. They give back rubs to the groom. That's what they do. That's what she told me they do."

Diane picked up her book. "I don't believe you."

"Do you think I'd get a back rub from another woman at my own wedding?" He nuzzled up close to her. "I'm married to you, pumpkin pie."

"Is it really their custom?"

"She was saying these weird words in my ear. I think she was blessing us."

"You telling the truth?"

"Scout's honor."

Diane let him kiss her on the cheek and snuggle with her on the sun chair. The remainder of the day they lounged by the pool, and when the sun sunk below the motel, they covered their legs with a towel. After showers, they ate dinner at a place called the Crab Shack. The waiter had on a black bowtie, and all the men at the other tables wore seersucker suits. Underneath the table, Diane kept pawing Chic's leg and hand. During one moment, when Diane had some difficulty cracking into a crab leg, grimacing as she applied more force, he recalled her laboring over a difficult test question in science class, pencil eraser in her mouth, her eyes tightly closed. He was going to make a life with this woman. He loved her, or he thought he did. He liked that she wasn't mad at him anymore. But, then again, there was Lijy. But he was going to push her way, way, way back in his mind, back there with the cobwebs and the dripping faucet, back there where he set things on a shelf to forget about.

When they got back to the room, Diane hung the Do Not Disturb sign on the doorknob. Chic climbed on the bed. Diane pulled her dinner dress over her head. She was near nude in her underwear and bra.

"Have you ever done this before?" she asked.

Chic shook his head no.

"Nervous?"

"Little bit."

She told him to get out of his clothes, and Chic quickly

kicked off his shoes and took off his chinos and shirt. He watched her unthread his belt from his pants. "You've been a bad boy, Chic Waldbeeser." She held his belt like a whip. "Turn around."

"You're not going to whip me with that belt are you?"

"Maybe."

"This isn't what I—"

"Go along with me, will ya, Chic? Please."

"Sorry." He turned around and noticed the curtain opposite the bed fluttering in the breeze. Outside, he heard the screen door at Jack's Hamburger Shack open and slam shut, the rustle of someone putting something in the trash can.

She smacked his butt with her hand. "You like that?"

"Not really."

"Chic. Please. Tell me you like it."

"I like it."

She whipped him with the belt.

"OUCH! Jesus Christ."

"No, more back rubs."

She whipped him again.

"Ouch!"

"You hear me?"

"Yes. I hear you."

She cracked the belt and gave him a sultry smile. "Isn't this fun?"

He reluctantly nodded, but thought about crawling underneath the bed or cowering in the corner. He swallowed hard.

She flipped off the light, and it was pitch black. He couldn't see her, could only hear the sizzle of grease in the kitchen of Jack's Hamburger Shack.

She was coming toward the bed. "Say something."

"Here," he whispered.

"Keep saying it."

"Here. Here. Here."

He felt a depression in the mattress, then she was straddling him. She pinned him down. Her wet mouth found his and she pressed into him so hard her teeth clinked against his. "Oh, I want you, Chic. Do you want me?"

He was trying to wiggle into a more comfortable position, but she had a hold of his wrists, his arms pinned above his head.

"Do you want me, Chic?"

"Yeah."

"Then what's the matter?"

"I can't move."

She let go, and he repositioned himself and propped himself up on his elbows. His eyes had adjusted to the darkness and he could see the outline of her sitting on the bed.

"Something's the matter," she said.

"I just . . . you know . . . I thought it would be a little different. Slower maybe."

She tossed the belt and the buckle thudded on the floor. "You take the lead."

He kissed her cheek, but she grabbed his hand and guided it to where it was warm and moist. "Get on top of me."

He did what she said, and she grabbed his behind, squeezing it and digging her fingernails into the skin. "That kinda hurts," he said.

"Come on, Chic. Get aggressive."

"I'm not really—"

"Pretend. Come on. Do me. Fill me with your sperm."

"What?"

"Fill me up with your sperm."

He didn't really like hearing his wife say that. It sounded dirty. He moved his hips this way and that way and up and down. He had no idea what he was doing or where he was shoving.

"That's not it. Here." She took his penis and guided him into her.

Chic froze. Oh my gosh. The top of his head tingled. He was inside of her. How did this feel? It felt . . . well, it felt . . . he couldn't really explain how it felt.

She bucked her hips. "Come on. Go."

He was afraid to go. She seemed . . . *experienced*. He thought of earlier that day in the bathroom of the penny arcade and immediately felt guilty.

"Go. Do it. Fill me up. Fill me with your sperm." She grabbed his hips and pulled and pushed and pulled and pushed. It was only two or three more thrusts, and Chic closed his eyes and his muscles tensed, and he saw a rocket on a launchpad, fire and smoke mushrooming from its bottom. He pushed into her as far as he could. The rocket lifted off the launchpad. His body went limp, and he collapsed on top of her. "Ohhhhh," he sighed.

She squirmed out from under him.

He rolled over on his back. "You like it?"

"Not really, but hopefully it did the job." She picked up her underwear and went to the bathroom and shut the door.

Chic & Diane Waldbeeser & Lijy Waldbeeser

■

September 1950–August 1951

When Chic and Diane returned from Florida, Diane's parents offered to help with a down payment on a house. The first one they toured was a Cape Cod with a detached garage on Edgewood Street, a dead-end street not far from Middleville's police station. While Diane and her parents sized up the three bedrooms and one bathroom with the real estate agent, Phyllis Glover, a woman they all knew since Phyllis's son and daughter had gone to school with Chic and Diane, Chic stood in the backyard, looking at the back of the house. Well, it wasn't the "new" part of Middleville, but the house had recently been re-sided with aluminum siding. Chic got down on his hands and knees and felt the grass with his hand. He put his cheek in the grass, letting the blades tickle his face. He'd walk on this lawn barefoot on summer mornings as his dog went about its business in the corner over there. He'd play with his kids in this grass. He ran his hands over the top of the blades. He stood up, wiping his hands. He heard a door open and a dog bark. Behind him, he noticed the neighbor, an older guy, watching him, his hands in his pockets and a cigarette dangling from his mouth. Chic nodded at the man. The man took the cigarette from his mouth and blew a wad of smoke. His dog, a small lapdog, squatted in the middle of the yard.

"My wife and I are thinking about buying the house," Chic said.

The man squinted at him.

Chic couldn't help but think that in a few years he and this guy could swap stories over the fence while their dogs frolicked in their yards.

"Hey, you know what kinda grass this is?"

"It's grass."

"Like is it Kentucky bluegrass? Crabgrass?"

The man stared at Chic. "You're one of the Waldbeeser boys, aren't ya?"

"That's right."

"How's your mother doing? I used to see her around town, but I ain't seen her in a while."

"My mother's a stinking polecat, and don't you ever ask about her again. You hear?" He left the man standing in his backyard with his cigarette and dog.

Inside, he found Diane and her parents standing in the living room, Phyllis Glover explaining something about south-facing windows. Diane made eye contact with Chic and smiled.

"We'll take it," Chic said.

Diane's father shot him a look, and Chic immediately felt like he'd done something wrong.

"Honey," Diane said. "We haven't even looked at the upstairs yet."

"Yeah, Chic. Patience," her father said.

"It's not like we're not going to like the upstairs. It's just bedrooms, right? We're just going to sleep up there."

They moved in three weeks later. Chic picked up his life where he had left off before the honeymoon, punching the clock every morning at the pumpkin cannery. He wore a hard helmet and white lab coat and stood in a giant, airy room watching cans of Junior's Pumpkins blur by on a conveyor belt. His job was to detect imperfections—dents, torn labels, anything that would diminish the appeal of a can on a store shelf. If he saw something, he stopped the belt and took a closer look. Chic had an impeccable eye for defects, and Mr. Meyers told him it was only a matter of time before he was promoted out of quality control to a management position on the second floor where he'd have a secretary who answered the phone and a desk stocked with pencils. In fact, Mr. Meyers told Chic that he was grooming his own son, Butch, for one of those jobs. A year younger than Chic, Butch was a senior in high school and already looked the part of management; he wore his hair combed to the side and horn-rimmed spectacles, and after school he spent two hours doing an "internship," which basically meant he emptied garbage cans.

Chic knew those offices on the second floor well. During his first week on the job, he had found himself on the second floor delivering some mail that had accidentally found its way to the production area. He asked an elderly woman, a secretary, which office had belonged to Bascom Waldbeeser. It had been nearly fifteen years since his grandfather worked at the cannery, but the woman pointed to a closed door. So, it was true. After his made-up story about the founding of Middleville, Chic wasn't sure if he should take anything his grandfather said at face value. Chic looked back at the woman and asked if he could go inside. She nodded that it was fine, and Chic took hold of the door. The room wasn't an office but a storage closet stacked with broken typewriters, boxes of pencils, and other office supplies. "He didn't have a desk," the woman said. "He had a cart."

Chic wasn't sure he understood.

"When he got too old to work on the production floor, he was moved up here to deliver supplies to the offices." She motioned to the office doors along the corridor. "Pretty much, though, he just kept the closet organized. You're BJ's grandson, aren't ya?"

Chic nodded.

"Didn't your mother just move down to Florida?"

Chic closed his eyes. He didn't want to talk about his mother. Everyone was always asking about his mother.

"How's she like it? Florida would be too hot for me. Nice in the winter, though. But, hey, are you okay? You don't look so good. You feeling okay?"

"I think I should get some air."

"Yeah. Right. Okay. Hey, when you talk to your mother, tell her Ellen Hastings said hello."

The Cape Cod needed fixing up, and Chic got to work. Up along the house, he planted box elder bushes. He cleaned out the gutters. He built a workbench at the back of the garage and hung some tools on the Peg-Board above the bench. He nailed up wainscoting in the dining nook. He painted the bedroom walls. Sometimes he'd be working and would feel like someone was looking at him, and he'd glance over his shoulder, and there would be his neighbor standing in a window, staring. Chic would wave, but the guy would just shut the shades.

Diane did light housecleaning, and every morning Chic showered and headed off to the cannery. Walking to the locker room, carrying his lunchbox, he often saw Mr. Meyers in his office that overlooked the production floor. He was always drinking a cup of coffee and looking down at some papers spread out on his desk, a pencil behind his ear, a look of fear on his face, like at any moment the pumpkin cannery could disappear into a sinkhole and be gone forever. Mr. Myers turned forty the week Chic started at the cannery, and Chic thought it was odd that he was already bald. Forty years old and totally bald. Chic didn't want to feel that same sort of fear that made a guy lose his hair. He wanted to feel like he felt right now, at nineteen. He lived in

Middleville, which was a bit of a misnomer, since the town wasn't exactly in the center of the state—it was a bit southwest of center, actually. If one flew over it in a plane, it probably wouldn't even be noticed. It was simply a cluster of houses and a school, a gas station, a couple of parks, and a few churches, all of which sprouted out of the Illinois dirt the way corn sprouted every June. Chic sometimes stood in his house and thought about how this was his town. He knew everyone—the teachers at the high school, the people at Stafford's, the grocery store. Everyone. And everyone knew him. Chic liked the comfort in that, even if everyone knew him as the son of the man who sat down behind his barn and froze himself to death. Knowing everyone took the surprise out of life, and Chic Waldbeeser didn't want life jumping out of the bushes and surprising him.

At Christmas, Mrs. von Schmidt decorated her house with an artificial, feather tree with gold balls and hung stockings on the mantel. When Chic saw the stockings, he stared at them, his hands in his pockets. When he was a boy, Christmas had never been anything but his mother clomping around in the kitchen, cussing under her breath. She would spend all morning making ham with slices of pineapple while his father sat in the living room drinking Scotch and staring at the snow. When dinner was ready, he, his mother, Buddy, their grandfather and his wife, June, Chic's grandmother, ate in the dining room. Their grandfather kept yelling over to his son to join them at the table, but he always ate in the living room, sitting in his chair, the plate in his lap. Their grandfather was always yelling at their father, although it wasn't really yelling because he couldn't really yell, but the tone was meant to be a yell. Their father just sat there in his chair while their grandfather went on and on about how he, Chic's father, needed to get his "act together."

Mr. von Schmidt owned a guitar, a nylon string model, and after Christmas dinner, Chic got it and plucked the strings, hoping he'd get the hint. Maybe they'd sing a Christmas carol, but

Mr. von Schmidt was asleep on the couch, his socked feet kicked up on the coffee table, and Diane and her mom were in the kitchen banging out the dishes. Chic put the guitar down and picked through his Christmas gifts—a pair of wool socks and a pewter statue of a father holding the hand of a little boy, a dog following behind.

About an hour later, when Diane asked Chic to run over to their house to pick up the ice cream, he was happy to oblige. It was a giant balloon of boredom in the living room, and besides, whenever Diane asked him to run an errand, it gave Chic a chance to check up on Lijy. Ever since the back rub at the reception, Chic couldn't stop thinking about her. He had no idea why it had happened, but he didn't care. It wasn't even the back rub, although it had felt so good, that fired his imagination. It was that she had grabbed him and pulled him over to the empty table and told him to take off his tuxedo jacket and untuck his shirt. No one had ever done anything like that to him—unprovoked and out of nowhere like that. Chic knew it was wrong that he let himself think about her, but he was weak. He was a dead tree branch in a thunderstorm. He was a goner when it came to Lijy Waldbeeser.

Buddy's house had classical pillars and a driveway that made a looping U so you never had to put the car in reverse. Chic slowed to a stop in front, then dug the binoculars out from under the seat. Through the living room window, he saw Lijy massaging Buddy's shoulders. Buddy didn't even seem to care about the back rub he was getting. He was reading the newspaper. Lijy leaned over and kissed him on top of the head.

The summer after Buddy graduated from high school, he packed his coin collection in two, hard-shell suitcases and ducked his head into Chic's bedroom one morning (Chic was sitting on the floor, leaning against his bed, reading a Batman comic book) and told him he was leaving. Before Chic could say anything, Buddy padded down the stairs. Chic heard the front screen door creak open and bang shut. He got up and glanced out the window and saw Buddy walking across the front yard carrying the two suitcases. When Buddy reached the gravel shoulder of Route 121, he sat the suitcases down and visored the sun out of his eyes so that he could see if a car was coming.

Chic pushed open the window and yelled down to him. "Ou-ay going tay?"

"Are you trying to speak pig Latin?"

"Maybe."

"Well, that's not right."

"Where are you going?"

"I don't wanna talk about it."

"Ou-tay back-ay?"

"Quit talking like that."

"Where you going?"

"Gettin' out of here. I'm done with Middleville."

"Ou-taaa back aaaaa?"

"Quit talking like that. It's not right. You're not doing it right." Buddy turned back to the road. There wasn't a car in sight, only pumpkin fields and a dusty ditch. Chic closed the window and went back to reading his comic book. Knowing Buddy, this was just a ploy to get attention. He'd get a ride into town, and by dark, he'd be back home, in his room, polishing his coins and waiting for dinner.

A few hours later, Chic was called to dinner by his mother. She'd set three places at the table. She told Chic that Tom Mc-Neeley would not be joining them for dinner. Chic picked up his fork and scooped up some mashed potatoes. His mother asked where Buddy was. Chic explained that he'd gone off to get out of Middleville and maybe he was going . . . he didn't know where he was going. He'd carried two suitcases out to the road. His mother shrugged and went about eating. "He'll be back," she said.

By the spring of 1951, Diane and her mother were spending a lot of time together in the kitchen nook. Sometimes, they both peeked in at Chic while he sat in his easy chair watching *The Life of Riley* or *The Lone Ranger*, then ducked around the corner out of earshot to whisper and giggle. If Chic could have quit daydreaming about Lijy, he would have realized that Diane was pregnant. But he couldn't quit daydreaming about Lijy. At first, he thought he could control it. When it was time not to think about her, he'd try to push her out of his mind and that would be that. But he couldn't stop, so he closed his eyes and thought about her standing on the edge of the dance floor picking lint off her sari. He thought about her rubbing his back. He thought about what she could possibly be doing while Buddy was out doing what he did with his coins. He wanted to feel her touch him again. It was almost too much for him to handle. Actually, it was too much for him to handle. So one night when he thought Buddy was out of town, Chic parked a few blocks away on Magnolia Street and walked up the sidewalk to the house and climbed the porch stairs. Before he knocked, he quickly fixed his hair.

She opened the door and blinked at him.

"I'm Chic. Buddy's brother."

"I know who you are."

"Well, you're looking like you don't."

"You see Buddy out there anywhere?"

Chic turned around. There wasn't anything happening on the street. It was eight o'clock on Tuesday.

Lijy grabbed his arm and pulled him inside.

"You sure you didn't see Buddy out there?"

"I thought . . . isn't he traveling?"

"I never know when he's here or gone or wherever. Did you talk to him today?"

Chic could tell she was upset. "I don't talk to Buddy very often."

"I don't know when he will be here. Maybe tomorrow. The next day. Maybe the day after that. So, I guess, you came over to talk to him."

"I came over to see you."

She should have realized—of course, he wanted to see her. She remembered the wedding reception, the back rub. Then an idea just kinda came to her all of a sudden.

"Why don't you come sit down?" She motioned toward the sofa.

Chic sat down. Lijy sat next to him, then felt odd and sat in the easy chair across from him.

"Do you want to listen to some music?"

Chic nodded.

Lijy got up and put on a record, "In a Sentimental Mood" by Duke Ellington. She closed her eyes and nodded along with the melody. When the song was finished, she told Chic it reminded her of Buddy. He had bought her the record, or maybe he'd already had it. She couldn't remember. She wanted to know if he liked it. Chic said he did, but he hadn't really paid attention. He couldn't believe he was sitting across from her in the living room. He got up and went to the window and peeled back the curtain and looked outside over the front lawn.

"Is it okay if I'm here?"

"If Buddy came in the front door, he'd walk right through the room and never even notice."

To Lijy, Chic had the same look as Buddy: puffy, sad cheeks that pulled his whole face into a frown. He looked sadder than sad. He looked defeated. Or actually that wasn't quite right. He was too young to be defeated. He looked on the road to defeat. Buddy was on that same road, pulled over to the ditch and broke down, the hood raised. She could be the one to change that—for Buddy. That's all she ever really wanted. She just wanted to be the one to help him, and she could; she knew she could. She tried to tell Buddy, but he wasn't ever really there, like *there* there, like present. She'd seen him hold animated conversations with no one, with air. Once, she heard him in the kitchen carrying on about this and that, and when she walked in, he was pointing his finger at nothing and snarling, "And that's not what you did."

Mostly, though, he stared off into some middle distance, some spot on the wall, and she'd ask him if he heard her, and he'd say, "No. I'm sorry. Were you saying something?"

Lijy thought that maybe Chic could help her. Maybe he could talk to Buddy. She was about to come out with it, just get it out there, just ask him to talk to Buddy for her, when Chic came out with an idea of his own.

"So, ah, I was thinking, um, do you think I could get another one of those back rubs?"

She sat there staring at him.

"You'd be doing me a favor. I got this awful . . ." He rolled his head this way and that to stretch his neck.

She got up and went to the record player. "Do you mind if we listen to the song again?"

"Actually, do you have 'Move It on Over'? Or 'Long Gone Lonesome Blues'? Or, hey, the B-side to 'Long Gone is 'My Son Calls Another Man Daddy.' I really like Hank Williams. I bet Buddy has some Hank records."

"Maybe we don't need another song."

Lijy got a chair from the dining room. Chic got up and quickly unbuttoned his shirt. He was wearing a tank top under-shirt, and he tore that off, too. He sat down on the chair. Lijy started out on his shoulders, kneading his tenseness, using her thumbs to work into the muscles on either side of his neck.

"Can you whisper those words into my ear?"

"Whisper what into your ear?"

"Those words. Ansa-something. And something else. I don't know."

"Ansa phalak."

"Yeah that. Whisper that."

Lijy moved her hands to the middle of his back. "This is your vri-hati," she whispered. "It's a bindu, a dot. It's mystical." She pressed on it with her thumb. Chic let out a sigh and felt his shoulders unravel. She moved her hands up to his shoulder blades. "Your ansa phalak."

"Keep whispering."

"Ansa." She held the *a* like she was letting out a long sigh.

Lijy had met Buddy at a restaurant on Grant Avenue in San Francisco's Chinatown. She'd come to San Francisco from Stockton, where her father worked as a day laborer for an asparagus farmer. Lijy had gotten on a bus without even telling anyone. She had aspirations. And then, in a restaurant in Chinatown, where she'd come in off the street to have a mug of tea, there was Buddy Waldbeeser leaning low over a bowl of pork noodles, trying to work the chopsticks, a napkin stuffed in the collar of his shirt. He was in town for a numismatic convention, and as soon as he spotted Lijy wearing her sari, he couldn't stop sneaking peeks. Whenever she caught him, he would avert his eyes and appear to be busy with his pork noodles. Eventually, she got up and approached him because that was the kind of woman she wanted to be. Buddy looked up at her and said, "You're not Chinese, are you?" He told her he was staying at the Mark Hopkins Hotel. He told her about the cocktail lounge, Top of the Mark, with a view of the San Francisco Bay and the Golden Gate Bridge. He was from Illinois, and in Illinois, he said, you had to get up on your roof to get any sort of view, and even then, there wasn't much to see but cornfields and other roofs, maybe an occasional bird flying by. He said he'd take her after he finished his bowl of pork noodles.

On their way to Geary Street, Buddy bought her a bouquet of roses from a flower stand. It was the first time a man had ever bought her flowers. Buddy insisted she cradle them like a baby, and she did. They caught the California Street Cable Car to Nob Hill. Lijy had never seen a place as gold and shiny as the Mark Hopkins. Neither had Buddy, but she didn't know that. They took the elevator to the nineteenth floor. At the bar, he ordered himself a Gibson while she walked over to the wall of windows. The view was something that hit her right in the middle of the stomach. The panorama, the vista, the buildings, the people, all of it in motion and happening nineteen stories below her, just rolling the way it rolled forward, and she could do nothing except witness it. She felt her knees go slack. Buddy got her a seat and handed her a bowl of nuts, but she didn't want any nuts. He sat down beside her, pointed to a spot where two windows met, and told her that was the Weeper's Corner. When servicemen shipped out to the war, he explained, their wives and sweethearts would stand in that spot dabbing their eyes with hankies, watching as their lovers' ships slipped out of the bay. He put his hand on her leg. She told him she wasn't a weeper, and he told her he wasn't in the service.

Chic hadn't put his shirt back on yet, hadn't even stood up from the dining room chair. Lijy sat down on the sofa. Now that the back rub was done, she could talk. She complained about Buddy being gone all the time and told Chic that he had promised her a life in Middleville where it was quiet and she would be able to do, as he said, "her own thing." It was true—Middleville was quiet, and she was doing her own thing. But she didn't like it, none of it, not even a tiny piece of it. She hated it, to be honest. She felt like she was in a dark room and the entire town was shining a flashlight on her. It was worse than Stockton, actually, where at least there were other Indians. Here, she couldn't even go to Stafford's without kids peeking around the corners of the aisles to watch her. And most people wouldn't talk to her and the ones who did talked very slowly, like she wasn't able to understand what they were saying. She hoped that Chic was getting all of this. (He just sat there smiling, every once in a while furrowing his brow.) She needed Chic to sound the alarm for her, to let Buddy know she was drowning. She thought she'd get him, really get him, if she came to Middleville. But she wasn't getting anything but a big, empty house and a lot of silence.

After Lijy was done, Chic went into the bathroom. He knew what it was like to be an outcast. He'd help her fit in; he'd help her become a real Middlevillian. That's more than Buddy was doing. He didn't care, not really; he was too busy doing whatever he did with his damn gold coins. Chic cared, really, truly, and he was convinced that all he had to do was make the first move and she'd lead him to the bedroom and let him slowly take off her sari. Then, she would kiss him—not like Diane kissed, rough and aggressive, but gently—and the two of them would giggle shyly between kisses because both of them would be nervous, and since he'd be the more experienced one, he'd have to take the lead.

Lijy was at the stove, her back to him. The teakettle was on.

"Excuse me."

She turned around.

Chic was wearing only his boxer shorts and black socks. His hips began moving back and forth, slowly, humping the air. He didn't even realize he was doing it.

"I could help you. Make it so people didn't stare at you."

She looked like she was on the brink of something, a movement, a lunge toward him, and they'd grab each other's cheeks and mash into a passionate kiss. Behind her, the teakettle began to whistle.

"Chic, what are you doing?" she finally said and shut off the burner. "Will you quit moving your hips like that?"

"Sorry."

"Chic, why are you in your underwear?"

"You rubbed my back."

"You asked me to rub your back."

"Not at the reception. You just grabbed my arm."

"I'm sorry if you got the wrong idea. I love your brother. I do, but you looked so sad tonight. I thought I could help you. And I thought you could help me."

"Sad?" The accusation dropped on him like a heavy weight. "I'm not sad."

"I can feel it in your muscles. I can feel it in your brother's muscles too."

"Feel what? What can you feel? What are you talking about? I'm not sad. Buddy's not sad."

"It's okay, Chic. You have Diane now, and your brother has me. It's going to be okay."

On the way home he stopped at Gene's Dairy Dream and bought Diane's favorite—a chocolate ice cream cone with sprinkles. He was determined to make this a good night: ice cream and *The Ruggles* or Ed Sullivan on the television and maybe he'd put his arm around his wife, like he should, like a husband should. Sad? He wasn't sad. He was the happiest man alive. He had a wife, and he was thinking about getting a dog and naming him Cody.

At home, he heard Diane sloshing in the tub. He tried the bathroom knob, but it was locked. "Honey."

"I'll be out in a second."

Then, he had an idea. "Unlock the door, honey."

"I'm in the bath."

"Open the door."

He heard her stand up out of the water. Her wet foot thudded on the linoleum.

"I want to carry you upstairs and lay you out on the bed and kiss you on the belly and your legs and your neck and cheeks and ears."

She unlocked the door. A towel was wrapped around her, above her breasts. Her hair was dripping. Behind her, the bathroom mirror was fogged with steam.

"You left the lamp by the couch on. I could see it when I pulled into the driveway." He held out the ice cream cone to her. "I made a mistake."

"What are you talking about, Chic?"

"I thought you were reckless, but now I see that you're not. I'm not sad. I'm really not."

"Reckless?"

"Wild is more like it. I want to hold you. That's what I want. We'll snuggle under a blanket and just be together."

She unwrapped her towel. She was about four months along,

and her stomach was beginning to bulge, a little rise like a hill in the middle of flat land.

His face turned white. "I . . . You're . . ." He swallowed hard. He thought about his father sitting in the living room staring out the window. He'd backed the family car down the gravel drive every morning and, at night, carefully pulled it back into the drive. He thought of his mother sweeping the farmhouse's porch with so much force, the shushing of the broom's bristles sounded like screaming.

"Chic, are you OK?"

He clenched the ice cream cone. It crumbled, and ice cream dripped over his hand and onto the hallway carpet. He started to waver.

"Chic! Honey?"

His eyes rolled back into his head, and he groaned a low, animal half sigh, half moan.

Then, he passed out.

Two

Mary Norwood, another beginning

1972–1990

In 1972, Mary Norwood and her boyfriend, Lyle Crabtree (who went by Lyle Style because he wore butterfly collar shirts and skintight polyester pants he thought gave him a bulge), rented an apartment in San Jose, California, but spent most of their time in Lyle's '69 Ford LTD hustling up and down the West Coast so Mary could shoot pool in the West Coast Women's Pool League, a semiprofessional pool league. Lyle didn't work, but that didn't mean he didn't bring in an income. He had a triangle head like viper, and his tongue could snap with the best of them. Somehow he always had a belt buckle, a pair of dingo boots, a pool cue, a Zippo lighter, or whatever to sell. This was nickel-and-dime stuff, but Lyle could stretch a buck. It was nothing for him to kick the LTD's seats back and sleep behind a movie theater. Mary, on the other hand, had big, blossoming dreams that didn't include sleeping in a car. Every time she started talking about what she called a "normal life," Lyle smiled through his mustache. "I'm with ya, babe. You think I like sleeping in my car?"

By the time Elvis died in August 1977, Mary was finishing in the top two of almost every tournament. Payouts were getting bigger—five hundred bucks here, seven hundred there—but she was still rubbing her neck and cursing the LTD's vinyl seats. Lyle didn't seem to mind sleeping in the car. He certainly didn't mind the increase in income. He bought himself new things, like a gold ring for his pinkie finger and a belt with his name stitched in back. He strutted around the pool halls striking a pose every few minutes—hip kicked out, cigarette dangling from his mouth.

During her matches, Mary often spotted him off in a corner talking to some girl, a look in his eyes like he was going to swallow the girl whole. She asked Lyle about the girls, and he told her he was just doing his job, working the crowd, trying to build up her image. Mary couldn't let herself believe he could be sneaking off with those girls. Even when she saw him one afternoon in Olympia, Washington, come back into the pool hall, a doe-eyed girl behind him carrying her high-heeled shoes, the girl's hair a tornado of mess, Mary told herself he was probably helping her fix a flat on her car.

All of this was about to change. Their—or rather Mary's—ship was about to come in.

In October 1978, after a tournament in Reno, Mary and Lyle were sitting at the bar having cocktails when they were approached by a slick-looking dude, his shirt unbuttoned showing gold necklaces. The guy had huge muttonchop sideburns that practically grew right into his mouth, and was built short and compact like a garbage can that fit under the kitchen sink. He introduced himself as Rod Alberhaskie, and he had a proposition. He talked to Lyle, looking at him directly, eyeball to eyeball like a high school principal. He and some folks were kicking off a professional women's pool league, WPPA, Women's Professional Pool Association. "Our league won't be a weekly event like this here. But the purses will be ten times as much."

"Ten times as much," Mary whispered.

Rod didn't even look at her.

"That's big bucks," Lyle said.

"The competition will be stiffer, so there's no guarantee, but I've seen her play. She's good."

Lyle turned an eye on her and smiled. "She's a damn good pool player."

Mary liked that Lyle was taking care of the business side of things, so she could simply sit there and sip her drink through the little cocktail straw. Who cared about sleeping in the LTD.

She wanted a man who could take care of business and Lyle was all about TCB.

Rod took a card from his inside breast pocket. Mary tried to get a glimpse of it, but Lyle pulled it away so she couldn't read it.

"More importantly, the good players will get sponsorship."

"A steady paycheck," Mary said.

Rod glanced at her, then back to Lyle. "About two thousand dollars a month." He snapped his fingers and motioned to a guy eating peanuts and watching them from across the bar.

"Which means we can sleep in hotels," Mary whispered, pretty much talking to her drink.

The peanut guy, a younger version of Rod, came over to the bar. He looked like he was all of seventeen. His suit pants were too short, what the kids called "high-waters." "I want you to meet Giles Alberhaskie. My son. He's a representative of Viking Cues."

"She uses a Viking cue," Lyle said.

"I know she does," Rod said.

"She likes it," Lyle said.

Giles shook Lyle's hand.

Mary slid off her barstool. "I'm going to use the ladies' room." None of the men looked at her.

Across the bar, she watched as Lyle's tongue pretty much went dog when Rod pulled out a contract and smoothed it on the bar. He signed it, then held up his glass for the other two men to toast him.

For the first few years Mary was a professional pool player, Giles Alberhaskie handed her a stipend check at every tournament. In fact, he picked Lyle and her up in his Oldsmobile Ninety-Eight and drove them to the tournaments. Mary usually rode in the backseat, watching the West Coast scenery blur by as Lyle rode shotgun and fiddled with the car's eight-track, playing rock and roll songs that he sang along with. At the tournaments, Lyle signed her in and carried her pool cue and ordered her tomato juice that she sipped while she ran a couple racks to warm up. There was enough money to afford hotel rooms and steak dinners delivered to the room on a cart. Lyle took care of those, too, signing the room service bill. Of course, it was Mary's money, but still, he kept a pen on him at all times.

Since the tournaments were monthly, the couple spent a lot of time at their apartment in San Jose (no more LTD), a modest place with air conditioning and a television set that Lyle, sitting in his tank-top undershirt, put to good use while he drank beer. It was shaping up to be a pretty good life. Mary worked one weekend a month, and when something like a clogged toilet needed taking care of, Lyle got the plunger from the hall closet. If that didn't work, he picked up the phone and called a plumber. All Mary had to do was sit on the couch.

Only problem was that Lyle had a knack for spending money, and he wasn't bashful about it. He bought a Ford Mustang Mach 1, seven polyester suits, a dozen silk shirts, a pair of Italian loafers, a ten-speed Schwinn bicycle, tennis lessons, a color television, golf clubs, a waterbed, a mustache comb, a hi-fi stereo, three lava lamps, two hundred rock and roll records, Chicago Cutlery steak knives, a bearskin rug, and a white leather couch. Mary said nothing about the purchases. She just kept collecting the checks and watched the new things make their way into her life.

Then, it was 1982, and Mary was attending most of the tournaments by herself. Giles Alberhaskie had moved to Los Angeles to represent television stars like Bernie Kopell and Jon Cypher, while Lyle stayed home to "keep an eye on things." The WPPA was on the decline; not many fans were showing up, even though the league sponsored promotional gimmicks like Kiss Your Favorite Pool Hustler. Mary hated those stunts—kissing a sweaty, fat guy for a dollar. Many of the women in the league had left and gone on to start families. This was what Mary wanted—her and Lyle and some little bambino and a house with a garage and a tree in the front yard.

Mary was jealous when a former WPPA player, Allison Whitman, showed up at a tournament in Reno with her seven-month-old son. The women cooed over the little guy, and it was right then that Mary made up her mind. She was going to down-shift out of this life. She was almost forty. What did she have to show for all these years? Sure, they had the Mustang Mach 1 and a white leather couch. But what were they doing? When she'd left the apartment earlier that afternoon, Lyle was sitting in front of the television playing Atari.

She didn't stick around to play her first match that day. She checked out of her hotel, leaving the key on the bed and not even bothering to get her money back. It was a five-hour drive back to San Jose. Mary did the drive in four hours and twenty-six minutes. At the apartment door, she could hear Journey's "Don't Stop Believing" blaring on the hi-fi. It was only 9:00 p.m. She'd burst in and lay it all out: "Lyle, we gotta make a change . . ." She dug in her purse for her keys. When she got the door open, her stomach turned inside out and a wave of shock spiraled through her body. A naked black woman with a huge, helmet afro was on top of Lyle. They were on the floor in front of the television, and Mary had a full-on frontal shot of this woman. Her eyes were closed, and she was pinching her own nipples while making a high-pitched whimper. Mary stood in the open door taking in the scene—the woman, Lyle, and the whimpering crescendo of Neal Schon's guitar solo.

She quietly closed the door and went down the stairs and out into the parking lot. It was a warm night. The traffic flew by on Saratoga Avenue, the busy street lined with fast food restaurants and dry cleaners that ran in front of the apartment complex. Mary found Lyle's Mustang Mach 1 in the parking lot. As she sat behind the wheel, her mind flashed to that afternoon when Lyle signed her contract to play professional pool. On the way out of the bar, he held the door open for her. In the car, he leaned over and grabbed both her cheeks with his hands and mashed his mouth onto hers. She loved it, the power, the aggression. Lyle was her man, and he was taking care of her.

During the next few months, Mary tried to get her mind off Lyle, but she couldn't; she loved him. Honestly, she did, but when she thought about going back to the apartment, her mind seized on the image of opening the apartment door and finding him fucking that woman. One afternoon she went inside a gas station to buy a pack of cigarettes. All she had to do was ask for cigarettes, but she couldn't move her mouth. "Lady, there's like four people behind you." She looked over her shoulder at a longhaired kid with a skateboard and a pregnant woman.

She wrote Lyle a letter. It was short and to the point and told him that she never ever wanted to see him again. He could have all their stuff, she didn't care, but he needed to get out of the apartment. In fact, he needed to get out of California. He should move to Virginia. Or New Hampshire. Somewhere. Anywhere but California or Las Vegas or Reno. She couldn't take the risk of bumping into him at a movie theater or grocery store. If she did, she didn't know what she'd do—most likely break down in tears.

Her new Viking representative, Pete Lemmingworth, was a chubby guy with curly hair who never showed up at any of her tournaments and didn't care if she stuck with it or not. He knew the league was a mud puddle and the sun was coming out. Mary called him for advice. Were there other pool circuits? What about Las Vegas? Los Angeles? Were any Bmovies looking for women who were good at pool? What should she do? When she started crying and blabbering about Lyle, Pete hung up. She called back, but he didn't answer. She called the next day, and he wouldn't take her call. She had enough money to do nothing but drive around San Jose, checking in and out of hotels, eating at restaurants by herself, going to movies, walking around the zoo.

A few months after she sent the letter, she stopped by the old apartment. There was a FOR RENT sign in the window. Mary still had her key, and it worked the lock. The living room carpet had indentations where the couch had sat. On the kitchen counter was a book of matches from a steak place on Hillside Avenue. She put the matches in her purse. The closet door was open in the bedroom. Lyle had left twenty or thirty wire hangers behind. Mary stood there, staring into the closet, imagining Lyle's silk shirts and polyester suits. In the bathroom, she sat on the toilet seat to feel the coldness of the plastic, to feel something, anger, betrayal, loneliness. She wanted to be in Lyle's LTD trying to sleep, listening to the hum of the interstate, Lyle in the seat next to her, snoring.

Over the next few years, there were other men, a lot of other men, too many other men. She got married to a guy named Jack, but that lasted six, maybe eight months. She couldn't remember. It didn't matter. She moved to Los Angeles, hoping to run into Giles Alberhaskie. She tracked down his number and gave him a call, hoping he could get her a part in a television show or some-thing, maybe a car commercial, but his secretary said he was "with a client." She was staying in a little roadside motel in Encino, but most days she sat in her car in some grocery store parking lot, smoking cigarettes and watching people get in and out of their cars. Some pulled their wailing, screaming kids behind them; oth-ers were alone, like her, and walked across the parking lot, hands in their pockets, looking around for something, someone, some sort of distraction from the loneliness that was crushing them.

After two months she left Encino for Eureka. After six months in Eureka, she headed to Portland, then Yuma, Arizona, then Las Vegas, then Reno, then Tahoe for the winter ski season of 1988. In Tahoe, Mary met Pierre Bontemps, who promised he'd take care of her. He wore a fur coat and drank champagne for no particular reason. But he didn't take care of her. He couldn't even take care of himself. Every morning he rolled over and asked her to make breakfast. She didn't want to make breakfast. Why couldn't they go out to breakfast?

All told, she was married and divorced nine times. There were also the men she never married, like the cowboy in Flagstaff, Arizona. This was in 1990, and she was working at a Chi-Chi's by I-40. When she got off her shift at ten, the cowboy was sitting at the bar eating a chimichanga. Mary sat next to him, and Julio, the bartender, brought her her usual—a shot of Cuervo and a Budweiser. The cowboy was a traveling salesman who sold power tools. They started talking while Julio kept setting shots in front of them. At midnight, Mary went back to his hotel, the Ramada Inn next door. The two of them rolled around on the king-size bed pawing at each other. Mary kept glancing at the hotel room door, thinking his wife or girlfriend was going to barge in.

Afterward, she couldn't sleep, but the cowboy nodded right off, sprawled out on his stomach, the bedsheets twisted around his body. Mary tried to remember if he'd put a condom on or not. She'd done too many shots. Her mouth was dry. It felt like a thousand angry bees were inside her skull. She checked the nightstand hoping to find a spent, shriveled rubber next to the clock radio. There wasn't one. She checked the bed, pulling the sheet back and exposing the cowboy's hairy white ass and his ugly feet with yellowing toenails. She checked the floor around the bed, then under the bed, then the garbage can in the bathroom. Nothing. She sat on the toilet and looked at her vagina and willed the semen to leak out. She tried to pee but only a little urine tinkled into the toilet water. She unrolled a mound of toilet paper and scrubbed her vagina. Then, she quickly got dressed and snuck out of the hotel room.

On the way back to her apartment, Mary stopped at a Walgreens and bought a pregnancy test. She pissed on the stick as soon as she got home, not even bothering to take off her coat. It came back negative, of course. You're pregnant, a loud voice inside her head said. It doesn't matter what the test says. You're pregnant. P-r-e-g-n-a-n-t. No you're not, a whisper voice said. You're forty-four years old. You are, the loud voice said. Mary sat down on the toilet. She could feel the baby inside her; it felt like a goldfish swimming circles in her stomach. Actually, she knew it was smaller than a goldfish—a minnow. Actually, smaller than a minnow, a guppy, actually smaller than that, a cell, a single cell orbiting in her womb, getting ready to multiply. The capper, the true indication of her pregnancy: her crotch was burning.

The next morning, Mary called her manager at Chi-Chi's and told him she wouldn't make it in for her lunch shift. She drove straight to the Brass Bull and ordered a double gin and tonic. Her plan was to carpet bomb the baby with G&Ts. She wasn't wearing underwear, and every hour or so, she went into the bathroom and smeared anti-burning cream on her crotch. By five o'clock, she was slurring her words and couldn't hold her head up. She began pounding her fist on the bar and repeated, "I need someone to take care of me. I need someone to take care of me. I need someone to take care of me . . ." The bartender at the Brass Bull, a woman with dream catcher earrings, started filling her glass with only tonic. After a while, Mary laid her head on the bar and started snoring so loud she could be heard over the jukebox. When the crowd thinned out around midnight, the bartender woke her up and told her she knew someone who might be able to help.

Mary perked up, wiped her eyes. "Who?"

"An herbalist. His name is Mr. Purty." The bartender leaned in to tell Mary that she'd suffered from night sweats and insomnia, but just last week, she'd gone to visit Mr. Purty out in the desert, and after only one visit, her symptoms disappeared. "Just one visit."

Mary sniffed, sucking up her tears. "Can he make a baby disappear?"

"Are you pregnant?"

Mary nodded.

The following morning, Mary followed the map the bartender had drawn on a cocktail napkin out of the mountains that surrounded Flagstaff and into the desert. Two hours later, she pulled into a gravel drive that led to a rusted trailer. She was in the middle of goddamn nowhere. A pack of dogs circled her car, barking. A tipped-over swing set sat in the front yard. A man who she could only assume was Mr. Purty peeked his head out the front door of the trailer. He wore an Indian headdress and a buckskin shirt that laced up the chest. He blew a whistle and the dogs sat down and stayed sitting when Mary got out of her car. Mr. Purty stood a little taller than a sixth grader. The first thing he told her was he was not Native American. He was old, maybe about eighty. He led her into the trailer where a morning game show was on the television and five or six cats slept on a ratty couch. He cleaned up some empty breakfast cereal boxes and threw away an empty milk jug before offering her a seat at the kitchen table.

"So what's the problem? Night sweats? Insomnia? Stomach pains?"

"I'm pregnant. And I don't want to be."

Mr. Purty looked at her for a long time, then removed his Indian headdress and set it on the table. He got up and went into the living room. He moved the coffee table out of the center of the room, turned off the television, spread a floral beach towel on the carpet, and shooed away the cats. Directly above the towel was a homemade skylight, a rectangle cut in the roof of the trailer that was fit with a piece of Plexiglas. There were scratches in the Plexiglas, and Mary could see the rusted heads of the drywall screws that held it in place. Mr. Purty motioned for her to lie down, and after she was on her back, he told her to close her eyes and imagine that she was standing in the desert.

Mr. Purty went into the kitchen for a moment, returning with a bucket of steaming rocks. Using a pair of tongs, he placed the hot rocks around the outline of her body. The heat radiated off them.

"Do you have a fan or something?" Mary asked.

"Quiet, please. No talking unless I ask a question."

The last rock, the largest, about the size of an oddly shaped bowling ball, was secured in a harness, and Mr. Purty winched the rock up into the air. He then pulled up her shirt to expose her navel and positioned the steaming rock about two inches from her skin. It felt like the sun was setting right into her stomach.

"Can I please get a fan?"

Mr. Purty kneeled next to her and whispered, "What does the man look like?"

"I don't think I can continue without a fan."

"The point is to sweat. Now, the impregnator. Imagine him."

She did. He was in the hotel room the morning following their rendezvous, checking the bathroom, the closet, to see if he had missed packing anything up. The television was on—MTV. Mary felt a coolness around her navel, and she opened her eyes to see Mr. Purty squirting hand lotion on her stomach.

After it was over, Mr. Purty made her drink a mug of water that had been boiled with lava rocks. He charged her a hundred bucks. Then she climbed back into the Mustang Mach 1 and sped off, the dogs barking behind her, chasing the car. She looked into the rearview to see Mr. Purty blowing his whistle and commanding the dogs to return. She put her hand under her shirt and felt the sliminess of the lotion on her stomach.

The next day at a clinic in Flagstaff, a nurse took her into a room and gave her a cup to urinate into. After she was done, the nurse asked her a few questions about her sexual history and showed her to a room. A doctor came in, carrying a clipboard, acting like he was in a hurry. Without looking at her, he flipped through some pages on the clipboard. "You've got a yeast infection," he finally said.

"I'm not pregnant?"

"The yeast infection is severe. I'll write you a prescription."

"Yesterday I went to an herbalist. Out in the desert."

The doctor stopped writing and looked at her.

"I was convinced I was pregnant. I mean . . . do you think . . .

do you think I could have gotten an herbal abortion?"

"Ms. Norwood, what made you believe you were pregnant?"

"Just a feeling, I guess. I didn't want to be pregnant, so I convinced myself that I was. That make sense?"

"When was the last time you menstruated?"

Mary shrugged. "A while ago. A year maybe."

The doctor tore off the prescription. "Take the pills twice a day."

Mary Norwood & Green Geneseo

■

April 9, 1998

Then, it was 1998, and Mary was sixty. It had been sixteen years since she had come home to find Lyle fucking that woman, and now she lived above a Mexican restaurant in Dustin, Nevada and worked as a cocktail waitress at the Frontier Casino in Vegas. She looked more like someone's grandma than a cocktail waitress, and the thing about being a cocktail waitress was you had to look good. In the afternoons, before her shift, it took every ounce of strength for Mary to drag herself to the Mountain View Mall to buy a new pair of earrings. Every time she stepped foot into the place, she was overrun by the California floozies who descended on Las Vegas like ants on a dropped Jolly Rancher. Mary knew she couldn't hold a candle to these women and their silicone breasts and spray-on tans—she saw how men would do a double take as they sashayed through the mall. She had this secret wish that an older guy would whisk her away to his suite where there would be a view of Las Vegas's shimmering lights. It would be like *Pretty Woman* (a movie Mary popped into her VHS and fell asleep to almost every single night), and she would be the Julia Roberts character, although the guy wouldn't be Richard Gere. Too subdued. She liked her men to be thick and sweaty, the kind of guy who had sweat stains under his arms after he mowed the lawn. That was not Richard Gere's character. He hired someone to mow the lawn, or if he did mow it, he probably had a special lawn-mowing outfit, something he kept in the closet next to his snow boots.

Cocktail waitressing didn't pay too well, so to supplement her income, Mary hustled pool at the Bowl-a-Rama out by UNLV. She could still handle a cue, and the railbirds who came to the bowling alley on Wednesday nights knew she could, too. They bought her drinks. They gave her high-fives when she won. They teased her each time she used a bridge. About five years before, Mary had tried to qualify for a Women's Professional Billiard Association (WPBA) tournament at the Riviera, but the women were so much better than they had been in the WPPA. She got knocked out in the qualifying round. At one time she could masse around an opponent's ball. She could double bank. She could draw the cue ball the length of the table. Now she was lucky if she could make the straight-in shots. Actually, she could make the straight-in shots, but sometimes she didn't feel like she could. Confidence was everything, and someone had gotten in her pocket and stolen hers, thrown it on the sidewalk and smeared it into itty-bitty pieces with the toe of his cowboy boot. Still, she was good enough to bring in fifty bucks or so at the Bowl-a-Rama on Wednesday nights. Every now and then, she had a really good night and won a hundred. At the end of those nights, while the shoe-counter kid sprayed the rental shoes with Lysol, Mary would buy all the railbirds a nightcap. They would pull together a couple of pub tables, and the younger guys would ask her about the WPPA. Mary didn't like to think about those days. They reminded her of Lyle and all the things that had happened since him, and she didn't want to be reminded of that. She hated what she'd become—a plump woman who looked like a waitress at Denny's.

Then, one Wednesday night, Mary pushed through the Bowl-a-Rama's glass front door, and Green Geneseo turned around on his barstool and gave her a head-to-toe once-over. Green Geneseo. She had no idea who he was, but she liked what she saw. He wore sunglasses and an emerald-green suit. A newspaper was spread out on the bar in front of him like he was studying the stock market or sport scores or something important. Her heart fluttered. She was glad she was wearing a new pair of earrings.

Green's trip to the Bowl-a-Rama wasn't chance or fate or whatever you want to call it. The previous Wednesday, he and his friend, Tim Lee, had been on lane three, a guys' night out, a couple of beers, a little bowling. Green kept getting distracted every time this woman shooting pool leaned over the pool table. She was a big woman, yes, but Green liked his women big (Jane had been an even bigger woman), and this woman's ass in her blue jeans looked like a mint julep, and he wanted to take it to Derby Town. Tim Lee asked him where his mind was, and Green motioned toward the pool table. Tim Lee saw Mary leaning over the table sighting up a shot. Tim tried to get Green to talk to her, but the time wasn't right. He needed a plan.

The sunglasses were Tim Lee's suggestion. The two of them had spent all afternoon at the Sunglass Hut, and the woman working the counter said they made him look "sporty." Green wasn't sure if "sporty" was the right look. While waiting for Mary to show up at the bowling alley, Green had caught a glimpse of himself in the bathroom mirror. He looked ridiculous. Who was he fooling? Wearing sunglasses inside? Vodka on the rocks? This wasn't him. He was a numbers guy. He was shy. What would Jane have said?

Green had spent twenty-five years working at the Las Vegas Bank and Trust, but after Jane died two years, four months, and sixteen days ago, he retired from the bank and got rid of his cardigan sweaters, khaki pants, and button-up Oxford shirts. A sixty-six-year-old in a cardigan sweater and a turtleneck was somebody's uncle, and no woman wanted to date somebody's uncle. Lately, Green had been telling women he was a bookie.

This was halftrue. In his life as a bank teller, he'd kept records—
"books"—and moved money from this "hand" to that "hand," so
he sorta was a bookie, kind of. Plus, he thought, telling someone
he was a bank teller sounded a little, well, a little boring.

After Mary won her fourth straight game, Green finally
slid off his barstool. He was a big man, about six foot two and
thick around the middle like a steak eater. Mary had her back to
him, talking to a guy wearing a Runnin' Rebels sweatshirt. Green
walked over and tapped her on the shoulder. When she turned
around, the bartender pushed play on the CD player. (Green
had tipped him twenty-five bucks.) It was Randy Travis covering Hank Williams's "I'm So Lonesome I Could Cry." Mary let
Green pull her close. He smelled like breath mints. All the railbirds hushed. A bowling ball rolled down the lane and crashed
into the pins. Green moved his giant hand down to the small of
her back and whispered, "I want to take you to dinner."

In the parking lot, Green unlocked the door of his Ford
minivan. He could tell Mary liked that he unlocked the door for
her. Jane had been the same way. She'd never asked him to do
things but had an expectation he'd do them. He had to have ESP,
or at least, always be studying her face for the slightest hint of
those expectations. Jane and Green had met in a divorcee support
group, and after a few months of dating, Green moved out of his
one-bedroom apartment and into her trailer—an Airstream with
an above-ground pool. Jane liked to sunbathe in the nude next
to the pool, and some of Green's fondest memories were coming
home from the bank and walking up the deck stairs to find her
soaking up the Nevada sunshine. He loved how she waved, rolling her fingers. They were married twenty-one years before she
got cancer.

Mary liked how this was starting out. At the diner, a twenty-
four-hour greasy spoon, he ordered for her—pancakes and eggs
and a mug of decaf coffee. How did he know she wanted decaf?

"If you drink regular, you'll never get to sleep tonight."

"How do you know I want to sleep?" She smiled, and he smiled. The waitress dropped off their food, two steaming plates of eggs and pancakes with an orange wedge and a sprig of parsley on the side. Mary picked up the hot sauce and bathed her eggs in it. Green watched her for a while, then finally said, "How about we get married?"

Mary almost spit out her eggs.

He took off his gold wristwatch and scooted out of the booth and knelt down. "Mary . . . what's your last name? Actually, forget your last name. You're going to change it anyway. Have you ever been married?"

She noticed how big his hands were as he tried to fit the watch on her wrist. He seemed like a guy who could take care of things.

Green was having trouble fitting the watch around her wrist. She was a big woman with wrists like plumbing pipes. "We'll get a bigger band. Or, you know what, I'll get you a ring. You probably want a ring."

"I'd like a ring."

"So that's a yes?"

The loud voice said, Do it. Yes. Marry him. The whisper voice said, You don't even know this guy. The loud voice said, Who cares? This is your chance, maybe your last chance. The whisper voice said, Get to know him. Play it slow. The loud voice said, Marry him. He held the door open for you.

"Yes," she said. "I'll marry you."

Green slid back into the booth and picked up his fork. "We're getting married." He looked for someone to tell the news to, but there were only two other people in the diner, and the waitress was sitting in the back corner working a crossword puzzle.

Mary took a bite of her scrambled eggs.

"Jesus, I have a headache," Green said. "You have any aspirin?"

"I think so." She dug in her purse and came up with a bottle of Tylenol.

"So, you wanna get married tonight?" he asked.

She shrugged. "Sure."

"This is great. Just great. I know just the right place."

Mary smiled. "So what do you do? For work. I feel like I don't even really know you."

Green thought about telling her about the bank. That would be a change. Honesty. But, in the end, he went in the direction he'd been going for the last few months. "I'm a bookie."

"A bookie?"

"Sports bets. A lot of basketball. College. Pro. You know . . ."

"A bookie in Las Vegas? Isn't that . . . redundant?"

"Redundant?"

"Unnecessary, I guess, is a better word."

Green took a sip of his coffee, then motioned to the suit he was wearing. "I got the clothes to prove it, if you don't believe me."

Mary & Green Geneseo

■

April–June 1998

Since the day he had driven back to the Airstream after burying Jane, Green's plan had been to find a woman, marry her, then ride east into the smack-dab center of Illinois: Peoria. At work one afternoon, he had overheard a young couple, both of them wearing a gleeful look on their faces like they had just gotten to the front of the line to ride the roller coaster, say to a teller, "We just moved here from Peoria." Green stopped doing what he was doing, which was entering some numbers into a ledger, longhand. He liked the word, Peoria. It rolled off the tongue. It sounded sung. A church choir could do something incredible with the word. Peeeee-or-i-aaaaaaaa. In a place like Peoria, he wouldn't have to remember watching his wife vomit into a bucket. The sun always shone in Peoria. The grass was green, the greenest of any place, and the wind whistled zip-a-dee-doo-dah through the trees. Everyone had a skip in their step. Gas was cheap. Green knew nothing about the place, actually, but he longed for it, dreamed about it. He did some research. Peoria—a city named after the Peoria Indian tribe, who were mound builders. He liked mounds. Mounds of blankets in the middle of a bed. A mound of mashed potatoes on a plate. Mounds were not cancer. Peoria. It was on the Illinois River. He liked rivers, boats, anything having to do with water. Peoria had also been a vaudeville stop in the early 1900s: *If it'll play in Peoria* . . . He loved to laugh. There was a college there—Bradley, the Bradley Braves. They had streets lined with houses, a minor league baseball team—the Peoria Chiefs. He liked baseball. He'd get season tickets. He imagined the pace of life was slower, the good life, flatland, cornfields stretching out to the horizon. Chain restaurants. Parking lots and strip malls. He loved those. Chili's and Bennigan's. The Gap. Starbucks. The people were probably so nice they blushed when you took the Lord's name in vain. He had daydreamed about Peoria, without actually knowing he was daydreaming about Peoria, about meeting a woman and taking her there, and it was happening, had already happened, and he was ready to leave all of this—Las Vegas, Jane, cancer, all of it—so he could go to this better place, Peeeee-or-i-aaaaaaaa.

"If it'll play in Peoria, it'll play anywhere," he told Mary.

She was floating in the pool. It was a Sunday afternoon, and they'd been married exactly eighty-seven hours.

"Did you hear me?" Green was shirtless, sitting under the shade of a deck umbrella, a blob of white sunscreen on his nose. He wore the sporty sunglasses.

"Yeah OK. Let's move to Peoria."

"Really?"

"Where's it at? Indiana?"

"Illinois."

"Oh, Chicago."

"South of there. Middle of the state."

"Fine," she said. She mouthed the word, "Peoria." It sounded exotic.

A week later, they hitched a U-Haul trailer to the mini-van and drove out of Las Vegas, through the Rocky Mountains, across Kansas and the high plains, through Missouri, and over the Mississippi into Illinois. At six in the evening, they cruised into Peoria and found Holt Street, in a part of town called the Greek Isle. When they pulled up to the house Green had rented, Mary's mouth dropped open. The place was nothing more than a brick bungalow, even smaller than the Airstream. One of the front windows was busted out, a piece of plywood the temporary (or permanent?) fix. The bushes up by the house were overgrown, and the walk leading to the front door was cracked, with weeds sprouting through the uneven concrete. There wasn't a porch, just a few concrete steps leading to the front door. There wasn't a storm door, just a smudged white door with a mail slot. Mary looked over at Green, who had this big, just-won-the-lottery grin on his face. "My gosh, isn't it great to be getting a fresh start?"

The place came "lightly furnished," which meant there was a well-worn couch in the living room. One side of the couch had obviously been a scratching post for a previous owner's cat. In fact, the smell of cat urine hung like an invisible fog through-out the house. There was an ancient double bed in the bedroom with a depression in the middle of the mattress that looked like it could hold water. Probably the most makeshift aspect of the house was the plastic patio furniture, a round white table and two white deck chairs, in the eat-in kitchen. When Mary saw that, she nearly burst into tears. Green said maybe they could put a vase with fresh-cut flowers on the table to spruce things up. Then Mary opened the fridge. Inside, there was a bottle of Heinz with crusted ketchup caked around the cap, a jar of pickles with two spears left, and a box of baking soda. Green smiled at her. "It's only temporary," he said. "Just a place for us to get started."

The plan was for Mary to make a little money while Green established himself as the man to see in Peoria if someone wanted to place a sports bet. Reluctantly, she filled out an application at the Pair-a-Dice, a riverboat casino docked on the East Peoria side of the Illinois River. Because of her Las Vegas experience, she was hired on the spot. The Pair-a-Dice was modeled after an Old West saloon. There were three mahogany bars, and the bartenders behind them dressed up in arm garters and suspenders. Different sections of the game floor had been given Old West names like the OK Corral, Dodge City, and Ghost Town. The place was stuffed to the gills with elderly people from nursing homes in neighboring central Illinois farm towns. Mary had never seen so many men in flannel shirts. The women had that bye-bye-Betty jiggle under their arms, and each time one reached up to pull the slot handle, the bye-bye-Betty jiggle-jaggled and made Mary feel sick right down to the bottom of her stomach. She was only ten years younger than these women—and Green was only a handful of years younger than the men.

She felt ridiculous in the waitress uniform she had to wear, a low-cut, madam-of-the-night costume complete with fishnet stockings which made her feel as if she'd fallen off a New Orleans parade float. She spent most of her shifts by an ATM in the corner pulling the skirt down to cover her butt and wobbling on stilettos that trembled under her weight of 225 pounds. *If it'll play in Peoria.* She hoped that someone, God maybe, was standing in the wings with a cane about to pull them off stage.

Peoria wasn't all that it was cracked up to be for Green, either. He put on a proud face for Mary, but he was already having some serious second thoughts. The sun certainly didn't always shine like he had imagined it would. In the six days they had been in Peoria, it had rained for five. He hated the rain, but as far as he could tell, the people of Peoria were fine with it, saying things like, "The plants are getting a good drink," or, "It sure is going to green up around here." But the worst part, the absolute worst part about Peoria, was that Green was having a hard time getting his gambling enterprise going. Sure, it had sounded good to tell Mary he was a bookie, but in reality, he had no idea how to collect a bet or "advertise" that he was collecting them. He'd bought an accounting ledger, which he kept under the front seat in the minivan, but other than that, he hadn't a clue. Still, he kept at it. He knew that Mary wasn't going to put up with the house situation for too long, as she was the type of woman who wanted things—a tablecloth covering the table and more than just soap and shampoo in the shower. In fact, she was probably more of a bath person than a shower person.

He started with the farm towns surrounding Peoria. Each day, he would walk into their Main Street bars and order a drink, waiting, hoping, for something to happen. He tried to look like a bookie, the way he stood, with a look on his face that was meant to say, *I'll take that bet.* The guys at the bar would gaze at him with sidelong glances, and, eventually, after they were comfortable, start talking to him, asking him questions, buying him drinks. A peculiar thing: these Midwesterners poured their bottles of Bud into small glasses. Green didn't understand this practice. How was he going to get these people to trust him with their money if they didn't even trust their bottles of beer? He had thought this was going to be easy, that he'd just have to walk into a bar, tell people he was from Las Vegas, and that would be that. Yes, they were impressed that he was from Vegas. They smiled and nodded their heads when he told them, giving him the look-over as they took in his suit. Then they would ask him if he worked for Caterpillar and had just gotten transferred to Peoria?

One day, Green went into a bar called Mike's Tap, on the south side of Pekin. It was eleven in the morning, and the place smelled like a locker room after it had been hosed down. The joint was empty except for the bartender drinking a mug of coffee and watching a morning talk show, and a guy sitting at a table reading the sports section of the *Peoria Journal Star* and drinking a bottle of Bud out of a small glass. The guy looked like someone who drove a grain truck and spent his weekends hunting deer.

Green sat down across from him. "What's with the small glasses?" he asked. "I gotta know. Everyone around here does it. I don't get it."

The guy looked over the top of his newspaper. "Do I know you?"

"No."

"Should I know you?"

"I see you're reading the sports page."

"Who told you about me?"

"No one. Why? Should someone have?"

"Do I know you?"

"Like I said, I don't think so."

"Did Mike send you over to talk to me?" The guy nodded toward the bartender.

Green looked over his shoulder. "Yeah. Mike did." He wanted to see where this was going.

"So, you wanna book a bet?"

"Wait a second. You're a bookie? I'm a bookie, too."

"You're a bookie?" the guy asked.

"In the flesh."

"You're not from around here, are you? You look tan."

"Vegas."

"So, you're a bookie from Las Vegas?"

"That's where I'm from. Yeah."

"How many suits you own?"

Green was wearing a maroon suit that day with a white pocket square in the breast pocket, a paisley tie. "About eight."

"They don't sell suits like that around here."

"They probably do. Somewhere. I haven't really looked around, but I bet they probably do. There were a few stores in Vegas."

"Rule number one. Drop the . . ." He motioned to the suit. "You sell cars?"

"I'm a bookie. I told you. I used to work at a bank, though. I'm retired."

"God does not see as you see. You judge by appearance, but the Lord looks into the heart."

"That's from a movie isn't it?"

"Something like that."

"So, you think the suit is too much."

"The Lord looks into the heart. You judge by appearance."

"What movie is that from?"

The guy rustled his paper. "I wanna get back to this article."

Green got up and took a stool at the bar and ordered a vodka on the rocks. He squeezed some lemon into the clear liquid, followed by a couple of packets of sugar. He wasn't quite sure what to make of the exchange he had just had—"The Lord looks into the heart." He had a headache, and gulped two Tylenol with his vodka.

Eventually, the guy got up from the table and put a Bonnie Raitt song on the jukebox, then went over to the pay phone to make a call. After he was finished with the call, he wrote something on a bar napkin, then stuffed it in his shirt pocket and sat down to do the crossword in the paper. Green watched him for a while, then ordered a cheeseburger. He offered to buy one for the guy, who declined Green's offer.

Green drank a beer with his cheeseburger, right out of the bottle, no small glass for him. At one point, the guy walked up to the bar and ordered another bottle of Bud. He nodded at Green, then carried the bottle back to his table and poured some in his glass. Then he went to the bathroom, and when he came out, he played the same Bonnie Raitt song he'd played earlier. Green had hoped that observing another bookie would help him understand how to become a bookie, but it didn't. The bookie seemed like just some guy in a bar. Then it hit Green: that was the trick. He needed to look like some guy in a bar.

Three

Diane & Chic & Lomax Waldbeeser
or, the Waldbeeser family extended, the first time

January–July 1952

Despite her rejection, Chic still had a hard time keeping his mind off of Lijy. Standing in the shower one morning, trying to push thoughts of Lijy from his mind, he became so consumed with guilt that he started weeping. Then, he felt guilty for weeping. Fathers didn't weep. They wore neckties and drank coffee and sometimes, by mistake, backed into a car in the grocery store parking lot, but even then, they didn't weep. They also didn't think about other women, especially their brother's wives, and they certainly didn't think about other women while they took showers. He shut off the water and stood there dripping. He could do this, he told himself. He thought of his grandfather telling his father to get his act together.

To try to and keep his mind occupied, Chic threw himself into projects for his newly born son, Lomax. He re-carpeted the basement and changed out the hinges on the closet doors and checked every shingle on the roof, which took him two full weekends and resulted in a sprained ankle when he lost his footing and fell into the backyard.

One night after dinner, Diane put Chic in charge of looking after Lomax while she scrubbed some pots and pans in the kitchen. Chic placed the baby on a blanket on the living room floor and switched on "The Lone Ranger." Lomax *withered* and giggled and squirmed, but after a few minutes, neither the television nor his son held Chic's attention as his mind drifted to an image of Lijy sitting in front of a mirror brushing her hair. Lomax started to cry, and Diane yelled from the kitchen to see if everything was all right. Chic didn't hear her because he was thinking about Lijy and didn't hear his son pretty much wailing bloody murder. Finally, Diane stormed into the living room and yelled, "Chic Waldbeeser!" She put the dish towel she was holding over her shoulder and scooped up Lomax and nuzzled him close to her chest and whispered baby talk into his ear. Chic felt so guilty that it was hard for him to breathe. He told Diane that he didn't know how to get Lomax to stop crying, didn't know the tricks she knew, and asked her to help him become a better father. Diane eyed him suspiciously, and Chic knew she wasn't buying it, so he told her that some of the guys at the cannery had talked about how unfair it was that women automatically knew how to take care of babies and men had to be taught. Diane cracked the slightest smile and told Chic to sit down on the sofa. She gently handed him Lomax and showed him how to cradle the baby close to his chest. As Chic held his son, Lomax looked up at him, and his wide eyes were so vulnerable that Chic could feel his heart melting. At that moment, he made a silent vow to put Lijy on a shelf in the back of his mind and never, *ever, ever, ever* think of her again.

However, one Sunday afternoon while Diane and Lomax were at church with Diane's parents, Chic found himself in his car across the street from his brother's house. He had his binoculars trained on the living room window, and through the part in the drapes, he could see Lijy sitting on the sofa, sipping a mug of tea and probably listening to that Duke Ellington song. The binoculars magnified her so that it looked like she was right there, right outside the window of his car, close enough that he could reach out and touch the smoothness of her cheek, the softness of her black hair. He kept the binoculars focused on the window while he undid his fly and worked his penis out. He was concentrating so hard on what he was doing that he didn't hear the police car pull up behind him, didn't hear the sheriff, Larry Hewitt, get out of the police car and walk up to the driver's side door.

Lucky for Chic, Sheriff Hewitt saw only the binoculars, which Chic dropped to the floor of the car when the sheriff screamed, "Waldbeeser!"

Chic reached down and grabbed the binoculars, setting them on his lap to cover his open fly.

"Isn't that your brother's house?" Sheriff Hewitt asked.

"My brother asked me to . . . ah . . . keep an eye on his house. He's out of town."

"Uh-huh." Sheriff Hewitt stared at Chic, a hard glare, piercing. He was holding his nightstick in front of him like he was about ready to whack something. "Are you sure you weren't peeping in the window at your brother's wife? The foreign woman."

"What? No. I wasn't . . . not at all."

Sheriff Hewitt nodded. "I'll let you go about your business this time. But don't think I'm not going to remember this, Waldbeeser."

In his rearview mirror, Chic watched Sheriff Hewitt walk back to his police car. He quickly zipped his fly. As Sheriff Hewitt slowly drove by, he pointed to his eyes with his index and middle fingers to show Chic that he'd be watching him. Then he took a left at the corner and was gone.

Chic was shaking. Before he started the car, he suddenly remembered a time when he was seven. He and Buddy were upstairs playing sock ball, a game played with a wadded-up pair of socks. The point of the game was to hit the other person with the wadded up pair of socks. The wrinkle was the person without the sock ball was allowed to hide anywhere in the house, and the person with the sock ball had to count to ten before starting his search. On this afternoon, Chic had the sock ball. After counting to ten, he went off in search of his brother. He first checked under Buddy's bed (his favorite place to hide), but he wasn't there. He then went out into the hallway and checked the linen closet next to the bathroom, throwing the door open and standing there poised with the sock ball cocked ready to throw.

But Buddy wasn't in the linen closet—he was behind the bathroom door, and right after Chic threw open the linen closet door, Buddy decided to make a break for it. He charged out of the bathroom, running the opposite way down the hall toward the master bedroom and the stairs that led to the living room below. Chic slammed the linen closet door shut, causing their mother downstairs in the kitchen to yell, "Don't slam the doors!" He took two steps in pursuit of his brother, then thinking better of chasing after him, stopped. Buddy was trapped between Chic and their parents' closed bedroom door. His only escape route was the stairs, and as soon as Chic wound up to throw the sock ball, Buddy dove for them. He slipped, however, and ended up taking a head-over-heels tumble down the stairs, a crashing somersault that made so much noise their mother set down the spoon she was using to measure vanilla extract and raced out of the kitchen. Buddy ended up on his back at the bottom of the stairs, a few feet from their father, who looked away from the window to Buddy at the exact moment that Chic reached the last step and dropped the sock ball on Buddy's chest and said, "You're it." His father smiled, a smile that Chic felt all the way to the bottom of his feet. The smile was quick but it had happened; Chic knew it had happened; then it was over, just like that, and his father went back to the window, and their mother came rushing into the living room to attend to Buddy who was beginning to cry, and Chic continued to stand there staring at his father and wondering what he could possibly be looking at out that window.

Chic started the car, and the engine roared to life. He looked over at his brother's house one last time. The drapes were pulled open, and Lijy was standing in the window. She held a mug; her lips were perfectly straight. A wave of fright rushed through his body, a sensation like hearing an unexpected noise in a dark house. He fumbled with the car's gearshift as she waved to him, holding up a hand in a sad hello. Chic ignored her wave. He pulled away from the curb and took a left—the same left Sheriff Hewitt had taken—and glanced in the rearview mirror to see Lijy still standing in the window, her left hand on the glass, perhaps, he thought, in an attempt to get him to stop.

Green Geneseo

■

June 12, 1998

About ten miles outside of East Peoria, down Creve Coeur Avenue, near the car dealerships, on the banks of the Illinois River—on the other side of the river was Peoria's skyline: the Jay Janssen Building, the Mark Twain Hotel, the Capital One building, the Pere Marquette—Green pulled into the parking lot of the Brazen Bull. He had passed the bar for the last week while driving Mary to the Pair-a-Dice. Just glancing at the place, even when crawling by on a road littered with stoplights and strip malls, Green noticed the structure had been home to a fast food restaurant in a former life, maybe a Hardee's or an Arby's. The building had huge, square windows on every side and a drive-through marquee, but those huge windows had been covered with sheets of plywood painted a park picnic table green, and the drive-through marquee had long since been abandoned and was now used as a storage area for a garbage Dumpster and empty beer kegs. An asphalt parking lot the size of an outfield spread out before the building, and at the turn-in off Creve Coeur Avenue was an overgrown landscape planter. In the middle of the planter, a large sign had sprouted up to announce to the drivers that there was a bar named the Brazen Bull offering happy hour from three to eight and all-you-can-eat hot wings on football Sundays, even though there hadn't been a football Sunday in seven months. A bar with a big parking lot usually had big bathrooms. Bad things could happen in bathrooms, and this was one of the reasons Green had been avoiding the place. But this morning he had a raging headache and needed a drink. Besides, he thought he had this bookie thing figured out—all he had to do was be Green. It was that simple. Just be a guy at the bar. So, that's what he was going to do, and this was where he was going to start.

Days of Our Lives was playing on a television set at the end of the bar. (Green knew the program because Jane had watched it every day in the hospital.) Cigarette butts polka-dotted the scuffed wood floor, and a cloud of smoke hung over the pool table in the back, where two guys were loudly battling it out. Green ordered a vodka on the rocks from the bartender, a young girl wearing a Harley Davidson tank top. He added some lemon and sugar and took a sip. Not enough sugar, so he emptied another packet into the glass. He then turned to watch the game of pool. One of the players was a kid in his early twenties, wearing a pink polo shirt, the three buttons undone so that his hairless chest showed. The kid leaned over to take a cut shot, seven ball in the corner pocket—a lot of table, and Green knew it was a difficult shot. When the kid missed, Green tried to show that he was into the game, saying, "Oh, that was close." The kid gave him the once-over, taking in the maroon suit and alligator-skin loafers. Green thought about what the other bookie had said about the suit. He held up his drink. "Nice try."

The kid turned his attention back to the table. He was playing against an older guy in a leather cowboy vest. The older guy sighted up a straight-in shot, the fourteen into the corner pocket.

"You got money on this game?" Green shouted. "This a money bar?"

The kid looked at Green. "You want next?"

"I'm more of a basketball fan, actually. Professional basketball. The playoffs are happening right now. You a basketball fan? Like either of the teams tonight? Chicago or . . . whoever they're playing."

"The Jazz."

"Right. So, you got a favorite?"

The older guy, whom Green later found out everyone at the Brazen Bull called Eight Ball, pulled out of his shot and glared at Green. "Hey, hombre. You mind?"

"Sorry." Green sucked a sip of vodka from his straw.

Eight Ball went back down on his shot, eyeing it up. He hit the cue ball with draw so that when it struck the fourteen and knocked it into the corner pocket, it reversed direction, as if it were on a string, and rolled backward so that it was in position for his next shot, the ten in the side pocket.

"Nice shot." Green turned around. "You got any aspirin, honey?" he asked the bartender.

She ignored his question, engrossed in *Days of Our Lives*.

"Excuse me. Do you have any aspirin?"

"There's a gas station down the highway sells aspirin," she told Green without looking away from the television.

A few minutes later, the pool game was over (Eight Ball won), and the kid took a stool next to Green and ordered a Miller Lite. The bartender got one from the reach-down refrigerator and in one fluid motion, cracked off the cap and set the bottle down on a coaster, then went back to staring at the television. The kid poured his beer into his tiny glass.

"What are you doing in a place like this?" Green looked the kid up and down, taking in his pink shirt and acid-washed blue jeans and flip-flops.

"I could ask you the same thing."

"Fair enough. My wife works up the road at the Pair-a-Dice. I just dropped her there. Thought I'd get a drink."

"At eleven in the morning?"

Green shrugged. "What can I say? I was thirsty."

"This is the only place you can play pool for money. Only place I know. I'm Seth, by the way." He held out his hand.

"Nice to meet you, Seth." Green wasn't sure if he should give his name. He paused for a second, and decided not to give it. "So, Seth, you a gambler?"

"I like winning money."

"You a basketball fan?" Behind Seth, Eight Ball was putting quarters in the pool table. "So, who do you like tonight? Chicago or Utah? Chicago is giving up three points."

"You a bookie?"

"You a cop?"

"Do I look like a cop?"

"Do I look like a bookie?"

"Not really. Not like a bookie from around here. I wouldn't really know, though. I used to bet with a guy who lived on my dorm floor, freshman year. I haven't in a while, though." Seth took a drink of his Miller Lite. "What's the over/under?"

"Bet a winner. That's where the true heart is. Chicago or Utah? Chicago's giving three points." Green stole a glance at the television. The *Days of Our Lives* theme music was playing, and the credits were rolling. "Tell you what, Seth . . ." He motioned with his head toward the front door.

Seth made a confused face. Green leaned in and whispered, "Meet me in the parking lot in five minutes. We'll talk lines or over/under. Whatever you want to bet."

"Why don't we . . ." Seth motioned toward a hallway that led to the bathrooms. At the end of the hallway was a door that went out to a deck with tables and a view of the Peoria skyline across the river.

"In the parking lot. Five minutes. I'll be in the minivan." Green slipped a five-dollar bill under his empty vodka glass. "Barkeep, honey." The bartender looked at him, and Green was positive she'd been crying. "Thanks for your hospitality."

In the parking lot, Green climbed into his minivan. His head was pounding and the corner of his vision seemed to waver. But he wasn't going to let a headache stop him. He was close to his first transaction, and it hadn't been all that hard; it was only a matter of breaking the ice and getting the person, the booker—was that right, booker? er, no . . . the bettor, yeah, the bettor—getting the bettor to start talking. Green opened the glove compartment and took out a bottle of Tylenol. He dry-swallowed two capsules and leaned his head back and closed his eyes. He hadn't felt like this, like a man, since he'd joined a gym the month after Jane died. While he strained through his reps, grunting, the complimentary trainer who that came with his six-month membership shouted, "Be a man. Come on. Be a man. Pump it out. *Pump it out!*" He was being a man again. He flexed his bicep and felt the hard bulge.

After a few minutes, Seth came out of the bar. He scanned the parking lot, spotted the minivan, opened the passenger-side door, and hopped in. He took five twenties out of his hip pocket and told Green he wanted to bet the Jazz. "I like Karl Malone."

"Utah's getting three."

"I'm a dog bettor. I like underdogs."

Green reached under the seat for his ledger. Bending over sent a jolt of pain up his left arm, through his neck, and into his left eye like someone had stuck a hotwire to the back of it. "Jesus Christ, I got a headache."

Lomax Waldbeeser

■

1952ish

Lomax's earliest memory was of a long-haired, red-lipped being who picked him up and said high-pitched incomprehensible things into his face after he finished sucking what the long-haired, red-lipped being stuck in his mouth, and a pudgy-cheeked being with a deep voice, who stuck its head into his vision every time the long-haired, red-lipped being laid him down in a room that looked like it looked when he closed his eyes. The pudgy-cheeked being said incomprehensible things for long periods of time and gave him rectangular items whose corners he liked to stick in his mouth and gnaw on. After a while, some of the incomprehensible things began to be comprehensible; he learned that the long-haired, red-lipped being was his mother and the pudgy-cheeked being was his father, and that his mother liked to say, "I love you and Daddy loves you and Grandma and Grandpa von Schmidt love you and Grandma Waldbeeser loves you." Although he'd never been held by Grandma Waldbeeser, his mother sometimes put a picture in front of his face and said, "Grandma Waldbeeser. She's in a place called Florida with a man named Tom McNeeley." Then his mother would touch his belly and say, "Goo-che-goo-che-goo," and his father would stand behind his mother mumbling something about Grandma Waldbeeser not being something something something and storm out of the room.

Chic Waldbeeser

■

1952ish

Since his run-in with Sheriff Hewitt, Chic had been a good guy. Anytime he started thinking about Lijy, he would wash his hands with hot water. Some days, he washed them seventeen or eighteen times, and as a result, they became dry and chapped. But it worked; he rarely thought about Lijy. Instead, his mind skipped to thoughts of his brother out on the road selling coins, and to his father, Bascom III sitting in the living room, staring out the window. His brother and father were one and the same, pretty much. Chic had a sense that something was wrong with them, like they were bearing crosses of infinite sadness. Maybe he had the cross, too, but Chic carried his differently. His cross was one of infinite denial. Push everything to the back of the mind. But he couldn't always do that because his mind often went in directions he couldn't control, though he tried. Oh, did he try. The worst thing was denying his feelings. He did everything he could not to feel. Do not feel. Feel nothing. Avoid feeling at all cost.

Even when doing something that should evoke the epitome of feeling, the penultimate of feeling, the zenith of feeling, the top of the feeling mountain, like kneeling next to his son's crib and looking over the top rail down on the sleeping boy on his stomach, sucking his thumb, Chic did not allow even the slightest, even the tiniest bit of feeling to wedge itself under the door that he'd closed on his emotions. But one evening, rubbing his son's back while shushing him to sleep, Chic tried to feel something. If he was going to feel something, this was the time. Right now. He was going to concentrate and feel what he was feeling while he rubbed his son's back. And what he felt . . . he felt . . . what did he feel? He tried harder. He felt . . . he felt like he was wearing a diving suit, one of those heavy, brass-helmet diving suits with an oxygen hose that uncoiled upward toward the water's surface. In his diving suit, he was suspended in the water, floating. There was no sound. No smell. No feeling. Nothing. Just him inside a heavy diving suit, protected from everything. Even when rubbing his son's back and shushing him to sleep.

Chic & Lomax Waldbeeser

■

1958ish

Lomax grew up quickly, too quickly, and filled out to be a roundish boy, not quite fat, but not skinny, either. Even though the elementary school fashion of the time was slacks and a button-up shirt, he dressed like a college professor, with a tweed sport coat and a bowtie. When he was just seven, he won the Jefferson Elementary spelling bee. After he spelled the last word correctly—*bildungsroman*—he ran off the stage and demanded that his second-grade teacher, Mrs. Nelson, and the other students, who looked at Lomax like he was some sort of space creature, call him Dr. Lomax.

Lomax carried a leather briefcase full of his great-great-grandfather's notebooks and unsent letters. The letters were written in German and addressed to Basom's parents, but for some reason, a reason no one knew, they had never been sent. When he passed away, he willed them to his son, Bascom Jr., who never read them (since he didn't know German), and before he passed away, he willed them to his son, Bascom III, who set them in the basement on a shelf next to some other not-worth-mentioning items to collect dust. Not long after his father's suicide, Chic found the box and took it up to his bedroom. He picked through the letters (there were over a thousand) and stared in bewilderment at the strange language and sloppy penmanship. A few days after Lomax's seventh birthday, Chic, for some reason, remembered the letters and dug them out of the attic and gave them to his son. Chic wasn't sure why he had given the letters to Lomax—it just seemed like a fatherly thing to do.

Being only seven, Lomax was too short to carry the briefcase properly, so for a time he dragged it behind him. At some point, he grew tired of dragging it (the constant dragging damaged the briefcase), so he took the rear wheels and axle off his Radio Flyer wagon and affixed them to the briefcase to create a contraption that predated the wheelie suitcase Brooks Walker would patent in 1976. Here's the thing: even at the young age of seven, Lomax's fuse had been lit. He had a destiny. He'd found the book *Middleville, Illinois: Our Town, Our Lives, Our Story* and seen the pictures of R.S. Archerbach and his sons. He wanted to be pictured in a book one day.

Chic, on the other hand, wanted his son to be like every other red-blooded American boy. He tried to get him to watch Cubs' games on the television, replicating Jack Brickhouse's famous "Hey-hey," home run call, but Lomax just sat on the couch ignoring the television and writing in a notebook. Chic also bought his son a baseball glove. Lomax, however, thought the glove was some sort of hat and put it on his head and sat down on his bedroom floor and opened the briefcase. "No, no," Chic said. "It's a glove." He slipped it on his own hand and smacked the palm with his fist. "A baseball glove."

Lomax looked at him, confused.

"For catching baseballs."

"What if I don't want to catch baseballs?"

"Every boy wants to catch baseballs. You just don't know how yet. Come on."

Chic led his son to the backyard. He walked about ten paces from Lomax and underhanded a baseball to him. The ball fell short and rolled up to Lomax's feet.

"Throw it back."

Lomax picked up the ball and looked at it, admiring the stitching on the seams. He shook off the glove and, with both hands, turned the ball over and over, studying it. "What are these?"

"The seams. Now, throw it back. Come on. Right here."

Lomax didn't throw it back. Instead, he walked inside the house, into the kitchen where his mother was making mashed potatoes and green beans. He reached up and took the paring knife she'd been using to peel potatoes off the counter.

When Chic came into the house a moment later, he found Lomax sitting on the kitchen floor using the paring knife, like a surgeon, to cut open the baseball.

"What's he doing?" Chic said.

Diane shrugged.

At dinner, Diane, Chic, and Lomax sat around the dining room table, a plate of mashed potatoes, green beans, and pot roast in front of each of them. The family dog, Cody, a one-year-old golden retriever, sat on the floor, nudging Chic's thigh, looking for table scraps. By this time, Lomax had removed the leather cover of the baseball—it was sitting next to his plate—and was unraveling the string that had been hidden underneath the cover. Every so often, he stopped unraveling the string and wrote something down in his notebook. When dinner was over, Diane picked up the plates and took them to the kitchen. Chic continued to watch Lomax, the string pile getting bigger and bigger; pretty soon, he had unraveled all the string and gotten to the core—a hard, gray ball.

"Hey-hey," Lomax said.

Chic smiled. "Hey-hey."

Lomax smelled the ball. "It's a seed."

"Not exactly."

"It's not a seed?"

"It's the center."

"A center?"

"The middle."

Lomax turned the ball over in his hands.

"Without that gray ball, there can't be a baseball."

Lomax was intrigued. "Do you have a center?"

Chic thought about this. "You and Mommy are my center."

"Do I have a center?"

"Me and Mommy are your center."

"The string needs its center back."

"Yes, it does."

Lomax began to re-wrap the string around the ball.

Mary & Green Geneseo

■

June 13, 1998

The morning after Green booked his first bet, he woke up with a splitting headache that felt like someone was stabbing a chopstick into his left eye. He and Mary had gotten horrible Chinese takeout from Ming Shee the night before (which was probably why he thought his headache felt like he was being stabbed in the eye by a chopstick). Ming Shee was the third Chinese takeout place they'd tried since they got to Peoria, and all three had served the shittiest Chinese he'd ever put in his mouth. Back in Las Vegas, he could get good Kung Pao chicken from three, actually four ... no, six different takeout restaurants. One in particular, in North Las Vegas, by Sunrise Manor, across the street from Lemming's Car Wash—Happy Wok was its name—had chicken strips of mouth-popping, juicy goodness with enough spice to make your forehead bead up. Green dreamed about the Kung Pao from Happy Wok, even though there was no point in dreaming about good Chinese takeout from Las Vegas when you lived in Peoria, Illinois, the world's worst city for Chinese takeout. And, to put a big cherry on top of this Chinese food mess, Green had a splitting headache, and the more he thought about the terrible takeout, the worse his headache got. Jesus Christ. Not to mention, the pain was affecting his vision. When he covered his right eye—which he was doing right now as he looked at the ceiling—everything became blurry. He rolled over and tried to read the digital clock on the nightstand, but the numbers were fuzzy.

"Mary." He shook her. "I can't see out of my left eye."

She moaned, shifted her weight, and pulled the comforter over her head.

Maybe he just needed some coffee and a couple of Tylenol. He got out of bed and, not bothering with his slippers, felt his way out of the bedroom and made it to the front porch and brought in the *Journal Star*. In the kitchen, he spread the sports page on the counter. He covered his left eye, opened to the box scores, and ran his finger down the page. The Jazz had won by eleven. Damn! That little preppie sonofabitch had made a hundred bucks off of him. "Goddamn it," he mumbled.

He opened the cabinet with the Tylenol just as Mary came into the kitchen. "Any coffee?" she asked.

"No. There's no goddamn coffee."

"Geez. What's the matter with you?"

"My eye. My frickin' eye . . . can you pop out your eyeball? Is that possible?" Green shook three Tylenol out of the bottle and dry-swallowed them.

"You should lay off those Tylenol. What are you taking, ten a day?"

Green grunted. "I have a headache, and I can't see out of my left eye. And it smells like oranges in here. Doesn't it?"

"It smells like horrible Chinese food. But I'll take an orange for breakfast. Do we have any?"

"No, we don't have any goddamn oranges. Oranges in Peoria? Are you kidding me?" He covered his right eye, then his left. "We're going to the Brazen Bull this afternoon. The bar I told you about."

"You know I don't want to hustle pool. That life is behind me."

"It's gotta be better than waitressing. All you do is complain about that."

"Yeah, well, the only thing bad about waitressing—other than waitressing—is that I gotta wear that horrible uniform. I feel like . . . like a . . . I don't even know if there's a word to describe it."

"Cheap slut."

"That's two words. And aren't you supposed to tell me I look good?"

"I like cheap sluts."

"Well, I don't like looking like one."

Green smacked Mary's ass, and she playfully slapped at his hand and gave him a don't-be-making-no-sexual-advances-this-morning look. "Take the garbage out, will ya," she said. "And get yourself established already. So far, this ain't playing in Peoria."

After taking a shower, Mary went to the kitchen looking for Green, but he wasn't there. She glanced out the window. Green was sprawled facedown in the driveway, not moving. A young girl was kneeling beside him, checking for a pulse on his neck. Across the street, Bradley students who had been on their way to class were forming a crowd. One girl had a hand up to her mouth, while her companion, a boy wearing a backward baseball cap, sipped from a to-go cup of coffee.

Mary thought about Green saying he smelled oranges. Wasn't smelling citrus a sign of something? She'd heard that, but couldn't remember what it was a sign of. The girl kneeling next to Green rolled him onto his back. He looked dead. Oh my God.

Don't be dead. Jesus. Please don't be dead. Mary heard herself whimper: *Green*. She reached out and touched the window. She took a deep breath. *Green*. His head rolled to look at the girl who was kneeling over him. He's not dead. He's alive. *He's alive!* But he was so pale, and his lips were almost blue. The girl shouted across the street for someone to get help, and the boy with the backward baseball cap handed his to-go coffee to the girl with her hand to her mouth and tore off down the sidewalk.

In the ambulance, the paramedic leaned over. "Can you hear me, sir?"

Green didn't move. He was looking at a cabinet in the front corner of the ambulance; there was a sticker on the door that said, DANGER, in red lettering.

"Sir?"

Green blinked.

"Can you talk, sir?"

Green grunted.

Mary had a wadded-up Kleenex in her hand. She dabbed at her eyes.

"Ma'am. Is he normally responsive?"

She nodded and sniffed. "Green, honey, it's going to be okay. Answer the man's questions."

Green turned his head to look at her—the fear in her eyes nearly broke his heart. He hadn't told Mary about Jane—or Sue or Leigh Ann, for that matter. The thing about Green was that when he fell for a woman, he fell hard. He fell hard for every-thing, and anything. Case in point: a move to Peoria at the age of sixty-four. Green didn't wear his heart on his sleeve; he pinned it to his forehead. He'd been married three times before he met Mary. The first one had been Sue Morris, a girl in his high school class, Lakeville High School, Lakeville, Montana. Three days af-ter graduation in 1953, they were married by the justice of the peace in Bozeman and didn't tell a soul, not even Mort Mor-ris, Sue's father, or Green's parents, church do-gooders Betty and

Bob Geneseo. Actually, Sue was supposed to tell her father, the young couple's hope being that Mort would reach out a hand and get Green a job in the silver mines outside of Lakeville, maybe help set them up in a little one-bedroom house by the railroad tracks. But each time Green asked Sue if she'd told her father, she hemmed, stuttered, tried to change the subject, and touched her nose a lot. Green knew why she was stalling. He saw the way Mort looked at him. The last thing he wanted was his daughter marrying some Lakeville townie destined to work the silver mines. Such was Mort's idea to improve his daughter's life—keep her away from guys like Green.

Green met his second wife not long after he had gotten out of the air force. He went in thinking he was going to fly planes but learned that he had a knack for numbers—"tracking" them, as his squadron commander liked to say. "Geneseo, what you can do with numbers is what them fighter pilots can do with riveted-together hunks of metal. It's a goddamn thing of beauty." Green earned the nickname Counter and was a finance clerk stationed at Clark Air Base during the Korean War. He liked the routine of the air force; he liked the chain of command; he liked shining his boots; he liked knowing what was going to happen every single day—the same as the day before, over and over and over. After Korea, he was stationed at Nellis AFB in Vegas, and when he was discharged (honorably) in 1961 after eight years of service, he got himself an apartment in town because he enjoyed the desert and the sunshine, and didn't want to go back to Montana. There wasn't anything but silver mines and snow in Montana anyway, and he didn't want any of that.

One night after imbibing his share of beer at Binion's Horseshoe Casino, he stumbled into the Glitter Gulch, a bottom-tier Vegas strip club (a "juicy joint", as the air force guys liked to call it). He didn't marry a stripper, but that night, he bellied up to the bar next to Leigh Ann Rogers, a roommate of one. Green was so smitten with Leigh Ann—the way she held her martini glass and wore a suede vest and kept saying "groovy" and threw her head back and laughed, showing a piece of pink chewing gum—that he married her two weeks after they met. The sex was amazing.

Then there was Jane. The night he met her in 1965, they went to a diner on Cypress Boulevard and drank coffee until three in the morning. She wore turquoise earrings, and Green liked the way the conversation sometimes got to the point that night where neither of them knew what to say so they didn't say anything but instead looked at each other, locking eyes, both knowing that they should be talking because you talk on first dates, even though neither would admit they were on a first date, they were simply getting coffee at a diner. In the parking lot, after she unlocked her car, Jane turned to him, and he kissed her on the forehead, and she wrapped her arms around him and hugged him, *really* hugged him, and he smelled her shampoo, which smelled fresh like a pile of just-out-of-the-dryer laundry. From the moment of that forehead kiss, their futures converged, and they walked the same path, helping each other, loving each other, connecting with each other, for thirty years. All he really wanted was another person like her. He hadn't seen this coming—a hospital bed in Peoria, Illinois. He couldn't wiggle the toes on his left foot. The left side of his body felt tingly. It made him want to scratch, and he did. He scratched the hell out of the left side of his face and head and his left ass cheek.

Mary sat next to his bed. The television was on—a edited-for-television version of *Pretty Woman*, the scene where Edward (Richard Gere) takes Vivian (Julia Roberts) to San Francisco by private jet to see *La Traviata*. Mary had seen the movie nearly a hundred times, and here she was watching it again in a hospital room in Peoria, Illinois. Green scratched at his face again as the opera character Violetta Valéry from the movie sang: *Gran Dio! morir sì giovane*—"O, God! To die so young." Mary looked at Green and forced a smile.

If it'll play in Peoria . . .

About an hour later, Green's doctor called Mary out into the hallway. Dr. Gannaway was a young guy, about thirty-five, with a goatee. He told her he didn't think Green would walk again, at least not for a while, not until he went through some therapy. He had acute hemiplegia on his left side with a mild case of dysarthria. Mary glanced over her shoulder—Green was asleep in the room behind her. She was having a hard time concentrating on what the doctor was saying. A loud voice in her head had been telling her all afternoon that she needed to pack her bags and get as far away from this as she possibly could. She was doing her best to ignore the voice, but it was getting difficult. The doctor continued to talk: *hemiplegia, dysarthria*. She felt like she was at Walmart, reading the ingredients on a tube of toothpaste.

"How about talking?" she heard herself say.

"He'll work with a speech therapist, but for the time being he can communicate through writing. He had a very severe stroke, Mrs. Geneseo."

"What about moving him? We're actually not from here. We're from Vegas."

"Let's see how things go. One day at a time, Mrs. Geneseo."

"You don't have to call me that."

Dr. Gannaway gave her a quizzical look.

"Mary is fine."

"Very well, then. Mary."

"One last question. Should I be looking for a home for him, an assisted living place or something?"

"He'll be here for a couple days, then let's see how things go. One day at a time."

That afternoon, a speech therapist gave Green a flip pad and a golf pencil and urged him to write.

He wrote, *Brazen Bull. Seth. $100*, and showed it to Mary.

"But we don't have a hundred dollars," she whispered.

Green looked at Mary with downtrodden, heavy eyes, and she knew what he wanted her to do.

Four

Buddy Waldbeeser

■

July 1, 1953

"He should have named the kid Bascom. That's what you did. That would have been the right thing to do. That would have honored you. Bascom V. In the line of Bascoms. I'm, of course, four: William Bascom IV Waldbeeser. BB. Buddy Bascom. You honored your father. Lomax Waldbeeser. I don't even know his middle name. Wait a second, I do. Archibald. Lomax Archibald Waldbeeser. He's going to grow up to hate his parents." Buddy went to the window and pulled the drapes shut. "Just like I hate you."

He turned around to face the chair he'd positioned in front of the window, giving the pillows stacked on it a view of the parking lot filled with traveling salesmen's cars and the neon sign proclaiming the HILLTOP HOTEL. Pine Bluff, Arkansas. Highway 81. Buddy carefully set his derby hat on top of the pillows and stepped back.

"I used to daydream about you calling me BB. I just wanted you to call me son. I mean, you never called me anything. You were there but not there, smoking your cigarettes or out in the barn cursing under your breath. Remember when you said to me, 'I know what I want to do, but when it comes to doing it, I can't?' Seems like a lie now. You did what you wanted to do. Remember that time in the living room when you squared off into a boxing stance? You and your father. A goddamn boxing stance. He was an old man and you go at him like you're Rocky Marciano. You were always . . . I don't know. You were always disappointed. In everything. It didn't matter what it was. Tom McNeeley wanted to talk about you. After you died. He tried to explain that I shouldn't think of you as less of a father for what you did. You were my father is basically what he said, like I should forgive you just because that's who you were. What was it about your life that you hated so much? It doesn't seem to be enough to say that I don't understand. I mean I'm mad at you. That's what I want to tell you. I just want the chance to tell you that. But I have to tell it to a stack of pillows. Look at us. Look at how you left us. Look at you. Your hat. Let me . . . there." Buddy adjusted the hat and looked at the pillows stacked on the chair, the hat on top of them.

Mary Geneseo
∎

June 16, 1998

The Brazen Bull was exactly what Mary had expected. The bartender wore a Harley Davidson tank top and dabbed at her eyes with a wadded napkin while the television at the end of the bar showed *Days of Our Lives*. Mary knew the type. She probably lived in an apartment above a restaurant, went to the mall once a week to get a new pair of earrings, maybe a new bra, a Victoria's Secret model if she could afford it, which she hoped to show off to the "right" guy.

Mary went up to the bar just as *Days of Our Lives* went to a Dove soap commercial. The bartender turned to Mary. "What can I get you?"

"Tomato juice. A few shakes of hot sauce. Two olives, pepper, and a lemon."

"A Virgin Mary?"

Mary smiled at her, though she hated when bartenders said "Virgin Mary." It sounded as if they were making an accusation.

The bartender stabbed two olives with a cocktail spear and dropped them in the red liquid and set the glass on a coaster in front of Mary. "Three dollars."

Mary had one hundred and seven dollars in her purse. That

morning, she had cashed in a large jar of change she'd found in the closet, which netted her seventy-three bucks, and had found eight dollars in the inside pocket of one of Green's suit coats. She also knew that Green kept an envelope with a twenty-dollar bill in the glove compartment of the minivan. The other six dollars she'd already had in her wallet.

"By any chance, do you know someone named Seth?"

The bartender pointed to a preppie kid lining up a pool shot. Mary thanked her and carried her drink over to the pool table. She set her hard-shell cue case on a pub table and stood off to the side, sipping her drink and watching Seth and the guy he was playing, a man wearing tight jeans and a leather vest over a white t-shirt. He looked like a cowboy. The cowboy was about her age and cute in a rough-around-the-edges way. What about this guy? the loud voice in her head asked. About your age. Seems your type.

Seth knocked in the shot he had lined up—an easy cut shot, four ball into the side pocket. He followed that up with a straight-in shot—seven ball in the corner pocket. He then put the cue ball into position to make the eight ball, which he did, in the corner pocket nearest the jukebox.

"Goldarnit, Sethy," the cowboy said. Some money exchanged hands, but Mary didn't see how much.

"Anyone have a winner?" Mary asked.

Seth and the cowboy looked at her.

"Go ahead," the cowboy said. "He's all yours, darlin'." He walked by her slowly, as if he were drinking her in with his nose. Mary hoped he was drinking her in. Maybe if she stood with her hip cocked out like so, he'd take a real good look at her. "He's a shooter." After the cowboy passed by, Mary glanced over her shoulder, hoping to catch him looking over his shoulder back at her. He was looking instead at the bartender, who was watching the soaps on TV, chewing on a sip straw.

Seth broke, and at the crack of the cue, the balls shot out

all over the table like scurrying ants. When they came to a stop, Mary looked at the break. There was good spacing between the balls, no problem areas like three or four balls clustered together or the worst, two balls off to the side against the rail, like they were in the corner on a date. The thing Mary liked about eight ball was that every game was a new game, a new start, but the objective never changed: clear all your balls, solids or stripes, and knock in the eight ball before your opponent did. What she didn't like, however, was that at one time, she used to think that pool, or any game for that matter, represented life, and that all it took to succeed at it (life) was some determination. That morning, she realized what she'd been denying for the past thirty years: no matter how much determination she had, there wasn't any point thinking her life was going to get better.

Seth missed his shot, and then Mary took over, making three balls in a row, all easy shots: six ball straight into the side, four in the corner pocket, and the one ball, a rail-runner, into the corner pocket by the jukebox. The cowboy whistled. "She's got your number, Sethy."

She was able to beat Seth with ease. When the game was over, he counted out fifty bucks and handed it to her. Mary in turn added another fifty and dropped the whole pile of cash on the pool table.

"That's a little steep for me," Seth said.

"Green owed you money," she said. "A hundred bucks. Now we're square."

"Green?"

"You made a bet with him last week," Mary said.

"The guy in the purple suit?"

"Yeah, he had an accident."

Seth said nothing as Eight Ball put three quarters in the pool table's coin tray.

"Is there a Mary Geneseo here?" the bartender called out.

Mary turned around. At the bar, a delivery guy held a bouquet of red roses. "You Mary?" he said.

Mary leaned her cue against the pool table, and the guy came over and handed her the roses. They were heavier than she'd expected. She stuck her face into the blooms and smelled their fragrance. Inside the bouquet was a small card that read, *Love, Green.*

"Hey, lady, just 'cuz you get flowers don't mean we don't get a chance to win our money back." Eight Ball said, racking up the balls. "Let's see if you're any good at nine ball."

Mary put the card in her cue case and started to unscrew her cue. "Sorry, I have to go to work now. But I'll be back."

Lijy Waldbeeser

■

Too many nights during the 1950s

Lijy woke up, and he wasn't in the bed. His side was cold like he'd been gone for a long time. She couldn't remember if they'd gone to bed together or not. Sometimes, she would wake up in the middle of the night wondering if he was home or not. Now she heard his voice coming from downstairs and remembered a few hours earlier, rolling over and wrapping her body around his, but he hadn't been asleep. He'd been staring at the ceiling.

Lijy threw back the covers, slid out of bed, and put on her robe. She thought she'd find him at the dining room table, piles of coins in front of him, a jeweler's loupe around his neck. However, when she crept down the stairs, he was standing in front of a dining room chair, which was stacked with sofa cushions. "Tell me," he said to the cushions. "Please. Just tell me what I'm supposed to be feeling."

"Buddy, are you OK?" she asked, walking into the dining room. It was just after two in the morning. "I can help you, Buddy, but you have to let me."

The first time she'd noticed this type of behavior was on the drive from California. They'd stopped at a diner somewhere in

Kansas, or maybe it was Nebraska; it didn't matter. When she came out of the restroom, she saw Buddy in the booth carrying on a conversation with the empty bench seat across from him. At first, she thought she was seeing things, but her eyes weren't deceiving her. He was talking to himself, and whatever he was talking about and whomever he thought he was talking to, it was getting heated. When she approached, he practically hissed through his teeth, "Right now you are the center of your universe. It won't always be that way." Then he looked up at her, smiled, and motioned for her to have a seat and stuffed a napkin into the collar of his shirt.

"I'm sorry you had to see that," he said now. He went past her, toward the stairs.

In the bedroom, he told her he didn't want to talk about it, then shut off the nightstand lamp. The room was dark. Lijy propped herself up on one elbow, waiting for him to say something, but she knew he wasn't going to say anything. He never said anything.

Mary Geneseo & Chic Waldbeeser,
the beginning of another beginning

■

June 16, 1998

There was this one guy at the Pair-a-Dice who spent whole afternoons—a green duffel bag on the floor next to his stool—playing video poker. He was a few years older than Mary, maybe ten years, but age didn't matter, the loud voice told her. At this point in her life, beggars couldn't be choosers.

The guy always arrived via one of the retirement home buses that flooded the Pair-a-Dice's parking lot. Sometimes, Mary saw him line up with a group of other old people while a young woman wearing hospital scrubs marked names off on a clipboard. He would tell the woman his name, but Mary never heard it clearly—

something with a C. It was a weird name. Mary had been thinking about him lately, after she beat Seth at pool, after she got the flowers from Green, in the hospital as she watched Green lying there and wondered how she could get herself out of this mess. To more than one guy over the years, she'd simply left a note on the kitchen counter—*I'm really sorry this didn't work out*—and hadn't looked back: a new break, a new spread of balls on the pool table. She told herself this time was different, but after the stroke, a part of her, that loud voice, kept nagging her, telling her to go. She'd heard this voice before. Like the time she caught Lyle in the apartment with the black woman. When she climbed behind the wheel of the Mustang and was about to turn the ignition key, the voice told her to do it, to turn the key, to just go already and get it over with. She didn't want to leave. She wanted to be with Lyle, but the voice screamed at her to turn the key, to go, go, go! But there was another voice, a competing voice, a whispering voice that asked questions like, if she had a stroke, would Green stay with her? It talked in clichés, too, like: *do unto others as you'd have done to you.* It told her that Green would be at the hospital holding her hand and feeding her ice cream. He wouldn't be thinking about running away. He might not ever talk again, the loud voice fired back. The whisper voice cleared its throat and told her that C, whatever his name was, lived in a retirement home, and Green had sent you flowers. That cowboy sure wasn't interested. He didn't check you out even once.

In the employee locker room, Mary stashed her pool cue in her locker and changed into the ridiculous waitress uniform. Out on the floor, she snaked between the slot machines and behind the craps tables and over by the blackjack tables where the pit bosses stood scanning the table games and, finally, by the video poker machines to see if C was there. She just wanted to look. She wasn't going to do anything. If he was at his usual machine, she'd let one of the other waitresses know that he was a good tipper.

Of course he was there. She watched him deposit a coin and pull the handle. The loud voice told her to do it, walk up to him, take a chance, who knows what's going to happen—roll the dice. Don't do it, the other voice said. Think about Green in that hospital bed, taking a nap, the television on, machines beeping. You can't do it to him.

"Hey." Mary tapped C what's his name on the shoulder. She set her tray down on top of the video poker machine and picked up the duffel bag—MIDDLEVILLE JUNIOR HIGH SCHOOL was written across it in white letters—from his lap. "Hey, don't touch that," he said in an agitated tone. She tossed the bag to the ground and threw a leg over him, straddling him. There you go, the loud voice said. Make a big splash. Get his attention. That cowboy at the bar doesn't know what he's missing. You are sexy.

C whatever his name was looked over his shoulder. "Where is he?"

"Who?"

"Morris."

"Who's Morris?"

"He put you up to this." He looked into the Chow Wagon, the buffet restaurant, behind them.

Mary put her arms around his neck and stuck her face into his face. They were nose to nose like they were about to kiss. "What's your name?"

"Mary, what are you doing?" Another waitress balancing a cocktail tray struck a grade-school teacher pose—one hand on her cocked hip. "This isn't a strip club. You know you're not supposed to touch the customers."

Mary slid off of C's lap and smoothed the front of her skirt.

"Don't make me report you." The waitress walked away toward the slot machines.

"Chic," he said. "Chic Waldbeeser. Now, where's Morris? How much did he pay you?"

"Who's Morris?"

"My roommate. There he is." In the Chow Wagon, Morris sat at a table eating a slice of watermelon, a plate heaped with fried chicken and mashed potatoes in front of him. He noticed Chic pointing at him and waved.

"I've never seen that guy in my life."

"Yeah, well, I don't believe you." Without bothering to get off his stool, Chic reached for his duffel bag but couldn't quite get to it. "Can you give me that?" Mary handed the bag to him. Chic unzipped it, took out a quarter, and put it in the video poker machine. The machine made beeping noises and dealt him a rainbow: three of clubs, nine of diamonds, seven of hearts, jack of spades, and ace of spades. "Goddamn it to hell. Look at that. Terrible. One ace and a bunch of junk."

"I know the feeling," Mary said.

Chic took another quarter out of the bag. Mary grabbed for it. "Hey what are . . . stop . . . don't." She pried his hand open and took the quarter and, giggling, dropped it down her low-cut blouse between her breasts.

Chic swallowed hard and stared at the cleavage crease that had eaten his quarter.

"You like these, don't you, Chic Waldbeeser?"

"You're going to get us in trouble."

"Hold on. Watch this." Mary could feel the quarter sliding between her breasts. Then it dropped out from under her blouse and landed, without a sound, on the casino's carpeted floor next to her high-heeled shoe. She expected Chic to reach for it, but he turned back to his poker hand, discarded everything but the ace of spades, and hit the deal button. The machine whirred to life and dealt Chic another ace and three other rags. It then beeped and dropped two quarters into the win tray.

Lijy Waldbeeser

■

September 1959

Lijy had known that Buddy needed help from the moment she saw him eating a bowl of pork noodles that afternoon in San Francisco. On the outside, he looked like just another typical guy wearing a suit and a derby hat, but on the inside, if you looked closely, if you peeled back the outer layer, he wasn't altogether all right. Lijy knew what she was getting herself into with a man like that, but she wasn't altogether all right herself, and perhaps, she thought, if you put two not-quite-altogether all rights together, that might somehow make them both right. And that's what she told herself she was doing. That's what got her through the days and nights sitting in the living room waiting for him. She'd wait an entire lifetime if she had to. No matter what, waiting for him was better than Stockton, California. Or maybe it wasn't. No, she wasn't going to let herself think like that, and besides, there were things she had to do like buy groceries, which she hated, but she would do it, for him. So she found herself, again, at Stafford's. She put a head of cauliflower into her shopping cart, a package of rice, a sack of potatoes. She felt a pair of warm eyes on her while she searched for a ripe cantaloupe. She glanced over her shoulder. A wiry man in a black turtleneck sweater stood a few feet away. He pushed his glasses up on his nose.

"There's so many to choose from," she said to him.

"Allow me." He took a melon and smelled it, then held it up high like it was a trophy. "Have you ever been to California?" he asked.

Lijy thought that maybe this was some sort of joke. She looked behind her, thinking she'd see someone standing there, laughing, but there was no one.

"In San Francisco they have these people called Beats. I can tell by looking at you,"—he motioned at her sari and Khussa shoes—"that you'd dig them." He smelled the melon again. "This one fits you. It's a gorgeous melon for a gorgeous woman."

Lijy blushed.

"My name's Lamar Jimmerson, the second." He held out his hand limply, like a woman, and Lijy noticed he was wearing a gold bracelet.

"Do you like tea, Lamar Jimmerson?"

"The second," he said. "Lamar Jimmerson, the second."

"Sorry," she said.

"Actually, I have a confession. My name is not Lamar Jimmerson, the second. It's Tom. Tom T. Shiftlett. I'm sorry I lied. It's just that . . . I normally don't meet women at the grocery store."

"I normally don't meet men at the grocery store." Lijy smiled at him. "Do you like tea, Mr. Shiftlett?"

"Please. Tom. And, yes, tea is beautiful. The world right now is so beautiful." He pushed his glasses up on his nose again. He was blinking so rapidly that Lijy thought he might pass out.

"Are you a priest?" she asked.

"No. I'm an athletic trainer. For the Rivermen."

Lijy had no idea who that was. "Rivermen?"

"The hockey team in Peoria."

Lijy nodded, feigning interest, and smiled at Tom T. Shiftlett. He was a slit of a man, like a small tear that could be fixed with needle and thread. She noticed that his hands were like a child's, soft and hairless. Buddy had big hands with hair on his knuckles, and stubble that grew down his neck and disappeared under the collar of his shirt.

Over mugs of tea in Lijy's kitchen, Tom explained that he was from Ohio and had a Doctor of Science from the Chicago School of Applied Science. He'd gotten the head trainer job with the Rivermen three months ago. The training room, he said, didn't have a whirlpool and he was a strong believer in whirlpools. He didn't understand the term, "the Middle West." "It isn't really west. It's more east than west. And it's gray. So terribly gray. A more accurate description would be 'the Gray West.'" In the Middle West, only 48 percent of the days each year were sunny. No wonder people were always complaining about back problems. They were scrunched up, tight-muscled, trying to fend off the elements. It snowed a lot in the Middle West, and anything that fell from the sky was not good, in his opinion. His plan was to move to California and open a private practice for aging weight lifters. He told Lijy that weight lifting was a beautiful sport, and that Yury Vlasov was, without a doubt, the favorite to win the gold medal in the 1960 Summer Olympics in Rome. He said he wasn't a communist, despite his admiration for a Russian weight lifter. He asked Lijy if she knew what the word California meant, and she said she didn't. He told her it meant "the perfect life" in Spanish. Then he told her that that wasn't true. He didn't know what California meant, maybe it was an Indian tribe. He said the houses were closer together in California because so many people wanted to live there. When he moved there he wasn't going to be just anybody. He was going to live out his dreams—the private practice, the weight lifters. He'd go out for dinner on Friday nights. He'd go to the movies. He'd buy two color television sets—one for the living room and one for some other room he hadn't decided on yet, maybe the bedroom. He'd put a hammock in the backyard.

"I'm sorry," he said. "I can tell you're not very interested in my description of California, but I have another confession. My name's not Tom T. Shiftlett. It's Ellis McMillion. This time I'm telling you the truth. I promise. It's just that I couldn't help notice your wedding ring and, well, it made me . . . one can never be too safe. Does your husband work out?"

"Work out?"

"Exercise. Lift weights. Push-ups maybe?"

Lijy shook her head no. She tried to remove her wedding ring and after some turning and pulling finally got it over the knuckle. Then, she thought better of what she was doing and put it back on. It didn't matter anyway. This would be a one-time thing and that would be that and she and Buddy would have a talk about it. She'd come clean, and then, *and then . . .*

"Anyway, my name is Ellis McMillion. That's the truth. I'm a mutt of a man. I'm Italian, Dutch, German, and British. A little Spanish, too. A speck of American Indian, Cherokee, on my father's side. My mother was 100 percent New Yorker, though. My family tree is a knotty pine, and frankly, I'm a little embarrassed about it. I'm sorry I lied."

Lijy wanted to tell him that Buddy collected coins and talked to himself and was on the road all the time and when he left her alone, she felt like a tiny part of herself, this very tiny little piece of herself, a piece that was invisible and only she knew about it, began to curl up and shrivel, and she didn't want that to happen anymore. She couldn't let it happen anymore. And that's why she'd asked him, Lamar or Tom or Ellis or whatever his name was, over for tea. She didn't care that what he was saying about California was not like the California she knew. He didn't know her California, the California she'd wanted out of, needed out of, had to get out of, but she didn't tell him any of this. She couldn't bring herself to say anything, except to ask a single question: "Would you like a little rum in your tea?"

"Oh, no! I never drink alcohol. It dehydrates the soul."

Lijy got up from the table and went over to the counter, where she uncapped a bottle of Buddy's rum and poured a big shot into her mug. What she was about to do was a scream to remind Buddy that she was still here. That's what it was, a scream, a *Hello I'm your wife; do you remember me?* She held up her mug. "Thanks for talking to me today," she said, then downed her spiked tea in one gulp. "Let's go to the living room."

Ellis pushed his glasses up on his nose. "My real name is Ellis McMillion. I'm not lying anymore."

"I know," she said. "Have you ever heard of Ayurveda massage?" When Lijy was twelve, her father had drawn the one hundred and seven Ayurveda marmas on a dress mannequin and instructed her to learn them. For nearly a year, she practiced on the dress mannequin while her father watched, correcting her, putting her hands in the proper places. He told her that knowing how to rub a person's back was like having a map to their soul. If she did it right, she could learn things about the person; she could feel his struggles, finger their fears, poke their pain;

she could help them. Lijy had felt Chic's sadness, and when she rubbed Buddy's back, her whole body quivered as his emotions pulsed through her until he shrugged off her hands and told her he didn't want to be touched.

"Heard of it? I've read a book about it." Ellis proceeded to cite from the book, saying the body was like a protein mass of intertwined muscles and if one muscle, one fiber, was blocked, the whole body's cosmic attachment to the world's core was interrupted. "It's a beautiful metaphor for a beautiful massage."

Lijy drew on the rum and told Ellis to lie facedown on the living room floor. She didn't really want to do what she was about to do, but she felt gripped by some invisible force; a hand, someone's hand was pushing her toward what she was going toward. She wavered a little bit, and Ellis suggested they center themselves with some meditation. They sat down on the floor and faced each other. He took her hands. He told her everyone did this in California.

"Why don't you take off your shirt?" she asked.

"That's probably better than meditation."

Ellis unbuttoned his shirt, and Lijy told him to take off his trousers too and lie on his stomach. She kneeled next to him and found his ansa; her father had taught her always to go for the ansa first. Her tongue felt swollen like a kitchen sponge. The rum pulsed through her. Her mind skipped to Buddy out on the road, probably checking into a motel or leaning over a table of coins. She wanted him to come in through the front door and find her kneeling next to this stranger, his shirt and pants off. She moved down to the vrihati and used the heels of her hands. She was being sloppy. She wasn't gentle with his bindus; she didn't care.

Ellis rolled over and smiled at her. "Disease does not go near the properly massaged body, just as the snake does not go near the eagle. I read that in a book."

Peeking out of the elastic waistband of his underwear was the head of his erect penis. It looked like a snake wearing a purple helmet. He saw where her eyes were looking. "This is very exciting for me."

"I want to own a massage parlor someday," she said. "A health food store and massage parlor." She'd mentioned this to Buddy one time before he left on one of his trips. For the next few days, she kept waiting for him to call from the road and tell her what a great idea it was. He never called, and then she hoped he would say something when he got home—maybe he was waiting to tell her in person. But when he got home, he didn't say anything. That was almost a year ago.

"Fantastic idea. I can see it now. Massage by Lijy, or something like that. That's just off the top of my head."

"Do you really think it's a good idea?"

"It's the best idea I've ever heard. I love everything about it. It's beautiful. Now, please," he said, rolling back over on his stomach. "Continue."

Five

Chic & Lomax & Lijy Waldbeeser

■

February 17, 1960

"But I don't know anything about hockey," Lomax complained.

"You can learn about it. You like learning. You're learning German. I bet Germans play hockey. Do Germans play hockey?"

"Dad ... "

"I bet they do."

"Lomax, honey." Diane was at the sink peeling a carrot. "Aunt Lijy sent the tickets. I think you should go to the game with your father."

"But I have class tonight." Every Wednesday, either Chic or Diane drove Lomax forty-five minutes to Bradley University in Peoria, where he took a one-on-one German language class with Dr. Fritz Dexheimer, the chair of Bradley's foreign language department. With Dr. Dexheimer's assistance, Lomax was translating his great-great-grandfather Bascom's letters. So far, Lomax had learned that Bascom came from Munich to New Orleans by way of Paris in the mid-1800s. In New Orleans, he'd felt like the only German within a thousand miles (a sentiment that Lomax could relate to). He wrote letters back home explaining his attempts to connect with others like him. He described approaching "German-looking" people ("men with high foreheads and walnut eyes" and "women with bosoms as soft as pillows") in the French Quarter, but these people just offered him puzzled looks when he spoke to them in German.

"Here, read this about the Rivermen's goalie," Chic said. "Igor Lupen-something or another. He's the best goalie in the history of the team, according to this article." Lijy had included the article from the *Peoria Journal Star* with the tickets. Chic slid the newspaper cutout across the table to his son.

"I already read it."

What Chic couldn't figure out and what had been bothering him was why Lijy had sent the hockey tickets in the first place. Maybe she had a thing for this Lupen whatever his name was. Chic knew that women sometimes got crushes on athletes. That was the problem, actually. Players like Lupen-whatever his name was were alpha males, big guys, with feet the size of loaves of bread. With these guys being heroes and such and roaming the streets and rubbing shoulders with the normal, average guy, how were men like Chic supposed to compete? They couldn't, so it was no wonder that Lijy had rejected him that night in the kitchen. She wanted him to go to the hockey game to come face to face with what he wasn't. But he'd show her. After all, he was sure he could have been a hockey-alpha-male-like type of guy if he had wanted to. Although he didn't really know how to ice-skate—but, how hard could it be? With a little practice, he could do it. With a little practice, he could have been just as good as that Lupen-whatever his name was.

"Dad, do you like hockey?"

"We're going to the goddamn game and we're going to enjoy ourselves."

"Chic!" Diane snapped.

"I'm sorry. That came out wrong. Lomax, I like hockey. I could have been a hockey player, you know."

"Really?" Diane said.

"I could have!"

"You played hockey, Dad?"

"Listen, Lomax, I'd like for you to go with me to the game. You can bring your whatever you're doing there, your German homework."

The seats weren't good—top row. Lomax brought his wheelie briefcase, and Chic brought binoculars. While Lomax kneeled down in front of the open briefcase and began sorting through the papers and a German-to-English dictionary, Chic scanned the arena for Lijy. It wasn't very crowded, about five hundred fans decked out in red sweatshirts (the Rivermen's colors). The Rivermen and the opposing team, the Lumberjacks, were warming up on the ice below. Chic found Lijy behind the Rivermen's bench. She had binoculars, too, and she and Chic spotted each other at the same time. She quickly lowered her binoculars, and Chic noticed that she looked different. For one, she wasn't wearing a sari. She seemed older somehow, and had lost that exotic edge. She looked Middlevillian.

The fans began shaking cowbells and stomping their feet as the two teams set up at center ice. A loud horn sounded—Lomax put his hands over his ears—a baritone blast that sounded like a ship navigating the sea on a foggy night. Chic offered Lomax the binoculars so that he could see the action, but Lomax shook his head and went back to translating Bascom's letters. Chic looked through the binoculars—Lijy's seat behind the Rivermen's bench was empty. He scanned the stadium and found her climbing the stairs.

Chic spent the first period waiting for her to return to her seat, but she never did. At the end of the period, neither team had scored. Chic suggested they get some popcorn. The lobby area was crowded with men in suits smoking cigarettes and kids waving Rivermen pennants. Lomax was pulling his wheelie briefcase. Chic asked him if he wanted a pennant. He did not. He asked him if he wanted a hockey stick. He didn't want that, either. He asked if he wanted a Rivermen team photo. Nope. He just wanted popcorn, so they got in the concession line. Chic surveyed the crowd—she had to be around here somewhere. Lomax opened his briefcase and took out a magnifying glass. Then, Chic spotted her coming out of the women's bathroom. A long piece of toilet paper was stuck to her left shoe. She knocked into a guy, who shot her an annoyed look; she collided with another guy, then another. It was like she was walking for the first time in high heels, though she wasn't wearing high heels. She finally noticed Chic watching her and nearly lost her balance, grabbing a guy's shoulder; the guy caught her under the elbow and steadied her, and she continued through the crowd, knocking into another guy and sloshing his beer. Then she was standing in front of him.

"I . . . you . . . Chic . . ." she hiccupped. "Hi Lowell."

"Lomax," Chic said.

"I know." She put a sweaty hand on Chic's shoulder. "I have something for you."

Lomax dug a Mason jar and tweezers out of his briefcase.

"I . . . ah . . . made . . . ever since . . . anyway. I'm . . ." She motioned toward the arena. "I'm . . . forget it . . . just . . ." She hiccupped again. "Excuse me." Lijy looked down at Lomax. He was studying the piece of toilet paper stuck to her shoe with a magnifying glass. "Lowell, please. I need to give something to your daddy." She opened her purse and started digging through it. "This will explain everything, if only I can." Lijy noticed that Lomax was trying to remove the toilet paper from her foot with a pair of tweezers. She shook her foot.

"Quit shaking your foot," Chic said.

She did, and Lomax was able to tweeze the toilet paper off her shoe.

Lijy looked up at the rafters where giant Peoria Rivermen pennants hung. She grasped Chic's shoulder. "Oh Jesus, listen. Do you hear that? It's the . . . It's the end of the world. The clock of time is stopping." Lomax put his fingers in his ears. It was the horn letting everyone know that the second period was about to begin.

"You're drunk," Chic said.

"No I'm . . . okay maybe a little bit, just a little bit, but do you blame me? You'd be drunk too if you knew what I know. The question is—why aren't you drunk? We should all be drunk. This godforsaken life would much goddamn better if we were all a little more drunk."

A man in front of them turned around and stared at Lijy, who was practically using Chic to hold herself up. He shook his head and grabbed his son's hand and led him away.

"You're making a scene, Lijy."

She held out an envelope. "I wrote this . . ." She dropped the envelope.

Lomax reached for it, but Chic swatted his hand away and picked it up. It had his name written across the front.

"Good luck," Lijy slurred. Then she zigzagged toward the seats. She cut in front of one guy, then cut back, going in the opposite direction.

"What's the matter with Aunt Lijy?" Lomax asked.

"She's drunk."

"I know but why?"

"Because she had too much to drink."

"I know what drunk means, Dad. Why did she do it?"

"I don't know," Chic said and folded the envelope and stuck it in his pocket.

Lijy's Letter

Dear Chic,

I've never understood your name. It seems short for something. Chicken, maybe. Chicken Waldbeeser. Although that doesn't sound like a name anyone would give a son.

I know I'm probably not starting out this letter the best way. But, I'm not sure how to write it. I'm scared. I made a mistake. I had this plan to get your brother's attention. In fact at your wedding reception, I used you to try to get his attention. I'm not proud of myself. I'm upset with myself. I hate myself, to be honest. I was using another man to make your brother jealous. Or, at least, that's what I was trying to do. I hoped that your brother would come home and discover us. Me on the floor and this guy on top of me. But he didn't. Now, I'm pregnant. I planned to tell you at the hockey game, but I probably didn't. Actually, I'm sure I didn't. I'm weak. I wish I were stronger.

Do you remember that night in the kitchen before Lomas was born? I'm sure you do. You tried to seduce me. Anyway, when I told you that I loved your brother, I meant it. I love him. Your brother is a hard person to be married to and an even harder person to love. Maybe we're all hard people to love. But I'm trying.

I'm going to tell Buddy the baby is yours, and I want you to say that it's true. I'm hoping you'll go along with this. I was going to tell him that I was raped, not by you, but by someone, some masked man, a night prowler, something random and senseless, like life, but then, after I thought about that, I realized that wasn't a very good idea. The shame. I don't think I could live with the shame. Then I considered immaculate conception, but realized how ridiculous that was.

So, why you? Well, you're his brother, and if he thinks it's your baby, he's not going to leave me. He absolutely can't leave me. If I tell him it's a stranger's, some guy I met at Stafford's while I was trying to pick out a canta-loupe, or if you tell him it's a stranger's, then you know like I know, he'll be gone. Long gone. We'll never see him again. Maybe you will, but I won't. I wanted to get his attention, not drive him away. If he leaves me, I'm go-ing to fill my pockets with rocks and walk into a body of water. And we both know that Buddy can't handle that.

I do really love your brother. I'll regret what I did for the rest of my life, but that is my hole to bury myself in. Please, just help me. I've been crying for three straight weeks and I hurt more than any living person should ever hurt, and I don't know what else to do. I'll never tell anyone, including Diane, if you never tell anyone. I'm going to tell Buddy the day after tomorrow. I'm sorry. Or, thank you.

Sincerely,

Lijy

Chic Waldbeeser & Mary Geneseo

■

June 16, 1998

Mary sat beside Chic in the minivan, his duffel bag in his lap. She didn't know a thing about him, except that he was interested in her, or she thought he was interested in her; she couldn't be sure. She was losing her touch; she used to be able to get any man's attention, but the cowboy at the Brazen Bull wouldn't even turn an eye toward her. Now she was down to this, a guy who lived in a nursing home—though he didn't seem like he should be living in a nursing home. He'd told her he didn't have to be there, but had moved there for the company. After the third time she called it a nursing home, he corrected her and said it was technically an "assisted living" facility. He said, with a smirk, that he needed assistance living; he said it like he was making a joke, but she wasn't sure she got the joke. Did he mean that he needed help going to the bathroom and stuff like that? She asked him, and he said that was not what he meant. She waited for the punch line, but it never came. Instead, he stared at her like she was supposed to say something, but she didn't say anything.

There was an odd smell in the van, musty and sweaty, and Mary knew it must be coming from Chic . . . or it could be Green's dirty suits, which were in a laundry bag behind her seat. Maybe the sun had baked them? She cracked the window. The whisper voice told her that this was a bad idea. Green was in the hospital, and she was in his minivan with a man who could be the reason, *who actually probably was the reason,* for the old man smell clogging up her nostrils. She looked at Chic and smiled. "Ready?"

"Ready as I'll ever be."

Mary turned over the ignition. The radio—Rock 106, Peoria's classic rock station—blasted Heart's "Barracuda" from the speakers. She loved this song and remembered a time when she thought of herself as a barracuda. She glanced in her rearview mirror and saw a retirement home bus. She backed out of the parking spot carefully, but before she could get halfway out, she had to stop to let a group of old people, walking single file toward the bus like a sixth-grade class, cross behind her. A white-haired lady with a walker made eye contact with her, while a bald guy in a flannel shirt wearing a loose wristwatch waved. Mary thought of Green in the hospital. She had held his hand last night, and it felt bony, like his long fingers were pencils. She hated what happened to the human body over time. You need to get back to the hospital, the whisper voice said. What are you doing with this guy?

Chic slouched down in the seat, hugging his duffel bag against his chest. "Don't say anything," he whispered. "There's Morris. Don't move." A guy wearing a Members Only windbreaker brought up the rear of the line. He was looking around with concern—right, left, over his shoulder. Chic was scrunched so far down in his seat he was practically on the floor. "I'm supposed to be on that bus. Jesus Christ, Morris is going to see me."

This was a new low. She was "kidnapping" an old man from a nursing home. His assisted living residence, the loud voice said back, and it wasn't exactly kidnapping. You asked him to come with you, and he agreed. He likes you. And you sorta like him or think you could like him, in time.

"You'll have to drive me back to We Care," Chic said from his slouched position. "In Middleville. When we're done."

"I know. You told me."

"It's a half-hour drive."

"That's fine."

"That's a half hour there and a half hour back."

"I know. I got it."

"I have to be back by ten."

"You told me. I remember."

"I'm just saying."

"I got it."

Once everyone had disappeared into the bus, Mary eased the minivan out of the spot and turned the corner into the lot where the valet guys were huddled by the entrance to the casino.

"Okay. It's safe now."

"You sure?"

"It's fine."

Chic sat back up and put on his seat belt. "That was close."

This is the biggest mistake of your life, the whisper voice told her.

"I haven't been to a bar in years. I never went to bars that much to begin with. My wife didn't like them. She's dead though. I'm a widower. Or a widow. Is it widower or widow? I'm widowed. Can a man be a widow?"

"You told me your wife died. Three times now."

Chic shrugged. "She hated me. Did I tell you that? Hate probably isn't the right word. I did some things that made her mad. That's probably more accurate."

Mary wasn't exactly sure why she'd decided to take Chic to the Brazen Bull. It had come to her during her shift, and she went with it. She told him that she was going to hustle pool and it would help if there was a man with her.

"Aren't you going to ask me why my wife hated me?"

"How about we don't talk about your wife."

"She didn't really hate me. I just said that. I haven't really been with a woman in a while, and I thought it would make you feel sorry for me, if you thought my wife hated me. I don't want you to feel sorry for me."

Mary kept her eyes on the road. She didn't care if his wife hated him or not. She was dead now, anyway.

"I got a confession. I should have told you this. I don't think I can fight anyone. I mean I've never been in a fight. Actually, I take that back. One time. With my brother. Wasn't really a fight. He pulled me out a window. What I'm saying is that I probably won't be much help with this pool hustle thing."

"I don't think you'll have to fight anyone."

They stopped at a light at Creve Coeur Avenue, about a mile down from the Pair-a-Dice. Next to them was a baby blue Mustang—Mary knew it was a '65. The driver, a guy with feathered blond hair parted in the middle, was wearing mirrored sunglasses. At that moment, Mary would have given anything—*anything*—to be sitting in that Mustang. The light changed.

"Oh, that's a good restaurant. We sometimes stop there on the way home from the casino." Chic pointed out the window at a Denny's, its parking lot half full. "I like the eggs over my hammy. Get it, like sun over Miami?

"I get it."

"What do you think of Florida?"

"I don't really."

"As a place to go. A destination. A place to live."

"It's hot."

"It's hot," Chic repeated. "I did my honeymoon in Florida. Did I tell you that?"

"How about we don't talk about our pasts?"

"I'm just trying to get to know you."

"But you're not really asking me questions. You're just telling me things about yourself. How about let's concentrate on the right now."

Chic looked out the window. "You have any kids?"

She didn't take the bait.

"Married?"

"I told you."

"Happily married?"

"Let's not talk. Okay. We're almost there. It's right up here."

Mary drove into the parking lot of the Brazen Bull and pulled into a spot next to a beat-up van with a ladder strapped to its roof. There was a bumper sticker on the ladder that read, IF ALL ELSE FAILS, USE A BIGGER HAMMER. The only other car in the parking lot was a Geo Metro.

"Looks like this place used to be a fast food restaurant," Chic said. "That's the drive-through right there. What was this, a McDonald's or something?"

"I don't know. It's a bar now."

"A fast food restaurant that's now a bar. Who would have thought? Things change, huh?"

Mary reached behind the seat and dug through the laundry bag until she found one of Green's sport coats, the maroon one. "Put this on," she told Chic. Under the laundry bag was a pair of alligator slip-on loafers. She handed them to Chic.

"My God, these are the worst shoes I've ever seen. Is this your husband's stuff?" Chic slipped on the sport coat over his windbreaker. The sleeves hung beyond his hands. "This doesn't fit me."

Mary rolled up the sleeves. "Let me see those shoes." She took them and stuffed tissues from her purse into the tips of the shoes.

"They're not going to fit me. I don't care how much Kleenex you stuff in 'em."

"Just put 'em on, okay?"

Chic took off his jogging shoes and put on the loafers. He was right. They didn't fit, not even close.

"Why are you making me wear all this stuff?"

"Just deal with it. Okay. Humor me."

On the walk across the parking lot, Chic's heels kept slipping out of the oversized loafers, and the soles thwacked the concrete.

Once they were inside, Mary put "Barracuda" on the jukebox. Chic tried not to move. He looked the place over. At the pool table, a college kid and an older guy dressed like a motorcycling cowboy were facing off. A couple sat at a table drinking brown liquor. A fat guy wearing a t-shirt with the sleeves cut off was belly up at the bar.

Mary ordered a tomato juice and was sipping it through a straw while she watched the pool game. Chic thwacked across the bar. The college kid stopped sighting up his pool shot to glare at him. Chic slipped into a booth, not even noticing the look he was getting, and set his duffel bag on the table and fished out a notebook. He opened to a poem he was working on. He'd been struggling with it for two days. So far he had one line: *Around the corner is the end.* He glanced up from his notebook to notice Mary staring at him. Her eyes seemed to say, what are you doing? Behind her, the bartender was wiping down the bar; the guy at the bar was watching television; the college kid hit his shot and the cue ball clicked into another ball. A line came to him, in the same way that all lines of poetry did, dropping out of the heavens and into his mind—*the end is the end is the end.* He reread the line. Nah. He didn't like it. He scratched it out. He flipped back a few pages. To get the juices flowing, it helped to look over old poems. He read one of his favorites.

> *My life is nothing*
> *but a large hole in the ground*
> *I can't get out of.*

Chic stuck the end of the pen in his mouth. The motorcycle cowboy walked up to Mary. They whispered to each other, and the cowboy took out his wallet. Mary motioned to Chic. The motorcycle cowboy turned around. "You want him to hold the money?" he asked. Chic picked up his club soda and set it down hard; some of the soda splashed out and got on his hand. Then he gave the motorcycle cowboy his best mean face.

"Jesus, what's wrong with him?"

The college kid, who was sighting up another shot, looked over at Chic, and Chic narrowed his eyes.

"Is he sick or something?" the motorcycle cowboy asked.

"I'm not sure," Mary said. "He might be."

Chic & Buddy Waldbeeser

■

February 18, 1960

It was the night after the Rivermen game, and Chic was tossing and turning in bed, thinking about Lijy's letter. She'd said she was going to tell Buddy "the day after tomorrow," which had been today. After he had gotten home from work, each time the phone rang, his heart had started thumping in his chest. Sitting in the living room, he couldn't concentrate on *Truth or Consequences* and was zoned out when Bob Barker uttered his famous sendoff, "Hoping all your consequences are happy ones." Chic knew that Lijy's news would bulldoze his brother's emotions, slay him, pull out his heart. He wouldn't be able to handle it if Buddy cried in front of him. At their father's funeral, Chic had heard Buddy sniffling, but couldn't bring himself to look over at him. Instead, he kept staring at the hymnal and bible in the book tray affixed to the pew in front of him. Tom McNeeley held their mother's hand, squeezing it and keeping it in his lap. At one point, Tom handed Chic a Kleenex, but it was Buddy, by then heaving and drooling and pretty much having an epileptic fit of sadness, who really needed one. Chic couldn't face that type of sadness again.

At two in the morning, Chic got out of bed. He hadn't gotten a single second of sleep all night. He walked down the hall and peeked into Lomax's room. The desk lamp was on, and Lomax was sleeping on top of his comforter, an explosion of papers on the floor, his briefcase open beside them. Chic tiptoed inside, shut off the desk lamp, and closed his son's bedroom door behind him. He then went downstairs to the kitchen to get a glass of water. Filling up his glass at the sink, he looked out the window. Stillness. A slight winter breeze through the trees. Scattered porch lights. The streetlamp on the corner. Then, from the backyard, Chic heard something. A light tap-tap-tap, like someone fudging a finishing nail into place. He walked to the back of the house, to the bathroom, and looked out the window. Someone was struggling to climb over the fence. The person was hung up at the top, and couldn't shift his weight to get over. When the person tried to throw his body over, the toe of his boot tapped the fence's wood planks. Directly underneath this person was a rosebush—shriveled and dormant for the winter but still full of thorns. The person turned his head, and Chic saw his brother's worried face. Buddy was wearing a drab-olive World War I uniform, the kind with the brass buttons and puttees. Chic immediately recognized the uniform as their father's, who had served in the Thirty-Third Infantry Division ("Prairie Division") in World War I. On the ground, upside down like a soup bowl next to the rosebush, was their father's doughboy helmet.

With a final burst of effort, Buddy fell into backyard, barely missing the rose bush. He scrambled and reached for the helmet, which he placed on his head, not bothering with the chinstrap. He then searched around for something else, and finally found what he was looking for: a butcher knife. What was he going to do with that? Before Chic could come up with an answer, Buddy was sneaking across the backyard and around to the front of the house. Chic went to the living room and flipped on the ceiling light. After a few seconds, Buddy periscoped up to peer in the window. Chic crossed the living room, and Buddy must have seen the movement because he quickly ducked back down. Chic opened the window. He could see his brother hunkering close to the wall, trying to hide.

"Buddy, what are you doing?"

He didn't answer.

"Buddy. I can see you."

He looked up at him. "Lean out the window. I want to tell you something."

"It's two in the morning. What are you doing? Why are you wearing that uniform?"

"Just lean out the goddamn window."

Chic could hear by the tone in his brother's voice that it would be a good idea for him to play along. As soon as he leaned out the window, however, Buddy grabbed Chic by the pajama top and pulled him out into the front lawn. He then pinned him to the ground, holding both of Chic's arms above his head. So, this was it. This was how it was going to happen. Of all the ways, Chic wouldn't have guessed this—dragging him out his living room window, a butcher knife, his father's military uniform.

Buddy pressed the knife's point against Chic's nostril. "I could cut off your nose."

"Buddy . . ."

"Shut up."

"Bud . . ."

"Shut up. You commie. You ankle biter. Keep your goddamn mouth shut." Buddy grabbed a handful of his own hair. Horrified, Chic watched him shear it off. Buddy then forced the sheared hair into Chic's mouth. "Buddy . . . don't . . . don't . . . stop it . . . I . . . please . . ."

"Eat it. Eat it, you serpent-tongued snake." He pressed the point of the knife into Chic's cheek, and Chic quit thrashing. A tiny bead of blood bubbled on his cheek. "Swallow it, you rat fink mother puss bucket pinko."

Chic swallowed the hair, or at least tried to, but most of it stuck to the roof of his mouth and got hung up in his throat. When Buddy took his hand off his mouth, Chic spit and gagged.

Buddy rolled off of him and stabbed the knife into the ground. The way he was hunched over and shaking, Chic knew he was crying. He put his hand on his back, but Buddy sloughed it off.

"Don't touch me."

"I'm sorry, Buddy," Chic said.

Buddy wiped his eyes. They were blown out, blazing with pain. Chic remembered a family photo shoot. Their mother had paid a photographer to come over to the house. Chic was five or six years old, and their mother dressed him and Buddy in matching tweed suits. Their father wore his military uniform with the overseas cap. He'd spent all morning polishing the boots, and Chic had watched him sit on the bed and wrap each of his calves with puttees. For the photo, Chic sat on his father's knee. Buddy stood next to him. Their mother stood behind their father, her hand on his shoulder. Chic remembered that the uniform smelled like mothballs and that his father kept pulling at the collar and complaining about how tight it was on his neck. During Chic's entire childhood, the photo hung on the wall going up the stairs. In his memory, it still hung on that wall.

"It was a mistake, Buddy. I made a mistake."

"She's pregnant. Did you know that? Of course you knew that."

Chic put his hand on his brother's shoulder. He wanted Buddy to know he was going to help him get through this. Buddy sloughed it off, again. Then he pulled the knife from the frozen ground, picked up the doughboy helmet and walked away, down the street toward the corner streetlight, the helmet under his arm.

Chic & Diane Waldbeeser

■

February 19, 1960

"Wait a second," Diane said. "I'm confused. Why did you let him believe you slept with Lijy?"

"Because of what happened in the kitchen."

"The kitchen?"

"I told you."

"You didn't tell me about the kitchen." Diane put her hands

on her hips. She knew something like this was going to happen. Ever since the wedding reception, she knew Chic Waldbeeser wasn't the man she'd thought he was. He said he wanted a normal life, she heard him with her own two ears, and then, he goes off and . . .

He told her everything, right down to the detail that he kept his socks on and his penis worked its way out while he was humping the air. "And that's what happened in the kitchen."

"Oh my God!"

"I'm not happy about it either. Trust me. In fact, it was embarrassing."

Lomax cracked his bedroom door open. He eyed his father, then his mother. He had a look on his face like he'd eaten something sour.

Diane looked at Chic. "Great. Lomax heard you. He knows that you tried to have sex with Lijy."

"Lomax, buddy, I didn't have sex with Aunt Lijy. I just told my brother I did. And, yes, at one time, a long time ago . . ."

Lomax stared at him. He put his hands over his ears.

"I can't believe this is happening." Diane's bottom lip quivered.

"Lomax. Listen to me. Take your hands off your ears. Let me explain. I'm doing the right thing here. Uncle Buddy is my brother, and he's in a lot of pain. He was crying last night, and Lijy, Aunt Lijy, remember the way she was acting at the hockey game? Well, she—as you heard—she made a mistake, and I'm worried about Uncle Buddy and to help out, because it's the right thing to do, I told him that . . . wait. Diane. Don't. Not the bathroom. No."

She slammed the bathroom door and locked it. Chic looked at Lomax. He wheeled his briefcase toward the stairs.

"I didn't sleep with Aunt Lijy, buddy. Someday, you'll see. When you have a brother, you'll see. This will all make sense."

Lomax pulled the briefcase down the stairs.

"Being an adult is hard, Lomax. You're going to see this someday, and you're going to think back on this day and you're going to realize that your dad was doing the right thing."

"I'll be in the car," Lomax yelled, slamming the front door.

From the bathroom, Diane said, "I hope you're happy."

"No. I'm not happy. This isn't how I expected this to go."

"And how did you expect it to go?"

"Maybe with a little more understanding. I'm trying to help my brother."

"Let me get this straight, Chic. You wanted to sleep with your brother's wife but you didn't because she didn't want to sleep with you. So you told your brother that you slept with her because you want to help him."

"Right."

"How is wanting to sleep with his wife helping him?"

"I feel guilty about that. I told you. That's part of the reason why I told him I did. But I didn't sleep with her."

"You wanted to and you told your brother you did."

"Because I wanted to help him and I felt guilty."

"She wouldn't sleep with you because she loves your brother. That's what she told you, even though she went off and slept with another man."

"She loves him. I can show you the letter. I believe her. She made a mistake. People make mistakes."

"Would you or would you not have slept with her?"

"I don't want to sleep with her. Not anymore."

"But would you have?"

"Honestly?"

"Yes, honestly, Chic."

"I know it's wrong, but . . . I can't believe I'm going to say this. I'm sorry. But—what? Diane? Don't do that . . ."

She shrieked a high-pitched scream that lasted ten or fifteen seconds. Even after screaming, Diane didn't feel better. She looked at the closed bathroom door and heard him on the other side, breathing. She didn't want to be hearing him. She didn't want to be anywhere near him. She wanted to go back in time to ten minutes ago when she was waking up and Chic was sitting on the edge of the bed next to her and said he had to tell her something. She knew by the way he was looking at her, by the way he put his hand on her leg, that what he was going to say wasn't going to lead anywhere good. So she tried to get away from it. She threw back the covers and got out of bed and went into the hallway, but he followed, asking her to stop, asking her to listen to him. In the hallway outside of Lomax's bedroom, she turned to him, and in turning to him, she knew that this was it; this was the moment when everything changed, when he was going to reveal to her things that she didn't want to know, things that were better left buried where she couldn't know they existed. When he began telling her what he'd done, her ears began to ring, her whole head buzzed and she felt woozy, her whole world wavered, the carpet beneath her feet appeared to be rolling, the walls closing in on her. She wanted to hold up her hand and tell him to stop, to quit talking, not to tell her. She didn't want to hear it; it would be better if she just didn't hear it.

"You said to be honest."

"I didn't *really* want you to be honest."

"I didn't sleep with her. That's honest."

"Your brother thinks you did. Your son thinks you did. You just said you would have if she'd let you. Buddy will spend his entire life thinking you slept with her. Unless you tell him otherwise. You have to tell him the truth."

"He's my brother, and his wife cheated on him."

"You can't change that."

"All I'm saying . . ."

"Just please, Chic. Quit talking. You're making it worse."

He tried the bathroom doorknob, but it was locked.

"Chic, I don't want to see you. I don't want to be around you. I don't understand you. I think I might hate you."

"Hate me? *Really?* My god. Don't tell me that."

"Please let's just . . . no more talking."

"I want to make it better. I'm trying to make this better."

"Chic please just . . . just please."

"But you hate me."

"I don't hate you."

"You said you hated me."

"Chic. Enough."

"I lied earlier. I wouldn't have slept with her."

"You're not making this any better."

"She's my brother's wife. Even if she wanted to, I would have said no. Really. Truly."

"You can't lie after you've told the truth. It doesn't work that way."

"I want you to think I did the right thing. Tell me you think I'm doing the right thing."

"Even if you're helping your brother, which you're not, but that's beside the point, the point is you're not helping me. You're not helping Lomax. And we're your family."

"It's just that . . . she slept with another guy." He put his forehead against the door, and mumbled. "And she didn't want to sleep with me."

"What's that? What'd you say?"

"Nothing. It's just that . . . I said, you can't tell Buddy. Don't ever tell Buddy."

Diane didn't answer.

"I know you're not going to say anything, but just know, if you tell him, if he knows the truth . . . even if you don't agree with what I did, you can't tell him."

Outside, Lomax honked the car horn, two long blasts— honk, honk.

Six

Buddy Waldbeeser

■

March–May 1960

The adulterous relationship between Lijy and Chic was just too heavy a cross for Buddy to shoulder. Each time Lijy walked into a room he was in, he walked out. He refused to drink the tea she made for him, and, of course, he wouldn't sleep in the same bed with her. He grew a beard, and took showers at odd times, spending large amounts of time in the steam-filled bathroom wiping the mirror and staring at his bearded face. He started smoking cigarillos. He had dreams in which he strangled Chic until his head exploded. He had other dreams in which he stabbed him repeatedly in the stomach with a dinner fork (and another in which he whacked him over the head with a sledgehammer). The two of them used to catch frogs in the creek behind the farmhouse when they were kids. Buddy stood up for Chic in high school when the other kids tried to knock his books out of his hands. Alone, out on the road, in motel-room beds, Buddy had often thought of Chic at home with their mother and Tom McNeeley, and worried about how he was doing. Then Lijy sat him down on the couch and told him that she and Chic had . . . had . . . he couldn't even replay it in his memory. He didn't want to think about it. It had happened right there on the living room carpet. Oh, Jesus. He wanted to kill himself. Maybe he should go behind a barn and sit down in the snow like their father. No, he couldn't do that. He wouldn't do that. He would never let himself do that. What was he going to do? He couldn't leave Lijy; she was pregnant. He needed some time to think. He had to clear his head and get this all straight.

One afternoon, Lijy ducked her head into the living room and asked Buddy nicely (too goddamn nicely, he thought) to "extinguish" that "awful-smelling cigarette." He told her it wasn't a cigarette; it was a cigar and it was supposed to smell this way, and besides, he liked the smell, and thank you very much, she really shouldn't be telling him what to do.

She stood there staring at him. "The smoke isn't good for the baby."

"Fine. That's it. *That's it.* Not good for the baby. Not good for the baby. Not good for Chic's baby." He stubbed out the cigarillo. "My God. My goddamn God. That maggot." Buddy went upstairs and got his suitcase from the bedroom closet and threw some clothes into it.

Lijy came upstairs and stood in the bedroom doorway holding a mug of tea. "So that's it? You're leaving?"

"If I can't smoke my damn cigars in here, I'm leaving."

"Does this mean it's over?"

"I don't know . . . actually, yes, it's over. Fini, as the French say. Actually, no. It's not over. I don't know what it means. I need some time to think."

"I'm pregnant, Buddy."

"That's why I'm leaving. You told me you don't want me to smoke around the baby."

"I love you."

He stood there, holding his suitcase.

"I do. It's true. I made a mistake. I admit it. A big mistake. I told you, I was just trying to get your attention. That's the truth."

He didn't say anything.

"Are you going to say anything? Say something. You never say anything. You have to say something, Buddy."

He stared at her, a hard stare with his eyes fierce like smoldering lumps of coal. "This would have been much easier if you wouldn't have slept with my brother."

Buddy took up residence at the Wel Kum Inn, a low-rent motel outside of Middleville on Route 7. It was by far the worst motel he had ever stayed in. There wasn't even a sign, just a sheet of plywood with the name WEL KUM INN spray-painted on it and propped up by a bucket. An old Mexican guy wearing a sombrero slept on a folding chair outside the lobby door. A transistor radio, the antenna extended so high it was a hazard for the eyes, sat on the counter beside a rack of dusty old Wel Kum postcards. Hanging on a single nail behind the counter was a 1957 calendar from Kneep's Automotive Shop. Buddy remembered going there as a kid with his father, who was trying to get a job at the service station. As the men who worked in the shop clinked around with their wrenches, his father sat there, staring straight ahead, not a single emotion on his face, just a wash of blankness, while he waited his turn to interview. Buddy asked the guy behind the hotel counter to move to his left in order to block the calendar from his line of sight. He paid for a room in cash and checked in under the name Nate West.

That night, Buddy pulled the shades shut and stacked pillows on the desk chair and set his derby hat on top of them. He heard scratching on the motel door. He ignored it at first, but it continued, so he opened the door. Down on the ground was a cat, a mangy thing, thin like it hadn't eaten for weeks. It darted into the room and hid under the bed. Buddy tried to shoo it out, snapping and saying, "Here kitty kitty kitty kitty." He got down on his hands and knees and looked under the bed—the cat's yellow eyes glowed back at him. He tried to grab at it, but the cat hissed at him, so he left it alone. Maybe later he could pet it. Petting a cat would make him feel better.

Buddy lit a cigar. "So," he said to the pillows. "So so so so. This is where you've taken us. Chic, your son, sleeps with my wife, impregnates her, and I'm on the brink of doing something horrible, worse than horrible, terrible, humiliating. Did you know that I couldn't even look at the Kneep's calendar in the lobby of this hotel? I had to ask the guy at the counter to step in front of it. Do you know why? Because of you—because it reminded me of you." The cat had come out from under the bed and was sniffing around the nightstand. "I need answers, Dad. What were you doing at Kneep's?" The cat sat down and looked up at him. Buddy ashed the cigarillo and took a drag. "I'm on my own, aren't I? Well, I don't want to be on my own. I want a father. In six or seven months, there's going to be another mouth to feed in Middleville—a bastard son, my bastard son." Outside, a car pulled into the Wel Kum's parking lot. The headlight beams raked over the wall and disappeared when the engine stopped. "What am I supposed to do?" he asked. "I just want some answers." There was a knock at the door. Buddy went to the window and peeked through the shades, carefully, so that he wouldn't be seen. In the parking lot, he saw Lijy's car parked next to his. She was standing at his motel room door. She was beginning to show her pregnancy, a bulge in her stomach. Buddy was shirtless, a cigarillo dangling from his mouth. His beard was straggly like a young Fidel Castro. He opened the window shades so that she could see him.

"Please come home," she said.

He inhaled a lungful of smoke and exhaled it into the window. He shut the curtains. The cat was looking up at him. It meowed. Buddy picked it up. "It's me and you, now, little fellow." He heard Lijy's car start and back out of its parking spot. Buddy went into the bathroom and filled up a glass with water and set it on the floor. The cat lapped at it. "A son should name his firstborn after his father. You know that, little guy. That's what my no good maggot brother never understood. He probably doesn't even like cats. I like cats. I like you, and you're my first cat, so I'm going to name you Bascom. Bascom the Cat. How do you like that name?"

Buddy squatted down to pet the cat between the ears. The cat continued to lap at the water.

Chic Waldbeeser

■

May 12, 1960

Chic had stepped in front of a bullet for Buddy, and now he and Lijy were probably spending their nights snuggling together and talking to each other in baby voices. They were probably holding hands at the grocery store. He had probably rekindled their love, blown into its mouth and brought it back to life. Forgiveness is powerful, and he was responsible for theirs. He'd nailed himself to the cross for them, and what sort of thanks had he gotten? Nothing—just a wife and son who were furious with him. It had been six weeks, and Diane still wouldn't talk to him, wouldn't look at him, wouldn't even share a bar of soap with him. (She'd put his bar in a coffee mug and left him a note taped to the medicine cabinet explaining that he shouldn't use, shouldn't even touch, the bar in the soap rack, her bar.) Each time he tried to nuzzle close to Diane at night, she scooted away. If he tried to give her a kiss, she ducked underneath it. When he sat down to dinner and asked Diane and Lomax how their days had gone, neither answered. She dabbed at the corner of her mouth, took a sip of water, and continued to eat; Lomax wouldn't even look up from his book. Chic couldn't handle it when people were mad at him. He needed to do something. He bought flowers. He made dinner—macaroni and cheese. One Saturday morning, he cleaned the entire house, even scrubbing the bathroom, by himself. He gave Lomax a twenty-dollar bill. He bought Diane a card. He drew funny pictures and left them around the house. None of it worked.

Then, it hit him one night. He got out of bed and wrote himself a note—*a swimming pool*—underlining the three words. The following morning, he dialed the operator and asked her to put him through to the Sea Shell Inn in Pensacola, Florida, the motel where he and Diane had stayed during their honeymoon.

"I'm sorry, sir. There's no listing for a motel with that name."

"What?"

"There's no listing for a motel with that name."

"I heard you."

"There's a Sea Breeze Inn. A Sea Side Motel. A Sea Beach Motel, but no Sea Shell Inn."

Lomax came into the kitchen.

Chic lowered his voice. "So, you're telling me the place closed down?"

"I don't know what happened. I'm just the operator."

Lomax got a bottle of milk from the refrigerator and carried it to the counter.

"Give me the number for the Sea Breeze Inn, then." Chic wrote the number down on the back of an envelope, then dialed the phone. Lomax turned to him.

"Dad . . ."

Chic held up a finger. "I'm sorta in the middle of something here. Can we talk later? Tonight maybe?"

Lomax picked up his glass of milk and left the kitchen.

On the line, a woman answered.

"This is Chic Waldbeeser in Illinois. I have some questions about your swimming pool. If you don't mind, can you describe it? The shape, the size. The furniture around it. How many gallons of water it holds?" On the same envelope he drew a picture of the pool based on what the woman told him.

After the phone call was over, Chic called William T. Daniels, who owned his own backhoe and did contract labor for Middleville Township, among other odds jobs. Chic told him what he had in mind. "I was hoping to get started this afternoon. Let's say noon."

"I have work scheduled for this afternoon. Water leak on Third and Jefferson."

"Then tomorrow. Sunday. Let's say 8:00 a.m."

"I can maybe get over there next weekend. But I think it's go-

ing to be too wet to start digging. Let's shoot for the first weekend of July."

"July! That's halfway through the summer."

"What's your hurry, Waldbeeser? Relax. I'll give you a call in
a couple of weeks to confirm a date."

Chic couldn't wait until July. He went right out to the garage
and dragged out the wheelbarrow, two shovels, a garden rake, and
some tent stakes. He then held up the envelope and tried to vi-
sualize how the pool would fit between the garage and the house.
There'd be a deck table with an umbrella by the back door of the
house, where he and Diane would sit and sip ice tea and watch
Lomax and the neighborhood kids, who, actually, didn't spend
a lot of time with Lomax; they were always playing baseball or
football in the empty lot a few houses down and Chic was always
trying to get Lomax to put away his notebooks and join them, but
Lomax never did; he always said he would, but he never did. If
they had a pool, though, the neighborhood kids would be hanging around all the time, and finally, maybe Lomax would get himself some friends. A kid shouldn't be by himself so much. Oh and
what was Lomax wanting to talk to him about in the kitchen?
He'd have to remember to ask him later. Anyway, the pool. He'd
invite Lijy and Buddy over, after the air cleared, of course. And it
would clear, he was sure of it. This pool would be the first step in
setting everything back on the right path. Diane and Lijy would
sit at the patio table under the umbrella with the new baby, while
he and Buddy soaked in the pool and Lomax did cannonballs off
the side (though he'd probably sit in the shade and mess around
with his German translations, but Chic could imagine him doing cannonballs off the side if he wanted to). He'd invite Diane's
parents over to sit under the umbrella's shade. Maybe he'd even
invite Mr. Kendrick, his neighbor. He and Diane's father were
about the same age. The two of them could talk about Middleville
and how it had changed, about the teenage kids and how they
were starting to grow their hair long and listen to rock and roll

music. They could lament the ranch houses popping up all around town. They could talk about the entire country changing, adding Alaska and Hawaii as states. He could just hear them now: two old men talking about the past. In the evening, he'd bring out the grill, and Diane would patty up some hamburger meat. Lomax and the neighborhood kids would eat fast because they'd want to get back in the pool, but Chic wouldn't let them go in for half an hour—he wouldn't want anyone getting a cramp and drowning. That would be horrible: one of the neighborhood kids drowning in his pool. That would upset Diane, and she'd blame him because it was his idea to put in the pool, blah, blah, etc., etc. But no one was going to drown, and he wasn't going to let his mind drift. He was putting in a pool and once it was finished, all the anger, all the ignoring, all of it, would be behind them, finally.

Chic set the envelope down in the middle of the yard and, using the back of a spade shovel, hammered a stake into it to keep it from blowing away. In about a month, that was his timeline, well before July, he was going to transform his backyard into a little slice of Florida. Diane couldn't be mad at him after he did that. They had honeymooned in Florida. They had conceived Lomax there. It was like their Garden of Eden. Chic went into the garage and got a spool of string and a hammer and staked off the shape of the pool, wrapping the string around the stakes like he was fencing off new grass seed.

Lomax came out the back door.

"Look, Lomax. A pool." Chic gestured to the stringed-off area. "I mean, it'll be a pool pretty soon."

"Mom know you're doing this?"

"Not yet. She will though. Imagine it. Our very own pool right here in the backyard."

Lomax shrugged. "I don't really like to be out in the sun."

"You're going to love it. We'll get one of those tables with an umbrella. Hey, by the way, I hear the neighborhood kids down the street playing baseball. Why don't you go get your glove and join them?"

"Yeah, maybe," Lomax said, then went back inside the house. Almost immediately, Diane came out the door and huffed and stomped until she stood just outside the stringed-off area. She glared at Chic, her hands on her hips. "A bomb shelter? You're digging a bomb shelter in the backyard? Don't you think that's a little extreme? I know you think you're protecting our family somehow by taking the blame for Lijy's affair, but a bomb shelter? You really think something horrible is going to happen, a nuclear bomb, in Illinois, and all of us will need to hide out? Is that what you really think? Really? I mean . . ."

"I'm digging a pool."

"A pool?"

"You remember that pool at the Sea Shell Inn? Well, this is going to be like that, or sorta like that. You know they closed the Sea Shell Inn? Or the name changed. Anyway, yeah, I'm putting in a pool."

"Here?"

"Yep."

"Chic, you can't change what happened. Nothing you can do can undo that. Nothing. Not one thing. Not a pool. Not a bomb shelter."

"I'm not building a bomb shelter."

Diane walked back toward the house, but before she went inside, she turned around and faced him. "All of this . . . .this pool. You may think you're doing the right thing, but you just keep making things worse."

Buddy Waldbeeser

■

June 7 and 8, 1960

Buddy locked the motel room door, put the key in his pocket, and nodded to the Mexican man wearing a sombrero sitting on a folding chair by the lobby door. He carried Bascom the Cat in a duffel bag; the bag wasn't zipped shut, and Bascom's head was poking out. That morning, Buddy had run across a real estate listing in the *Journal Star* for an abandoned Central Illinois Light Company—CILCO—switching station. The ad said that the building was ten thousand square feet and overlooked the Mackinaw River. This would be all he needed—a giant empty brick building with concrete floors. He'd be so far outside of town that people would leave him alone. He could smoke his cigarillos and no one would bother him.

At Wyman's Hardware Store on Main Street, a few blocks from the pumpkin cannery, he bought a flashlight, extra batteries, and a black ski mask. The cashier, Mrs. Wyman, looked over the top of her glasses and asked him how his mother was doing. Buddy shrugged and told her she was fine. He, of course, didn't know how she was. He hadn't talked to her in years.

In the car, Buddy had a hard time keeping his head clear. Everything he'd worked so hard to achieve had slipped through his fingers. He'd gone on the road and ended up in California, and come home with a wife, a wife he loved, a wife who . . . he couldn't even let himself continue. "I had a goddamn plan," he said aloud. The cat looked at him with big yellow eyes. Was he really talking to a cat? He drove by the cannery and slowed the car down. In the parking lot, he spotted Chic's car. He stepped on the gas and sped around the block and came back around again, like a shark circling its prey in the water. He was going to get even with Chic. He wasn't done. He tore around the corner and sped across town to Chic's house. In the front yard, Chic's odd son, Lomax, was on his hands and knees scooping dirt into a mason jar. Buddy wanted to roll down the window and tell him what a horrible man his father was. He wanted to tell Lomax that he hated his father, hated Diane, hated him, Lomax, hated Middleville. He had so much hate inside of him it felt like a small animal was nipping at his heart. He choked back tears. There wasn't any time to cry. He sped away.

When night fell, Buddy parked in front of the Stebbenthal house, which was next door to his home. The living room light was on, and Lijy was sitting on the couch drinking tea. His mind flashed to her on top of Chic. Buddy shook his head to erase the image, but he couldn't get it out of his head. Jesus Christ. Jesus H. Christ. He put on the ski mask. "I'm going to make this better, buddy," he told Bascom the Cat.

The morning—a sunny blue winter morning—his father was discovered frozen to death behind the barn, Buddy was upstairs in his bedroom eating a Baby Ruth candy bar. It had recently stopped snowing, and a white blanket spread out in every direction from the farmhouse. Looking out his bedroom window, Buddy saw a black station wagon he didn't recognize pull into the drive. He didn't have a view of the back of the house from his bedroom, so he went into the upstairs bathroom and, standing in the claw-foot bathtub, watched as two men bundled in wool coats got out of the station wagon and went around behind the barn. His mother and Tom McNeeley were already in the backyard. A toboggan leaned against a tree. Buddy didn't understand what was going on; it looked like his mother and Tom McNeeley were preparing to go sledding, but why was that station wagon there? Tom McNeeley tried to hug his mother, but she pulled away. Just then Chic came into the bathroom and wanted to show Buddy his hands. He'd been tracing them on a piece of paper, and they were covered with different colors of ink. Buddy didn't care about the ink on his brother's hands, and kept on looking out the window. The men from the station wagon came around the corner of the barn carrying his father on his side, his legs out and his back straight as a ruler, his body forming an L. He was wearing his pajamas and no coat. The pajama pants were tucked into his untied snow boots. Buddy noticed that his father's eyes were open and that tiny icicles hung from his mustache. His mother yelled something and shook her finger at his father. Buddy couldn't make out what she was shouting about, but he could see the anger in her jerky motions. Tom McNeeley tried to hold her back, but she shook him off and continued to wag her finger at his father. Even when the men put his father down on the ground behind the station wagon, she continued to rant at him. Finally, she turned away and buried her head in Tom McNeeley's chest. Through it all, his father's expression never changed. Buddy whispered, "Stand up," even though he knew his father was dead. He whispered it again, louder this time, "Stand up." Chic, who was washing his hands, asked Buddy who he was talking to. Chic then said he wanted to see what was happening outside, but Buddy told him to go to his room. Chic insisted that he wanted to see. The sink water was running and soap was lathered on Chic's hands and he was dripping on the bathroom tile. Buddy turned and gave his little brother a look that said if he asked again, he'd tell Mom and then he'd be in trouble, so Chic said, "Fine," and finished washing his hands, dried them on his pants, and went down the hall to his bedroom. The two men from the station wagon positioned themselves on either side of Buddy's father, hunching over, preparing to pick him up again. Buddy suddenly realized that he hadn't seen his father since Friday night, when he had been in the kitchen fixing himself a drink, getting ice cubes from the aluminum tray in the freezer. Buddy had been in his room polishing his coins and had gone to the kitchen to get a glass of water. His father was whistling when Buddy came into the kitchen, and he said hello, which was strange since his father pretty much ignored everyone even if they were standing right next to him. His father poured some Scotch over the ice cubes and the warm liquid made the cubes crackle. He capped the bottle and held up the glass to Buddy and said to him, "America. You have to love it. Someday, you'll see. It's not worth it. None of it." He downed the Scotch in one gulp and set the glass on the counter and put on his winter boots (he was wearing his pajamas) and told Buddy he had to check on something in the barn. He went out the back door. The men picked up Buddy's father, and like they were loading a piece of furniture, they turned him this way and that, trying to find the right angle to shove him into the back of the station wagon. Downstairs, Buddy heard the back door open and his mother and Tom McNeeley come into the house, both of them stomping the snow from their boots. Chic's bedroom door opened, and he ran down the hall yelling, "Mom, Mom, Mom, Mom." Finally, the men found the right angle—his father on his side, head first— and pushed him into the station wagon.

When the living room light finally went out, Buddy knew that Lijy had finished her tea and gone to bed. He waited about five minutes, then told Bascom the Cat that he'd be right back. He quietly got out of the car and softly closed the door. He snuck through the neighbors' backyards, going tree to tree and climbing over fences. When he reached the back of his house, Buddy climbed up on the gas meter and shined the flashlight into the kitchen window. Lijy's empty tea mug was upside down in the sink. He tried the window, knowing it would be open, and pushed it up as far as it would go. He slid through the opening, being careful not to make too much noise. Once he was inside, he could hear the ticking wall clock in the living room. The house smelled like one of Lijy's curry recipes. He crept upstairs to the master bedroom, shining the flashlight off the walls, the floor. At the end of the hallway, the bedroom door was closed. Standing outside, Buddy listened to Lijy shift her weight, the bedsprings sighing. His hand was on the doorknob. He wanted to burst into the bedroom and tell her how bad she'd hurt him, how angry he was, how sad she'd made him. He wanted to cry into her chest, and he wanted her to pet his hair and tell him it was going to be all right. How could she, how the hell could she? She was ruining him. Did she know that she was ruining him?

Instead he went to the basement. He shined the flashlight around until he found his coins, stacked like poker chips on a card table. An ironing board piled with folded laundry was next to the table. His white shirts hung on hangers from the ceiling rafters. Buddy picked up an Indian Head penny and shined the beam on it. He quickly scooped the rest of the coins into the ammunition boxes he used to transport them. Back in the car, Bascom the Cat was curled up on the front seat but immediately woke up when Buddy opened the back door and loaded the first of the ammunition boxes.

The next morning, Buddy called the real estate agent, Phyllis Glover, who was listed in the *Journal Star* ad. Buddy had gone to school with the Glover kids. He tried to disguise his voice. Phyllis put him on hold, saying she needed to pull the spec sheet. When she came back, she asked what sort of business he was in.

"Storage," he said.

"I can't quite hear you. It sounds like your hand is over your mouth."

Buddy didn't say anything. He looked at Bascom the Cat sleeping on the unmade motel bed.

"Are you there?"

"Storage."

"Oh. Okay. What sort of storage?"

"Human, Phyllis. Human storage."

"Is that a polite way of saying a funeral home?"

"I'm going to live there, Phyllis. It's going to be my home. A big, goddamn house. Human storage. Get it?"

There was silence on the other end of the line, a buzzing sound.

"Look, Phyllis, do you want to sell me the place or not?"

"Of course, Mr., ah—"

"Waldbeeser. Buddy Waldbeeser."

"Oh."

"Yes, Phyllis. My father froze himself behind the barn. Thank you for your condolences. It's been twenty years. And my mother's fine. She's great. I have no idea where she's at but I'm sure she's wonderful. Can you just meet me at the property in an hour?" Buddy hung up the phone.

The CILCO plant was down Route 7 about six miles from the Wel Kum Inn. A chain-link fence enclosed the property, with barbed wire coiled around the top. Sumac and locust trees hid the building from view. The gate was unlocked, and Buddy walked down the gravel drive about a quarter of a mile, until the drive opened into a parking lot. The building, a square, squat, one-story brick thing, looked like an automotive garage. It was clearly abandoned. The front door was boarded shut, and some of the windows had been rocked out. Buddy wiped dust away from one window and looked inside. In one corner was an abandoned Steelcase desk with a wooden chair on top of it. In the middle of the room was a lone metal garbage can stuffed with scraps of wood. Sunlight streaked through the windows illuminating floating dust particles. Buddy picked up Bascom the Cat up so that he could see in the window too, petting him between the ears. "Look at that. This is going to be our home."

Buddy was leaning against his car smoking a cigarillo when Phyllis pulled up.

"Can I show you the building?" she said.

"I already saw it. I walked up there. The gate was unlocked."

"Well. What do you think?"

"You take cash?"

"Of course. We'll have to fill out some paperwork. And then there's a closing, but the owner is a motivated seller. If you have some money to put down today, we can get the ball rolling."

Buddy flicked the cigarillo on the ground and went around to the trunk of the car.

"You know, my son was a few years younger than you," Phyllis said. "Or maybe it was your brother. You Waldbeeser boys both look so much alike."

Buddy took a deep breath, then put on a smile. "Let's not talk about family." He opened the trunk. Sitting next to the spare tire were eight ammunition boxes. He opened one to show Phyllis that it was full of coins. Buddy picked up a coin, flipped it, and showed it to her. "Took me twelve years to amass this fortune. Twelve years of driving all over the country. I had a plan, Phyllis, but that plan has changed a little bit."

She was eyeing him, looking at the coin, at his face.

He studied her worried face. This wasn't going the way he wanted it to go. "These are rare coins. Collector's items."

She fidgeted with her pearl necklace. "I can't accept your coin collection, Buddy."

"Wait a second. Hold on. Just hold on." He went to the car and scooped up Bascom the Cat. "I can give you my cat."

"You want to give me a cat for the building?"

"This isn't just any cat. This is a very special cat. His name is Bascom."

"Come see me when you get some money, Mr. Waldbeeser."

"I have money, Phyllis. My coins."

"Is everything all right Buddy?"

"What do you mean is everything all right? Of course everything is all right. It's just that . . . I think that . . . my brother. You know I . . . he . . . why? Do I look like something is wrong? Nothing is wrong."

"Why don't you sell the coins and come and see me when you have cash? And keep your cat. It's a cute cat, and it's named after your father."

Buddy watched her get back into her car.

"He's named after all the Bascom'," he yelled after her. "My great-grandfather, grandfather, dad, and me. All of us. He's named after all of us."

Buddy Waldbeeser

■

June 8, 1960 (ten minutes later)

What was he thinking, trying to pay for a building with a coin collection? He was too busy thinking about his brother sticking his dick in his wife to actually think; that was the problem. He needed to think. He needed to stay focused. Think happy thoughts—think of waking up with the morning sunlight streaking through the CILCO building's windows, think of the wind whispering through the trees, think of the Mackinaw River in the distance. Think calming thoughts. The car drifted toward the ditch. Buddy opened his eyes and jerked the wheel to swerve the car back onto the road. Bascom the Cat was curled next to his leg, and he scratched him between the ears. "Hang on, buddy." He turned on the radio, and Chatty Jim Melvin the radio preacher shouted, "You should love your neighbor like your brother." Buddy shut off the radio and stepped on the accelerator. He looked at Bascom the Cat. "Is this how you felt?" The cat looked at him. "Before you went off behind the barn? I'll tell you what. I feel like going off behind the barn. You're listening to me, aren't you? Dad? You're hearing me, aren't you?"

Buddy glanced in the rearview mirror. He thought he saw someone in the backseat, but there was only another car approaching, coming on fast. He looked down at his speedometer. He was going fifty. The other car had to be going seventy, maybe eighty. Buddy glanced over his shoulder. The car was in the left lane making a pass. He tried to speed up, but he couldn't go any faster. When the car was parallel to him, he looked over. "Dad?" Buddy whispered. "Is that . . . ?" The guy was looking straight ahead, both hands on the steering wheel. "Dad!" The car pulled into the lane ahead of him. Buddy floored the gas pedal, but it was no use. The car kept getting farther and farther ahead. "Don't leave me." The car disappeared over a hill. "Dad! Please!" He slowed down and pulled the car over to the side of the road, the gravel crunching under the tires. He got out. It was dusty and hot. The sun was high in the blue sky above him. It was the kind of heat where your pants stuck to the backs of your legs. He loosened his tie. He was going to show his father. He was going to show Phyllis, Lijy, Chic. The entire town. He was going to buy that goddamn CILCO building. The cat was looking at him. "You," he said to the cat. "Get out." The cat cocked its head like it was confused. "Get out of the goddamn car." Buddy grabbed the cat by the scruff of the neck and pulled him out. The cat scurried underneath the car. "Leave. Get out of here." He kicked the side of the car hard, which hurt his toe. "Goddamn it." He grabbed his foot. "Jesus Christ. Get out of here, you goddamn cat. I don't need you. I. Don't. Need. You." He got on his hands and knees. The cat was cowering, looking at him with his big yellow eyes. "Go on. I don't need you. Scram." He stood up and clapped—three quick smacks—which scared the cat. He bolted into the ditch weeds. "Now, please. Leave me alone." Buddy got back into the car and pulled away. He glanced in the rearview mirror. The cat had crept back onto the road and was watching him.

Seven

Mary & Green Geneseo

June 16, 1998

Mary had promised to be at the hospital at five with a bucket of Kentucky Fried Chicken. It was now almost six. It wasn't so much the lateness that bothered Green, but that he couldn't complain to anyone about it. Complaining made him feel better, and what he really wanted to do right at this minute was run at the mouth to someone, the nurse most likely, since she was around. He could write a note. But then she'd have to read it. That had been a disaster this morning, when he'd had the nurse send flowers to the Brazen Bull for Mary. Green couldn't spell worth a dang, and he hadn't wanted the nurse to know that because then she'd judge him and he didn't want to be judged. So he purposely wrote sloppy, hoping the nurse wouldn't notice that he couldn't spell. But she couldn't read what he wrote. And, to make matters worse, he didn't know the address of the Brazen Bull and had to have the nurse look it up. While she was out of the room, he took his time with the note, trying not to misspell anything. Jesus, it took him like five minutes to write that note. It was bad enough he'd had a stroke. But, then, to have people know that he couldn't spell. He couldn't deal with that. Not to mention that writing a note delayed the complaining, and complaining needed to be immediate, a stream of consciousness kind of thing. Green wanted very much to spew a batch of complaints, like, for example, that Mary should be sitting in that chair, the one right over there. And that she should have been here an hour ago—one hour and three minutes ago, according to the clock in the hallway, which he had a view of if he leaned over on his right elbow. She should be feeding him. She should be dabbing the corners of his mouth with a napkin. She should be holding his hand. She should be talking to him in a gentle, soothing voice, making him feel loved, making him feel wanted, making him feel like he didn't almost goddamn die on the driveway of some stupid rental house in Peoria goddamn Illinois.

She was probably with some guy. That's why she was late. Maybe he had his arm draped over her shoulder like some baboon, holding her close like she belonged to him. Maybe they were driving in his car, a Cadillac probably, with the windows down, and she had her head on his shoulder. Maybe right now they were in this guy's Cadillac, sitting in the drive-through of a Kentucky Fried Chicken. That was his goddamn stinking luck. The one woman he ever loved gets cancer and dies, and two years later, he has a stroke and the woman he married because he couldn't stand to be alone runs off with a guy who drives a Cadillac. Green wanted to voice these complaints to someone, but couldn't write that on a goddamn Post-it Note.

It was now 6:07. She was one hour and seven minutes late. He wanted to get out of the hospital. That's what he really wanted. Get out of here and away from that stupid television that was affixed to the wall and was unwatchable for three or four hours in the afternoon because of the glare, which meant that for three or four hours in the afternoon he had to read, which he didn't want to do. He hated reading. It was work, and he didn't want to work, he just wanted to lie in bed and watch reruns of *Friends*. He liked that show. He liked Joey, though he identified with Ross. He was so nice, like Ross, but he was always getting the shaft, like Ross. No matter what he did, things never went his way. Except for Jane. Things went his way with her. Except for the cancer.

Green wished he had never come to Peoria. He wished he was back in Las Vegas at the hospital where Jane had been treated. He used to visit her every day after he got off work. She had a roommate, a woman named Laura, who also had cancer.

Laura had flowers all over the room and cards pinned up on the bulletin board. Green used to bring Jane flowers (and he was the only one who did) and put them in a vase on her nightstand, and each time he walked in with flowers, Jane would smile, even if smiling was the last thing she wanted to do. Luckily, he didn't have a roommate. That would make it worse—some guy recovering from surgery with his whole family sitting around his bed and flowers all over the place and cards pinned to the bulletin board. Maybe he should have bought more cards for Jane. She only received a couple the whole time she was in the hospital, one from her sister who lived in New Mexico and another from her cousin Becky. Green wished he had a family sitting around his bed and a bunch of flowers. Jane, she would be here, and if he were in Las Vegas, Tim Lee would be here. Jane's cousin, Becky, would be here, maybe, or at least, she would have sent a card. The only person he knew in Peoria hadn't shown up with his fried chicken. God he missed Jane.

Out in the hallway, he heard a nurse say, "He's up." Then he heard Mary's voice. "He wanted fried chicken." She sounded happy. She was happy? "Hey there," she said, coming into the room.

Green pretended to be watching television, but the set wasn't on. He'd shut it off when the glare was so bad he couldn't see the picture.

"You look mad. I'm sorry. I got caught up at work. But I got the chicken like you wanted." Mary set the bucket down. "You want a leg or a breast?"

Green grunted and picked up the golf pencil and the Post-it Note pad and wrote, *Leg*.

Mary put a leg on a paper plate. He wrote, *Get any rolls?*

"I got coleslaw."

Hate coleslaw.

"Sorry. I didn't know that. I can go back. You want me to go back?"

Green shook his head no. He took a bite of the chicken. Jane would have known to get rolls, and she would have gotten butter, too.

The nurse walked in. "When you're done, we need to take your blood pressure. And take these." She set a pill cup on the nightstand and left the room. Mary peeled a straw out of its paper wrapper and jabbed it into the large soda she'd gotten for them to split. In the hallway, an old woman pushed an old man in a wheelchair. The old man wore the standard-issue purple hospital gown, and the woman had her purse over her shoulder. The guy looked downtrodden, an admittance bracelet around his wrist, his hospital gown riding up showing his pale, hairless leg. This was what he had to look forward to—Mary pushing him in a wheelchair. About six months, maybe a year, in a wheelchair, that's what the doctor thought, and even after that, he might not ever walk without a walker or cane. It just really depended, the doctor said.

"How's the chicken?"

Green nodded that it was fine. He wanted to ask Mary where she had been, what she had been doing, why she was late. He had a lot of questions, but he'd have to write them down, and he didn't feel like doing that. Besides, his fingers were greasy. He picked up a fresh chicken leg Mary had set on his plate and gnawed the meat from the bone.

When they were finished with dinner, Mary cleared away the mess and dumped the bones and soiled napkins into the garbage can in the bathroom while Green licked his fingers. She washed her hands, then wet a washrag and wiped off his hands.

"You need to take those." She looked at the pills.

Green didn't move.

"Green, you know what the doctor said."

He grunted and picked up the pills and popped them in his mouth and looked around for something to drink. Mary handed him the giant soda and he put the straw in his mouth and sucked in some soda.

"That wasn't so bad was it?"

Green rolled his head away from her and looked out the hospital window. There was a view of the parking lot and beyond the parking lot, a parking garage and beyond that, to the west, the skyline of Peoria.

"What's the matter with you?"

Green rolled back over and looked at her.

"I told you. I got tied up at work. I wouldn't lie to you Green. I'm late. I'm sorry. I hurried. You wanted fried chicken. I brought that. It took me some time to find a Kentucky Fried Chicken."

It occurred to him that he didn't know anything about her past, except for some guy named Lyle, a guy she married when she was in her thirties, a guy she caught cheating. She made Green promise he'd never cheat on her. He promised. He meant it, too. He wouldn't cheat on her.

Green picked up his Post-it Note pad and wrote, *Take me to Brazen Bull.*

The nurse walked into the room again. "Mr. Geneseo, did you take your medication?"

"He took it," Mary said.

"If you don't mind, Mrs. Geneseo, I need to change him."

"Sure." Mary stood up.

Green looked away from her and out the window again. He wasn't sure what going to the Brazen Bull would prove, but he felt like he had to go. At the same time, he was afraid to go, afraid of everyone's reaction, afraid everyone would laugh at him. Or, if they didn't laugh, they'd feel sorry for him. He'd see it in their faces. He didn't want anyone looking at him and feeling sorry for him.

"OK, Mr. Geneseo. I need you to sit up. Can you do that for me?"

With the nurse's help, Green sat up in his bed. He felt lightheaded, and the sides of his vision were tunneling in on him. He felt like he might pass out. It took a moment, as the nurse got some wet wipes from the container next to the soda, for the dizziness to pass. After it did, Green noticed the nurse was using the wipes to clean him off like he was a baby.

Lijy Waldbeeser & Ellis McMillion
Or, the Waldbeeser family extended, the second time

■

July 10, 1960

Ellis McMillion was waiting in front of the house in his Ford Fairlane, eating an orange, the peels scattered on his lap. His shoes were off and the driver's seat was reclined. Beside him on the passenger seat were several issues of the *Journal Star* and a paperback book, *How to Improve Your Softball*.

Lijy noticed the Fairlane as soon as the cab turned onto the street. She told the driver, an elderly black man wearing jazz sunglasses, not to stop.

He looked at her in the rearview.

"Keep going." She tightened her grip on the baby. As the cab passed Ellis's car, she tried to slump down in her seat, but he saw her and started up his car.

"Don't let that car catch us," Lijy told the cab driver. "Go, go. Step on it."

"Lady, this is a residential area."

"I don't care. Lose him."

Rather than speeding up, the driver stopped at the intersection and looked both ways. The pause gave Ellis time to glue his car to the cab's bumper.

"This boy's got some sorta fire in his eye. I don't wanna test 'im," the cab driver said.

"Fine. Pull over."

The driver pulled to the curb. Ellis jumped out of his car and ran up to the cab and stuck his beady, unwashed face in the rear window.

"That's my son. I know that's my son." He pushed his glasses up on his nose. "I followed you to the hospital. They wouldn't let me see you. Did you get the teddy bear I sent?"

Lijy wrapped her arms around her son and turned her back on Ellis, hoping he wouldn't see the baby, hoping he'd get the hint, hoping he'd go away. The cab driver was eyeing her in the rearview mirror. Ellis cupped his face in the window, the oil on his forehead smearing the glass. "I'm not leaving until you talk to me, Lijy."

She opened the opposite door and slid out.

Ellis hurried around the back of the cab. "Let me hold him."

"Your hands are dirty. You can't touch him like that. He doesn't like that."

The driver rolled down his window. "Somebody needs to pay me my money."

Lijy looked at Ellis. He sighed and took out his wallet. The cab driver hopped out and keyed open the trunk and took out two hard-shell suitcases. He then accepted the bills from Ellis, shoving them in his pocket and not asking him if he wanted any change.

"Wait a second. Before you go." Ellis held out a camera to the driver. "Can you take a picture of us?"

"No pictures, Ellis," Lijy said. "I don't want any pictures."

"One picture. Geez." He pushed the glasses up on his nose and put his arm around Lijy. The cab driver stared at the camera. "It's that button there on the top," Ellis told him. "There. Yeah. That's it."

The cab driver put the viewfinder to his eye. "Ya'll ready."

"Cheese," Ellis said.

"Tell your woman to smile, Commander."

"Lijy, please."

"The woman's still not smiling."

Lijy forced a quick smile. The cab driver snapped the picture, then handed Ellis the camera, hopped back in his cab, and sped off.

Lijy started to walk away, not even bothering with the suitcases on the sidewalk. Ellis picked them up. They were heavy, and he struggled with them. "What the hell do you have in these things?"

She didn't answer him, walking down the middle of the street holding her son close to her chest. The last person in the entire world she wanted to see was Ellis McMillion. This whole situation felt like something spilled, a mess that kept spreading all over the floor. His tongue had been in her mouth. She'd touched his penis. Actually, she'd done a whole lot more than touch it. She couldn't believe she'd let him do the things he'd done to her, experimental things, strange things, things that hadn't felt very good. She had only wanted to get Buddy's attention, and now she was forced to live this horrible, godforsaken lie. Chic had done the biggest favor anyone had ever done for her. She knew that, and she owed him. A few weeks ago, she had tried to call him, but Diane answered and immediately hung up. She called back. Diane said they must have been disconnected and told her she would go get Chic. Lijy waited. She could hear activity in the background. Someone filled up a glass of water from the tap. The back door slammed. Lijy said hello a few times, but no one picked up. She waited ten minutes before she finally hung up. Poor Chic. He had no idea. She knew what she had done was wrong. And selfish. She needed to thank him. Maybe send him a card. Or maybe put a gift or something in his car. She had so much to do. She had to start getting her life back in order.

When she reached the house, she glanced over her shoulder. Ellis was still halfway down the block, struggling with the suitcases. He would pick them up, take a few hurried steps, set them down, then pick them up again and take a few more hurried steps and set them back down.

Lijy unlocked the front door. Inside, she sat down on the sofa, cradling the baby, and waited. He was coming, and she'd have to deal with him. She started to sing quietly to the baby:

Shoo, fly, don't bother me,
Shoo, fly, don't bother me,
Shoo, fly, don't bother me,
Shoo, fly, don't bother me,
For I belong to somebody.

There was a knock on the door. "Let me in," Ellis called from outside. "I need to talk to you."

Lijy opened the door. Ellis used a hanky to dab the sweat on his forehead, then straightened and pushed his glasses up on his nose. "What's that smell?"

"I don't smell anything."

He sniffed at the air and looked at the baby.

Lijy smelled the baby's bottom. Sure enough, he had pooped. She laid him on the sofa. It was the first diaper she'd changed by herself, and she had some trouble with the safety pins. Ellis hovered behind her, breathing heavily.

"Do you know what you're doing?"

"Yes, of course I know what I'm doing."

"Here, let me help."

"Don't ... no. Ellis. I don't need your help." The baby squirmed, and Ellis tried to muscle his way in, but Lijy elbowed him in the chest.

"Jesus. You don't have to hit me."

"I don't need your help. You've already made this difficult. My brother-in-law had to take the rap for this, you know."

"Your brother-in-law? What are you talking about?"

"Nothing. Forget it."

After Lijy got the diaper changed, she picked up the baby and snuggled him close to her chest. "You know, Ellis, if that's really your real name ..."

"It's my real name."

"You seduced me that afternoon."

"I did nothing of the sort. You wanted to give me a massage. You told me to take my shirt off. I thought that was an invitation."

"I was using you, Ellis. The whole time you were doing that . . . that . . . I didn't like that, by the way, but that's beside the point. The point is the whole time you were . . . you know . . . I was thinking about Buddy."

"Who's Buddy?"

"My husband."

"His name is Buddy?"

"Yes. His name is Buddy."

Ellis smirked.

"What?"

"Don't you see the irony?"

"His real name is Bascom. Bascom IV."

Ellis chuckled to himself, then started nodding. Lijy thought he was going to say something, but he just kept nodding.

"Why are you nodding like that?"

"Nice try. Very good, Lijy. Buddy. Bascom IV. That's a real laugh. You're making this up. You don't have a husband."

"I have a husband."

"I have been in front of your house for two days, and I have not seen anyone enter or leave this house."

Lijy pointed to a framed photograph on the end table next to the couch. In the photo, Buddy was leaning against the rear quarter panel of a 1957 Coupe de Ville. When she and Buddy were driving from California, he'd seen the car in a parking lot of a motel, and for some reason, Buddy had wanted his picture taken with it.

Ellis sat down on the rocking chair across from the couch. "Look, I don't care if you have a husband or not. I have a plan. Do you want to hear it?"

"No," she answered, but he told her anyway. That week, he'd quit his job with the Rivermen. The job had been a stepping stone, a rung in his climb for the future, but his future had changed. He was going to California. He loved it there. And it wasn't just the state. It was the word: California. When he got to California, he planned to get a job teaching American history and coaching girls' softball. After he secured this job, they'd get married. He didn't want a religious wedding. He didn't believe in religion, but he thought it was important for their son that they had a legal marriage. He also wanted the tax breaks, and besides, people looked at you strangely if you were living together without being married.

That was phase one of his plan.

Phase two involved a farmhouse and some animals, goats mostly, but cows and chickens, too, perhaps some horses. Lijy would write a book about Ayurveda massage. Their son would play baseball. If he didn't want to play baseball, he could take up table tennis or golf, perhaps. Basketball was acceptable too, as was football or bowling. (Was bowling really a sport?) He needed to play a sport. He was going to be good at a sport. That had always been his problem, he told her. He wasn't good at a sport, and he saw how others, guys especially, looked at him. They knew he wasn't good at sports. He had his parents to blame for this, and he wasn't going to have his son blame him for anything.

Phase three would start when Lijy published her book. If she couldn't get a publisher, they'd self-publish and take the books to where people would appreciate them. They'd buy a van. By this time, his girls' softball team would have won a state championship or two. He'd been reading a book on softball strategy and believed that the key to a winning team was having a strong infield. He asked Lijy if she knew anything about baseball. Had she ever heard of Roger Maris? He was having a great season for the Yankees. He and Mickey Mantle were two of the best baseball players of all time.

Lijy stared at him, stone-faced. He waited for her to make a move, to do something, bat an eye, crack a tiny smile, maybe go into the kitchen and uncap the bottle of rum. Instead, she just glared at him.

California! She hated that place, and she wasn't going back there, back to where people called her "Hindoo" and did miserable things to her and her family, catcalling at them, snapping their fingers, shooting rocks at them with a slingshot, standing in their front yard wearing white robes and whistling strange music that she never wanted to hear again. California was not a place she ever wanted to think about again. She hadn't even told Buddy about her past there; she hadn't told anyone.

"What's the baby's name?" Ellis asked to break the silence. "I was thinking we'd name him Ellis. Ellis Junior. Call him EJ. I came up with that this morning. Actually, I lied. I've secretly always wanted to name my son after myself. I know naming a baby is important in your culture. Maybe he should be named after your father. What was his name?"

"I was thinking Buddy," she said.

"Your husband's name? Not a good name."

Lijy didn't say anything.

"Do you mind if I lie down?" Ellis asked. "I've been sleeping in my car for two days. I could really use a little nap."

"I don't think that would be a good idea."

"I just need to rest my eyes."

"Ellis, I don't care about your plan, and I'm not going to California with you."

He pushed his glasses up on his nose. "Do you want to hear phase four?"

"I think you should go."

"In phase four we open a health food store like you've always wanted to."

Lijy felt herself go momentarily dizzy.

"I know you don't want to be with your husband. If you did, that afternoon wouldn't have happened."

Lijy thought about Buddy pacing the living room and smoking his mini-cigars. She thought about the night she had visited him at the Wel Kum Inn. She'd never intended to hurt him, to hurt anyone, to get Chic involved or any of it. It just, somehow, the next thing she knew, it had happened. Ellis rolled off her, sweating and quivering, and she was staring up at a crack that ran from one edge of the ceiling to the middle, directly above her.

"This is what you've always wanted. I can see it in your face."

"I think you should go."

"You can't deny our son his father, Lijy. He's going to want to know me."

She showed him to the door. "Good-bye, Ellis."

He stepped onto the porch. "But . . ."

She shut the door. She could deny him his son, and she would. He was not the father. He would never be the father. She peeked out the window. Ellis was standing in the driveway. He appeared confused, looking up and down the street like he'd forgotten where he'd parked his car.

Lijy & Buddy Waldbeeser

■

July 11, 1960

Next to the entrance gate of the CILCO building, Buddy had set a plywood sandwich board that read: BUDDY WALDBEESER'S RESIDENCE. NO TRESPASSING. KEEP OUT! PUT THE MAIL IN THE BOX. TO BE ANNOUNCED, TALK INTO THE CAN. An arrow pointed to a tin can hanging from the chain-link fence. A piece of red string ran from the can and disappeared around the bend of the gravel road. Lijy picked up the tin can and eyed it suspiciously. Then she spoke into it. "Hello. Buddy? Buddy Waldbeeser."

Her voice traveled down the string, around the bend, through the window, across the concrete floor, and out the second can, which sat next to the secondhand couch Buddy was sprawled out on. He was using a magnifying glass to look at the only coin he'd kept, his first coin, the gold Double Eagle his grandfather had given him.

"Buddy? Buddy Waldbeeser."

He picked up the can. "Buddy's not here. Go away."

"Buddy, I recognize your voice."

"This is not Buddy."

"Don't play games." She shifted the baby's weight to her other hip. "I brought your son to meet you."

"He's not my son."

"So you're admitting you're Buddy?"

"Fine. Yeah. I'm Buddy. What do you want? I'm very busy."

"Open the gate. I want to come up there."

"Nope. I told you. I'm very busy."

"Doing what?"

"Things."

"I want you to meet your son."

"He's Chic's son. Remember? You had sex with him."

"This is a baby we're talking about. A real baby. Not some doll." She held the tin can in front of the baby. "Hear him."

"I don't care if he's real. I don't care if he's cute and I don't care if he slobbers all over himself. I don't care, Lijy. I don't care. I don't care. I don't care."

"Buddy, I'm sorry."

"That doesn't help."

"I want you to help me name him."

"Name him Chic. Chic Junior. CJ Waldbeeser. He'll grow up to enlist in the navy and die when his ship sinks in the Indian Ocean. Only then will you hurt like I hurt. You tore out my heart. You're a devil woman. I hope you fall in a deep hole and are buried alive."

"It's a boy, by the way. You always wanted a son. Can you please just help me? What do you want to name him? I want to name him after us."

"Who's Russ?"

"What?"

"Is that your boyfriend? Is he taking care of you? Why did

you come out here to tell me that? Haven't you put me through enough? Who is this Russ?"

"Russ?"

"You said you want to name him after Russ."

"I said after us. *Us,* Buddy. We're a family. The Waldbeesers. I love you. I do. Honestly I do. I'm sorry—I'm so sorry, Buddy. I was only trying to get your attention and I made a mistake. A horrible, terrible, unfortunate mistake."

Buddy opened his mouth to say something, but nothing came out. He felt like someone was looking at him. He sat up and looked over the top of the couch and hoped that his father was standing there, a ghost, ready to finally at last be his father. But there was nothing.

"Please forgive me and come home and be this baby's father."

His voice was frozen in his throat. The only sound he could get out was a squeak, and it traveled down the string like it was using a cane and never made it out the other side.

Lijy waited, but nothing came out of the can. She'd said that she loved him, and he'd met her apology with silence. She dropped the can, and it clinked against the fence and hung there, dangling and swaying back and forth like a pendulum. She felt sick to her stomach. Maybe he couldn't forgive her. Maybe—and this was the worst possible thought she could have—he didn't love her. She loaded the baby into the car and got behind the wheel and backed onto the highway. Before she put the car into drive, she screamed, a piercing, high-pitched wail that was so profound, so full of pain, that her baby son didn't even respond. He simply sat there too overwhelmed by his mother's emotion to make a sound.

After Lijy drove off, the tin can continued to dangle. The crickets chirped in the ditch weeds. The cloud of dust the car had kicked up settled on the road. Finally, Buddy's voice came out of the can, softly. "I want to come home." Not finding any ears, his words floated down to the gravel. "I want to come home," he said, again. "Lijy?" He stood up from the couch and screamed, "Lijy!"

Lomax Waldbeeser

■

July 15, 1960

On the morning of July 15, 1960, Chic watched proudly as William T. Daniels maneuvered his backhoe into the yard. After he got the machinery in place, William T. stretched the bucket out as far as it would go. Chic, who was leaning on a shovel, smiled. He was going to have a pool, his own pool, his own slice of Florida, right in his own backyard. William T. lowered the bucket into the ground; the teeth of the bucket dug into the earth. Diane watched from the upstairs bedroom window. Chic saw her and waved, but she didn't wave back.

Around noon, Lomax came out of the house. He was wearing a scuba mask, which was pushed up on his forehead. A towel hung around his neck. He was carrying scuba flippers and a duffel bag that read MIDDLEVILLE JUNIOR HIGH SCHOOL in white lettering. William T. was taking a break, reclining in the backhoe and eating a sandwich.

"Whoa," Chic said to his son. "You're a little early there, kiddo. Pool's not done. Couple more weeks."

"I'm going to Kennel Lake," Lomax said. He kneeled down by the water spigot and unscrewed the garden hose.

Chic wondered what he was going to do with that hose. "If you wait a few hours, I'll drive you."

"I'll just ride my bike."

Lomax went into the garage and got his bike, a red Schwinn Phantom with a banana seat. Balancing his load—the hose, the flippers, the duffel bag, the swimming towel, and the scuba mask—he wobbled down the drive and took a left.

"I have a strange son, Willie," Chic said when Lomax was out of view. "What's he going to do with a garden hose at Kennel Lake?"

Willie took a bite from his sandwich.

"The other night, I walked past his room, and he's hunched over something, kneeling on the floor. I stopped and watched him. He's got a pocketknife and a cutting board from the kitchen and he's cutting something. I went in for a closer look, and he's got a pile of fingernails. He told me he'd been collecting them for a year. Imagine that."

"Didn't you have a collection of something in your desk in Mrs. Horn's class?" Willie said. "What was it again?"

"I didn't have a collection of anything ..."

"Spitballs, that's it. You had a collection of spitballs."

"I did? The things we forget."

"He's a kid," Willie added. "He'll grow out of it."

"Yeah, maybe."

Later in the afternoon, after William T. had knocked off for the day—he'd gotten about half the pool dug—Chic wheeled the Weber grill from the garage into the driveway. He went inside the house and got his barbeque apron, a spatula, and a plate of burger patties. The sun was beginning to set and the shadows from the trees were stretching out across the driveway. He put the burgers on the grill, the meat sizzling on the wire rack. From down the street, he could hear the kids playing baseball in the empty lot. Chic put the grill lid on and walked down the driveway toward the street. There were six kids playing ball. There wasn't any sign of Lomax among the group, not that Chic had really expected him to be there. He never was, but Chic had hoped Lomax would be there this time because he had been gone for hours and Chic was starting to get a little worried.

Diane came out the back door and put her hands on her hips. She seemed worried too. "See what you did. You're too busy digging a pool to pay attention to your son. So now he's ... where is he?"

"He said he was going to Kennel Lake."

"You let him go by himself?"

"I told him I'd drive him." Chic picked up the lid and flipped the burgers.

"You're overcooking them."

"You don't think I know I'm overcooking them? Do you wanna cook them yourself?"

"You don't have to yell at me."

"You don't have to tell me what I already know."

"Someone is in a bad mood."

"Yeah, well, I'm trying to make this better, you know. I'm trying."

Diane turned and went back into the house.

The sun sunk behind the neighborhood trees and roofs. The streetlights came on. Diane had made up a plate for Lomax and poured him a glass of milk. The kitchen window was open, letting in the sound of the summer crickets. Chic told Diane he was going to drive out to Kennel Lake, but he didn't move. Both of them stared at the empty chair, their plates in front of them, the kitchen getting dark and neither of them getting up to turn on the light. Chic wanted to hear his son coast up the driveway on his bike. He wanted to hear him park his bike in the garage. He wanted to hear him come in the back door, stomping his feet the way he stomped his feet.

Finally, Chic stood up and looked around for his keys. Just then the phone rang.

It was Sheriff Hewitt.

Kennel Lake was a sportsman's paradise that featured trap shooting, a clubhouse for fish fries, a canoe launch, and a beach with a floating dock that the kids did cannonballs off of. At one end of the lake was a bunch of cattails. Diane and Chic pulled up to the clubhouse. The one streetlight in the middle of the lot was on, and there were three police cruisers and a fire truck near the boat launch. A half-dozen men were raking their flashlights over the bank and the black water. Sheriff Hewitt came up to the car carrying a cardboard box containing several mason jars and an empty MIDDLEVILLE JUNIOR HIGH SCHOOL duffel bag.

He told Chic and Diane that the night watchman had found a johnboat beached in the cattails by the spillway. He said they had some men getting ready to go in the lake. He motioned to two guys putting on their scuba fins. Diane put her hands over her face. Chic wanted to know if he was sure Lomax was in the lake. Couldn't he be in the cornfield? He probably just left the boat and got distracted chasing a firefly or something. He had to be around here somewhere. Did they check the clubhouse bathroom? Did they check along the bank? How about the cattails? Or a creek—wasn't there a creek around here? Did they check the road? He's a good kid, and he's got to be around here. He has got to be. Sheriff Hewitt reached through the window and squeezed Chic's shoulder. Diane was softly crying in the passenger seat.

Diane's parents showed up a few minutes later, and the four of them stood by the car waiting, watching the flashlights bob around the lake. The two men in scuba masks floated on the surface of the water. A boat was next to them, and a guy trained a flashlight on the water. A couple of other men waded in the shallow water poking cane poles in the mud. Diane looked dead-eyed, staring out over the lake. Her father kept rubbing her back and telling her it was going to be okay. Sheriff Hewitt checked on them. He couldn't bring himself to look Chic in the eye. He told them they were doing their best and that some state officers were on their way.

"It's going to be all right," Chic said. "They're going to find him."

Diane's eyes welled with tears.

"I have this image of him coming out of those trees over there. He's fine. Everything is going to be fine."

Diane's father looked at Chic.

"It is," Chic said. "It's going to be fine."

Diane's mother hugged him.

About an hour later, Chic heard a diver on the opposite side of the lake yell, "Over here." His voice was tiny, echoing. The flashlights raced toward him. He was standing in waist-deep water, not far from the canoe launch, not far from the patch of cattails where they had found the abandoned boat.

A man with a cane pole waded out to him, poking the pole up and down in the water. "It's something."

The diver went underwater and was gone for a few seconds. When he resurfaced, standing up, he cradled something, lifting it out of the water. A body. Water cascaded off of it. Lomax's body. He was wearing his socks and one scuba flipper. He squeezed the garden hose in one hand. Seaweed was stuck in his hair.

Diane's body went limp. Her father caught her and gently set her down on the grass next to the car. Diane's mother grabbed Chic to hug him, but he didn't want to be hugged. He didn't want to be touched. He stepped away from her. The diver carried Lomax out of the lake and up the muddy bank and laid him down in the grass. His son's body was lifeless like a washed-up seashell. Chic wanted to reach out to him. He wanted to touch him. He wanted to run to him and kneel down and breathe life into him. He wanted him to stand up. Stand up. But he just lay on the bank, the men surrounding him, looking down at him, shining flashlights on him. The hose was still in his hand and trailed out into the water. His son was no longer the boy pulling a briefcase behind him, the boy dressed in knickers and a paperboy hat, the boy who spent his evenings sitting on the floor of his bedroom translating Bascom's letters into English, the boy whom had once unraveled an entire baseball to get to the core, the boy who he held when he was a baby, the boy who was his son, the boy he, Chic, should have protected. Diane was right. He'd made a mistake. He'd made a lot of mistakes. How could he keep making so many mistakes? Diane's mother and father knelt next to her, hugging her, petting her hair as she cried. Chic didn't have a mother and father to console him. He had no one. He was alone, his emotions bubbling inside of him, throbbing in his chest. He felt like he was going to cry, but he couldn't let himself cry. He had to be strong. He had to be strong for Diane. She needed him. He needed to finish the pool and be strong. That's what he needed to do now. He looked up into the night sky—the stars. His son was up there somewhere. He hoped it was a better place. It had to be better than this, a place that allowed Chic to feel alone and hurt the way he was hurting. What kind of place was this? A tear trickled down his cheek, and he wiped it away with the palm of his hand.

The morning his father died, he had gone downstairs into the kitchen after he heard someone stomping snow off their boots. His mother was crying, and Tom McNeeley told him that he should go to his room, but Chic didn't go to his room. He wanted to do something, but he didn't know what to do. He wanted to console his mother but he didn't know how to console her. His mother squeezed Tom McNeeley, hugging him, clawing at his back. She gasped as she cried, sucking in air, and Tom McNeeley whispered to her. Upstairs, Chic heard his brother come out of the bathroom and pad down the stairs. Buddy was on the verge of tears. His voice cracked. "He went behind the barn and killed himself, didn't he?"

Tom McNeeley looked at Buddy. "Go upstairs," he said.

"That's why those men are here?" Buddy said.

"Just go upstairs," Tom McNeeley said.

"What are we going to do now?" Buddy said. " Just go upstairs," Tom McNeeley said.

Chic stared at his brother. He was trying to make sense of what was happening. He tried to slow it down and stop it. But he couldn't. His brother was right: what would they do now? Out the kitchen window, he could see the snow in the field behind the house and the blue sky and the backyard tree branches swaying in the wind and the arrow of the weather vane on top of the barn pointing in the direction the wind was blowing.

Eight

Buddy & Lijy & Russ Waldbeeser
Or, the Waldbeeser family, a funeral

■

July 19, 1960

While getting ready for the funeral, Buddy drank two Bloody Marys and smoked three cigarillos. He didn't feel drunk. He pinched his cheek to make sure. He wasn't, not yet at least. He put on a racy Hawaiian shirt and a straw hat. This was what happened when you betrayed your brother, when you violated him, when you stomped on his toes and sucker punched him in the stomach. This was the what-goes-around-comes-around.

On the drive to Roth Cemetery, Buddy thought he saw his father in the backseat. He squeezed his eyes shut, then opened them and checked the rearview mirror. The empty road stretched out behind him. He swerved over the center line, then jerked the car back into his lane.

At the cemetery, he kept his distance, standing under the shade of a sycamore tree about fifty yards away. The hearse pulled up, and men in suits unloaded the small casket. Buddy uncapped his flask of bourbon and took a quick nip. Chic and Diane wore sunglasses and looked like they'd been ravaged by a massive wind. Diane was wearing only one shoe; she'd lost the other one while walking to the gravesite. Lijy was bringing up the rear carrying her bastard son. He didn't want to see her. He didn't even want to be within a thousand feet of her.

The funeral was officiated over by Father Eugene, a frail old man with shaky hands who continually blessed everyone and spoke in Latin. As the coffin was lowered into the ground, Diane's father squeezed Chic's shoulder while Diane unleashed a high-pitched banshee scream that echoed out over the cemetery and made a neighborhood dog howl.

Buddy held up his flask. "Ashes to ashes. Dust to dust. It's gonna rain and we'll all turn to mud." He took a pull and wiped his mouth. His father was also buried at Roth Cemetery, in the plot beside Lomax's. (The mourners were actually standing on his father's grave.) Buddy remembered his father's funeral—his mother standing with Tom McNeeley, the wind whipping off the surrounding pumpkin fields. (The fields were gone now, replaced by houses; the backyards of some of these houses abutted the cemetery: swing sets, dog houses). When his father's casket was in the hearse and no one was around for a moment, Buddy peeked inside. His father was dressed in a black suit, white shirt, and red tie, his hands folded over his belt buckle. His eyes were open and he had that same look on his face that he had when the men carried him from around the barn. Buddy hated that look. It taunted him, telling Buddy that his father knew something he didn't. "What do you know?" Buddy whispered. Just then, he felt a hand on his shoulder. He turned around. "You okay?" Tom McNeeley asked.

After the funeral, Buddy approached Chic and Diane as they were getting into the limousine. Chic's sunglasses were mirrored and reflected Buddy's image back at himself—Hawaiian shirt and beach hat.

Diane grabbed Buddy's forearm. "Chic's putting in a pool. A pool! Ha. The irony."

Her mother put a gentle hand on Diane's shoulder.

"Why are you dressed like that, Buddy?" Diane's mother asked.

"I'm sorry, Diane. Chic. Mr. and Mrs. von Schmidt." He took off his straw hat and put it over his heart. "I don't do well at funerals."

"Does anyone?" Chic asked.

"Mom did pretty well. You did, too, at Dad's."

Chic remembered his mother talking to people, smiling,

laughing, Tom McNeeley beside her, his hand on the small of her back. Afterward, they went back to the church and had a pot-luck dinner. Chic spent the afternoon running around the church basement with some of the kids from the congregation while Buddy sat on the front steps scowling and muttering to himself.

"My son's dead, and you don't have the decency to wear the color of mourning. Shame on you, Buddy Waldbeeser," Diane scolded, sliding into the back of the limousine. Her mother and father followed.

"I could tell you something," Chic said when they were alone.

"Yeah? What can you tell me?"

"I'm not going to say."

"You can't say you're going to tell me something and not tell me."

"Yes I can and I just did."

"What were you going to tell me?"

"You're welcome."

"For what?"

"For being your brother."

"Like I asked you to be my brother. And by the way, you've been a terrible brother. The worst. You know, I could ruin your life. Right now. All I have to do is tell Diane about what happened. But, I won't. I can't. I'll never say anything. Never. Zip my lip potato chip."

Chic touched his brother on the bicep, then got into the limousine, which pulled away. The other cars filed out behind it. Buddy was now alone. He pulled out the flask and took another pop. He didn't feel like going over to the church. He was beginning to think that he was making things worse, and he didn't want to make things worse. He just wanted things to be better. He just wanted to go back to the way it had been with Lijy, before all this. Sadness bore down on him like the weight of a giant boulder, like he was under the thumb of God. If only someone could pick him back up, brush off the dirt, and tell him everything was going to be all right, tousle his hair, squeeze his shoulder.

The lot was now empty except for a single car parked on the far side under a maple tree—Lijy's car. The back door was open and she was putting the baby in his car seat. Buddy uncapped his flask and took another hit. He felt like he was about to cry. He took another sip. Suddenly, he noticed something. His father was crossing through the cemetery, carrying a derby hat in his hands, wearing the black suit and red tie he had been buried in. He got to the gate and lifted the latch and let himself through. Buddy took another drink. He felt the alcohol pulsing in his head. He shook his head and closed his eyes. When he opened them, his father was standing in front of him, the same look on his face as always. "Dad?" Buddy asked. He reached out to touch him. "I wish I had an axe so that I could break you out of this icy silence. I sold all the coins and live in an abandoned building. I'm sure you know that. Chic had sex with Lijy and impregnated her. I'm sure you know that, too. I'm sure you know everything. You're probably up or out or wherever you are watching us make fools of ourselves. I don't want to make a fool of myself. I want to do the right thing. Tell me, what's the right thing? Please." His father looked like he was on the verge of talking. Buddy's heart surged. "Yes. Tell me. Go on. Please. Go on."

His father said, *Othing-nay o-tay ay-say.*

"That's . . . you are . . . you're speaking . . . that's pig Latin."

Othing-nay o-tay ay-say.

"Nothing to say. But you're my father."

Orry-say, Uddy-bay. Hats-tay ife-lay.

"No it's not. That's not life. It has to be better than this. Look at us. We're a goddamn wreck. Ravaged. I want to know what to do, how to stop it. What am I supposed to do? Tell me what I'm supposed to do."

Ou-yay re-ay oing-day hat-way ou-yay eed-nay o-tay o-day. Eel-fay he-tay ain-pay. Eel-fay t-iay. Nd-ay orgive-fay e-may. Then his father turned around and walked back toward the cemetery.

"Hold on. Wait. Don't go. Come back."

But it wasn't any use. He wasn't coming back, and Buddy knew it.

He was gone.

From across the parking lot, Buddy noticed that Lijy was watching him. She wasn't dressed in a sari but a black dress, her hair up in a funeral bun. He went up to her.

"Why are you talking to yourself, Buddy?"

"I wasn't talking to myself."

"You were talking and carrying on, and . . . you were talking to yourself. I saw you."

"I'm a lone wolf. One-lay olf-way."

"One-lay . . . huh? What are you saying? Are you drunk?"

"I-ay ove-lay ou-yay."

"I don't have time for this, Buddy."

"I'm trying to tell you I forgive you."

A smile started to break out on her face. "Does this mean you're going to come home?

"You can move in with me, yes."

"And you're going to be Russ's father?"

"That's what it means."

"Do you want to hold him?" Lijy leaned into the backseat and scooped the baby up. The exchange was a little awkward, and she had to help Buddy, had to show him where to put his hands. "There," she said. "Like that. You're a natural."

The baby looked up at him.

"Hold him against your chest, so he can feel you. He wants to feel you. He wants to feel his father."

Chic & Diane without Lomax, part 1

■

August 1960

Whenever Diane tried to get out of bed, she fell right back on the mattress. She didn't have the strength to move. She couldn't even reach over and pick up the bottle of soda pop on the nightstand. She just lay there, staring, blinking, thinking. She hated thinking. Thinking was remembering and remembering was a knife slitting open her heart. She wanted to forget. But she couldn't. She remembered him in the kitchen, in his bedroom, in the backyard, at school, in the bathroom standing at the sink brushing his teeth. She remembered his smell, the smell of his hair, kissing him on the head and smelling his hair. The sound of the latches opening on his briefcase. Rustling papers. She remembered him at the bottom of the stairs calling for her. She closed her eyes. Nothing she'd ever done in her entire life could have prepared her for this. She put the corner of the pillow in her mouth. She wanted to rip it open and spread its guts all over the room; she wanted to make it rain pillow feathers. She wanted something. A change. Something. Chic. If only he would have taken him to Kennel Lake. *He should have driven him.* He should have driven him. But . . . no, he had to dig a pool. A goddamn pool. What the hell. She rolled over and pounded her fists into the mattress. Her head felt like it was about to burst. She wanted to get past this. She needed to get past this. There had to be a way to get past this. Her mother had sat on the edge of the bed and told her that she'd get past this. She'd rubbed her back, her shoulders, her back again, run her fingers through her hair. She told her again that she'd get past this. She'd brought her a book, *The Power of Positive Thinking*, and left it on the nightstand. She turned on the radio and told her about a program she should listen to, on WMBD. Diane said nothing. She couldn't talk. She couldn't even bring herself to roll over and look at her mother. Her father sat on the edge of the bed later on. His voice was low, confident, yet searching. It held a flashlight and tried to find her. He told her a story about loss. She didn't pay attention. He said, "Do you catch what I'm saying." The story was supposed to make her feel better, but he didn't know how she was feeling. No one knew how she was feeling. Not one person. How could these people sit on her bed and tell her she would get past this? She wasn't going to get past this. This was an ocean of sadness and she was floating in the middle of it, bobbing up and down. She was swallowing water. She was sinking. The pain had taken root inside of her. It had bloomed in her brain. It kept knocking on the door of her consciousness, surprising her, pulling a bouquet of sadness from behind its back. Chic sat on the edge of the bed. He didn't say anything. He got into bed and spooned her. She didn't have the energy to not let him. She didn't want him to touch her. She wanted to scream. He was digging a pool. A hole full of water, like a lake, like Kennel Lake. Why did they need a hole full of water in their backyard? He got up. She heard him in the shower. She heard him leave for work. She lay there staring at the ceiling. The day passed, he came home, made her dinner and brought it to her. She didn't eat it. He lay down next to her. They fell asleep. She heard him leave for work the next day. The day passed, he came home. He made her dinner. She didn't eat it. He lay down next to her. They fell asleep. She heard him in the shower. She tried to get up. This would be the day that she went on with her life. This would be the day that she got mad and told him that their son had died because of him. She would yell at him. She would pound her fists on his chest. She stared at the ceiling. Blinked. Thought. She hated thinking. Thinking was remembering and remembering was ... She looked at the radio. Was it on or off? Was she hearing a voice, or was she thinking? The radio was on. Chic must have turned it on, or maybe she had. She didn't know. It didn't matter. The radio squawked voices that weren't her thinking and that was a little better. She was drawn to one voice in particular. A man's voice. Norman-something-something. She liked hearing him. Hearing his voice was not thinking and not thinking was better. The voice belonged to Norman Vincent Peale, a psychiatrist and minister, and from what she gleaned, he'd written a number of books. During his radio program, she kept hearing a commercial for his book, *The Power of Positive Thinking*. Diane picked up the book her mother had left on the nightstand. It was the same book. On the radio, Dr. Peale said, "Become a possibilitarian. No matter how dark things seem to be or actually are, raise your sights and see possibilities—always see them, for they're always there." Diane heard Chic come home from work. He was not a possibilitarian. He was a wreckatarian. A pool digger. Goddamn him. She should throw off the bedsheets and run down the stairs and punch him in the stomach. She should spit on his feet. She should grab both of his ears and scream her hot, vengeful breath in his face. She should jump up and down in the middle of the living room, then on the couch, and after gaining enough momentum, hop to the coffee table and finally leap on him and tackle him to the ground, where on top of him, she'd scream into his face, "Chic Waldbeeser, this is all your goddamn fault!" But she didn't move. She heard Chic go into the downstairs bathroom and lock the door. Dr. Peale said, "The life of inner peace, being harmonious and without stress, is the easiest type of existence."

Chic & Diane without Lomax, part 2

■

August 1960

Chic wasn't really sure how to be sad. Diane, on the other hand, felt her sadness. It consumed her. She cried. He tried to cry but couldn't. He told himself, "Now is the time to cry." The doorbell rang. It was another neighbor dropping off a casserole. Chic set the casserole on the counter with the other casseroles and went back to looking at the pile of dirt, the wheelbarrow with the shovels and rakes, the half-dug pool in the backyard.

Diane's parents came over. Her mother went upstairs to comfort Diane. Chic and his father-in-law sat in the living room. Chic tried to look sad.

"So," his father-in-law said.

"I'm very sad," Chic said. What was he supposed to say here?

He needed to be strong to show his wife's father that he was strong. Earlier, before his in-laws had arrived, Diane was wailing and pounding her fists into the mattress. "It's tough. But we're managing."

"You're like a rock," Diane's father said. "Diane needs your strength right now."

Chic nodded, but wanted to tell him that he needed Diane's strength, too. He needed somebody's strength. He needed more than strength—he needed a map, a guide, some direction, a book of directions, something to tell him how to feel this sadness. "I was out earlier. In the garage. Hot out there. Whew. A boiler."

"It's going to be OK, son. You're going to get through this."

His father-in-law had never called him son before. Chic got up and moved to the couch next to him. He wanted Diane's father to touch him. Hug him, maybe. Touch his leg even. He wanted to be comforted by him. He wanted to be loved by him. Chic put his face in his hands. More than anything he wanted to be touched on the back by this man.

Diane's mother came downstairs. Diane's father stood up. "I'm going to go check on Diane," he said. Chic watched his father-in-law go upstairs.

Diane's mother had been crying. She dabbed at her eyes with a tissue and said she needed some air.

"It's hot out there," Chic said.

She smiled and went out on the porch, pulling the door shut behind her.

Chic went to the back of the house and stared at the hole in the backyard. He wanted to be in that hole, lying there, looking up at the sky, the moist earth cooling his back. The sound would be muffled. He could stare at the clouds. He wanted to feel what it felt like to have someone shovel dirt on him. He heard Diane's mom come in the front door. He wanted to sit with her, but he couldn't take wanting to be touched and not being touched again. Alone was better. Alone he wouldn't be disappointed. He felt like he was going to cry, but he wasn't going to let himself. Crying was being out of control and he needed to stay in control.

Chic got a bottle of beer from the fridge. It tasted good, cold, good and cold, and he took another drink, a longer drink, sucking down half the bottle. Diane's father came down the stairs. He called out for Chic, but Chic didn't answer. He took another drink of beer. Diane's parents whispered to each other in the living room. His father-in-law called for him again. Chic edged himself into a corner of the kitchen, hoping they wouldn't come looking for him. He heard the front door open and close. He heard his in-laws get into their car. He heard the car start. He went out into the living room. Diane's mother's used Kleenex sat on the coffee table. Chic went upstairs and stood in the doorway of the bedroom and looked at Diane lying on the bed. She had a pillow over her head. He should go to her. He knew it. It was so obvious. He took off his shoes and placed them side by side next to the bed in front of his nightstand. He slid into bed and nuzzled close to her and put his arm around her. He wanted to share the feeling with her, wanted her to roll over and face him and acknowledge that they were both feeling this terrible awful sadness and it was like a bomb exploding in their hearts, like a thousand bees stinging their hearts, like a million trillion billion nails being pounded into their hearts. But she didn't roll over. It was another day in the life of his life and he was lying in bed holding his wife like he was expected to hold her. He squeezed her, but she didn't squeeze him back. He just wanted to make a connection with her. Feel one with her. He squeezed her again, hoping she'd squeeze him back, but she didn't move, so he got up and left the room, went downstairs to the kitchen and got another beer.

Chic Waldbeeser

■

June 16, 1998

Morris Potterbaum couldn't sleep again. He rustled around in bed, fighting the covers, rolling over, rolling over again. Finally, he sat up, put on his slippers, and got out of bed. Most nights, Chic slept through Morris's insomnia, but tonight he was already awake, thinking about the afternoon he'd spent with Mary. Before they'd gone to bed, Morris had asked Chic why he had missed the bus back to We Care earlier that day. Chic shrugged and told Morris that his son, Russ, had picked him up and taken him to dinner. Morris told Chic he was lying, and that Carol hadn't made a note of it on her clipboard.

Morris put on his robe and went out into the hallway. You weren't allowed to leave your room after lights out, but Morris always went into the hallway and down to the common room when he couldn't sleep.

The digital clock on the nightstand glowed 11:43. Chic rolled over. He wanted to go to sleep, but his mind was a rollercoaster, climbing up and dropping down, banking to the left and to the right, and all the passengers were screaming. He liked Mary; she was sorta, kinda, nice. And, best of all, she talked to him, and nobody talked to him, especially since Jessup had died and Morris had become his roommate. Jessup Anderson had been a talker; Morris, on the other hand, pretty much ignored Chic even when he asked him direct questions like, "Have you been outside? Do I need a jacket?" One night, about four months ago, at around three in the morning, Jessup had let out a howl, held his throat, gurgled a couple of times, and taken his last breath, which sounded like air hissing out of a tire tube. Chic always thought that someone's last breath would make a wheezing sound, like the person was clinging to a rope and didn't want to let go, but Jessup's wasn't like that; it was just an exhale, and that was that. A week later, Morris moved in. As Morris carried in a cardboard box full of personal items, clothes and a pair of gargoyle bookends, Chic tried to strike up a conversation, but after just a few questions, Morris told him not to ask any more questions. Later that day, Morris drew an imaginary line down the middle of the room between the beds and told Chic that they'd get along a lot better if they just didn't speak to each other unless they absolutely had to.

The only person who really talked to Chic was Russ. Sometimes, he and Ginger would visit, or else Chic would go over to their house for dinner. Ginger usually made pot roast. Chic didn't like pot roast, but he didn't say anything because he didn't want to not be invited back. After dinner, Chic would sit in the living room with the television on until Russ fell asleep and Ginger knocked out the dishes and Chic knew he had to go back to We Care. It was then that he would get this sinking feeling, this emptiness, like someone had dug out his soul with a garden shovel. He was feeling that way right now. He wanted to see Mary again. She made him feel—how should he say it?—she made him feel wanted. He hadn't felt wanted in . . . well, he hadn't felt wanted since he was eighteen years old and Diane had come up to him at that football game and told him he was going to take her for ice cream. Chic was serious about what he had said to Mary about taking her to Florida. He hadn't thought about Florida in . . . well, he didn't know the last time he had thought about Florida. A long time ago, that's for sure. He hadn't really thought about anything or even done anything since Diane had died, and that was—what was it . . . fifteen years ago or something like that. He'd sold the house. That was something. And he had moved into We Care because Russ told him that maybe he wouldn't be as lonely. But We Care was like a holding cell for death. That's what really scared him. He was on the cliff's edge of death—what'd he have left, ten, fifteen, maybe twenty years if he was lucky? And what did he have to show for his life? The role of a son is to save the family, and he had killed his, strangled it, cut off its oxygen supply, held its head underwater . . . Jesus, he couldn't believe he'd let his mind wander that far. But it was true—everyone he'd touched had turned blue in the face.

He should try to be more like Morris. Outside of their room, in public, he was hello, how are you? and blah-blah-blah to everyone and smiling and shaking hands and making little jokes and saying the right things at the right time and touching people on the back and winking at the old ladies and flirting with the nurses. Chic once asked Morris why he was so unfriendly with him in their room, yet so upbeat with everyone else in the place. Chic hoped that if he asked this, Morris would open up to him, but he just went about doing what he was doing, which was polishing his shoes. Chic then told Morris about his son, Lomax, how he had lost him, and about Diane, hoping that the two of them could share things that had happened over the course of their lives, but Morris said, "I don't want to know anything about you, Chic. What happens out there is what happens out there. But in here, leave me alone." And then he went back to polishing his shoes.

Chic rolled over to face Morris's rumpled bed. One of his pillows was on the floor. Chic got out of bed and picked it up. The green duffel bag was hanging on the coat tree by the door. Chic went over and fished out his poetry notebook. Then he heard Morris say something to the security guard in the hallway. Chic quickly put his notebook back into the bag and got into bed and rolled over so that his back was facing the door. The door opened, and light from the hallway splashed into the room. Chic heard Morris get into bed and adjust the covers. Then, it got so quiet. Chic rolled over to face Morris, who was curled up in his bed, the outline of his body under the blanket. He liked Morris. Or he envied him, actually: Morris could put on a face when he went out into the world and pretend that nothing was wrong. That was a better way to be. Just walk right into the wind and hold on to your hat.

It was 11:56. He was going to the Pair-a-Dice tomorrow. He was going to try a different approach with Mary. The Morris approach. He was going to be the person she wanted him to be. Then she'd want to be with him, would agree to go to Florida with him. Chic closed his eyes, but he knew he wouldn't fall asleep. But that was all right. At least he was looking forward to something. It had been a long time since he'd looked forward to anything.

Lijy & Buddy & Chic & Diane Waldbeeser

■

May 1, 1961

As a sign of their reconciliation, Buddy and Lijy decided to renew their vows at Blessed Sacrament Church. Buddy had asked around and found Dr. Himanshu, a "cosmic" spiritualist, in Chicago. His idea was for both Father Eugene and Dr. Himanshu to conduct the ceremony together. Father Eugene was skeptical. He'd been a Catholic priest for fifty-four years, and he'd never been asked to do such a thing. Still, Buddy pressed him, telling him that it would be good for the Waldbeeser family, as they—everyone—had been through a lot, what with Lomax's death, their father's death, their mother . . . wherever she was. Father Eugene said that this was asking a lot. Buddy kept pushing, and Father Eugene finally agreed, under one condition: that the ceremony be held in the dead of night.

Diane and Chic arrived on foot. Chic had lost their car keys, so they walked the two miles to Blessed Sacrament. When they arrived, Lijy was talking to Dr. Himanshu outside the church. Lijy introduced them. Dr. Himanshu was a short man, about five feet tall, and bald. He wore a salmon-colored dhoti and was eating sunflower seeds.

"Is it Halloween?" Chic said. He wasn't sure. He didn't think it was, but he'd spent so much time staring at that hole in the backyard that he'd lost track of time. Maybe it was Halloween. He looked at Lijy for confirmation.

"It's May," Lijy said.

"Who is this guy supposed to be?" Diane asked.

"Dr. Himanshu," Lijy said.

"Is someone sick?"

"We will all be sick someday and maybe someone is sick right now," Dr. Himanshu said. He spit out some sunflower shell and giggled and excused himself to go inside the church.

The three of them stood there thinking or not thinking about what Dr. Himanshu had said. Finally, Diane wandered into the church, leaving Chic and Lijy alone. Chic was still mad at her, although he hadn't remembered his anger until this moment. He'd made a sacrifice for her, and now his son was dead and he was sure that Lijy had something—all of this had something—to do with what had happened, that there was this big cloud hovering over him, ruining his life, because of her.

"You're welcome," he said.

Lijy cocked her head.

He motioned to the church. "This is because of me, you know. You're getting a second chance because of me."

"You're welcome, too."

"I didn't say thank you."

"I'm a person. A real person. Not someone in your imagination."

"Of course you're a real person. Did I say you weren't?"

"Chic . . ."

"I almost lost my wife because of this. I was digging a pool to make it up to her. My son died. My son, Lijy. He's never coming back. Never. I want some recognition. I mean, no one knows. What good is doing something if no one knows about it?"

"I could tell everyone that you stood in my kitchen with your . . ." she dropped her voice to a whisper, a harsh whisper, " . . . boner hanging out of the front of your boxers. And about the time you were spying on me from your car."

"You lied, though. Why?"

"You made it true. You confirmed it."

"But it's not true."

"It's true to him. And to me. We made it true. Thank you. Really, I thank you from the bottom of my heart. I do. But he can't ever know the truth. Not now, not ever. I'm thankful that you helped me. Really, I am. And I'm sorry about Lomax. So sorry, but these two things don't have anything to do with one another."

Chic could tell that she was being sincere, but that didn't make it any easier. He went inside the church and found Diane in the back row. He slid in next to her and kneeled down. How different his life would have been if he hadn't let Lijy rub his back at his wedding, if he hadn't tried to seduce her. How different it would have been if he hadn't married Diane . . . if his father hadn't committed suicide . . . if his brother hadn't disappeared after that, then showed back up in Middleville with Lijy . . . if his mother hadn't run off with Tom McNeeley . . . if he hadn't been born.

The organ started. Dr. Himanshu walked around, throwing rose petals into the air, while Father Eugene stood at the front and welcomed everyone. He said he wanted to have a moment of silence for Lomax Waldbeeser, nephew of the groom and son of Chic Waldbeeser.

Chic stood up. "He would have been a scientist," he said.

The congregation turned to look at him. Next to him, Diane was zoned out, staring straight ahead.

Chic stretched out his arms. "My son died because of me."

"Praise Jesus Lord and Christ forever and ever," Dr. Himanshu blurted out. "Amen." He then cupped his hand over his mouth like he'd accidentally burped.

Chic sat back down. "Did you say something?" Diane asked.

"The truth."

Then, Dr. Himanshu clanged a tambourine and made everyone chant, "Rama-rama-esch-a-lam." Father Eugene, not approving, snuck out the back door. Buddy held baby Russ, bouncing him to the beat of the tambourine. Dr. Himanshu motioned for everyone to chant louder. Diane fell asleep, and Chic lost focus after Dr. Himanshu began speaking about how marriage was a bond that transcended this life and went into future lives. "You may come back a frog," he said giggling, before regaining his composure. "And one of your wives may be a hawk." He giggled again. "Enemies marry . . ." he put his hand over his mouth, " . . . eventually in due time. That is the power of love, the power of connection."

Chic stared at the crucifix hanging behind the altar. He knew the pain of a nail in the palm, not the physicality of it, but the mental anguish. Lijy didn't understand. He had done what he had done to save the family. His brother would have left her, and he prevented that. He'd done it to redeem himself, but now his brother was mad at him, his son was dead, and his wife hated him, or at least, he was pretty sure his wife hated him. So much for redemption. He felt like a car had dropped him off in the middle of the desert and he had to walk back to civilization. He stood up again. "Let me off this cross," he shouted.

Buddy glared at his brother. He was about to march off the altar and show Chic a thing or two. Lijy grabbed his arm.

"He's hurting," she said.

"He should keep that sort of thing inside his house. No one wants to see it."

"We're good people," Chic said. "Why is this happening to us?"

Dr. Himanshu continued to clang the tambourine: "Rama-rama-esch-a-lam. Rama-rama-esch-a-lam. Rama-rama-esch-a-lam. Rama-rama-esch-a-lam . . ."

Nine

Diane Waldbeeser

1961

Chic wanted to have another child, but whenever he tried, Diane would just lie there. She could be dead. She could have been hit in the chest with a cannonball (she had been hit in the chest with a cannonball). It was bad enough that they slept in the same bed, but he wanted to touch her, too. She just wanted to be left alone, to curl up on the bed and not think, not do anything, not even move. She wanted to be as still as possible. Still, and alone. At one time, she had wanted to be a mother more than anything. Now, only a part of her, a very small part of her, like a sliver, like a fingernail, like a single strand of hair, wanted a family. She couldn't go through it all again. Not with Chic. Not with anyone, actually. The worry. The fear. It would consume her. It was consuming her. She wasn't going to do it again, but then Chic's mouth was all over hers, his breath stinking of beer. Then his pants were off. He pushed her back on the bed and rolled on top of her. He stuck himself inside of her. The radio on the nightstand squawked and hissed. Dr. Peale was talking about changing the negative thoughts into good thoughts, positive thoughts, productive thoughts, sunny thoughts, blue sky thoughts, beach thoughts, winning thoughts, smiling thoughts, laughing thoughts, but all she could think about was Lomax underwater, holding the garden hose, kicking and thrashing and struggling and not being able to breathe. Not being able to breathe. *Not being able to breathe.* Then going limp. No more thrashing. Just limp. Sinking to the bottom. No more struggling. Just limp and sinking. His hand clutching the hose, the unmanned boat on the surface of the water drifting toward the cattails.

Mary Geneseo

■

June 21, 1998

She had driven to Middleville to visit some guy she hardly knew. Take a good long look at yourself, the whisper voice said. Do unto others as you would have them do unto you. Oh, shut the hell up, the loud voice said. It's a dog-eat-dog world. Get in there and get your bone. Yeah, she thought, get in there, seize the opportunity. Chic was opportunity. Mary dug through her purse trying to find her lipstick. She was going to march in there and talk to him. She was going to make him like her. The whisper voice cleared its throat. You're about to do it again. Another guy. Another change. How many times have you been married? The loud voice said, Go inside and talk to him, sit with him for a little while. Take him to the Dairy Queen you passed on your drive through town. Buy him a cone, a milkshake, whatever the hell he wants. The whisper voice butted in: Go back to Peoria, to Green. He's getting discharged tomorrow. You married him. The whisper voice was right, she thought. She wasn't going to do it like that this time. No more running. She was going to stay with Green. It was the right thing to do and it was about time she started to do the right thing. That's bullshit, the loud voice said. You've lived your entire life trying to find something better. The "right thing" has never stopped you before. Why now? Why this time? Are you feeling sorry for that putz in the hospital? Don't feel sorry for him. He'll be better off without you, and you'll be better off without him. That's right, she thought. You made Green promise he'd never cheat on you, and here you are about to cheat on him, the whisper voice said. Talking to someone isn't cheating, the loud voice said. True, the whisper voice said, but it's a slippery slope. Very slippery. Green's been good to you. This was true, she thought. You're going to up and leave him, the whisper voice said. Why? You moved to Illinois with him. You moved to Illinois because you thought it would be better, and it's not, the loud voice said. It's terrible. Are you kidding? Green may die in a month, six months, a year . . . then what?

Mary put her hands over her face. She hated when she couldn't think clearly. She needed something to help her think. She leaned back in the seat and closed her eyes. The voices kept snarling at each other. She didn't even know if she really liked Chic. He annoyed her, actually. He wanted to tell her about things from his past that she didn't want to hear. At least, with Green, he never wanted to talk about his past. She knew nothing about him, and she liked that. It was simply the present with him—the moment, the right here and now. The past muddied everything. Wait a second, had she just made a decision? Yeah. She was going back to Green. That was it. It was settled. She was going back to him. Hold the phone, the loud voice said. You really want to take care of him? Give him sponge baths? Feed him? That's what you want for the rest of your life? You don't want to take care of anyone. Heck, you want someone to take care of you. "Stop," Mary said aloud. She looked around. Had she actually said that out loud? She needed to stop letting her thinking control her like this. She put the minivan in reverse and backed out of the parking spot and turned left onto Jackson Street. Bravo, the whisper voice said. This is the right thing to do. You're doing the right thing. And tomorrow you can take Green to the Brazen Bull. That's what he wants. It'll help. You gave Green's loafers to Chic, the loud voice said. You'll get new shoes. Right now—find a mall. Then, you'll clean the house and prepare it for Green's arrival. That's the irony here. You've never taken care of anyone in your life.

She needed to find a mall. She stomped on the gas pedal and refused to look in the rearview mirror.

178

Chic & Diane without Lomax, part 3

■

June 1961

Chic was shuffling through life like a zombie. He couldn't go on, but he had to go on. He was drinking six or seven beers a night and taking the empty bottles to the garage and hiding them in the garbage. He needed something, anything. The pain he felt, the loss, the hole, consumed him. He wanted to box up the pain and put it on a shelf in the back of his mind and turn out the light. He wanted to forget, but he couldn't forget: the pain was always buzzing around him like a pesky mosquito. He wanted to swat it, slap it, kill it.

Chic decided to continue Lomax's translation project as a way of running head-on into his grief, as a way of better understanding his son and his great-grandfather, as a way of better understanding his family. Understanding would help him forget, or something like that. Chic called Dr. Dexheimer, but as soon as he heard the professor's voice, he remembered driving Lomax to his German classes. He hung up the phone. Perhaps it was too soon. It hadn't even been a year. Chic sat there staring at the phone, considering his options. He got another idea, to rid Lomax's room of every object that held a memory: the poster of the periodic table on the wall, the desk, the nightstand, volumes one through seventeen of Lomax's "Scientific Findings" notebooks, the dictionary, the pocket watch, the magnifying glass, the wheelie briefcase, and, of course, the crate of Bascom's German letters and notebooks. He'd take the crate to his brother and Lijy's. Let them have it—he couldn't stand to be under the same roof with those letters.

Chic started with the desk drawers, dumping the contents into a garbage bag. Next was the dresser: all of Lomax's clothes, his underwear and socks, everything into the garbage bag. Then he got down on the floor and looked under the bed. Underneath there was a lot of useless junk (Lomax had not been clean): dress slacks with the belt threaded through the loops, a German-to-English dictionary, a single sock filled with kernels of un-popped popcorn. He threw it all in the trash bag. Then he found a photograph of Lomax with a fake mustache, spectacles, and an outfit with red suspenders. For Halloween a few years ago, Lomax had dressed as the ghost of Bascom. The picture was taken after Diane had whitened his face with makeup. Chic remembered that night. He'd walked with his son around the neighborhood, waiting for him on the sidewalk while he knocked on people's front doors. On Nelson Street, a group of kids hiding in the bushes ambushed them with eggs. Chic covered his head and took refuge behind a parked car; Lomax, defiant, stood on the sidewalk and tried to catch the eggs in his trick-or-treat bag.

In the closet, Chic found the crate of Bascom's letters and notebooks. Mixed in with the yellowed papers were mason jars—some with dirt in them, some empty. There was a pocket folder of Lomax's translations. Chic took one out.

April 14, 1855

Dear Mother and Father,

I've been in New Orleans for 1,427 days. Have I told you about my system for keeping track of the number of days I've been in America? I think I have. Have I? I can't remember. I'll tell you again. Every day I take a kernel of corn and put it in a sock. I just finished counting the kernels. It took me nearly three hours. I kept losing count, but that's fine. I have nothing else to do. I'm bored with New Orleans. I miss Germany. I didn't think I'd miss Germany. I know you told me I'd miss Germany, and I didn't believe you. I argued with you. I will not miss Germany, I said. But in this, my 364th letter, I'm finally ready to admit that America isn't what I thought it was going to be. I had very high expectations. Last week, a man in the French Quarter sold me a vial of liquid. He told me that if I went home and put the liquid on my tongue I'd be able to make a wish which would come true within three days. Well, it's been a week, and that wish still hasn't come true. I'm not going to tell you what I wished for. Actually, I'm going to tell you because you should know. I wished to come back to Germany. I want things to be the way they were. I want to live at home with you both. I want my old bed back. If I could only come back to Germany, I think everything would be better. I know I said the same thing about coming to America. There is one thing I should tell you, though. I think I've met a girl. And mother, I know what you're thinking. She's a nice girl. I like her. Or I think I like her. I don't really know what it feels like to like someone. I sometimes sit in my room and close my eyes and think very hard about how I'm supposed to feel when I like someone. I have a confession: I actually haven't met this girl. I've seen her almost every day for about a month. Every day at noon she feeds the pigeons in front of St. Louis Cathedral. I go there, and I watch her. I haven't talked to her. I plan to. If I talk to her, I think I'll be happier than I am now. I know, I know. How many times have I said something like this? Too many to count, I presume. I should also mention that I've been doing a fair amount of gardening. I'm growing geraniums in terra-cotta pots. I set them in the south facing windows of my apartment. I've been collecting feces in the French Quarter, animal droppings mostly, to mix with the soil. I think I'm getting very good results. I've been keeping a notebook where I record my observations. I shall copy my observations and send them to you, in detail. Maybe if I lived elsewhere, I'd like America better than I do. There are many Germans in states north of Louisiana. I'm saving money to go there. That's how people do it here. If you don't like one place, go to another. It will be better when I move north, I think. The great thing about America is that everyone is after the same thing. They are all trying to make a better life. Is it working for me? Is my life better? No. Do I think it will get better? I can hope. I do, however, think that my geranium growing is better here in New Orleans. I think the air is right for it. It's humid and the geraniums seem to like that. That's more than I can say about my attempts at geranium growing in Germany. I just don't think the sun is right in Munich for geranium growing. Or maybe it was the house, the placement of the house, how the sun hit the house. I do not know. I'll continue to think about this. I've just now taken off my shoes. My feet are beginning to hurt. I wouldn't wear the damn things if I wasn't afraid of stepping on something in the French Quarter. I've noticed that the shoes need mending again. I'm constantly mending my shoes. Anyway, I've nothing left to say. I'll write again. I conclude my 364th letter.

Love,

Bascom William Waldbeeser

The picture of Lomax dressed like Bascom's ghost was on the floor. Chic picked it up and stared at the fake mustache. He'd glued that mustache to Lomax's lip. Lomax had tilted his head up, and Chic had rubbed Elmer's glue on his upper lip and gently affixed the mustache. As he'd done it, he could feel Lomax's hot breath on his fingers. His son's eyes had been closed, and at that moment, Lomax had been absolutely dependent on him. A lump rose in his throat. From down the hall, Chic heard Dr. Peale on the radio: "Our happiness depends on the habit of mind we cultivate. So practice happy thinking every day. Cultivate the merry heart, develop the happiness habit, and life will become a continual feast." Chic stood up. He needed to get out of this room. He needed to get rid of these things.

Lijy & Baby Russ & Chic & Buddy

■

June 25, 1961

Lijy was sitting on the floor playing a hand-clapping game with Russ when a "hello" floated out of the tin can. She looked at the can dangling next to the door. She wasn't expecting anyone, and Buddy was out floating on the river in a canoe. Another "hello" came from the can; it sounded almost apologetic. She got up and went to the window. Because of the trees, she couldn't see much, but at the gravel pull-in off the highway, she was able to make out someone standing next to a car. She hoped it wasn't Ellis McMillion. The other day, she had been in town and glanced in her rearview mirror, certain that he was following her.

"I see you at the window," the tin can said. "I have binoculars."

Lijy recognized that voice and picked up the can. "Chic?"

"Let me in."

"Are you alone?"

"Of course I'm alone. Who isn't alone? We're always alone."

She told him where the gate key was hidden. Chic left his car at the pull-in and carried a cardboard box down the gravel road. When he reached the front door, Lijy was waiting for him.

"This is for the baby. It's Bascom's stuff," he said. "Not the mason jars, though. Those are Lomax's. Were Lomax's." He held the box out to her, but she didn't make a move to take it. "This is sorta heavy."

Lijy stepped out of the way, and Chic set the box down on the dining room table. Since Lijy and Russ had moved in, Buddy had done some work on the old CILCO building. He'd erected drywall to room off the open space, creating a living room of sorts. Out of plywood, he had built a kitchen counter and shelves. Off the back of the building, Buddy had put in French doors that led to a patio area with a view of the Mackinaw River and a path that went down to a makeshift dock.

Lijy reached into the box and picked up a folder containing Lomax's translated letters. Chic looked at Russ, who was playing with Lincoln Logs on an Oriental area rug in front of the sofa. "Diane and I are trying to have another one," he said wistfully. "Begin again. Return to return. It's not going well. Last night I slept on the couch. Imagine that, will you? My back is killing me. *Killing me.*"

Lijy wasn't paying attention, instead reading one of the letters:

January 12, 1854

Dear Mother and Father,

This is my 217th letter, and I'm writing to tell you that I want to accomplish something. Anything. If I accomplish something, anything, then I'll feel much better about myself. When I think of myself, I'll think of what I have accomplished. You could probably say that coming to America is an accomplishment, but it's not. I simply rode on a boat, and now, 972 days later, I'm still without accomplishment. Maybe you'd say that these letters are an accomplishment. I disagree. I need to set my sights on a direction. A path. I need something, otherwise I'm just adrift—a young man among many young men . . .

Lijy looked up from the letter when she heard Chic utter Buddy's name. "I saw Buddy a few days ago," he said. "I ran out of gas on Jackson, by the post office. He pulled up behind me, and I glanced up and saw him in the rearview mirror. I waved to him, but he sped off."

"He probably didn't see you."

"We made eye contact."

"It's going to take time. He's still upset."

"At that moment, more than anything, I needed a brother and he left me."

"At night," Lijy said, "I find Buddy out here talking to himself. He just stares at me with this look like he's there, but not there."

"He's always been like that. Ever since our father . . ."

"What happened to your father? I thought he moved to Florida with your mother."

"Our father froze himself to death behind the barn. Buddy didn't tell you?"

She shook her head—no.

"We were young. Buddy was eleven."

Now it all made sense to Lijy—the talking to himself, the staring off into space, the time in the parking lot after Lomax's funeral, the sofa cushions stacked up on the chair.

"We all need our diversions," Chic said. "Diane listens to the radio. And you know what? I think it helps her. People need something, you know."

"Buddy bought a canoe," Lijy said, motioning to the French doors, which opened onto a view of the river and a steel bridge in the distance. "Sometimes you can see him. He's just a little speck out there, casting his line into the water."

"That sounds biblical . . . *casting his line into the water*."

"I can't believe he didn't tell me about your father."

"I can't believe he drove off and left me there. That's the thanks I get after I helped him. I know he doesn't know, but think about how that made me feel."

"Do you ever feel like people are watching you?"

"You mean, from the bushes? Like someone is going to jump out and, I don't know, sucker punch me? Yeah. I do. I mean, I got sucker punched."

"That people are studying you? Scrutinizing your every move?"

"From the bushes?"

"No, not from the bushes. From everywhere. Like there's an audience. Like we're on stage."

Chic looked behind him. "There's no one here. Except . . ." He motioned to Russ, who was gnawing on the end of a Lincoln Log.

"Maybe things don't make sense and that's the point. Maybe they're not meant to make sense. I know you're trying to make sense of what happened to you. Buddy is too. Everyone is trying to make sense of what's happening."

"Are you talking about me-and-Buddy everyone, or the-whole-world everyone?"

"I'm sorry about the church, about our argument."

"I didn't really think it was an argument, but thank you for your apology."

"You look horrible, Chic."

"I feel horrible. I'm exhausted. I could lie down on that sofa right now."

Lijy went up to him. "Let me rub your back."

"I don't think that's a good idea."

"I owe it to you. For what you did."

"We can't. I mean—I want to, but we can't."

Lijy ignored him and went right for his shoulders. Chic closed his eyes. His knees went slack.

"Don't think about me, Chic . . ."

"I'm not thinking about you."

"Concentrate on the touching. You want to be touched. It's what everyone wants."

The back rub stirred up something that had been dormant for a long time. Chic felt himself start to pulse and get a little lightheaded. The blood halted in his veins, reversed course, and made its way to his groin.

"I'm sorry that I put you in this position, Chic. I was desperate. I had no idea what I was going to do, and then it dawned on me. You. You were the answer."

She was right. He was the answer. Him. Chic Waldbeeser. He had always thought of himself as the answer and it was about time that someone else thought of him that way too. Surely Diane didn't.

"And it worked. Or, it's beginning to work. So, thank you, Chic. I know I've tried to tell you this a couple of times, but really, thank you. We will always have this. You and me. This . . . whatever you want to call it."

"Bond."

"Right."

Just then, Chic noticed his brother watching them through the French doors. He was holding a stringer of bullhead catfish, which were dripping on the patio. His eyes were full of fierceness like there was a boxing match going on in his brain.

"What the hell? Lijy! What the . . ."

"It's not what it looks like," Chic said.

Buddy darted across the living room. "I'll tell you what it looks like . . ."

"Buddy, I'm helping him," Lijy said.

Russ started crying.

"He has an erection."

"I don't have an erection."

Buddy swung the stringer of bullhead catfish, but Chic ducked underneath it. Water splattered on the wall and peppered the French doors. Russ's crying grew louder.

"I'm going to kill you, Chic." Buddy swung the stringer again, the fish whizzing above Chic's head.

"Buddy, find your daddy place," Lijy said firmly. "Rub your shankh."

"Will someone shut that kid up," Buddy yelled.

Lijy went to Russ and picked him up. "Control yourself, Buddy," she said.

Buddy closed his eyes and took a deep breath. Then he opened his eyes. "Were you going to have sex with my wife again?"

187

"Buddy Waldbeeser," Lijy said.

"Let him answer."

"I came here . . . I dropped off Bascom's letters . . . and we started talking and I told her about the other day when you abandoned me."

"I didn't abandon you."

"I ran out of gas and you left me there."

"Buddy, is that true?"

Buddy looked up at the ceiling. It appeared as if he was about to cry. "You slept with my wife, Chic."

Lijy went up to Buddy and touched his temple. "Rub your shankh, honey."

"Don't touch me. I don't want to be touched." He turned and stormed out of the room.

"Buddy!" Lijy gave Chic a look. "Here, hold Russ."

"Do you really think . . . ?"

"Just hold him." She handed him the baby and chased after Buddy. Chic heard the bedroom door open and close. He looked down at the baby. Russ tried to grab his cheek, his hair. Chic told him no, but Russ kept trying to touch him. Chic pulled his head back, to avoid being touched.

A few minutes later, Lijy came back into the living room, Buddy behind her. He'd changed clothes and was wearing a salmon-colored dhoti. He was barefoot.

"Buddy has something to say to you," Lijy said. She took Russ from Chic.

"I'm sorry," Buddy said. "I overreacted."

"Now, why don't you boys sit down, and I'll make some tea."

Chic sat down on the couch. Buddy sat next to him. Lijy handed Buddy the baby, who grabbed at his father's cheek.

Buddy turned to Chic. "Orry-say, Hic-cay."

Chic looked at his brother.

"This is your shankh." Buddy touched Chic's temple. "Close your eyes." Chic did, as his brother rubbed his temple. The last time his brother had spoken to him in pig Latin had been the day their father was found behind the barn. Chic was in the kitchen, watching Tom McNeeley hug his mother. Chic wanted someone to hug him. He went upstairs. Buddy's door was closed. He knocked, but Buddy didn't answer. He called Buddy's name. He tried the doorknob, but it was locked. "Uddy-bay," Chic said. "Lease-pay open-way he-tay oor-day." It was their secret language, and Chic hoped that speaking it would tell his brother how much he needed him. He waited. "Uddy-bay?" Nothing. Chic then went to his own room across the hall and sat down on his bed. He had a view of Buddy's closed door. He waited. Finally, Buddy opened the door, crossed the hall, and came into Chic's bedroom. Chic wanted Buddy to sit down next to him on the bed. Instead, Buddy said, "I-way ink-thay om-may as-way aving-hay an-way affair-way."

Chic grabbed Buddy's hand to get him to stop rubbing his temples. "O-nay, Uddy-bay, I'm-way orry-say."

"I know you are."

Lijy was standing in front of them with a tray of mugs and bowls of yogurt. Buddy took a mug and handed it to Chic, then took one for himself.

"You ever had yogurt?" Buddy asked.

Chic picked up a bowl and sniffed it. He spooned a little taste. "Oh, Jesus . . . it's sour."

"You should read this book, *Look Younger, Live Longer* by Gayelord Hauser. Lijy got it for me. It's all about how to age well."

"Age well?"

"Age gracefully."

"This stuff will help you age well?"

"That's what Gayelord Hauser says."

Lijy began to rub Buddy's shoulders. "Tell Chic the good news."

"We're opening a store," Buddy said. "After we save up some money."

"A health food and massage store," Lijy added. "It's always been my dream."

"We're also going to sell wheat germ, blackstrap molasses, and powdered skim milk," Buddy said. "And Lijy's going to give massages."

They smiled at each other, and Buddy laid his head on Lijy's shoulder and she rubbed his hair and kissed his forehead. They were going to open a store and sell yogurt. Chic took a sip of his tea. He hated tea.

"Do you have any beer?"

"No," Lijy said.

"Drink your tea and eat your yogurt," Buddy said. "It'll make you feel better."

Chic tried some more yogurt. He didn't think this stuff could help anyone age gracefully.

Mary & Green Geneseo

■

June 23, 1998

Mary wanted Green to have the motorized wheelchair, but he told her, actually wrote, that he wanted the manual wheelchair, the someone-stand-behind-him-and-push wheelchair. The motorized wheelchair was brand-spanking-new and more comfortable and heavy-duty, etc., but Green didn't want brand-new and comfortable and he'd be goddamned if he was going wheel himself around in a motorized wheelchair while Mary pranced around Peoria with some guy who drove a Cadillac. No, he was going to make sure she had to push him so she wouldn't be able to do whatever she did when she left him lying in the hospital bed. Anyone with a good heart, with one single caring bone in her body, even Mary—who Green was beginning to suspect had neither a good heart nor a caring bone—would stick around the house to push him to the bathroom or the kitchen or wherever he wanted to go. So he didn't want the motorized, deluxe, comfortable, brand-spanking-new wheelchair, even if the hospital was willing to do a lease-to-own contract for zero percent interest for five years. He wasn't stupid—he knew why Mary wanted him to have the motorized wheelchair.

Here was the thing, though: the manual wheelchair was uncomfortable. Really uncomfortable. Even with a pillow wedged behind him, Green's left ass cheek went numb if he sat in the thing for too damn long. Anything that folded up and fit in the trunk of a car wasn't meant to be lounged around in all day. Green wanted to tell someone about this. Complain about it. He looked around for Mary. She was in the bathroom, doing her hair, or maybe brushing her teeth. The water was on. She'd got him up an hour ago, and while he was still in bed, she'd brought in a bowl of warm (although it wasn't warm enough) water and a washrag and had given him a quick bath, wiping off his face, armpits, arms, stomach, legs, and feet, even his penis. A nurse was bad enough, but now every single goddamn morning it was going to be like this. She had rolled deodorant under each arm, dressed him in a suit. It was all pretty much goddamn humiliating, but the worst part, the absolute goddamn worst part, was when she tried to pull him out of bed and into the wheelchair. She'd positioned the chair right next to the bed, but the thing kept moving. After a few minutes of pulling him up then putting him down, she finally found the wheel locks and managed to get his bag-of-sand body into the chair. She then picked out a tie, but had a hell of a time tying it (cussing under her breath) and ultimately tossed it on the bed and wheeled him out to the living room and opened the drapes to give him a view of the driveway and the Bradley students on their way to class. As soon as she opened the drapes, Green wanted to scream, "What the hell do you think you're doing!" He could have written a note, but he would have had to get the Post-it Note pad out of his pocket and the golf pencil and then take the time to write what he wanted to say. It was easier to sit there fuming, his head steaming, his mind whirling, his anger churning like a blender. He had to pick his battles, and he had his sights set on a bigger battle. So he stared at the place on the driveway where he had collapsed, behind the minivan. Right there. That's where this all began. The downfall. The beginning of the end. The slow demise.

"You ready?" Mary yelled from the bathroom.

Was he ready? Could he physically answer that question? No. So if he couldn't physically answer that question, why was she yelling it to him?

She came into the living room carrying a rectangular box wrapped in newspaper. "I got you something." She set the box in his lap, and he looked up at her. He felt a rush of sentimentality flash through him, and his eyes welled with tears. She'd got him a present.

"For your big day."

His left arm wasn't a hundred percent. He couldn't make a fist, couldn't wiggle his fingers; it was like a paperweight, so he just set it on the box to steady it and used his right hand to tear into the newspaper wrapping.

"Here, let me help." Mary took the box and got the paper off and removed the lid and moved the tissue paper so that Green could see inside. "They're suede. I saw them at the mall and they reminded me of you."

They were shoes, boots actually: taupe-colored chukka boots. Instead of laces, they had a zipper on the inside seam.

"Here, let me . . ." Mary kneeled down in front of the wheelchair and wiggled the boots onto Green's feet. Since the stroke, his body had shriveled into little more than skin stretched over bone. His knees poked through his maroon suit pants, and his cheeks sunk in, making it look like he was starving himself to death. She stood up and stepped back.

"I like them," she said. "Very sharp."

Green leaned over. The boots were narrow and pointy, like elf shoes. He tried to move his feet but could move only the right one; the left foot stayed planted where it was like it was cemented into place.

He wrote, *Thank you.*

"You're welcome, Green. I knew you'd like them." Mary got behind the wheelchair and pushed him onto the porch. It was a sunny morning, warm and humid, and there were birds singing in the trees and students passing on the sidewalk in front of the bungalow. Since there wasn't a wheelchair ramp, Mary turned the chair around and carefully backed it down the steps. She then wheeled Green over to the minivan and, like last night, like this morning in the bedroom, had trouble with his weight while lifting him out of the chair to get him into the passenger seat. Green thought that people were snickering at the sight of him.

On the way to the Brazen Bull, Mary went over the ground rules. She'd set him up at a table with a drink and the newspaper. Other than Seth and Eight Ball, who arrived around eleven, most people usually didn't show up at the bar until after lunch. It was only ten now, so they'd probably have to hang out for a while. When there was a crowd, she'd ask them—she'd make it covert— if they wanted to place a bet. If they did, she'd point to him sitting in the booth, the newspaper spread in front of him.

He wrote, *Don't tell anyone I can't walk.*

"Nobody will have a clue about that."

Who's going to help unload me?

"I can get you in the chair. I got you in it this morning. And I got you in the minivan."

You can barely do it.

"I'll get the bartender to help."

Green didn't like this. Sure, he may have said he wanted to do it, but that was in the hospital, that was when he thought that there might be another guy. Maybe he was wrong about the other guy, and if there wasn't some other guy, then . . . then . . . he was dressed up in this ridiculous maroon suit, and Mary was going to unload him from the minivan like a piece of meat and strap him into a wheelchair and push him into the bar. Why would he want to subject himself to this?

I don't want to do this.

They were exiting off the bridge onto Creve Coeur Avenue. At the bottom of the ramp was a stoplight.

She read the note and drove at the same time. "You said you wanted to book bets, Green."

He looked out the window. They took a right onto Creve Coeur Avenue.

"You have to quit feeling sorry for yourself."

He stared out the window: the strip mall parking lots, Kmart, Denny's, the Illinois River running parallel to them, and, on the other side of the river, Peoria and its downtown skyline.

"So this is it? You're giving up."

Green rolled his head to look at her. At that moment, he wanted her to be Jane. Jane wouldn't be talking to him like this. She'd be nurturing him. She'd have her hand on his leg.

They pulled into the parking lot of the Brazen Bull and found a spot close to the door. There were no other cars in the lot.

I'm sorry, Green wrote.

Mary put the minivan in reverse and backed out of the parking spot. "Yeah, well, Green, well . . . you know . . . if you think I'm going to sit around the house and feel sorry for you, you're wrong. I'm not going to do that. I refuse, Green. I goddamn refuse to do that."

Ten

Mary & Green Geneseo, continued

June 23, 1998

Mary unfolded the wheelchair next to the minivan and locked the wheels. Green watched her through the window. She hated it when he watched her, with that look on his face. She opened the passenger-side door and grabbed him under the arms. "On three, shift your weight." The loud voice in her head was laughing at her. *This is your future. You're going to be stuck taking care of him for the rest of your life. You need to get out of here. Leave him.* "One. Two. Three." She pulled him out of the seat and got him standing in front of the wheelchair. He was like a puppet on strings. Though he was slim as a razor blade, he was taller than she was by about two heads and still heavy. She struggled. "You're not helping me. Stand up," she snapped. Gravity brought him forward, and she did everything she could to keep him standing while pulling the wheelchair into place behind him. *This is what you have to look forward to,* the loud voice said, *every day for the rest of your life.* She misjudged his weight, and he fell forward, his upper body buckling at the waist. She caught him, and he folded over her shoulder like a rag doll. She tried to lift him up in a fireman's carry while at the same time positioning the chair, but his body shifted, causing his weight to overwhelm her, and they both collapsed to the grass, overturning the wheelchair, Green landing on top of her.

Mary wiggled out from under him. "This isn't easy, you know. You have to work with me."

Green put his hands over his face.

She grabbed him under his arms and dragged him across the

front yard. One of his ankle boots slipped off. She pulled him up the porch stairs and propped him up against the front door. She then ran back to the minivan, retrieved the wheelchair, and picked up the ankle boot.

Green's maroon suit was covered with grass stains, and a black sock was hanging off his left foot. Mary unlocked the front door of the house and dragged him inside, leaving him in the middle of the living room.

"I don't understand you. You want to go to the Brazen Bull, then you don't. What do you want to do? You can't sit around and feel sorry for yourself all day."

Mary went outside and got the wheelchair. When she came back inside, Green was lying on the hardwood floor, staring up at the ceiling. She turned on the window air conditioning.

"I'm done helping you. I'm not getting you in that chair."

"Ma-eee. Eeeeppp."

"You lie there and think about it."

"Ma-eee."

Mary went into the bedroom and sat down on the bed. From where she was sitting, she had a view of Green's feet, the black sock half off his left foot. The quiet voice told her to go back and help him. No, the loud voice said. If you go back, you're sunk. Ruined. He's a man who can no longer function as a man. He isn't whole.

It was almost eleven in the morning. She knew that Chic would be at the Pair-a-Dice by now. She could be there in half an hour, then to the Brazen Bull by noon. Quit thinking that way, the quiet voice said.

She went out into the front room and kicked the golf pencil. It shot across the hardwood floor. Green rolled his head and looked at her.

"I'm going out," she said.

He looked away from her.

She didn't say anything else. You're doing the right thing, the loud voice said. He'll be just fine without you.

Chic & Diane Waldbeeser

■

November 22, 1963

The afternoon that every radio and television program was interrupted to announce that John F. Kennedy had been shot in
Dallas, Chic was looking for his car keys. He usually put them on
the kitchen counter next to the sugar jar, but they weren't there.
He was down on his hands and knees checking under the coffee
table when, from the upstairs bedroom, Diane called out for him.
"Chic. My God! Chic. Chic!" For a moment, he thought that
maybe she'd turned a corner and had finally come out of her funk.
Maybe she wanted to have sex? He started to get aroused.

She came to the top of the stairs. "Kennedy has been shot. I
just heard it on the radio."

Chic stood there looking at her. He scratched his head.
"Yeah?"

"The president, Chic."

Then it clicked. Right. The president. Kennedy. "That's too
bad. What a terrible thing. Hey, have you seen my car keys?"

Diane came downstairs and turned on the television. On the
screen, Walter Cronkite took off his glasses. "President Kennedy
died at 1:00 p.m., central standard time, 2:00 p.m., eastern standard time, some thirty-eight minutes ago."

"I'm going to the store. I can't find my keys so I'm walking,"
Chic said.

"The store? The president is dead."

"Well . . . we still need food."

Stafford's was empty. At the checkout counter, Chic set down
a stack of TV dinners and took out his wallet. The cashier, a woman he knew but whose name he couldn't quite remember, asked,
"Did you hear about the president?"

"I heard," he said, taking some bills out of his wallet.

"It happened *just like that*," she said, snapping her fingers to signify the suddenness of his death.

Chic stopped straightening out his bills. Her snap, and the phrase, *just like that*, had triggered something. He felt like someone had smacked him in the knees with a baseball bat. He wanted to kneel down, but he had to get through this. It was going to pass. He was all right. He pressed two fingers against his jugular vein. Stop thinking about it. Move on. Stop. Don't think. Stop thinking. Concentrate on your heart. Your heart beating. Be in the moment. Stop thinking.

"Mr. Waldbeeser, are you all right?"

He concentrated on his wristwatch. Tick. Tick. Tick. He took a deep breath and removed the fingers from his neck. He smiled at the woman. "I'm fine. How much do I owe you for this stuff?"

The cashier gave him a concerned look.

"Beautiful day out there." Chic motioned toward the windows overlooking the parking lot; a misty rain was falling. He felt another rush coming on. He imagined a bulldozer pushing the thought out of his mind. He smiled at the cashier, whatever her name was. "You know, I don't think I actually need this stuff. Thank you for your help." He left the stack of TV dinners sitting on the counter and walked out of the store.

Chic at Work

■

1960s

Chic didn't like his job, but then again, he didn't not like it. Sure, he daydreamed sometimes about something bigger and better, something with more responsibility, maybe an office where he could kick up his feet on his desk, but he was a cannery man, his father had been a cannery man, his grandfather had been a cannery man, and Chic knew that he would die a cannery man.

This simple fact gave him a small bit of comfort. At least he knew what he was going to do for the rest of his life.

Every morning, he went to the locker room where he put on his hard helmet and white lab coat and punched the clock before heading out to the production floor. Every day at noon, he took lunch with the other workers in the break room. He unpacked his sandwich. Sometimes someone sat across from him, and he smiled at the person and made small talk. That person, whoever it was, after engaging in pleasantries, usually started complaining at some point: about work, the government, family, etc. and would solicit Chic into complaining along with him. Chic would then chime in about whatever the other person wanted to complain about, such as the town's decision not to line Main Street with American flags during the Fourth of July weekend. It was un-American. Unpatriotic. A travesty. Etc. There was companionship in complaining. So, Chic complained, until the other person finished up his sandwich, shut his lunchbox, and went back to work, leaving Chic looking around for someone else to complain along with.

Sometimes the whole ordeal—work; lunch; small talk; complaining; the death of Lomax; his wife's hatred of him, which he felt but kept locked away in the deep dark part of his consciousness; his brother's thoughts about him, whatever they were; Lijy's disappointment in him, which he couldn't understand since he had done what she had wanted him to without getting so much as a thank you in return (actually, he had gotten a thank you, but not a real, honest-to-goodness thank you); every single thing in his life, actually—got to be so much, so heavy, that he couldn't hold his head up anymore and he would push his half-eaten sandwich aside and put his forehead down on the lunch table and close his eyes. He knew the other workers were probably watching him. Some might even be nudging each other—*What's up with Waldbeeser?*—but he couldn't help it. He felt numb. He felt hollow. It was like he was a seashell and his insides had crawled out and left

199

an empty body behind. If a penny was dropped inside of him, the noise would echo forever. He was nothing. Chic Waldbeeser was nothing. He was there but he wasn't there.

Then, he picked his head up off the table. He pinched his arm. He wiggled his toes. He blinked his eyes. See, he was there. He wasn't hollow. He was something. He was a body. He was Chic Waldbeeser. He filled his lungs, drinking in the oxygen. Oh, that felt good. He took a deep breath and held it. He heard the hum of the other employees complaining. Someone deposited a dime in the soda machine. Someone crunched into a potato chip. Someone crumpled a paper bag. Someone laughed. He put two fingers to his neck and felt the consistent throbbing of his beating heart. He was alive. *He was alive.* He lifted his head. His co-workers were talking, eating, complaining. No one had even noticed he'd put his head on the table.

Diane in Bed

■

1960s

One afternoon when Chic was at work, Diane sat up in bed and looked around the room. Clothes piled on the dresser; soda bottles cluttering the nightstand; empty cereal bowls stacked on the floor (a half-eaten hot dog beside them); a layer of dust covering the furniture; the tangle of sheets at the bottom of the mattress; the dog, Cody, lying on the floor, his drooping eyes looking back at her. She decided that she didn't want to live this way any longer. She wiped away the crumbs from the front of her nightgown, noticing her thigh, the largeness of it, the ripple and jiggle of flesh. She didn't remember it being this big. She tried to wrap both hands around it, attempting to measure its girth, but she couldn't get both hands around it. Her thigh had to weigh fifty pounds; that was a hundred pounds for both legs. Add in the rest of her body, and she probably weighed three hundred pounds.

She pulled up her nightgown. Fat rolls. How could she have let this happen? She picked up a soda bottle with a small amount left in the bottom and took a sip. It was warm and flat and syrupy. She picked the hot dog up off the floor, sniffed it, then took a bite. That morning, she'd heard a news segment on the radio about the first heart transplant. The surgery had lasted nine hours and had been performed by a South African, Christiaan Barnard. Diane had always taken it for granted that her heart would continue to beat. She didn't think about it beating, or not beating. On the other hand, she always thought about thinking. If she thought about it, thinking had gotten her in this mess, or rather, her thinking in response to what had happened. If she didn't think, she wouldn't be feeling the way she did—simple as that. If she had a mind transplant, she'd have a different mind, like that person in South Africa had a different heart. She'd be better off that way. Sure, she'd still be thinking, but her thoughts would change, and that was the solution, according to Dr. Peale. But she knew better: thinking was thinking no matter what the thoughts. The question was whether it was the thinking or the thoughts that caused the problem. She wasn't so self-absorbed to think that others had better thoughts. They all had it bad, everyone, the whole world. Everyone thinks, so it must be the thinking, not the thoughts. It was this thinking stuff that had to stop. That was the problem. She thought it curious that most people thought that the heart was the soul. *The heart of the matter. The heart is a lonely hunter.* But really, it was the mind. *It's the mind of the matter. The mind is a lonely hunter.* It was thinking that made people who they were, not the heart. People felt in their minds, not their hearts. It wasn't heartache; it was mindache. Thinking the way she was thinking made her ache. She needed to stop thinking. She sat as still as she could and closed her eyes. Stop thinking, she thought. But then, just like that, she had a thought; it came in from somewhere and then it was there, in her mind, and she was having it: *thinking about thinking was thinking.* This was like digging in sand. Maybe it was best if she distracted her thinking so that she wasn't thinking about her thinking. She stood up, walked to the window, and pulled back the curtain. A few inches of muddy water covered the bottom of the half-dug hole for the swimming pool. She bent down and touched Cody on top of his head. "Come on, boy," she said. "Lunch time."

In the kitchen, Diane opened the fridge and took out the milk. She found a TV dinner in the freezer. She got a box of macaroni and cheese from the cabinet and started a pot of water. An hour later, the dishes were in the sink and she was back upstairs in her bedroom. Again, she noticed the mess around her. Cody was on the bed and she shooed him off. He loped out of the bedroom. She tore the sheets off the bed and piled them next to the dresser, next to a pile of clothes that had been there for she didn't know how long. She had to go to the hall to get clean sheets. However, that took effort, so she just curled up on the bare mattress. Cody came back in and looked at her like he needed to go outside. The newscaster on the radio was talking about Christiaan Barnard's heart transplant again. She felt her heart, then rolled over on her back and stared at the ceiling. The light was on. She should shut it off. Cody barked. Chic would take him outside when he got home. He would be home in a few hours. She'd hear him come in the front door. Dr. Peale would be starting soon. She wanted to hear his voice. She needed to put sheets on the bed, throw away the soda bottles, and straighten up the room. There were dishes to be done downstairs in the kitchen. She turned and reached for a bottle of soda on the nightstand. A single drop was left in it. She put the bottle to her lips and watched the drop roll toward her mouth. She waited, getting excited, already tasting the sugary goodness of the soda, wanting the taste, needing it. This drop was going to taste so good. The drop touched her lips; the liquid was warm and nearly tasteless. She licked her lips, but there was just a hint of sugar. She picked up another bottle and, holding it up, checked for liquid. Closing one eye, she peered through the bottle's mouth. There wasn't anything left. She tried another bottle. It was empty, too. She could go downstairs and get a fresh bottle, but she didn't have the energy. She rested her head back down on the bare mattress. Cody stood next to the bed looking at her. She turned over so that her back was to him. She noticed the mess of the bedroom. Tomorrow she'd clean it up. She'd have the energy tomorrow. She closed her eyes and started to think about thinking again, about how thinking was the problem. She stopped herself. She wasn't going to think about that. She wasn't going to think at all. She rolled on her back and opened her eyes. She needed to turn off the light. Stop, she thought, stop. Stop. Stop. She was thinking again. Stop. Stop thinking.

The Bathroom

■

1960s

Chic locked the bathroom door. Upstairs, he could hear Dr. Peale's voice on the radio. Diane's dry-skin lotion was in the medicine cabinet. He unbuckled his belt and pulled down his pants and underwear, sat down on the toilet. He'd been watching *I Dream of Jeannie*, when he remembered his honeymoon, the night he and Diane went to dinner, then came back to the motel where he seduced her for the first time. He squirted lotion into his palm. That night had been perfect. He'd laid her down and kissed every part of her body—her feet, her inner thighs, her stomach, her breasts. She giggled. He could tell she was nervous. He pulled her nightgown over her head, revealing his wife . . . oh, his wife. He was rubbing his penis; the friction and the lotion combined to make squishy sounds. He climbed on her. They kissed. He rubbed—faster, faster. He felt himself getting close. She moaned. She was into it and into him; he was into it and into her; they were into each other, and it was the closest he'd ever felt to someone in his entire life. He felt connected to her. His head tingled, and he started to orgasm. "Ohhhhhh." He shot the se-men into the bowl—one squirt, two squirts. He whimpered as a wave washed over him and he forgot where he was for a moment. Then, he came back. He was in his bathroom. Upstairs he heard Dr. Peale on the radio: "Imagination is the true magic carpet." He washed his hands and flushed the toilet. He zipped up his pants and buckled his belt. He looked at himself in the medicine cabinet mirror. Everything was going to be okay. He was going to be okay.

Mary Geneseo & Chic Waldbeeser

■

June 23, 1998

Mary had lost a hundred bucks playing pool, and she was pissed. Ever since they'd left the Brazen Bull, she'd been running her mouth about men and how they didn't appreciate a good woman. Chic was doing his best to keep up with what she was saying, but she talked so fast that spittle sprayed out of her mouth like a garden sprinkler. "They want this and they don't. They want to go here and then they don't. This wheelchair is expensive, and this one isn't. You can't leave me. You have to stay with me. Let's move to Peoria. What the hell is in Peoria? Nothing is in Peoria. Look around. Have you had the Chinese food? Gone to the mall? Jesus Christ. I don't know. Do you know? You're a guy. Give me some insight."

Chic didn't say anything.

"What?"

"Nothing."

"That's what I thought."

She lead-footed it and ripped through Creve Coeur past the car dealerships, strip mall plazas and beyond the city limits into a landscape of farmhouses, barns and cornfields. From the air, from a bird's view or God's view, there may have been some symmetry to this, but down on the highway, it was just a mishmash of farms and corn flowing into each other. The ditch along the road was overgrown with weeds, broken up by the occasional plastic garbage bag.

Coming up on a slower car, Mary glued the minivan to the car's bumper and honked and mumbled obscenities before jerking the minivan into the opposite lane and flooring it. Chic noticed that the car was driven by a man about his age, a woman of similar age seated next to him. Mary leaned over Chic and yelled out the passenger window, "Speed the hell up," and shook her fist. "That's the problem," she said. "Right there. They're the problem. They do everything so slowly. You know why? Because they don't want to die. They think if they go slowly, they can ward off the inevitable. Well, you can't."

Chic glanced in the side mirror and saw the car dropping back. Mary jerked the wheel, and the minivan shot into the correct lane, the tires biting into the gravel shoulder and kicking up dust. They came dangerously close to barreling into a sign announcing their entrance into Tazewell County. About a week after her arrival in Peoria, Mary had found herself out this way with Green, after he had picked her up one afternoon from the Pair-a-Dice. They were looking for a bar or something, but mostly playing grab-ass. Green kept grabbing her leg, and she kept swatting him away, playfully, hoping he'd drive them back to the bungalow so they could do what they both wanted to do. Then the DJ on the radio said, "Here's an oldie, but a goodie," and "I'm So Lonesome I Could Cry," came on the radio, the same song that Green had had the bartender play at the Bowl-a-Rama. (And this was the original version, not the Randy Travis cover.) Green looked at her, and she knew what his look meant. He turned off onto a gravel road and pulled up behind two silos. It was the middle of the afternoon, and the sun was high and hanging over the surrounding cornfields.

Mary slowed down. She looked this way and that and over her shoulder and around like she was trying to find something familiar. She passed a pickup waiting to turn onto the highway. The driver kept a sharp eye on her; after she had passed, he pulled onto the highway going the opposite direction.

"Are we lost?" Chic asked.

"No, we're not lost."

The minivan crossed a creek and passed a cemetery, then went up a hill. There was a farmhouse about a hundred yards up the highway. Mary pulled into the gravel drive. A dog chained to a tree in the front yard lunged and barked at the minivan. Mary put the car in reverse, backed out of the drive, and left the way she'd come, past the cemetery, across the creek. Chic wasn't sure where they were. Wasn't Russ's farm out this way? Or maybe it was over that way? There was a water tower in the distance. He was sure that was Farmington. Maybe he should suggest they stop by Russ's? They could all have a beer or something. He wanted to get her in the right mood so that he could bring up Florida. He'd been thinking about how to bring it up. Could he just say it? Come out with it. Blurt it out. She seemed a little flustered right now. The timing had to be right, and maybe this wasn't the best time. Maybe she and her husband had gotten into a fight? Maybe that was reason enough to bring it up? He should tell her more about Diane. If this was going to be an honest relationship, he needed to start being honest with her.

"My wife's name was Diane. She was seventeen when we got married."

"You told me this."

"We had a son. Lomax."

"Chic . . . not now. I'm looking for something."

"He died."

She looked around—right, left, then at him. He was rubbing his thumb and index finger together nervously, like he was rolling something into a ball.

"I said he died."

"What I'm looking for has got to be around here somewhere."

"I'm trying to tell you my son died."

"Yeah. I heard you. I'm sorry to hear that."

"He drowned."

The quiet voice in her head told her that this required a response. Make him feel like she cared. But she kept looking around instead, trying to spot the gravel pull-in.

"My wife and I, we never . . . It was just one of those things that we just never . . . have you ever had anyone die?"

She hadn't stuck with any guy long enough to have had one die on her. Her father had died, although she hadn't been around when it happened. He had been living in Bakersfield. It was ten years ago. His third wife, a woman Mary didn't know, called one afternoon. They'd already had the funeral. Her father hated churches, so Mary found it odd that he'd had a church funeral, but then again, maybe he'd changed since she'd seen him last—she hadn't been in the same room with him for seven or eight years. She'd talked to him on the phone only once in the past five years, Christmas or his birthday or something, and she could hear the television on in the background. For a long time, she told herself she was trying to find a man like him. Truth be told, her father hadn't really been a good man. That afternoon she called him for what turned out to be the final time, the first thing he said to her was, "What are you calling for? You need money or something?"

Up ahead was a gravel road that cut into a cornfield and led to two silos about fifty yards off the highway. Mary took her foot off the gas pedal. "Look," she said. The sun was setting, a massive blazing ball sliding down below the horizon, casting a golden light on the silos, making them glow, making them seem so promising and new, two towers of hope, two rockets sitting in the middle of a cornfield about to blast off to a better place.

"That's what we've been looking for?" Chic asked.

After she and Green had sex that afternoon, they lay together on the floor of the minivan, her head on Green's chest, the carpet scratchy against her naked skin. The radio was playing country music. Lying next to Green, their clothes scattered around the minivan, the radio on, she felt forty years younger, like she'd never aged, like the years had melted away, and she was simply a girl with a boy on the floor of a minivan.

She cut the engine and an orchestra of cicadas and corn bugs filled in the silence. She began unbuttoning her blouse. Chic swallowed hard. He remembered Diane, the weight she had gained after Lomax died, the two of them in the messy bedroom, Peale's voice on the radio, Diane so far removed from him that she could have been in another country. Mary put her hand on his leg and drew close. She closed her eyes. She wanted to kiss. He noticed she was wearing a men's watch. She opened her eyes. He was leaning away from her.

"Aren't you married?" Chic asked.

"How about we don't talk about my husband?"

"You bring me out in the middle of nowhere and you unbutton your shirt and you don't want to talk about your husband?"

"Can we not talk about this?"

"But you're married."

"Do you want to do this or not?"

"It's been a while."

"Me, too." She touched his cheek with her meaty hand.

"I can't stop thinking that you're married."

"I wouldn't be here if I didn't want to be here." She climbed in the back between the seats. "Come on." She unbuckled her jeans and shimmied them off.

"I don't know about this."

"Will you please shut up and take off your pants." She was down to her bra and underwear. She was a big woman, rolls here, there, and everywhere. She took off her bra, and her breasts spilled out.

Chic unbuttoned his shirt. Underneath, he wore a white tank top, which he left on. He took off his pants.

"Come here." She was on her back reaching up to him, and he crawled onto her.

"My wife and I, for a while, tried to have another kid, but I don't know. It was . . . it just didn't . . . I wanted to, but . . ."

"You're kinda ruining the mood here."

"I told you it's been a long time."

She grabbed his penis through his boxers. "You're not hard."

"It's just that my brother's wife, Lijy, she . . ."

"Can we please quit talking like this?"

"Sorry."

She fondled him until he was erect. "Here we go."

"Can I ask you something?" he said.

"No."

"I want to go to Florida with you."

She sighed. "Can we talk about this later?"

"Do you think you've aged gracefully?"

"Take off your boxers."

"I don't think I can."

"What do you mean?"

He looked embarrassed.

"What?"

"I think it was 1965, that was the year when I knew something wasn't right with me and Diane."

Mary sat up on her elbows. "Can we please not talk about you and your wife's marriage?"

"I'm sorry."

She reached for her bra. "You've ruined the moment."

He was about to say something. He opened his mouth to talk.

"Chic, please . . . no more talking," she interrupted.

Eleven

Buddy & Lijy Waldbeeser

1970

Middleville was growing up. The town had doubled in size since 1950, and in what had once been the surrounding corn and pumpkin fields, subdivisions with names like Whisper Creek and Shady Grove had sprung up. A new high school was being built on the east side of town under the water tower, and traffic lights had been installed at both ends of Main Street. Buddy thought the timing was finally right for a health food store, which was what Lijy had always wanted, always dreamed of. Besides, if he was going to be a real father, he couldn't spend his days staring out the window like his father had. He wasn't going to be his father. He had a son, or at least, or rather, he was a father, which meant that he had a son, *a son*, which meant he was a father, *a father*, a man with a kid, heavy stuff not to be taken lightly.

He and Lijy leased a store on Main Street between Ray's Hairport and Witmer Insurance. Across the street from the store was Middleville Community Bank and Witzig's department store, which showcased a modest selection of conservative fashions. (Those who wanted colorful polyester jumpsuits or bell-bottom Levi's had to make the drive to Bergner's in Peoria.) The plan was to split the store in two: in the main area, they'd stock healthy fare like blackstrap molasses, brewer's yeast, nuts, honey, vitamins, herbal teas, and steel-cut oatmeal; while in the bac room, Lijy would give massages. Buddy sanded down the wood floors and snapped together the aisle shelving. Along one wall, a small commercial refrigeration unit was installed for yogurt, eggs, and milk. Lijy hung a beaded curtain in the doorway behind the counter and made sure the towels were stacked on the shelf by the massage table. For a final touch, Buddy propped a copy of Gayelord Hauser's book next to the cash register; for ninety-nine cents, a customer could walk out with a paperback copy of *Look Younger, Live Longer*.

On May 1, 1970, Buddy and Lijy hung balloons on either side of the front door and a grand opening banner in the front window. To make the place look familyfriendly, Russ, who was now ten, put on his Little League uniform and stood on the sidewalk with free cups of fresh-squeezed orange juice. By noon, however, not a single customer had stopped into the store. Lijy was still holding a tray of yogurt samples, while Buddy, wearing a dhoti and flip-flops, kept looking at his watch. At one o'clock, Mrs. Witmer came out of Witmer Insurance and stopped on the sidewalk in front of the store. She gave the place a long look before getting into her station wagon and driving away. At three o'clock, Lijy set the yogurt samples on the counter and went into the massage parlor to lie down. She took one of the massage towels from the shelf and put it over her head. Russ came inside the store. Out front, a Chevy Impala parked next to the curb, and a man Buddy recognized as the high school football coach, Coach Reiser, hopped out. He wore sunglasses and a flat-top haircut. "I think we might have our first customer," Buddy yelled. Lijy burst through the beaded curtain and picked up the tray of yogurt samples. Coach Reiser stood out front, rubbing his chin. He looked up at the hand-painted sign that read GENERAL HEALTH FOOD AND MASSAGE STORE. Buddy waved him in. "Come on in, Coach." Instead of being the first customer, Coach Reiser turned around, got back into his Impala, and drove away.

For the next few months, the residents of Middleville walked past the store, scratching their heads, not sure what to make of it. A few did venture inside to have a look around; they would pick up the odd items, like the herbal teas, eye them suspiciously for a few moments, then put them back on the shelf and leave. (A few brave customers did buy some stuff, mainly jars of honey or pints of yogurt.) Coach Reiser came back one day and wanted to know if they sold creatine or any other weightlifting supplements. They did not, but Buddy did offer him a complimentary package of licorice tea, which the coach declined.

One afternoon, Buddy saw Chic walk by, heading south toward Ray's Hairport. Buddy thought maybe he was in the neighborhood to get a haircut. A few minutes later, Chic passed going the opposite way. A couple of minutes after that, he passed by again. This back-and-forth went on for another few minutes, until Buddy went outside. Chic's car was parked out front, and Diane was in the front seat of the car, wearing Jackie O. sunglasses and holding a doll. When Chic saw Buddy, he slowly walked toward the car.

"Maybe you two can come in for some yogurt," Buddy said. "I bet Lijy would like to see you both."

Chic stared at his brother. "Do you really think that's the best idea?"

Then, it dawned on Buddy—he'd been so focused on the store, he'd forgotten about the affair. Actually, that wasn't true. He hadn't forgotten about it, but the years had dulled the sharpness, the pain, the agony, the betrayal. Occasionally, though, it would all come pouring back for a moment. This faraway look would appear on Buddy's face, and he'd get very quiet. He'd have to sit down, close his eyes, and rub his temples.

Chic got in his car, and Buddy watched him drive away. Diane hung her head out the window and looked back at him. They weren't okay. They weren't even close to okay. Buddy had heard from a few people in town that Chic hadn't mowed his lawn all summer, and that he was going into Stafford's and buying two dozen frozen TV dinners at a time.

By September 1970, after being open four months, the health food store had netted ninety-seven dollars. Lijy suggested they cut their losses and sell all the inventory at half price. They could call the whole adventure a "learning experience." In retrospect, the idea seemed so half-cocked, misguided, and selfish. How could she have been so stupid? A health food store in a small town in the middle of Illinois. Buddy wasn't ready to cut his losses, though. He told Lijy to have some patience. People needed time to get used to change. He reminded her of when she first moved to Middleville, how everyone used to stare at her. Did she not remember that first week—the goons on the lawn cackling and threatening to make their life miserable? How they tossed eggs at the porch and toilet-papered the trees and yipped like excited dogs until Buddy got his BB gun from the closet, cracked the living room window, and shot one in the leg, knocking him to his knees. All of them then jumped in their cars and sped off. It was the last time they gave them any problems. Of course, that didn't mean that people stopped looking sidelong at her, but at least they did their staring in silence. So, no, he didn't want to sell off the store's stock at half price. Quite the opposite: he was going to print up some flyers and stuff them in people's mailboxes. He was going to get a PA speaker, affix it to the roof of his car, and drive up and down Main Street. (Those things kept him busy for a little while, although they didn't really help. It would be another three years before the store got a foothold, when, in the summer of 1973, a fitness craze swept through Middleville. A health club featuring a weight room and stationary bikes opened on Main Street, and in the early mornings, small groups of men and women dressed in tracksuits and headbands would jog through town, dodging lawn sprinklers and barking dogs and stopping in the store to eat yogurt and wheat berries and vitamins and purchase copies of Gayelord Hauser's book.)

One afternoon in October, Buddy was standing at the cash register talking to Russ, who was sitting on the counter, when the bell above the store's door rang, announcing a customer. Buddy looked up to see a man wearing aviator sunglasses, a beige raincoat, and a jet-black Halloween wig.

"Can I help you?" Buddy asked.

The man waved him off and picked up a shopping basket and darted down an aisle. In front of the cereals, he spent several minutes studying the ingredients on a box of granola. Buddy could tell that he wasn't actually reading the ingredients but looking over the box at him and Russ.

"Daddy, why's he looking at us like that?" Russ whispered.

The man put down the granola and disappeared down another aisle.

"Can I help you find something?" Buddy asked.

The man crept around the aisle. "I'd like to schedule a massage."

Buddy noticed the man was strangely puffy, as if, under his raincoat, he was wearing a few sweatshirts to make himself appear larger than he actually was. The man pushed his sunglasses up on his nose.

Buddy was suspicious. "Have you ever had a massage before?"

"No. I mean yes. Once. A long time ago."

"My wife practices Ayurveda massage."

"I know. I mean, okay."

Russ reached out to touch the wig, but the man took a giant step backward. "The boy. Your son? He has a ... how do I say it ... an aura."

"Aura?"

"I'd like to come in on Friday. The last appointment of the day. What would that be—five o'clock?"

Buddy ran his finger down the page of the schedule book. He glanced up at the man and forced a smile. "I don't know about Friday. Let me check with my wife." He gave Russ a glance, and motioned with his head toward the beaded curtain. He grabbed Russ's hand, and they both went into the back. The man pushed his sunglasses up on his nose.

Lijy sat on the massage table, a magazine open on her lap.

Buddy lowered his voice. "There's a guy out here. I think it's . . . it might be Chic."

"Chic?"

"He's in disguise."

"Why would Chic be in disguise?"

It was a good question. He hadn't considered this. "Well, it's probably not Chic, but it's someone . . . someone odd. He wants a massage."

"I'll take care of this." She handed Buddy the magazine.

"Wait a second. Before you go out there." Buddy leaned in to whisper. "He said Russ has an aura."

"Aura?"

Buddy nodded.

Lijy knew then that it was Ellis. She wasn't going to stand for this. She had finally gotten things moving in the right direction. She had her health food store; Buddy was coming around; she wasn't waking up and finding his side of the bed cold and empty; and just that afternoon, she had eavesdropped on Buddy and Russ having a father-and-son conversation about the benefits of a daily multivitamin. She needed to give Ellis the narrow eye and shoo him back to his life. But when she pushed through the curtain, he was nowhere to be found. On the counter, he'd left an empty shopping basket, and next to the basket was a small, rectangular box, the kind with a pad of jewelry foam and a necklace inside. She picked it up. She shook it. She looked over her shoulder. Behind the beaded curtain, Buddy was telling Russ that the world was full of strange people. She could see that he was kneeling down in front of him.

She opened the box, and inside was a wallet-size photograph of Ellis McMillion wearing a softball uniform. In cursive letters across the front of his jersey was the town name, LEXINGTON. He wore a mustache and had a wooden bat over his shoulder. On the back of the picture, he'd written, *Phase one is almost over.*

Mary & Green Geneseo

■

June 23, 1998

Green remained sprawled on the floor, his head turned so that he could stare at the front door. He waited to hear her key in the lock, watch her walk in the door. When she did, he was going to let her have it. Lay into her. He might even cuss. He was going to get loud, which meant he'd write in capital letters. He was fuming. She was going to regret that she set him off. She was messing with fire. He was going to rise up. Rise up! And he was going to rage. Rage! She wouldn't ever—EVER!—leave him on the floor again. Ever!

He'd been on the floor all afternoon. Outside, he heard a lawn mower. He listened to the hum of the motor for a half hour or so, before it stopped. He heard cars, occasionally, pass the house. He kept thinking one of them was going to be Mary, but none were. The shadows grew longer and the sun took on that late afternoon, soft, hazy glow. At six o'clock, the driveway was still empty. Green practiced what he was going to say when she came in the door. *And where the hell have you been. Where? Who have you been with?* He then realized that what he was rehearsing in his head was pointless, since he couldn't talk. How was he going to get mad at her by writing notes? Jesus Christ. He couldn't even get angry anymore. He began to feel sorry for himself. What if she came home with the guy, some dealer from the Pair-a-Dice or whatever, some guy making her promises about how he was going to make everything better? Ha. She had just about as perfect a guy she was going to get with him. Didn't she see that? What if she and the guy opened the front door and found him on the floor? "My husband can't feel the left side of his body." Hardy-har-har. "He can't talk." Hardy-har-har. She was mistaken if she thought some dealer or whatever from the Pair-a-Dice was going to whisk her away and make everything better. Nothing was going to be better.

Better only lasts a short time—like two months, in this case, in his case, with her. He could not believe that she had left him on the living room floor. Just left him. Where the hell was she? He crawled over to his suit jacket and fished the Post-it Note pad out of the inside breast pocket. He wasn't going to stand for this. He wasn't going to let himself be treated this way. He wasn't going to be made a fool. HE WAS NOT GOING TO BE MADE TO LOOK LIKE A FOOL. The living room was starting to get dark. He heard laughter—Mary and her new man. *Quit laughing at me.* He looked around. It was quiet.

He was still on the floor when the minivan pulled into the driveway. He was ready. He'd prepared various notes anticipating an argument. He heard her key in the lock. She burst through the door.

"Oh, Jesus, Green. What are you doing? You're still on the floor."

He reached out to her and shook the note in his hand.

She took it. Read it. The note said, *Quit laughing at me.*

"No one is laughing at you."

He held out another note. *What's his name?*

"There's no one else, Green."

He still had five or six notes, but he pointed to the one she was holding.

"There's no one else. How many times do I need to tell you that?"

He pointed, and emphasizing his anger, grunted.

"I'm not lying to you."

"Wuh hiz aim?"

"Green Geneseo."

You're lying.

"Let me help you back into your chair."

He slapped her hand away.

"Green, you have to get back in your chair."

He shook his head no.

"Don't be this way."

He turned toward his wheelchair; it was across the room, about six or seven feet away, just out of arm's length. Despite the distance, he reached for it; he had visions of wheeling himself away from her, going into the other room, leaving her behind like she left him behind. He wanted her to know that he didn't need her. He wiggled his fingers, reaching, reaching, but of course, he couldn't reach the chair and collapsed on the floor.

Mary grabbed him under the arms, and he let her. She helped him into the wheelchair. Sweat had beaded on his upper lip, and he wiped it away. He was so mad he tasted metal. He narrowed his eyes at her.

"Stop looking at me like that."

He continued to narrow his eyes until they were completely shut. He saw darkness and popping flashes of anger. He knew she was looking down at him. He hoped she was feeling guilty for leaving him while she did whatever she did with her new boy-friend. Hardy-har-har. "He's in a wheelchair. He can't talk. And here I am, driving around in your convertible." Hardy-har-har. "I love the way the wind feels whipping against my face. I feel so free. So alive." Hardy-har-har. He opened his eyes. She wasn't standing in front of him like he thought she would be, like he se-cretly hoped she would be. He heard her in the kitchen. She was getting a glass from the cabinet. She turned on the tap.

Chic & Diane Waldbeeser

■

1970

Chic found the first doll at a Salvation Army in Peoria. It was ratty as hell, with a missing eye and crayon scribbles on its bald head. He called the counter lady over and asked her if women liked to receive dolls as gifts.

"Does it make them want to be mothers?" he asked. "Is that

why you give little girls dolls?"

The woman stared at him.

"Well," he said, "I thought it prepared them to be mothers."

"You give little girls dolls so they have something to play with."

"Yeah, well, sure, but it also prepares them to be mothers, right?"

When he arrived home, Chic put the doll in a brown paper bag and left it at the bottom of the stairs. He sat down on the couch to wait for the news to come on, then Johnny Carson. Diane would be down soon for some soda and peanut butter toast, maybe a couple of raw hot dogs. Chic looked at the bag at the bottom of the stairs. The doll was a fantastic idea, a stroke of brilliance, if he didn't say so himself. This was going to get them headed in the right direction. They'd been spinning their wheels for too long. Heck, they hadn't had sex in he didn't know how long.

Sometime after midnight, while half dozing on the couch, Chic heard Diane's footfalls across the ceiling. She came down the stairs quietly. Seeing the bag, she stopped. Chic pretended to be asleep, but kept his eyes open slightly. He watched as she picked up the bag and tested its weight. Then she peered inside and took out the doll. Chic had done his best to clean it up— scrubbing the crayon markings from the head and gluing a button to replace the missing left eye. She took the doll with her back upstairs.

Many more dolls followed over the next few months. Chic scoured estate sales and trade papers to find them. He hung a notice on the bulletin board at Stafford's—WANTED: YOUR OLD DOLLS. In order to make room for the dolls, he moved the furniture in Lomax's room down to the basement, vacuumed the carpet, and reassembled the crib. He carried a rocking chair up from the basement and placed it next to the crib. He hung shelves on the walls and a mobile in the corner.

At night, when the house was quiet and Chic was downstairs

watching the *Tonight Show*, Diane would sneak down the hall to ad-
mire the doll collection. They lined up on the shelves, stone-faced,
staring out over the nursery. She remembered Lomax waking her up
in the middle of the night when he was a baby. He wanted her. He
cried for her. She went to the dolls and took one off the shelf, then
another, and another, and held them close to her, hugging them. She
sat down on the rocking chair. She used to hold Lomax in this chair,
daydreaming about what he'd be like when he got older. It had been
ten years. A whole decade had blurred by in a snap, and she had wast-
ed it in bed, lying there and listening to the radio. She didn't want to
feel like this anymore. She needed to move on. She needed to get out
of this house; she needed to pull herself together.

Chic heard his wife in Lomax's old room. He set his can of
beer down on the coffee table and crept up the stairs. The door
was cracked just enough so that he could see her sitting in the
rocking chair, holding three dolls tightly against her chest. Her
eyes were closed, and she was rocking back and forth. He wanted
to put an end to the depressing cloud that hung over the house
like a swarm of gnats. He wanted to take her right there in Lomax's old room. Right there. On the floor in front of the rocking
chair. He wanted to take her, like he had taken her in Florida. He
ducked his head in and cleared his throat.

"I was thinking that maybe . . . you know . . . maybe it was
time to . . ." he looked at her and winked " . . . give it another try."

"I don't think so."

"Come on. It's been . . . Diane . . . let's . . . it's why I got you
the dolls."

"I haven't forgiven you, Chic."

"Forgiven me. For what? Lijy?"

"I don't think I'll ever forgive you. For any of it."

He stood there staring at her. "Diane . . ." he began, but she
interrupted him.

"No. Don't say anything. Don't say another word. Just, please,
get out. Just leave me alone. I want to be alone."

He shut the door and stood in the dark hall. He didn't know what to think. He wanted to turn around and throw open the door and yell at her, raise his voice and scream at her. This wasn't his fault. None of this was his fault. Not one bit of it. Couldn't she see he was trying here? She had to work with him. She had to try, too. But he didn't open the door. He didn't do anything. He simply went down the hall to the bedroom, but he didn't want to sleep in the bedroom, so he went downstairs to the living room. He finished his beer and went into the kitchen and turned on the faucet to disguise the noise he was about to make. He crushed his beer can as quietly as he could and hid the can at the bottom of the garbage. Then he made himself a bed on the living room couch.

Lijy & Russ & Ellis McMillion

■

October 8, 1970

Lijy looked up Lexington on a map and saw that it was a tiny town, a mere gas stop on I-55 in the sea of corn between Middleville and Chicago. She left Buddy in charge of the store—telling him she was going to take Russ to the park for the afternoon—and made the hour-and-a-half drive.

The high school was on the edge of town, and the softball diamond was behind the school by the bus lot, which abutted a cornfield. Lijy parked the car on the street. Russ, who was eating raisins in the backseat, wanted to know where they were, and Lijy told him that they were on a secret mission and that he was never, ever to tell his daddy about it. Russ said he liked secret missions and popped a raisin in his mouth.

Lijy and Russ sat in the bleachers behind home plate. Down on the field, Ellis, his hair pulled back in a ponytail under a baseball cap, Ray-Ban sunglasses wrapped around his face, was hitting grounders to the infielders. Last year, his team had won the

Class A State finals, and over the past three seasons, their record was fifty-seven wins and only seven losses. This year, they were poised to make another run for the state championship. That would make two state championships and one-third place finish over the past four seasons. Deep down, however, Ellis knew that the team's success had little to do with his coaching and, more to do with the fact that Illinois's best female softball player, Colleen Popper, happened to live in Lexington. Colleen Popper was a broad-shouldered, beefy catcher with blonde hair and a .584 career batting average. She'd grown up the only girl in a family of five boy, and by the time she was seven was playing in the boys' Little League; by twelve, she was the tailback on the town's traveling peewee football team. In only ten games, she rushed for over a thousand yards.

Ellis noticed Lijy and Russ as soon as they took their seats in the bleachers. Seeing the two of them, he felt something inside of him move. He'd waited for this day for a long time. He'd dropped off the picture hoping to jumpstart things into action, and here it was happening; it was officially in motion. After he was done hitting grounders, he went to the bench, which was enclosed by a chain-link fence, while the girls took batting practice. He continually looked over at Russ and Lijy. Lijy kept a sharp eye on him as well. She thought she had made it clear that she didn't want anything to do with him and his phases and plans. If she hadn't been clear enough that afternoon at her house, she was going to be more than clear this time.

A big, blonde-haired girl went to the bench to put on her batting helmet and select a bat. Lijy noticed that there was something peculiar about the girl's interaction with Ellis. She kept nuzzling up to him, rubbing against him like a cat. Ellis kept stepping away from her and looking over at Lijy, smiling nervously. At one point, the big girl put her hand on Ellis's rear end, gave it a squeeze, then slipped her hand into his back pocket. She left it there until it was her turn to bat. She took her place in the batter's box. The pitcher, a small girl, looked worried. The blonde-haired girl tapped her bat on the plate and took an aggressive stance, rear elbow out, squatting. The pitcher tried to speed an underhanded fastball by her, but the big girl ripped it over the centerfielder's head, the ball clanging against the chain-link fence. She sent the second pitch deep into the cornfield in right field. She pulled the third pitch foul, the softball skipping down the third base line, but she crushed the next pitch over the scoreboard in center. Then she was done. She went back to the bench, dragging her bat behind her. Ellis clapped and said, "That a girl. Good hittin'." Passing Ellis, the girl craned her neck upward and tried to give him a kiss on the cheek, but he ducked away. Lijy couldn't believe what she was seeing. She'd known Ellis was a perverted snake who had seduced her with his quivering tongue, but . . . a high school girl? What was she thinking, coming here to Lexington? She didn't want to talk to him. She couldn't talk to him. A high school girl?

Lijy nudged Russ in the shoulder and told him it was time to go. Down on the field, the softball team huddled together on the pitching mound and did some sort of rah-rah cheer before sprinting off across the outfield toward the high school. The only player who didn't run off was the blonde girl. She put her glove on her head and moped around home plate, kicking dirt while Ellis picked up the batting helmets.

"Go," Ellis said, waving her on. "I'll meet you in the parking lot." Hanging her head, she slowly crossed the outfield.

After she had disappeared into the school, Ellis came over to the fence by the bleachers. Lijy had hung around just so she could tell him what a snake he was.

"Is that him?" Ellis asked.

"Of course it's him. Who do you think it is?"

"It's me," Russ said.

"Do you know who I am?" Ellis poked a finger through the chain-link fence and wiggled it. "Hello. I'm me. You're you."

Russ looked at his mother, not sure what was going on. "Who is he, Mom?"

"No one," Lijy answered. "Russ, can you get my purse—I left

it in the bleachers." Lijy had intentionally left her purse behind, knowing that she would need a minute alone to talk to Ellis.

She waited until Russ was out of earshot.

"I saw you—you and that girl, the big girl," she said angrily. "She stuck her hand in your back pocket. She tried to kiss you."

"I've been alone for ten years. Ten years! It's like I've been in the desert. I'm Simon of the Desert. Do you know that movie? That's me. I'm Simon. And you're the devil. The world is the devil. Everyone is the devil."

"She's in high school."

"She's gonna be eighteen in three months. And besides—you've seen her—she's a softball goddess."

"No more disguises. No more visits to the store. I'm not part of your plan. I never have been and I never will be. I thought I made myself clear. I do not want to have anything to do with you ever, *ever* again."

"From the moment we were together, you have been a big part of my plan and I have been a big part of your plan. You're the mother ship. You have radioactive flesh."

"Look, I don't want you in my life anymore. Or Russ's. I don't want to be your mother ship. And what are you talking about, radioactive flesh?"

"I'm his father. You can't change that."

"I've changed it. His father is Buddy. He actually has two fathers. He thinks his father is my brother-in-law. But anyway that's beside the point. Neither of them would let a high school girl grab his behind in public." She thought that maybe Chic would allow this, but she wasn't sure.

"I'm blood. I'm the blood father. I'm the sperm. Look at him. He looks just like me."

It was true. Russ looked like Ellis; he had his beady eyes and lanky long limbs. Later, when he got to college, he'd start pushing his glasses up on his nose when he was nervous and would have no idea it was a genetic tic passed down to him.

"I wanted to hurt Buddy. You were a warm body. You're right. You were sperm. That's it. That's all you were. It was a mistake, and I'm trying to clean that mistake up. That's my plan. I have a plan, too, you know."

"I love when you get feisty like this."

"Good-bye, Ellis."

"Wait."

"Leave us alone. Let us live our lives. And go about your life. Just . . . we're through, Ellis. And if you ever try to get into my life again, I'll . . . I don't know what I'll do, but I promise you won't like it." Russ returned with the purse, and Lijy grabbed his hand and pulled him away.

Ellis threw his hat on the ground, jumped on it, then yelled, "You are ruining the plan, Lijy. This isn't part of the plan."

"What's he talking about, Mommy?" Russ asked.

"Just ignore him, honey."

"Give me your tired, your poor," Ellis continued, getting dramatic, "your huddled masses yearning to be free. You want to be free, Lijy. I know you do. Come to me. Come back to me. You need me. I'll set you free."

She kept walking toward the car with Russ, away from Ellis. "We're going to get some ice cream," she told him, "and I'm going to tell you something that you can never, ever tell anyone." Over ice cream, she'd explain everything. Of course, Russ wouldn't understand. He was only ten, but in time, he would understand. Maybe he'd never understand. No one really understands, really, why they do what they do. She wasn't sure she fully understood. Maybe he'd get angry. Maybe he'd cry. Maybe he'd cross his arms and stare at her. She couldn't take that. Her little boy, glaring at her. She could not take that. How could she tell Russ the truth, especially since she and Buddy had already told him the "truth" about her and Chic when he was four years old? Buddy had demanded she tell him, and even though she didn't really want to, she did it. The news about Ellis would spin Russ's world like a top. It would mess him up. He might never recover, and she couldn't have that. Today wasn't the right time. Today, they'd just get ice cream, and she'd tell him how much she loved him because she did love him. She was protecting him. That was what she was doing. She was protecting him, and wasn't that what love was? That's how much she loved him. Buddy, too. She'd protected him. Both of them. Yes, she had hurt Buddy in the process of protecting him, but she had lessened the hurt with a lie, so that was still protection, still the truth. What was truth, really, if you wanted to get philosophical about it? Buddy was Russ's father, maybe not the biological one, but he was his father, and that was truth enough.

Twelve

Diane Waldbeeser

■

1971

Diane stood on the bathroom scale. She waited a moment for the dial to settle. Two hundred and eighty-seven pounds. She'd dropped fifteen pounds. For the past two weeks, inspired by something Dr. Peale had said on his program—"Have great hopes and dare to go all out for them. Have great dreams and dare to live them. Have tremendous expectations and believe in them."—she had been on a drastic diet, trading in raw hot dogs and soda for black tea and bananas.

Energized by her weight loss, Diane threw herself into getting the house in order. She started in the bedroom, picking up the clothes that were strewn about like a garage sale, the soda bottles on the nightstand, the old plates of food that had been pushed under the bed. She cleaned the baseboards and wiped the dust from the blades of the box fan. She reorganized the shoes in her closet, lining them up by style. She folded the clothes in her drawers, and in Chic's drawers, too. Then she moved to the bathroom, scrubbing the tub, sink, and toilet. In the kitchen, she cleaned out the fridge. She swept the front porch and the driveway and the sidewalk in front of the house. She cleaned out the gutters and weeded the barren patch of ugly earth in the backyard where Chic had tried to dig a pool. She cleared out the attic, pulling out the boxes and labeling them with black marker—CHRISTMAS DECORATIONS, OLD PHOTOS, etc. She vacuumed the whole house. The cleaning fit took three days. Once or twice, Chic asked if he could help, but she said she didn't want his help. The house hadn't been this spotless since the day they moved in. She demonstrated how clean it was by wiping her finger in random places and showing Chic. "See, no dust here."

Diane felt rejuvenated—alive, fully conscious. She stopped listening to the radio. She did sit-ups. She took drives in the car. She stood in the backyard and took big, deep breaths of fresh air. She walked around the block, waving at her neighbors and shouting, "Hello there!" She painted her toenails. She sat on the front porch and drank ice tea. She went to Stafford's and pushed a cart up and down the aisles. Stafford's had changed. They'd expanded and rearranged the store, putting the frozen food section in the back and bringing the produce to the front. And the produce! There were now exotic items like pineapple and mangos. There was also an entire section devoted entirely to vitamins. (Diane didn't know this, but this was Stafford's reaction to Buddy and Lijy's health food store.) When her alarm clock buzzed at a quarter to six in the morning, she threw back the covers and announced, "World, I am Diane Waldbeeser, and I am getting up now." And with that, she sprang out of bed. She'd spent over a decade in that bed. She tried to recall the thoughts she'd had while lying there, listening to the radio, but when she closed her eyes to call them up, there was just darkness. But that life was over now—she was moving forward.

One night, she invited her parents over for dinner. They were very old now. Her father had retired in 1968, and he could barely hear anymore. Diane had to shout at him across the table, and several times, he turned to his wife and asked, "What'd Diane just say?" At one point, before dessert, he stood up and began to speak. He said he'd been a math teacher for thirty-five years and felt that he'd served the town well. He had had a purpose, and had a gold watch as proof of his value and a commemorative plaque hanging in his living room. He didn't know what a health food store was, but Middleville now had one, thanks to Chic's brother. He asked Chic and Diane what they thought their purpose was, and both of them looked down at their laps. He said he was sorry that they'd lost their son. He said he thought about him from time to time. He said when it was time for him to go, he'd go peacefully, hopefully in his sleep. He hoped it would be soon. He was getting tired.

"Oh, sit down," Diane's mother said. "He gets like this sometimes."

"Daddy," Diane said. "You're not going to die." She couldn't handle another death, not now, not after she'd finally gotten herself up and off the ground.

Her father sat down and put his napkin back in his lap. He looked at Chic and smiled.

After her parents left, Diane did the dishes and wiped the table, while Chic sat in the living room to watch *All in the Family*. After she turned out the lights in the kitchen, she went upstairs and sat in the rocking chair with a doll. She wanted to think about what her father had said, but there was a barrier around it—like a scab over a wound—that protected her from thinking about it. However, she did allow herself a few moments of imagination: her father and Lomax in heaven, both of them laughing. Her father throwing Lomax a baseball, Lomax catching it. Then, she snapped back into the present and looked down at the doll she was cradling.

After a while, Chic ducked his head into the nursery and asked Diane if she wanted to come to bed, but she wasn't ready yet. He went into the bathroom, and she listened to him getting ready. After he was finished, she called him back into the nursery.

"Yes?" he asked.

"I think I want to join a bowling league," she said.

"A bowling league?"

"We never get out and socialize. We should do more of that."

"OK," he said.

"I'm going to sign us up. Wednesday nights."

"Very good, then. Wednesday nights." He watched her for a while. They probably weren't going to have another kid. He shouldn't even bring it up. It occurred to him that he wasn't sure if he was in love with her. He thought he was, but maybe he wasn't. Maybe he only felt like he loved her because of what they'd gone through. Maybe that was all love was. Anyway, it was much easier if he didn't think about it. Just go with it. Get in the river and float along with it. Wednesday nights. It was settled, then. Bowling.

Mary & Green Geneseo

■

June 24, 1998

Green woke up. His neck was killing him. He'd been too stubborn to sleep in the bedroom, so he'd slept in his wheelchair, with his head slumped over on his chest. The sun peeked through the Venetian blinds. The house was quiet. What time was it? He heard a car start up on the street. He peeked out the blinds—the minivan was in the drive. He rolled into the kitchen, but she wasn't there. The coffeemaker hadn't been used. In the bedroom, the bed was made. The bathroom. He pulled aside the shower curtain. There were droplets of water in the tub, and it smelled like she'd recently washed her hair. In the back of the house, out the sunporch window, he had a view of the backyard—the grass needed mowing—and the neighbor's house with its garden shed and picnic table. No Mary. Then he heard the door open. He glanced over his shoulder, sending a sharp jolt of pain through his body.

"There you are, sleepyhead." She was holding a cordless phone. She saw Green eyeing it, and put it behind her back.

He dug out his Post-it Note pad but didn't write anything. He didn't feel like talking. He thought about asking about the phone, which she was obviously hiding behind her back, but what was the point. He was tired of arguing with her. He wanted to wheel himself away so that he didn't have to be in front of her and feel like such a little man.

"So, I'm going to the Brazen Bull later today. I know you

don't want to go, so I'm not gonna make you. But I thought we could go have dinner tonight. Me and you. I shouldn't be home too late. Around six. Seth and that guy they call Eight Ball are usually there until about then."

Green felt the anger rising up inside of him. He knew she wasn't going to the Brazen Bull. The Pair-a-Dice guy, or whoever, was probably going to spring for some sloppy hotel where they'd spend all afternoon watching soap operas on the television while he took her from behind.

Mary sighed. He didn't even have to write anything. She could see it in his face.

The sigh made Green feel like a scolded dog, but he couldn't help himself. He wanted to know the truth. He dug out his notepad and wrote, *I'm sorry I didn't turn out the way you wanted me to.*

She put her hands on her hips. The way she was looking at him, he could tell she was at her breaking point. He was pushing her too far.

Chic Waldbeeser

■

October 18, 1971

While Diane had her dolls and now bowling, Chic still had nothing. His desire to connect with someone, something, was so great that it felt like a blender was whirling inside of him, constantly churning, churning, churning with longing. He needed to find it, whatever it was. Maybe it was books, he thought. Or yogurt? Maybe that yogurt book or whatever it had been that had done the trick for Buddy? He should pay him a visit. Maybe he could recommend something. He was his big brother after all, and wasn't a big brother supposed to help the younger brother? Wasn't that how it worked?

Chic got as far as standing on the sidewalk in front of the health food store when he glimpsed Russ standing by the counter. He was ten now, pretty much the same age that Lomax had been when he drowned. Chic froze. He couldn't breathe. His heart was doing a crazy dance—pitter-pat, glug, glug, beat, beat, beat. His mind flashed back to the time he took Lomax to the high school gymnasium for Little League tryouts. Lomax had brought along his briefcase and spent the morning sitting in the bleachers, shuffling papers. When it was his turn to take some grounders, he stood under the basketball hoop, his legs crossed at the ankle, his glove hanging limply at his side. The coach could tell Lomax wasn't a ballplayer, so he rolled the ball at him instead of smacking it with the fungo bat. Lomax didn't even try to make a play on the ball—he simply watched it bounce off the wall behind him. His own son couldn't—or wouldn't—even scoop up a slow roller! Chic wanted to go turtle and put his head into his shell. All the other fathers turned the death eye on him as if he'd raised some kind of oddball. And it was true. His son was different. Chic knew it. Diane knew it. Anyone who spent three minutes with the boy knew it. Maybe that was the problem. Maybe if he had pushed Lomax to hang around with the boys in the neighborhood more, he wouldn't have gone off to Kennel Lake on some lake-diving mud-gathering science study thing. He'd be in college now, maybe down at the University of Illinois, and there wouldn't be a room full of goddamn dolls at home, and his wife wouldn't be dragging him to a Wednesday night bowling league, which, by the way, he hated. He was terrible at bowling. They were both terrible at it, and he knew the other bowlers were laughing at them just like the fathers had laughed at him that afternoon at the Little League tryouts. He should have forced Lomax to become a normal, red-blooded, American boy. Now, the worst thing, the absolute worst thing, the knife twisting in his goddamn stomach, was that his brother was raising a son who played baseball. A real son. A normal son. An alive son. Chic couldn't go inside the store. He couldn't make small talk with Russ—ask him about Little League and school. No goddamn way. And he certainly didn't want to ask his brother for advice.

He wanted to be alone—alone with this heavy rock sitting on his chest, alone with his thoughts, his memory, his disappointment in himself as a father. He'd find his own book.

There was a can of beer under the seat, stashed there for occasions when he needed something to loosen the strings, take a little weight off. Chic cracked the beer. It was warm, but he guzzled it anyway; a little bit dribbled out the corners of his mouth. There was another one in the glove box and three more in the spare-tire well in the trunk. He pounded them all and crushed the cans and hid them under the seat. He wiped his mouth. He felt woozy. The feelings of disappointment subsided a bit. The beer always helped. He drove to the library.

Chic tried pushing through the library's glass front door, but it wouldn't open. Closed! The library was closed. He couldn't believe it. But what were those people doing inside? He stood there scratching his head until someone pushed through the door and excused himself past Chic. (He hadn't realized that the door needed to be pulled open.) He opened the door and went inside. In his head, he heard trumpets. He was here. His salvation! Books! Which, to be honest, he didn't really enjoy. The last book he had read was *Great Expectations*—in high school.

He walked toward the card catalog, stumbling a few times along the way. He was trying not to appear drunk, but he was too buzzed to be able to pretend. Across the library, he noticed his former English teacher, Mr. Haze, reading a book at a table. He had to be around one hundred years old. He had been old when Chic was in school, and that was twenty-five years ago. Chic acknowledged him with a shy wave. Mr. Haze gave him a stern look, then went back to reading his book.

Chic thumbed through the cards quickly. He wasn't really sure where to start or what type of book he was looking for. He flipped the cards in the T drawer—*Taproot. Tarrytown. Tennessee.* He was looking for *temple.* His body was a temple; for some reason, that phrase stuck in his mind. He felt a tap on his shoulder.

He turned around, but no one was there. Then he noticed a girl looking up at him, a tiny girl with straight dark hair and feet the size of dinner rolls.

"Have you been drinking, sir?" She had a squeaky voice.

Of course he'd been drinking. In fact, if he had any beer left, he'd be out in his car right now still drinking. But he had no beer left, and besides, he was looking for something different, a book or something. This is what he wanted to tell her. He wanted to tell her other things, too. The baseball tryouts. Lomax. The death. His brother. Russ. Lijy. Dolls. Bowling. Everything. She could pull up a chair and they could have a conversation. He tried to talk to her, opening and closing his mouth like a fish, but the beer had stolen his voice.

"We don't allow intoxicated people in the library."

Chic looked around for something to write on. He had to tell her how he was feeling. He had to tell someone. His feelings wanted out. On a table were little squares of paper.

"I said you can't be here," she hissed at him. "You're drunk. I smell it."

Chic picked up a square of paper and wrote: *My life is nothing but a large hole in the ground I can't get out of.* He handed the piece of paper to the girl. She read it. It had a rhythm, and although it didn't have the right number of syllables, it was pretty close to a haiku. "Are you a poet?" she asked.

Chic had never been asked that question before. In fact, he'd never given that question an iota of thought. Chic Waldbeeser, a poet? Was she saying that he'd just written a poem? Maybe this was it. Poetry. He'd be a poet, and poetry—words—would chisel him out of the icy sadness that surrounded him.

The girl, whose name was Lucy Snell, had a thing for poets; she, herself, was trying to be one, and her boyfriend was trying to be one, too. They spent their Friday nights at One World Coffee in Peoria, near the Bradley campus, reading poems and hawking the poetry journal the two of them edited. She led Chic to the back of the library. It was quieter here, out of sight from the other patrons. The shelves reached the ceiling and were packed tight with books. She carefully picked out eight titles for him. "These two are good. And so is this one. Everyone needs to read Shakespeare's sonnets. Ginsberg's *Howl* is a must. You can only take eight out at a time," she said. "You'll have to come back for more. Oh, here's a good one. Emily Dickinson. I love Emily Dickinson."

Suddenly, not paying attention to titles or authors, Chic started grabbing books off the shelves and handing them to Lucy. The stack of books grew precariously tall in her hands, higher than her head, and she needed to peek around it to see him.

"You can only take out eight," she said.

"I have nothing. Nothing," he said, "and I need something. This might be it."

Maybe it was his admission that he had nothing and Lucy Snell's belief that poetry was the injection of "something," maybe it was because no one ever came into the Middleville Public Library looking for poetry, maybe it was the throw-me-a-rope look in his eyes; whatever it was, Lucy made an exception and let Chic check out forty-seven books of poetry. It took him four trips to carry them all to his car.

He slid into the driver's seat and picked up the first book, John Berryman's *77 Dream Songs*. He looked at the cover. He smelled the book. It smelled like it hadn't been opened in years. He liked the title, though. He could use a dream song. That's what he really needed right about now—dreams, some sleep. The beer had run its course. He reclined the seat and set the book aside. His eyes felt like they were being cranked shut. He'd get to the books in a little while. He closed his eyes. Everything went black.

One by one, people left the library. The sun set. The streetlights came on. Lucy Snell locked the front door and went through her closing routine. When she was done, she went outside, unlocked her ten-speed bicycle from the bike rack, and hopped on. She noticed a lone car in the far corner of the parking lot under a streetlight. She rode up to the car and saw Chic asleep in the driver's seat. Leaves blew around the parking lot. It was starting to get chilly. She circled around and came up to the driver's side door and knocked on the window.

Chic startled awake and saw Lucy looking at him.

"Are you all right?" she asked.

He rolled down the window.

"I'm fine. I have all these . . ." He motioned to the pile of books on the seat next to him. "My eyes got heavy, and I just closed them for a second. What time is it?"

"Almost eight."

"Oh, my gosh. My wife is going to be worried. We have bowling league tonight."

"I liked those words you wrote."

Chic cocked his head in confusion.

"In the library."

"Oh yeah, right." He took the scratch piece of paper out of his pocket and handed it to Lucy. "You can have it. It's yours."

"If you put a line break here after 'nothing' and another one after 'ground,' it's a haiku, or close to one."

"A haiku?" he said, accepting the piece of paper back from her.

"Take a look at that book there. Basho. He said haiku is what's happening in this place at this time."

Chic thought about that. He felt like so much was happening in this place and at this time.

"I publish a poetry chapbook with local poets. Mostly, it's just me and my boyfriend's poems, but we're always on the lookout for other work. Maybe, you know, if you don't mind, we could publish your haiku."

"This?" He held up the scrap of paper.

"Yeah. If you want us to."

"Other people are going to read this?"

"Well, yeah. A few other people. My boyfriend and his sister. And me. Maybe a few students at Bradley."

"Take it." He held the poem out to her. "Do whatever you want with it."

"Let me just . . . just a second." She got a notebook from her backpack and copied down the poem.

"You really think that poem is good?"

"It's heartfelt. Confessional. I like that kind of stuff. Hey, I need a bio for the chapbook. What do you want me to say about you? So, after someone reads the poem, they'll know a little more about you. Like, you know, who you are."

"A terrible father. Put that. Chic Waldbeeser was a terrible father."

"Really."

"I don't know. Who knows anymore?"

She put her notebook away. "Come back in a few weeks and I'll give you a copy of the chapbook."

In the rearview mirror, Chic watched Lucy ride across the parking lot. He liked what she had said about haiku being what was happening in this place and at this time. He put his fingers to his neck and felt his pulse—the thudding of the blood in his veins. He tried to center himself. Concentrating on his pulse almost always helped him do this, but he couldn't relax. It felt like he was running at the bottom of the ocean. Fish were watching him. A shark swam by. Diane would be waiting for him at home to go to the bowling alley. He re-read his haiku:

> *My life is nothing*
> *but a large hole in the ground*
> *I can't get out of.*

Mary Geneseo

■

June 24, 1998

Mary was in the minivan, staring at the house and the closed mini-blinds in the front window. She'd told Green she was going to the Brazen Bull and that she'd be home by six, and then they'd go to dinner at Avanti's or some other shitty Peoria restaurant. The loud voice in her head told her to run. Get out of Peoria. Go to Florida with Chic. Just turn the key, back out of the driveway, and drive away. If she stayed with Green, she was going to be stuck here. She would be trapped playing pool at the Brazen Bull, watching *Pretty Woman* alone after Green went to bed, slinging drinks at the Pair-a-Dice, wiping Green's ass, giving him a wash-cloth shower, and taking out the garbage for the rest of her life. Jesus, she hated this town. Hated it. *Hated it.* Do you really hate it or do you just hate what has become of your life here, the whisper voice asked. Flagstaff was bad, the loud voice said, waitressing at Chi-Chi's, but Peoria is even worse. The Pair-a-Dice. A hus-band who had a stroke. This is Muckville. What would happen to Green if you ran? the whisper voice asked. Who the hell cares about him, the loud voice said. Take care of yourself. He needs you, the whisper voice said, and you need him. You actually like taking care of him. That's horseshit, the loud voice said. You do *not* like taking care of him. Go to Florida with whatever his name is. Chic, the whisper voice said. His name is Chic, at least learn his name. She saw Green peek through the mini-blind. Green needs you like no one else has ever needed you. And you need him. You've always wanted someone to need you. Bullshit, the loud voice said. You want someone to take care of you. You don't want to take care of someone. Never the caregiver, always the cared for. Don't listen to that voice, the whisper voice said. It's the part of your mind trying to convince you to do something you don't want to do. You have run away your entire life. You haven't loved anyone but yourself your entire life, the loud voice said. Why start now? You loved your father, the whisper voice said, and the loud voice made you run away from him. Remember. You were eighteen, the loud voice said. It was the right thing to do. He was dating that woman and he was choosing her over you. Now look at you, the whisper voice said. You're still thinking, all these years later, if you did the right thing. What about all those men you ran from? You loved them but you were afraid. Don't be afraid. Just be with him. Be with Green. He needs you. She was right, or it was right, the whisper voice was right, she thought to herself. You're coming to your senses, the whisper voice said. Look at him peeking through the mini-blind, the loud voice said. He doesn't trust you. He thinks you're going to run. Trust is the most important part of a relationship, and he doesn't trust you. He said it himself. You saw it yourself. He's accusing you of having an affair. Because you are having an affair, the whisper voice said. You have to put an end to it. You can't be around Chic anymore. Tell him this afternoon. You met him for a reason, the loud voice said. Everything happens for a reason. Don't you believe that? I'm not leaving Green, she thought. He needs me. So does Chic, the loud voice said. Green peeked out the mini-blind again. She had to get going before he suspected something. He already suspects something, the loud voice said. Wave to him, the whisper voice said. She waved to him. Then, she started up the minivan and backed out of the driveway.

Diane & Chic Waldbeeser

■

October 1971–July 1972

A poet! This changed things, and Chic began to change. First, he started dressing the part, wearing a brown corduroy blazer over a black turtleneck. He found a black beret at a hat store in Peoria. He wore argyle socks. He grew a little sliver of hair under his lip; a "French beard," he called it. He also started carrying a notebook, in which he jotted down ideas or lines or simply words he wanted to use in his poems. He would sit on the couch in the living room with his legs crossed, wearing his blazer and beret, his notebook out and at the ready as he listened to Diane in the kitchen, doing the dishes or mopping the linoleum floor.

*My wife cleans and
cleans and cleans but she is
sad about her life.*

He began working on a book or, as Lucy Snell called it, a "chapbook." He spent hours at the kitchen table taking his ideas from his notebook and typing them into what he called "haikuetry." The poems were his feelings, his past, his life. He thought about the people who would read them. Diane. Lijy. (He actually didn't want to imagine her reading his poems. Then, again, he did want to imagine her reading them.) His brother. He wanted them all to be impressed. Poetry was his purpose, like Diane's father had said that night at dinner. Chic had thought being a brother was his purpose. Then, he thought fatherhood was. But now it was clear to him: poetry was his purpose.

One afternoon at the library, Lucy Snell gave him a copy of the chapbook with his published poem inside. He read the poem three times in front of her. Reading it made him feel whole, complete—accomplished. He was no longer a cannery worker. He was a poet. He asked Lucy who else had read the chapbook, and she told him that so far, only her, her boyfriend, Syd, his sister, Samantha, and him. And oh yeah, she almost forgot: Mr. Haze had taken a copy with him into the library's public restroom. Chic imagined Mr. Haze reading his poem. He had done terrible in his class in high school, but now he was a poet. That had to give Mr. Haze some satisfaction. How many of his students were poets?

When Chic got home, he read his poem to Diane, who told him it was very nice. He wasn't sure if she was listening to him. The radio was on. He started to read it again. "Shhhhh," she said. "I heard it the first time. It's nice, Chic. I'm listening to the radio." He told her he'd leave the chapbook for her so that she could read it later. A couple of days later, he found the chapbook in a pile of newspapers for him to carry out to the trash. He was livid.

He wanted to march upstairs and tell her that she was not—
not ever—to throw away his chapbook. Never. Never. Never. He
opened up the book, just to make sure his poem was still safe.
Next to the poem, Diane had written a note. *Chic, you're not a terrible father, and your hole is not as large as you think. You need to quit
feeling sorry for yourself. Remember, we're bowling tonight at 8 p.m.*

Over the next several months, as fall became winter and 1971
became 1972, Chic read every single book of poetry at the Middleville Public Library (and ordered the ones Lucy recommended
from the library in Peoria). Without a doubt, his favorite poems
were Basho's haikus. He also liked poems by the Beats. He hated
Shakespeare's sonnets—too much structure. A poem, Chic had
decided, should be sharp and refreshing like a pull of beer from a
cold can. He liked ones that hit him over the head and dropped
him to his knees, ones that yelled in his face. Whenever he read
a good poem, he felt the need to laugh. Sometimes when he was
reading in bed and Diane was sleeping, he'd start laughing. The
laughing would wake her up, and she would ask him what was so
funny. He laughed sometimes at Stafford's while thinking about
certain poems, or at work, or at the bowling alley. People would
ask him what was so funny, and he'd say, "Everything. What
you're doing right now. That's funny, if you think about it." He
was so grateful to Lucy Snell. Whenever he went to the library,
he grabbed her hand and thanked her. She blushed and told him
she was glad that she could share such a wonderful thing with
him. He told her about his chapbook. It was going to be called
Onward Toward What We're Going Toward, which was a line from
one of Bascom's letters that had always stuck with him. Lucy told
him that she couldn't wait to read it, but that the title was a bit
morbid. Chic told her it was intended to be funny. "We are all going toward the same thing," he said. "We're all marching into the
same battle, behind the same bugle player. Off the same cliff." He
also told her he was going to revise the poem she had published.
It was going to be the first one in his chapbook:

Our lives are nothing
but a deep hole in the ground
we can't get out of.

Some of the other poems were:

Florida is a long
way away in miles and in
memories.

And:

A heart is
a canister that holds more
than pain.

When Chic finished his chapbook there were twenty-seven poems in it. He dedicated it to Lomax. He typed up eight copies and took six to Stafford's, where he fashioned a stand out of a clothes hanger and propped it next to the magazines at the checkout. The cashier, a high school girl with a ponytail and braces, watched him.

"Want one?" Chic asked.

"What is it?" she asked, taking a copy from the makeshift stand.

"What I like to call haikuetry—haiku and poetry."

"Isn't haiku poetry?"

"Well, I don't always follow the haiku pattern."

"Wouldn't that just be poetry?" The cashier then read the last poem out loud:

Chic Waldbeeser
onward toward what you
are going toward.

"Who's Chic Waldbeeser?"

"Me."

"Are you leaving town or something?"

"No."

"Then where are you going?"

"I'm going toward what we're all going toward."

"But I don't know where you're going." She flipped through the chapbook, counting the syllables in the poems. "Aren't haikus five-seven-five?"

"I said I don't always follow the pattern." Chic snatched the book back. "Haiku is what's happening in this place at this time. And frankly, that can't always be contained to some stupid pattern. Do you know Lucy Snell?"

The cashier stared at him.

"The librarian. Up at the library."

She shook her head. "No."

"She published one of these. She and her boyfriend and her boyfriend's sister all have read it. And they liked it. Do you know who I am?"

"Chic Waldbeeser. You just told me your name."

"I'm a poet. Look at me. Look how I'm dressed."

"You're wearing a beret."

"Take this. Read it," Chic said. "Give me a dollar."

"Why?"

"For the chapbook."

"I don't really want it."

"Forget it. Don't give me a dollar. Just keep it. You should read more poetry. It's good for you. *Onward Toward What We're Going Toward.*"

"What does that mean exactly?"

"It means . . . how old are you?"

"Eighteen."

He placed his hand on hers, but she quickly pulled it away.

"Are you getting fresh with me?"

"Right now, at this moment, things are happening that you don't have any control over. There are cells in your body dividing and dying and being born. Right now. That's happening. Sometimes, in the morning, my urine is a very dark yellow. Do you think that's bad? I think that's bad. Maybe that means I'm going to die. At some point, I am going to die, and so are you, and that's scary as hell, but that's the easy part. You will do things that you're not proud of. Embarrassing things. Hurtful things. People will not like you. If you're lucky, someone will love you. You will disappoint that person. The same person who loves you may someday hate you and there's not a thing you can do about it. But you'll try. And you'll keep trying. All of this you probably already know. But, here's the hard part, this is the part that the poems are about, you won't be able to stop any of it. None of it. It has momentum, this life. Onward toward what we're going toward."

Thirteen

Mary Geneseo & Chic Waldbeeser

■

June 24, 1998

After the previous day's debacle in the back of the van, Chic was surprised when Mary called and asked him to go to lunch. Since she had given him a second chance, he had to impress her, had to show her he was "legitimate," the kind of guy a girl would want to be with. And what kind of guys did women want to be with? Well of course they wanted to be with guys who took them to nice places, places where there was a basket of breath mints on the bathroom sink counter. Chic knew of only one place where there was a basket of breath mints on the bathroom sink counter. Jim's Steakhouse was a Peoria institution, an old-school restaurant that served slabs of beef and refused to bring ketchup, A1, or barbeque sauce to the table. With its thick carpet and wood-paneled walls, the place looked like a set piece from a gangster movie. The bar area was dimly lit, even in the middle of a sunny afternoon, and the bartender wore a bowtie. Oh, and not only was Jim's the finest, most expensive (and most talked about) restaurant in Peoria, it also (and this was really why Chic wanted to take Mary there) boasted the world's largest antler chandelier.

Chic thought he should wear a suit, but his suit was in storage. He settled instead for his corduroy blazer and beret, his old poet uniform, and polished the alligator-skin loafers Mary had given him and stuffed the toes with wadded-up newspaper. She picked him up a little before one, and on the ride over, Chic yakked on and on about the antler chandelier, saying it was about twelve feet in diameter and looked like "a primitive spaceship." Most of what he said was made up, as he didn't really know much about antler chandeliers. Mary didn't seem interested, smiling and nodding and saying, "Uh-huh," and "Yeah," and "No kidding."

"Are you paying attention?" Chic asked her.

"Yeah, of course." The voices in her head were droning on endlessly. Run. Stay. Chic. Green. Run. Chic. Stay. Green.

"Have you seen one?"

"Seen what?"

"An antler chandelier."

"Oh, ah . . . maybe, those are those lights made out of deer horns?"

"Antlers, actually. And you're going to love this one, as it's the biggest one in the world. By the way, sorry about yesterday. It wasn't good, I know. There I said it. I had to say it. I feel better now."

He's apologizing, the loud voice said. He likes you. Go. Get on with your life. Pull a U-turn on this Peoria fiasco and go to Florida with this guy.

"What I was trying to tell you yesterday, and the reason I was having such a hard time was that . . . what I was trying to say was . . . I mean what I want to say . . ."

Jesus Christ, just come out with it already, the loud voice said. What did this guy do? It can't be much. He's a milquetoast for crying out load. Did he wash some darks with whites? Forget to put the toilet seat down? Mary looked at Chic and gave him her best forced sympathetic smile.

"My brother thinks I slept with his wife," Chic finally said. "I didn't though. I just said I did. I'm not that kind of guy. I don't cheat on people. Unless masturbation is cheating, which, I don't know, I think my wife thought it was, but anyway it kind of sounds stupid saying it out loud—I know. I was trying to help him. Now that sounds really stupid."

"Is this the restaurant?"

"Yeah. That's it." Across the street, valets wearing yellow polo shirts shuffled on the curb, waiting on customers. "Park in the garage, over there," Chic added. "So, as I was saying, I lied to my brother, and the kid—their son, his name is Russ. I've told you about Russ."

"Right. Russ. Russ and . . ."

"Ginger."

"Right."

"He thinks I'm his father."

She didn't remember him talking about Russ. Maybe he had, at some point. She gave him that fake smile again. "Russ," she said, "he lives in Arizona."

"No that's my brother. Russ lives here."

"Right. Russ is your brother's son. Teddy and Lily's son."

"Buddy and Lijy."

"Okay. Do you have money for parking?"

"I have money." Chic fished out his wallet. "As I was saying, I wish I wouldn't have done it, looking back on it. I did it for my brother. He needed me to do it, or I thought he did. Now, I don't know. My wife, she never really understood. She held a grudge. Not really an outward grudge, but it was there. I could feel it be-tween us. But we just kept . . . she locked herself in the bathroom the morning I told her. She did that a lot actually. Anyway then, our son died. I told you this."

"You did. A few times." She gave him that smile again.

"And we stayed together through it. We were married for thirty-five years. Something to be proud of, I guess. Anyway, my brother, who I did all of this for, he and Lijy moved away about ten years ago."

"Arizona."

"Right. They've been married almost fifty years, if you can be-lieve that. Fifty goddamn years. To the same person. I'd go crazy. Or, actually, that's not true. It's sorta admirable really, if you think about it. Do you ever think about that, being with someone for a long time like that?"

"Sure. Who doesn't?"

"I like to think I had something to do with them staying together. I don't talk to him much. Every once in a while Lijy calls me. I think she's just making sure I don't tell the truth to Russ. He still doesn't know. Which . . . anyway, I promised her I wouldn't tell anyone. But here I am telling you. It feels good, actually. I've never told anyone this, except Diane."

Whoa, wait a second, the whisper voice said, red flag: what kind of guy keeps a secret like this for so many years?

The maître'd showed them to a table in the middle of the restaurant directly under the antler chandelier, as had been Chic's request when he made the reservation. While Chic spread a napkin in his lap, he craned his neck to look up at the giant chandelier. It did look like the underside of a primitive spaceship. He liked to think it was a spaceship, like he was in a spaceship, like he was headed somewhere new, a new frontier. He liked Mary. He did. She was nice, the way she was smiling at him in the van. She was really listening. He was making a connection with her. He really was.

Mary looked up at the chandelier, too. "It just looks like a bunch of bones to me."

"Technically, its hair," Chic said. "Antlers are hair. Not bones. Or maybe it's the other way around, maybe horns are hair and antlers are bone." He picked up the menu but set it down immediately. "I know what I'm having. A rib eye steak and a baked potato. Don't tell me you're one of those salad girls."

"I don't know if I feel like steak."

"Well, I'm definitely having steak."

Mary shrugged and looked around the restaurant. Across from her was a man in a wheelchair. She stared at the guy, who was forking a piece of meat into his mouth, and was reminded of Green peeking out the blinds earlier that day. He was probably still at the window, waiting. The whisper voice said, You shouldn't be here. Nonsense, the loud voice said. You're sitting under the biggest antler chandelier in the goddamn world. The guy wants to buy you a steak. He's a nice guy, who obviously likes you. Give him your best forced sympathetic smile and order a goddamn steak. Laugh at his jokes and ogle the stupid antler chandelier like it's the most impressive thing you've ever seen.

Chic cleared his throat. "You okay?"

"Fine," she said. "I'm just taking in the scenery."

"I know I said I was sorry about yesterday . . . you know . . . but I was thinking, maybe after lunch, maybe . . . " He raised his eyebrows.

"Maybe what?"

"We could maybe . . . " He raised his eyebrows again.

"Go somewhere?"

"Yeah. Like, maybe, I don't know, a hotel room or . . . I don't know. That silo again."

"Maybe," she said.

"Right, maybe. Okay." Chic took the green duffel bag off his lap and put it on the table. He unzipped the top. Mary tried to get a peek inside, but all she saw was a mess of papers and what appeared to be Polaroid pictures. Chic took one out, a photo of a woman sitting in a rocking chair holding a doll. "This is my wife. Was my wife. Diane. She had a doll collection."

In the photo, Diane was looking down at the doll she was holding as if it were a real baby. Mary noticed she was a large woman, even bigger than she was.

"Here's another." In this picture, Diane and her girth were stuffed into black, lacy lingerie. She was making a Bettie Page pose, squatting flirtatiously, her hands on her knees, her chin on her shoulder. She looked happy. Content with her life. You could have that life, the loud voice said. You could be her.

Chic dug deep into the duffel bag and pulled out a letter. "My great-great-grandfather wrote this to his parents back in Germany in 18-something. My son translated it." He smoothed the paper out. There were phrases underlined in red ink, and Mary noticed that one—"onward toward what we're going toward"—had been circled.

The waiter appeared, and Chic stuffed the letter back in the duffel bag and placed the bag on the floor.

"Can I get you anything to drink?"

"A bottle of wine," Chic said proudly.

"It's the middle of the afternoon," Mary said.

"Red wine, please."

"Any particular type of grape?" The waiter picked up the wine list from the table and handed it to him. Chic knew nothing about wine and, in fact, had never ordered wine at a restaurant in his life. "Something French. French wine is supposed to be good." He looked over at Mary and winked. It hadn't occurred to her until that moment that he had brought her to this restaurant to impress her. She looked down at the Polaroid of Diane in her lingerie and slipped it into her purse without Chic noticing.

Chic ordered the rib eye, and Mary, in the end, decided to ride the afternoon like a parade float and ordered steak, too, the filet mignon wrapped in bacon. Instead of a baked potato, she had pommes frites, which, the waiter told them, were French fries, but she already knew that. Chic then changed his order from a baked potato to pommes frites. As soon as the waiter walked away, Chic sat back in his chair and looked across the table at Mary. He felt his attraction to her starting to take root. Hell, he'd just ordered a fifty-eight-dollar bottle of wine. Hopefully all of this would pay off, and he could get her to Florida. The two of them could stay in a place like the Seashell Inn, maybe one of those motels with the beds that shook and vibrated. They could close the shades and do the things that he and Diane did when they were on their honeymoon. They'd have fancy dinners, and order wine and pommes frites. They'd go to an orange grove and pick oranges. They'd sit in sun chairs and rub sunscreen on each other's back.

"I went to Florida on my honeymoon," Chic said. "That's why I want to go there. In case you were wondering why I keep asking you to go there."

This wasn't the first time she'd been with a guy who wanted to relive something. What was it with guys wanting to do things they'd already done, like doing it a second time would make it better? The whisper voice sighed and told her she should march out of that restaurant and back to Green and clean off his mouth with a washcloth and push his wheelchair in front of the television and take care of him all afternoon. Mary picked up a roll from the bread basket and tore it in half, then smiled as Chic told her about Buddy's cookbook, which was really part cookbook and part meditation on life. It was also a memoir. It was also about their father. It wasn't finished, and it might never be finished. He told her that his father had frozen himself to death behind a barn. He said it was best if he didn't talk about that anymore or even think about it. The wine arrived. Chic tasted it. He was more of a beer drinker he told her. He told her about his mother. She'd run off to Florida with Tom McNeeley when Chic was nineteen, and he'd never forgiven her. He told her again about taking the blame for Lijy's infidelity, and about Lomax's drowning. He told her about taking the blame for Lijy's infidelity again. Even after the waiter put their plates on the table and wished them bon appétit, Chic continued to talk. He talked with his mouth full. He took gulps of red wine and talked some more. He said that he wished they had barbeque sauce because he preferred his steak with barbeque sauce. He poured himself more wine. He poured her more wine. Mary smiled. She scanned the restaurant. The man in the wheelchair was being pushed out by a younger woman, his daughter perhaps. Chic said something about poetry, that he could have been a great poet but he didn't have the mental focus. After that, she didn't hear a word of what he said. She thought about Green, sitting at the window, looking out over the street. The loud voice said, Why are you thinking about Green? Focus. This guy is pouring his heart out to you. You want him to like you. Make him like you. She picked up her wineglass and tuned Chic back in. He was talking with his mouth open, laughing, and saying how much fun he was having. She smiled.

"I haven't had this much fun since . . . I don't think I've ever had this much fun. You know why I'm having such a good time?"

"Why?"

"Because I'm being honest with you. I'm telling you everything, and you're listening. You care."

"Cheers." She held her wineglass out for him to clink.

"And what about you?" he asked, leaning back in his chair. He'd finished his steak. He took the napkin that he'd tucked into his collar and crumpled it up. "I don't feel like I know you at all, but I feel like we're making a connection. I see you looking at me. I saw the way you looked at me at the Pair-a-Dice before we met. I felt it then. Like you were pulled to me. Like you were, like I was, like both of us were meant to be sitting here in this restaurant right now. I like you. I don't know if it's too soon to say that. But I do. I like you, Mary . . ."

She smiled. "Geneseo."

"Like the town?"

"What town?"

"Geneseo, Illinois. Ha. There is a God, and he's having a great time messing with us."

She had no idea what he was talking about, but she knew he'd fallen for her. She'd seen this before. "Well," she said. She could open up like he had opened up. She was on the verge. She felt it. If she quit thinking for a second, she could gush like an open fire hydrant. But then she remembered Green. "Can I show you something?" she said.

"Sure."

"Not here. Somewhere else."

"Oh. Like the silo."

"Something like that. A little different, though."

Chic spotted the waiter on the other side of the restaurant. He put his hands in the air and did that thing he had seen on television where people write in the air like they're signing the check.

Chic Waldbeeser

◼

July 18, 1972

So what if some stupid cashier at Stafford's didn't understand his poetry! A lot of people didn't understand poetry, and that was part of its appeal. Lucy Snell would understand it. He had waited a long time to do something he could share with the world. Sure, he had created Lomax, but the world had been unforgiving. Now, finally, round two. Diane walked into the kitchen and saw him holding up the stapled pages. He'd drawn a star in the center of the cover page, and under the star he'd written the title, *onward toward what we're going toward*, in all lowercase letters, like the poetry of E.E. Cummings.

"Is that where we're going—to the stars?" Diane asked.

Chic hadn't really considered the correlation. He'd simply drawn the star because the page had looked empty. "Right. Yeah. That's what it means."

"I didn't know you believed in heaven."

"I don't. Or, I don't know." His beret was sitting on the table and he put it on his head and slipped on his corduroy blazer and snatched the keys off the counter. "I'll be back."

"Where are you going?"

"The library."

At the circulation desk, an elderly librarian told him that Lucy would be with him in a moment. She stamped a due date and handed a book to a woman, who kept staring at Chic like she'd never seen a grown man wearing a beret. He couldn't wait to show Lucy the chapbook. Her boyfriend would probably want to read it, too. She might have friends who would be interested. Then he saw her, across the library, shelving books. He didn't even bother to tell the elderly librarian he'd found her.

"Lucy," he said loudly, "I did it."

A couple of people looked up from their books and shushed him.

"This is a library, sir," the elderly librarian called after him.

Chic zigzagged his way among the reading tables. When he reached her, he held out the stapled together pages. "My own chapbook."

The elderly librarian came up behind him. "I don't know how many times I need to tell you, Lucybelle. No visitors."

"I'm not a visitor," Chic said. "I'm a poet."

"You're Chic Waldbeeser. I know who you are. Your brother opened that weird store on Main Street. And she, Lucybelle, has a visitor almost every single day."

"My boyfriend," Lucy said.

"I don't care who it is. It's against the rules. No visitors until your break."

"I can wait over here." Chic pointed to an empty table.

"I don't care where you wait as long as you don't talk to her while she's working."

"I go to lunch in half an hour," Lucy said.

For the next half hour, Chic sat at a table in the middle of the library and watched Lucy shelve books. He could hardly contain himself. Someone who actually knew poetry was going to read his chapbook. She was going to love the poems. She was his mentor, or was it muse? She was his mentor and his muse. Actually, she wasn't really his muse, just his mentor. She lit his fire, but that would be something like his muse. None of the poems were about her. But he found her cute. He stole a glance at her. She was cute. He realized it had been several days since he had last masturbated. He looked over at the bathrooms. He looked at his watch. She was going on break in a few minutes.

Lucy finished shelving and pushed the empty book cart to the circulation desk. He jumped up and followed her. He practically shoved the chapbook into her hands.

She took it to an empty table, and he followed her again and sat down across from her.

"Do you like the title?"

"Yeah. It's good. It reminds me of a Flannery O'Connor title." She opened to the first poem. Chic studied her face as she read it, looking for a reaction. He couldn't tell if she liked it or not. "Did you like that one?"

She smiled at him, then turned the page and read the next poem. She wiped her nose; she chewed on her thumbnail. She turned to the third poem.

"How was that one?"

"It's probably easier if you don't ask me if I like every poem."

"You want me to move? I can move."

"If you don't mind. That way I can concentrate."

Chic moved to an empty table and opposite a teenage girl who was reading a book. He kept trying to watch Lucy but had a hard time seeing around the girl; she was big, and when she read, she rocked back and forth. "She's reading my poems," he whispered to the girl. She smiled at him, then went back to reading and rocking.

When Lucy finished, Chic jumped up and snaked his way back to her table. He sat down across from her.

"So . . . ?"

She started to chew on her thumbnail.

"What'd you think? Did you like them?"

"I really like the energy. And the title, as I said."

"I was going for the way people talk. You know, how when someone just starts to talk and pretty much just runs at the mouth without really thinking about what they're saying."

"I get that. So, why are you trying to evoke that?"

"Because that's the way people talk."

She nodded her head. "I'm not sure what you're saying with these poems. There's some nihilism, some self-hatred, some awe, some confession, some plagiarism. There are all sorts of different things happening. It's kind of all over the place. Let me ask you something. What's your relationship to other people?"

"My relationship is fine with other people."

"What's your relationship like with your wife."

He shrugged. "We've been married for twenty-two years."

"You have this one poem . . ."

"I know which one you're talking about."

"It doesn't portray her very well."

"I was afraid of that. I think maybe I should change it."

"Is it honest?"

"Maybe."

"So you think your wife is overweight?"

"She eats a lot."

"What about your brother and his wife? I get this feeling that you're infatuated with your brother's wife."

"No, no. I'm not infatuated with her. That's . . . no. I'm not."

"Are you being honest?"

He thought about the question. "I don't covet my brother's wife."

"Do you want to have sex with her?"

"What kind of question is that?"

"Do you wish you had more sex?"

"I have sex."

"There's a longing to have sex in almost every single poem."

"How did you get that? I don't ever use the word sex."

"Also, it's unclear what you think about the people in these poems."

"I love the people in these poems."

"It doesn't seem like it. Well, actually, Lomax. You love Lomax. That's clear. And maybe Lijy, but it's more of a desire than love, per se. But the other people—your brother and your wife, mainly. There's this disconnect between you and them. It's like you don't understand them, and you don't think they understand you."

"Just tell me. Do you like the poems or not? Are they any good?"

She put her hand on top of Chic's hand. Chic looked down at it. Her nails were painted red. She had a ring on every finger, including her thumb. He looked up and locked eyes with her.

She was making a pass at him. Was she making a pass at him? She was making a pass at him. He smiled slightly. She smiled slightly back at him. She was definitely making a pass. She liked his poems. He could tell. She really liked his poems. He could feel himself being pulled into her eyes. She had the brownest eyes he'd ever seen. He wasn't really sure if he'd ever been in a moment like this. He could be in this moment forever. He didn't want it to end. But then it did. She pulled her hand away.

"Did you feel that?" she said.

"Yeah, I felt it."

"That was a connection. I was making a connection with you. I have a boyfriend, by the way. That was just pretend."

"Oh, yeah. I know. Me too. I was pretending too. Practicing. It's good to practice those things."

"You were looking at me like you were about to kiss me."

"I wasn't going to kiss you."

"I have a boyfriend."

"You said that."

"So, I'm going to get back to work."

"Yeah. You should. The librarian ... she's probably looking for you."

Lucy stood up.

"Oh, hey." He held out the chapbook to her. "I want you to have this. Thank you for reading it. I don't think anyone really actually read it. I gave it to my wife, but ... anyway ... thanks."

"Good luck, Mr. Waldbeeser."

"Chic. Call me Chic."

"Good luck, Chic."

Chic Waldbeeser

■

July 18, 1972, two hours later

Chic couldn't stop thinking about the moment he had shared with Lucy. It had lasted only a few seconds, but during that flickering fraction of time, he had felt so locked into her, so drawn to her, like he was in some sort of trance or something, like her eyes were magnets that were pulling him toward her. He wanted to capture that feeling in a poem. How could he capture that feeling? He needed to find the right words. The telephone rang. He looked at it. He knew Diane wasn't going to answer it. From upstairs, he could hear the voice of Norman Vincent Peale. He wasn't going to answer it, either. It was probably Diane's mother, or worse, someone from the bowling league. The phone continued to ring. Diane yelled for him to answer it. He put down his pencil and went to the phone.

It was Stan Landry, the owner of Stafford's. He wanted Chic to pick up his chapbooks. What did Chic think Stafford's was, a bookstore? Besides, he'd sold only one—to Diane—and also and more importantly, the book hadn't really been published. It was just a bunch of pages stapled together.

"Wait. Diane bought one?" Chic said.

"Two days ago. Another was stolen, I think. There are four left. Didn't you drop off six?"

"I gave one to a cashier," Chic said.

"Well, then, come pick these four up, please? Or I can throw them away."

Stan met Chic in the parking lot. He was dressed in a brown leisure suit, polka-dot tie, and horn-rimmed glasses. His hair was carefully messy, and he had a giant, blond mustache. He took a long look at Chic, up and down, seemingly making note of the beret and corduroy blazer.

"Want some advice, Waldbeeser?"

What did Stan know that he didn't? He hadn't gone to college or anything. He had just graduated from high school and gone to work for his father. And, in fact, in high school, Stan had been good at math and everyone made fun of him because of that, but no one remembered Stan Landry the kid everyone made fun of because he was good at math; they knew him only as the son of the owner of Stafford's, and apparently this gave him the right to offer advice.

Stan shook out a Pall Mall cigarette and offered one to Chic. Chic thought hard about taking it. In time, if the road kept this course, then, yeah, cigarettes, but for now, he'd hold off. (And besides, Diane wouldn't like it.) Stan lit his cigarette with some sort of fancy Zippo trick. He took a long drag, then waved his hand in front of Chic like he was conducting an orchestra. "Look at yourself. You're wearing a beret."

"I like the beret."

"Have you ever seen anyone wear a beret in Middleville? This is the Midwest. Illinois. A small town. Look around. We have farm acreage within the city limits. Tractors drive down the street. There are no poets here. The kids don't even study poetry in high school. We didn't study poetry in high school."

"We did a unit on poetry," Chic said.

"Yeah, well, but we were snickering in the back of the room."

"How do you know I'm not a poet?"

"I read those poems. Trust me. You're not."

"So, is that your advice?"

"Look, Waldbeeser, what are you, forty? You have twenty-some years left at the cannery. Don't rock the boat. Just fit in. Play the part. Put in your time. Hug your wife when you need to. Then, I don't know, do what your mom did—go down to Florida and retire. Sit on the benches and watch people ride by on bikes."

"My mother didn't retire to Florida. She ran away with Tom McNeeley."

"Wasn't he a janitor at Blessed Sacrament?"

"That's him."

"Look. Shave that little bit of hair under your lip. You look ridiculous. And your brother. His health food store. What happened to you guys?"

"What's this have to do with my brother?"

"Nothing. Forget it."

At home, Chic found Diane upstairs in the nursery. She was in the rocking chair, cradling a doll. It was a good thing Stan Landry didn't know about this. Or maybe he did. Chic took off his blazer and hung it on the doorknob. He took off his beret, threw it on the floor, and stomped on it.

"What are you doing?" Diane asked.

"Stan Landry offered me some advice, and I think he's right."

"What sort of advice?"

"He said I wasn't a poet, and other things. I have a question for you. Why won't you have sex with me?"

"I have sex with you."

"Ha. We haven't had sex in, I don't know, a long time."

"Chic, I feel sorry for you."

"For me? Don't feel sorry for me. I'm fine. I'm perfect. I'm living my life. I feel sorry for you."

Diane gave him a hard stare, and Chic thought maybe she knew something he didn't know.

"What?"

"Nothing."

"Tell me."

"Chic, I know you're masturbating in the bathroom."

"What are you talking about—masturbating in the bathroom? Are you kidding? That's not true. That simply isn't true. I am not masturbating in the bathroom."

"I hear you. Grunting."

"You what . . . grunting?"

"Like every day. Sometimes twice a day."

"Well. I can't believe you're listening to me masturbate."

"And I know you're sneaking beers and hiding the crushed cans in the garbage."

"That's . . . how do you . . . did you find the cans?"

"Chic, we need to move forward, move on, change, grow up. Onward toward what we're going toward. Like the title of your poems."

Chic picked up the beret. "Did Stan Landry say something to you?"

"No."

"He did."

"No, he didn't."

"We used to make fun of Stan Landry because he was good at math. In your dad's class. You remember that?"

"What's that have to do with anything?"

"This has not been helpful. You know, I came to you because I was upset, and you made me more upset."

She tried to snatch the beret away.

"Don't!"

"Give it to me."

"I want it. It's mine."

She let go.

He put the beret on his head and walked out of the room.

"Quit using all my lotion when you masturbate," she called out after him.

Diane & Chic Waldbeeser

■

July 22, 1972

It was Wednesday night, and like every Wednesday night for the past year, Chic and Diane went bowling at Middleville Lanes. A haze of smoke hung from the ceiling like a low-hanging cloud. Chic noticed the smoke every week, and every week, he wondered why no one else noticed it, or if they did, why they didn't seem to mind.

Diane shook her ball out of her pink bowling bag, while Chic picked a community ball, a nine pounder with holes that didn't squeeze his fingers. He sat down at the scorer's table and watched Diane laughing with a few of the women on their team. A couple of the guys shook Chic's hand. One guy bought him a bottle of beer. He saw Diane looking at him. How long had she known he was sneaking beers at home? He should have stored the cans in the trunk of the car and ditched them in the Dumpster at work.

The guy keeping score, Mitch Watkins, told Diane she was up. Chic and Diane had gone to high school with all the people in the league. They lived in houses not far from the houses they had grown up in. They had kids who would someday most likely end up in a similar Wednesday night bowling league. Stan Landry and his wife were in the far lane. Stan made eye contact with Chic and pointed to his head—Chic had worn his beret. Stan wagged his finger. Stan's wife threw her ball and got a strike. She leapt into Stan's arms and gave him a big hug. Chic was up next. He picked up the ball and without really thinking, rolled it down the lane. It picked off one pin in the far right corner before clunking into the gutter.

"Good try, Chic," Mitch said.

"Pick up the spare now. Come on," someone said.

Chic waited at the ball return. He watched Diane. She was talking to Leslie Soderstrom, and they were both laughing. What did they have to be laughing about? This wasn't fun. His ball came back. He picked it up. He aimed. He took three steps and rolled the ball down the lane, knocking down seven pins. An eight in the first frame.

"Get 'em next time, Chic," someone said.

Stan Landry and his wife clinked their beer bottles together, still celebrating her strike. Chic walked up to Diane and held his beer up to her so that he could clink it against the glass of water she was drinking, but Diane looked at him like she didn't know what he wanted her to do. He sat down. Ever since Diane had told him she knew he was masturbating, he kept picturing her standing outside the locked bathroom door listening to him. Or, maybe, when she was lying in bed listening to Dr. Peale, the sounds of his masturbation wafted through the heating vents. Whatever, Chic told himself that he was just biding time until she was ready to have sex again. Masturbation was like a warm up lap, like knee bends before a big race. It was a way to keep loose and focused. Who was he kidding? It was pathetic. And look at Diane over there, laughing and having a good time, drinking her glass of water, laughing again, slapping her knee. He needed to quit lying to himself. He needed to be honest with himself. You need to be honest with yourself, he told himself. Your life is not the life that you wanted to live. Whoa, that was direct. But it felt pretty good. He tried it again. You're mad at your father for committing suicide. You blame your mother for it. You hate her for leaving you. Your son died. You blame yourself for that. You masturbate in the bathroom every day. Your son probably knows that you masturbate in the bathroom. Your father, too. Actually, that made him feel small, imagining that dead people knew what he did. Maybe he was being too honest. This wasn't really working, come to think of it. He didn't want to be honest. He wanted to put the lid on these thoughts, he wanted to live in a cloud of smoke like all of the people here at the alley and not notice that he was living in a cloud of smoke. Next to him, a cigarette smoldered in an ashtray. He picked it up and took a drag. He coughed. Diane made a nasty face. The guy sitting next to him, Larry Stevenson, whose cigarette he'd picked up, looked at him.

"I didn't know you smoked," Larry said.

"I don't." Chic handed the cigarette to him and stood up.

"Hey, where are you going? You're almost up."

"Bathroom."

On his way to the bathroom, he stopped at the bar and bought two beers. In the bathroom stall, he guzzled them both. He thought of Diane out there laughing—all of them, Stan Landry, his wife, the people he had gone to school with, every single one of them, laughing. At the end of the night, they'd get in their cars and drive home, where they'd laugh some more. In the morning, in the afternoon, and at night when they watched television, they'd laugh some more. Weren't these people depressed and sad and overwhelmed with their existence? Didn't they know there was a war going on? People were dying in the jungle in Southeast Asia. People were dying everywhere. Someone came into the bathroom. The person was whistling. He wanted to take that whistling and shove it right down the guy's throat. The guy burped. He unzipped his fly. He was in the stall next to Chic. The guy did his business and Chic listened to the tinkle of urine in the toilet water. This was what it had come to—sneaking beers in a bowling alley bathroom and listening to people piss. The guy in the next stall finished up and washed his hands and left the bathroom, whistling again on his way out. Chic put the bottle to his lips and finished off the beer, swishing the last drop in his mouth and letting it roll on his tongue and down his throat. He wiped his mouth with the back of his hand. Someone else came into the bathroom. He held still.

"Chic?" It was Diane. Oh, Jesus. What was she doing in here? "I know you're in that stall, Chic. I can see your shoes. I know you're drinking beer. I saw you buy it."

He didn't say anything.

"Quit feeling sorry for yourself," she said, then left the bathroom. He was alone, holding two empty beer bottles. Had his wife just come into the men's bathroom to tell him to quit feeling sorry for himself? He wasn't feeling sorry for himself. He was feeling sorry for her, for them, for the bowlers, the people, all of them. He was feeling sorry for how they didn't even notice what was obviously right in front of their goddamn noses.

When he got back to the lanes, he took out his notebook and flipped to an empty page. Everyone was watching him, but he didn't notice. He tried to write a line, but his mind was a blank. He closed his eyes. He wanted to capture what he was feeling in a poem. He wanted to frame it so it could be hung on a wall, so others could look at his feelings and understand him. He wanted to hand the poem to Diane and say, "Here. This is how I'm feeling. Read this. Right here. This is me. My innermost feelings walking right into your imagination."

"You can shatter glass with your concentration, Waldbeeser," Mitch said.

Chic looked up. Everyone was staring at him.

"It's your turn."

"Oh, sorry." He smiled. He got up and bowled a seven. He sat back down. He looked at a cigarette smoldering in the ashtray next to him. He thought about Diane coming into the bathroom. He couldn't tell if that had really happened or if he just thought it had happened. He didn't really know how much he had had to drink. His head felt stretched out like a balloon with too much air. He felt a little bit different, older somehow, or actually, that wasn't quite right. He felt like he'd already finished a book that everyone else was just starting, and he knew how everything was going to end.

On the way home, he wasn't paying attention and drove past their house.

"You just passed our house," Diane said.

Chic slammed on the brakes. He backed up and pulled into the driveway.

"You don't like bowling league, I know. I can tell, but to-night—were you drawing a horse in your notebook?"

"No."

They both got out of the car and stood in the driveway. It was dark. The crickets chirped.

"Don't you notice?" he said.

"Notice what?"

"The bowling alley. The smoke. There's this cloud of smoke that hangs over everything."

"What do you expect? It's a bowling alley. People are smoking."

"It's hard to breathe."

"What are you talking about Chic?"

"The bowling alley."

"No you're not. You're talking about something else."

He sighed. "I can't go on like this. I can't. I won't. It's not natural."

"Maybe you shouldn't come to the bowling league anymore."

"I'm in this hole. This big deep hole that I can't get out of."

"You need to stop feeling sorry for yourself."

"Why? Why do I need to stop feeling sorry for myself? Why is that so bad? Everyone feels sorry for themselves."

"Keep your voice down. We have neighbors."

"Why do you think I'm masturbating in the bathroom?" he whispered.

She shrugged. "Desiring other women?"

"Other women? No."

"Not this again. Please. A baby isn't going to change anything."

"Let's just have sex for the sake of having sex. For fun. People do that, you know."

She stormed off into the house. He followed after her. She was going towards her old bunker, the bathroom, and he headed her off. She did an about-face and went up the stairs and into the nursery and slammed the door. Chic pushed it open.

"Do you know how long it's been since we've had sex?"

"July 1, 1964. It was morning. Independence Day. You had the day off work."

"You remember the date?"

She left the nursery and crossed the hall to their bedroom. Chic followed. "A good man is hard to find," he said. "I'm a good man, Diane, but you know what? A good woman is even harder to find. Think about that, will you."

She turned to him. "Chic, sometimes, you know . . . I'm hurting too. Just like you. Do you think I like bowling? I don't. But what else are we going to do? We're stuck, and I'm tired of feeling sorry for myself. I'm tired of it."

Chic kicked off his shoes. "Get undressed." He pulled his shirt over his head.

"No."

"Go with it. Go with the moment."

"I'm not going to have sex with you."

"Remember Florida. How I seduced you. How I kissed your entire body. Your feet. Your legs, and how I sucked on your toes and licked your earlobes and how you giggled. Remember how I nuzzled into your neck. How we batted our eyelashes together. How I smelled your stomach. How I whispered 'I love you' into your ear. Remember. That bed. That room. We had seafood for dinner and we were one. One. We were connected. It was beautiful."

"That's not what happened."

"Oh, it's what happened. We made Lomax that night. I think about it every single day."

"Chic, I took advantage of you in Florida."

"You did not. We connected in Florida."

"I whipped you with your belt. I made you shut off the lights."

Chic thought about this. The haze of his memory began to lift. He recalled what had really happened that night. It was buried down deep, back in the hollows of his memory where the floor was concrete and cold. He put two fingers to his neck and felt the blood thumping through his veins. He closed his eyes, then opened them. It all flooded in on him. She was mad at him because of Lijy, and locked herself in the bathroom. There wasn't any cuddling. There weren't any nuzzle kisses or pecks on the cheek. It was quick and he had no idea what he was doing and afterward she pushed him off of her and picked her panties off the floor and went into the bathroom. He'd sandbagged the real memory, changed it, tried to erase it by building a new memory on top of it, a false one, a lie. He was about to cry. His bottom lip started to quiver.

Chic Waldbeeser

■

July 22–23, 1972

Chic sat on the couch in the dark living room, his mind replaying and looping. His entire relationship, his entire marriage, his "love" for Diane, was built on lies and false memories. His fingers tracked the throbbing in his neck. He couldn't sleep. At some point, very late, around two in the morning, Diane came to the top of the stairs and whispered for him to come to bed. He didn't say anything, then listened as she padded back down the hallway to the bedroom and shut the door. The sun began to blue up the sky a few hours later. It was Thursday. He called work and said he wouldn't be coming in. Diane came downstairs and made coffee. She asked if he wanted any. He did not. She went back upstairs, and he heard Peale's voice on the radio. What was the big deal about this guy? He put on his beret and corduroy jacket. He should go see his brother. He was the only person he knew who had pieced together his life after a major setback.

He parked in front of Middleville Community Bank, directly across the street from the health food store. He dug out binoculars from under the seat. Inside the store, Buddy was wearing a maroon toga robe. He looked ridiculous. A lady took a container of yogurt from the cooler and paid for it. She left. Russ came out from behind the beaded curtain. He had a bowl haircut and was wearing striped athletic socks pulled up to his knees. He sat down on the floor to examine a potted parsley plant. Chic remembered that Buddy still thought that he was Russ's father. Another lie. Chic lowered the binoculars and remembered the afternoon of his father's suicide, sitting in his room, on his bed, staring at his brother's shut door, waiting for it to open, waiting for his brother to come for him, to sit next to him on the bed, to put his hand on his leg, to put his arm around him, to hug him, to make him feel better—to do anything. But when his brother's bedroom door opened, he only made it worse. He told him their mother was having an affair with Tom McNeeley.

Inside the health food store, Russ plucked a sprig of parsley and ate it. Buddy laughed and came around the counter. Russ started laughing, too. Then Lijy came through the beaded curtain.

She walked slowly, haltingly, her stomach swollen. It was obvious she was several months pregnant. She started laughing as well. Chic threw the binoculars down on the passenger seat. He suddenly felt very cold, even though it was the middle of summer. The inside of the car began to spin. He took a deep breath. He closed his eyes. He had a choice—to keep living the lie, or start living the truth. An idea came to him. It was perfect. All he needed was an hour. One hour. All of this would be behind him in an hour.

He started the car and stepped on the gas, squealing out of the parking spot. He sped through town and got onto the interstate, heading toward Peoria at eighty miles per hour, cutting off several other cars along the way. (One driver shook his fist at Chic.) When he reached Bergner's, he pulled up in front of the store—ignoring the parking lot—and shut off the engine. He took the binoculars with him. He banged into a woman coming out of the store, nearly knocking her over. Once inside, he looked right, left. In each direction were racks of women's clothes. He put the binoculars to his eyes. He scanned the store. Nothing. He spotted an employee folding pants at a display and ran up to her. She was older, with gray hair, and wore a pantsuit.

"Where are the dolls?"

Without looking up, she pointed toward the back of the store.

Chic trained the binoculars in the direction she was pointing. "I don't see them." He turned the binoculars on the woman.

"Why are you looking at me with those things?"

"I can't stand to see reality for what it is. It's ugly. Where are the dolls?"

She pointed toward the back of the store again.

"You know what? You're not helpful. No one is. We're in this alone. All of us. My father died. My son died, too. And do you know what? There's nothing I can do about it. That's the truth."

"I'm sorry."

"No you're not. No one is sorry. We say it but we don't mean it. What we mean is, 'I'm glad it didn't happen to me.'"

"I'm just trying to make you feel better."

"You can't. And that's the problem. Now, tell me, the dolls?"

When Chic burst into the house an hour later, Diane was upstairs in the bedroom. He was carrying a shopping bag from Bergner's, and the binoculars dangled from around his neck. He was grinning and sweating.

"Turn off the goddamn radio and get down here," he yelled.

"Chic, you know not to interrupt me when I'm . . ."

"Get down here!"

The radio clicked off, and a few seconds later, Diane came down the stairs.

"I bought you a present." He put his hand into one of the bags. "It's in here somewhere. Hold on. Wait a second. Here it is."

Diane noticed that what he took out of the bag was still on a hanger and small, like a dishrag, maybe smaller. He put it behind his back.

"Guess which hand."

"Chic, I don't want to guess."

"Guess."

"I don't want to."

"Will you just guess?"

"The right."

"Nope. The left." Then he revealed his gift—a pair of stringy, black underwear. "I got medium, but they look, I don't know—maybe they'll be a little tight, but that's the point, I guess."

"Chic . . ."

"I don't know why I didn't think of this earlier. Look at these. I mean . . . if these don't put you in the mood . . ."

"I've gone through menopause. A little early. The doctor said. Who cares what the doctor said. I've gone through menopause early."

Chic looked at the underwear. He looked at his wife. She was a long way from that delicate high school girl she used to be. "Menopause?"

"That's when women stop having their . . ."

"I know what it is." He sat down on the coffee table.

"Are you going to pass out? You look pale."

He set the lingerie down and put his fingers to his neck. He'd tried, but now it was official. Nature was taking its course, and he was stuck in the eye of the storm. Everything was crashing around him.

"We're going to get past this, Chic. We just need to change our attitude. It's just going to take a little effort, but we can do it."

"Do you believe that?"

"I want to believe it. Imagination is the true magic carpet."

"Did you come up with that?"

"No, that's Dr. Peale."

He took out his notebook.

"So, are you going to be all right?"

He put his fingers on his neck. "I haven't passed out yet."

She smiled. "Remember when I told you I was pregnant?"

"I do."

"You got ice cream all over the carpet."

Chic smiled. He looked up at her. "Diane, I'm sorry."

"I'm sorry, too."

"I'm truly sorry."

"Me too."

"I really am. I didn't . . . I mean . . . who would have known . . . it's just that . . . you know . . . how could we have . . . it's just . . . I guess . . . I'm sorry."

"I know you are."

"I'm very truly sorry."

"I know."

He stared at her, trying to lock eyes. She looked away. He waited for her to look back at him. When she did, he made an intense, squinty face, trying to lock eyes again.

"Why are you looking at me like that?" she asked.

"I'm sorry."

"Quit looking at me like that. What are you doing?"

"I'm sorry."

"Chic, please."

"I'm trying to make a connection with you."

"You're overdoing it."

"I'm sorry."

"Stop it."

Fourteen

Mary Geneseo & Chic Waldbeeser

June 24, 1998

Mary parked the minivan across the street from a tiny brick bungalow surrounded by oak trees and giant Bradley frat houses. Chic figured this was where she lived. The bungalow reminded him of the house on Edgewood Street where he had lived all those years with Diane. It looked lonely and sad. He could hear Peale preaching on the radio and imagine Diane sprawled out in bed, eating cookies dipped in peanut butter.

"What are we doing here?" he asked.

Mary didn't answer. She was lost in thought, the voices screaming at her. "Shut up," she whispered. "Just shut up."

"I'm sorry. You brought me here."

"Nothing. Not you. Come on." She got out of the minivan and hurried across the street.

Chic slid out of the passenger door and followed her across the street. In the front yard, she crouched down next to a tree. She stood up and hurried across the yard and around the side of the bungalow. Chic trailed after her, cradling the duffel bag close to his chest. They huddled against the side of the house. He was out of breath.

"What are we doing?" he asked. Rock 'n' roll music—whining electric guitars—blasted from a third-floor window next door. Two co-eds passed on the sidewalk and didn't notice them in the side yard.

"Follow me. Stay down." Mary crept along the house, avoiding the basement window well and a coiled garden house. She reached the rear of the house, where she sat with her back against the bricks. Chic sat down, too, and tried to feel his pulse in his neck, but Mary knocked his hand away. "What are you doing?"

"Taking my pulse."

"You're not dying. You're fine. It's him." She motioned toward a window directly above them.

Chic looked up. All he could see was a cloud of gnats swarming above their heads.

"Look!"

"What are we doing?"

"Just look, will ya."

Chic periscoped his head through the cloud of gnats, so he could see into the sunporch that overhung the backyard. Sitting on the porch was Mary's husband. He didn't look at all like what Chic had expected. Instead of a big, burly guy with hands like a railroad worker's, he was older—about Chic's age—and rail thin like a slice of lunch meat, with a head full of white hair. He wasn't wearing any socks, and Chic could see his bony, white feet. He was sitting in a wheelchair with a blanket in his lap and seemed to be asleep or . . . wait a second, was he? Chic had seen dead people before. Is this what she wanted to show him?

"You see?" Mary asked.

"Did you . . . you didn't?"

"What?"

"Kill him?"

"No. Jesus. I didn't kill anyone. He's sleeping."

"Who takes their lover to see their husband sleep?"

"We're not lovers."

"We sure seemed like it in your minivan yesterday. And what about this afternoon? All that stuff at the restaurant."

"We're friends."

"You have an odd way of showing friendship." He swatted at the gnats, which had descended on them like a rainstorm. "Do you like me, Mary?"

"Of course I like you."

"What do you like about me?"

"Well, you're . . . you're honest. Very honest. I'm not used to that."

"So you like honesty?"

"If you're going to bring up Florida again, please don't."

"I'm just saying that if you like me, even a little bit, you have to consider it."

"I'm thinking about it."

"Truthfully?"

She nodded.

"I have a masturbation problem. And I'm afraid of women. Sex, I mean. Both. It's a long story, actually. Do you know why I want to go to Florida?"

"You don't have to tell me. I think I get it."

"It's symbolic. Do you know what that means?"

"Yes, I know what that means."

"Some people don't. Florida represents a new start. For me. For you. For us."

"I know."

"But it's ironic, too. Do you know why it's ironic?"

"Because we're old."

"I didn't expect you to know that. We're old. That's right. And old people don't get new starts."

She looked at him. "I hear these voices in my head."

"Like crazy voice?"

"More like thinking voices. This constant chatter. They're always arguing."

"I've got that. Everyone does. That's nothing."

"But, I don't know which one to listen to. I used to know. But now I don't."

"Is one of the voices telling you to go to Florida?"

She nodded.

He swatted again at the gnats. "These things are driving me crazy."

"Why do you live in a nursing home?"

"It's assisted living, not a nursing home. I could leave if I wanted to."

"You don't have to live there?"

"I signed myself up. Lots of people do. You could."

"How much is it to stay there?"

"Let's not talk about that. Let's . . . are these gnats bothering you?" He swatted at them again.

"Quit swatting at them."

"I'm trying to get rid of them."

"You can't get rid of them."

"Jesus. They're everywhere. They're getting in my eyes."

"I think I should take you home."

"What . . . why? Let's just . . . my God. Get these things away from me." He was using both hands to swat at them.

"Stop doing that. You'll make it worse."

Chic kept swatting at them, but it wasn't any use. They had engulfed his head and were orbiting around him like hundreds of tiny moons.

Chic & Diane & Buddy & Lijy & Russ & Baby Erika

or, the Waldbeeser family, fast-forwarding through some years

■

1973–1982

One evening in early 1973, Chic drove out to the Mackinaw River. He parked on the gravel turnoff and walked out onto the bridge downriver from his brother's house. With the binoculars, he had a straight-on view into Buddy and Lijy's life. Lijy was sitting on the sofa, holding their new baby, Erika. Russ was sitting on the floor beside them. Buddy came into the living room and scooped his baby daughter out of Lijy's arms and held her up in the air. She smiled and slobbered. Lijy laughed, and so did Russ and Buddy. The laughter made Chic so jealous that he had to calm himself for a moment so that he didn't fall over the bridge railing into the river. Putting the binoculars back to his eyes, he saw that the entire family was now sitting on the sofa. A camera was set up on a tripod across the room. Erika was in Buddy's lap, Lijy's arm was around Russ, and Russ's arm was around Buddy, who was holding a cord to snap the camera shutter.

Dr. Norman Vincent Peale's radio program, *The Art of Living* was still going strong in 1977, forty-two years after its premiere. (It would air for a total of fifty-four years.) Diane owned almost all of his books, *The Power of Positive Thinking, Stay Alive All Your Life, Reaching Your Potential.* She spent entire days sitting on the couch, holding a doll and listening to Dr. Peale or paging through one of his books. She wasn't bowling anymore. She wasn't doing much of anything. She watched *Hee Haw* on Friday nights. Occasionally, she cleaned, or cooked (if putting a pot roast in the slow cooker was cooking). She went to the grocery store once a week. She ate all the time. Chic would often discover her in the middle of the night leafing through one of Peale's books and eating peanut butter toast or Twinkies. When he came home from work, she'd be eating popcorn or potato chips or hot dogs, a mess of bun crumbs on the front of her nightgown.

Chic became curious about Peale's appeal. If Diane was getting insight from him, maybe he could, too. So he started listening to *The Art of Living*. During the program, he kept looking over at his wife, hoping to spot something in her face—merriment, understanding—but she just sat there with a dull half smile on her lips and a glazed expression in her eyes. One night, he asked her what it was about Peale, what the attraction was. "Does it help?" he asked.

"Does it look like it helped?" she answered. Listening to Peale's message of positive thinking for the past twenty years hadn't made a positive difference in her life. Yes, she was still here, breathing (though even that was getting harder, as she was starting to get short of breath often, like when she climbed the stairs or pushed the grocery cart to the car in the Stafford's parking lot). However, she was still a very big woman, had been a very big woman for almost fifteen years, would be a very big woman until the day she died. Every single day, she still went into Lomax's old bedroom and held one of the dolls. (Lomax would have been almost thirty now, and probably married, maybe with children of his own.) Peale wanted her to think differently about her life, to think positively, and if she did that, everything would change. She had tried to do as he asked, but the only thing that happened was she got older. For a time, she blamed Chic. Now, what was the point? She was too tired to blame anyone. She just wanted to be left alone; she just wanted to eat, to feel the fizzle of soda in her mouth, to chew a hot dog and taste the sharpness of the mustard mixing with the tanginess of the ketchup. If she could just sit on the couch and eat forever, that would be better, that would make everything better.

Across town, Buddy and Lijy rocketed into their future, the proud parents of Erika Waldbeeser. When she was a baby, Buddy had loved to hold her and make faces at her. Now that she was older, he liked to hold her hand while the two of them walked up and down the gravel driveway. He read books to her. He sat on the floor and helped her learn shapes and colors. He carried a wallet picture with him, and whenever a customer came into the health food store, he took out the picture and talked and talked and talked about his daughter. Russ took a real interest in his sister as well. He took her for nature hikes along the Mackinaw River and pointed out the different kinds of trees. When they got home, he showed her pictures of the trees and quizzed her on what type they were. She entered kindergarten the smartest kid in Middleville, according to Buddy. In class one day, she made a crayon drawing of her family. Each member—Buddy, Lijy, and Russ—was represented as a different-color stick figure with a different geometrical-shaped head. Buddy swooned over the drawing. He marched it into the bedroom where Lijy was taking a nap, woke her, and insisted the drawing was the work of a young genius. He called Erika's teacher and asked her if she'd ever seen something so creative in her entire teaching career. The teacher told him that it was a "solid effort." Buddy framed the picture and hung it behind the counter at the health food store. He told customers that Erika was destined to paint or draw or maybe do clay sculptures. One day, he bought her some clay and sat her down at the kitchen table and encouraged her to make something, but she told him she just wanted to go outside for a walk.

Sometime in the early 1980s, Lijy received an envelope in the mail without a return address. She knew immediately that it was from Ellis McMillion. She took the envelope outside, dug a hole in the ground, and buried it. That chapter was behind her now, and she never, ever wanted to think about Ellis McMillion or her mistake again. They—all of them—were in a better place. Buddy had gotten beyond her mistake, and Russ was a well-adjusted boy who accepted the lie she had told him about who his father was. (Even if the lie was built atop another lie.) Sometimes, she felt guilty about lying to her son. She'd always meant to tell him the truth, but somehow the right time never presented itself, and then he was in high school, and she tried to imagine herself sitting him down for a talk, but she always anticipated it going terribly. He'd be mad at her. He'd be sad. He'd be hurt. He'd be so many things, so she chose not to say anything, and she did her best not to think about it, even when he did something that offered a painful reminder, like pushing his glasses up on his nose.

Russ graduated from high school in 1978 and went off to Illinois State University, where he majored in botany. He spent a lot of time by himself, studying in an unfurnished room in the basement of his dorm, next to a couple of coin-operated washers and dryers. To help alleviate his loneliness, he joined a socialist group and grew a mustache because all the other guys in the group had a mustache. He didn't really believe in socialism. If he worked hard, why should someone else receive the fruits of his labor? He told one of the leaders of the socialist group, a guy who didn't attend ISU but audited philosophy classes, his beliefs. The guy told him that he was a capitalist, and that capitalists were the scum of the earth. Russ didn't like being called the scum of the earth. At the next meeting, in the basement of the theater building, the guy told the group that Russ had something to say. Russ said that he didn't have anything to say. The guy said, "Go on and tell them what you told me the other day." Russ then told the group he didn't think it was fair that others should receive the fruits of his labor. The group suddenly became very agitated, demanding that Russ explain why he was attending a socialist meeting when, in fact, he wasn't a socialist. Russ told them he attended the meetings because he didn't have any friends. (Not to mention that the group threw potluck-style dinners where Russ was always a big hit because he brought vegetarian treats that Buddy had sent him in the mail.) This was Russ's last socialist meeting. The next semester he threw himself into his school-work and made the dean's list with straight As. However, he still wanted to be a part of something, as he always had this under-the-surface feeling that he wasn't quite a part of anything. Maybe this was because Chic was his father. He didn't really know, but he didn't like the way he felt.

Back in Middleville, the health food store was a smashing success. The health fad of the seventies had never gone away, and people were driving to Middleville from Peoria and Mackinaw and other small Central Illinois towns to purchase tofu, vita-mins, herbal teas, bulk honey, unsalted peanut butter, and dried fruit from the store. Buddy also bought a commercial juicer and concocted new recipes like the Spinarrot (spinach and carrot), the Middleville (pumpkin, chili powder, honey, and carrots), and the Waldbeeser (ginger, apple, kale, lemon, and carrot). Kids and adults alike loved Buddy's juices; even people who didn't buy their groceries from the store would swing by for a fresh juice. The popularity of the juices catapulted the store into an entirely different level of success. The store was doing so well that Buddy was able to transition out of working the counter, spending more of his time on a cookbook/memoir about his life. Lijy encouraged him, but Buddy wasn't a natural writer, so it took him a long time to construct a sentence. Sometimes, Lijy would find him at his desk in the back of the store, a mess of papers spread out before him. She thought that he was thinking about the next sentence, but he was in fact daydreaming about the day that he could sell the store and move his family to a state like Arizona. Maybe they'd open another health food store there? Or a store that sold diet books? Or fresh-squeezed juice? Even though he was past fifty, retirement was not in his future. He wasn't about to sit idle and spend his afternoons fishing in the river.

Russ Waldbeeser

■

February–July 1982

One day during the spring semester of his senior year, Russ spotted a flyer for something called Greenleaf hanging on a bulletin board in his dorm. There was no meeting advertised on the flyer, just a phone number handwritten at the bottom. That night Russ called the number. Jacob Honness, a senior and political science major, answered and told Russ that Greenleaf hadn't held a meeting in a year and a half and that, in fact, he was the only member of the group. He further explained that he didn't want the club to require a large time commitment or make its members march through campus protesting this or that. Russ didn't want to belong to a club that required a large time commitment or made its members march through campus protesting this or that. He asked about the next meeting, and Jacob said they could get together the following Saturday.

The meeting was held at Jacob's one-bedroom apartment, a messy place not far from campus with empty soda cans on the coffee table and a big fish tank. The meeting didn't turn out to be much of a meeting. Russ completed some paperwork, and Jacob collected a ten-dollar fee from him and gave him a button to hang on his bag or coat or wherever. After that, Jacob shook his hand and said the meeting was over. He looked at Russ like he wanted him to leave, but Russ wasn't ready to leave. He wanted to talk about Greenleaf, about what the group was going to do next. He told Jacob that he was a botany major and was interested in the group's efforts and wanted to know how he could help. Jacob told him he could hang some flyers. Russ had hung flyers for the socialist club; flyer hanging was tedious and boring. He wanted to organize something. Jacob pretended to share Russ's enthusiasm, while at the same time slowly ushering Russ toward the door. At the door, Jacob asked Russ to write up a proposal. On the spot, Russ blurted out, "Maybe we can plant a tree or something. For Arbor Day." Jacob shrugged and said he'd check with his Greenleaf contacts in Portland, Oregon. Then, he wished Russ good day and shut the door.

Two weeks later, Jacob interrupted Russ while he was study-ing in the library and told him that he'd talked to his contacts in Portland and that they thought an Arbor Day event was a good idea. Jacob, however, said he didn't have the time to help plan the event. This was his final semester, and he was taking a 300-level political science class and a linguistics class that required him to read two hundred pages per week. Russ said he'd be happy to plan the event by himself. Before Jacob left, he gave Russ an application. "The Greenleaf people said to give this to you. Since you seem to like this stuff, they thought you might want to do it."

"What is it?"

"An internship or something. I don't really know."

Russ stuffed the application into his backpack without read-ing it. He was too excited to concentrate on anything other than the Arbor Day event.

The Greenleaf Arbor Day Event was set for April 6, 1982, at noon. It would take place on the east side of campus behind the football stadium; the closest dorm was half a mile away. Russ had hung flyers all around campus announcing the event, and he had roped off the area—a square about five feet by five feet—where the tree was to be planted. Jacob rode up on his bicycle a few minutes before noon, joining a few other people around the rope: Dr. Spenser, Russ's mentor in the botany department, who lived with his four dogs outside of Normal, Illinois, in a school bus converted into a trailer; a student Russ didn't recognize; and a guy and a girl from Oregon who said they were affiliated with Greenleaf and had driven there for the event on a spring break trip. With the help of Dr. Spenser, Russ had gotten a local tree nursery to donate a blue spruce, a sapling about the size of a five-gallon bucket. At noon, Russ and Dr. Spenser dug a small hole in the center of the roped-off area. It took about five minutes to plant the tree. After they were finished, everyone wished each other, "Happy Arbor Day," and then scattered back to their lives. Dr. Spenser had to take care of some things in his office; the unknown student waved and said he needed to meet up with some friends. Russ was tying a ribbon on the tree when he noticed that the two Greenleaf representatives were watching him. They suggested getting a drink to celebrate Arbor Day.

At the Thirsty Scholar, the three of them cozied up together in a booth. The two Greenleaf representatives, Tyler Wilcox and Ginger Beauchamp, wanted to know what Russ's major was. When he told him that it was botany, they both looked at each other and smiled. They wanted to know his plans for after college. Russ shrugged and said that lately he'd been thinking about farming Christmas trees. The idea had come to him that past winter, when he saw Christmas tree stands being set up around campus. He told them that those trees needed to be grown somewhere, and that he wanted to be the person to grow them. This idea troubled Ginger and Tyler; they asked Russ if he wouldn't rather grow trees than cut them down. Russ told them that he had to make money somehow. They suggested a tree nursery instead. Russ said that a tree nursery could be part of the business, but the real money would be made harvesting trees and that there probably wasn't enough demand for a tree nursery because once a tree was planted it lasted for a long time, like fifty years, so he'd basically sell one or two trees to a customer over the course of their lifetime, and that, according to Russ, was no way to run a business. But, he told them—and here was the "good part"—for every Christmas tree he cut down, he'd plant two new ones. In his mind, he was being ecologically prudent, and he was making a little money, which, for any business, he said, was the goal. Both Ginger and Tyler nodded. Tyler took a sip of his beer. At that moment, Russ felt a light tapping on his leg. He looked under the table and saw the toe of Ginger's boot tapping his shin. She winked at him. Then she asked, "Have you given any thought to the Canadian internship?"

Russ didn't know what she was talking about.

"The tree-planting internship Greenleaf sponsors every summer in Alberta, Canada," Tyler said.

Then Russ remembered the application Jacob had given him, which he'd stuffed in his backpack and forgotten about.

"We could use someone like you," Ginger said. "Someone with a business mind."

Tyler slid another application across the table. "Give it some thought," he said.

Russ did give it some thought. In fact, he thought about it so much that he couldn't sleep that night. But it wasn't the prospect of planting trees in Canada that was keeping him awake, although he did think that would be pretty cool. Rather, it was Ginger Beauchamp. Had she been flirting with him that afternoon? She had to be. Why else would she be kicking him under the table? Wasn't that called "footsie," and wasn't "footsie" considered flirting? He'd had two girlfriends during his four years at ISU, but both of them had wanted him to shave his beard and cut his hair, and he didn't want to shave his beard or cut his hair. He wanted to be who he wanted to be—a guy with a beard and long hair. Not to mention, when he told a girl he was a botany major, she would usually get this faraway look in her eyes and walk away from him while he was in the middle of talking. Ginger was different. She had tapped his shin with the toe of her boot. She had winked at him. He got out of bed, turned on the light, sat down at his desk, and filled the application out.

The internship was on the eastern slope of the Rocky Mountains, several hundred miles from Calgary. Russ arrived a few days after the Fourth of July; Tyler picked him up from the train station. There were six Greenleaf members participating in the internship: Tyler, Ginger, Russ, and three other guys from colleges around the country. They all stayed in a hunting cabin without electricity or indoor plumbing. The cabin was one big open room with a kitchen area. On one wall were four bunk beds, and in the middle of the room was a table with an overhead light that was powered by a camping generator. Every few days, someone needed to go into the nearest town, Luscar, to get gas for the generator. At night, the group played cards; in the morning, they woke early and alternated making skillet breakfasts on a camping stove. After breakfast, they drove into Jasper National Park, where they spent the day planting trees and ramming long spikes into the Canadian ground to "feed" nutrients to the trees. Russ loved the work. There was a problem, however, and that problem was Ginger.

Ginger Beauchamp was a twenty-two-year-old Canadian girl who did her work without complaining, and each time it was her turn to pick a card game, she picked Hearts. She had a gap between her front teeth, but despite the gap, she was a pretty girl with a slight build, like a cheerleader's, and auburn hair. She was fond of wearing cutoff jean shorts around the cabin and a gingham shirt that she tied up to show her belly button. Most nights before bed, she would lie in her bunk and read. Russ would lie on his side, his head on his arm, watching her hold the tiny penlight, her eyes raking across the pages. He imagined a life with her unfolding like the narrative of a novel: event after event; good days, bad days, and in-between days; conflict, tension, and resolution. They'd buy a house, a farm, something outside Middleville, where they'd grow trees together, maybe have a couple of dogs. Cows. Chickens. They'd have a baby one day. It all seemed so clear in his imagination, so perfect.

Unfortunately, the other guys in the group had fallen for Ginger, too, and it seemed that Tyler was the frontrunner. They'd gone to high school together, and from conversations with the other guys, Russ found out that the two of them had once dated, though they weren't currently a couple. One of the other guys, Nathan, from upstate New York, who'd started a Greenleaf charter at Syracuse, said he was "lying in the weeds, just waiting for his time to pounce." They all were. Around the card table, Russ could feel the tension. All eyes were on Ginger, on every move she made. When she shuffled the deck, the guys watched her, their tongues basically hanging out of their mouths like dogs. Russ kept looking under the table to see if Ginger was tapping anyone else's shin. She was always sitting Indian-style in her chair. Once, when Russ looked under the table, she asked, "What's under there, Russell?" For some reason, she called him Russell, although Russ was his full name, and after a while, the other guys took to calling him Russell Muscle.

Russ knew he needed to stake his claim, needed to prove himself. So he started to do what any guy would do: he "flexed his muscles" to show Ginger he was the type of man who would be good for her. When they all sat around at night, passing a joint (something Russ now liked doing, although he'd never done it before coming to Canada), he tried to be funny, lively, a good time kind of guy. When they planted trees, he planted twice as many as anyone else. At meals, he ate twice as much as anyone else. When they played cards, he played to win; a few times, he even cheated to make sure that he won.

And then, one afternoon while they were out planting trees, Ginger spotted a pinecone hanging on a branch about three stories up, dangling like a Christmas ornament. She pointed it out to everyone. The other guys admired the pinecone and went about unloading sandwiches and sodas from the cooler and spreading out a blanket. Tyler rolled a joint. Russ, however, knew that he had to climb the tree and get that pinecone for her. He started climbing. Ginger watched him while she ate her sandwich; the other guys ignored him, or did their best to ignore him, as they passed around the joint. The smell of cannabis wafted up to Russ's nostrils. He wanted to be down on the ground with them, smoking the joint. He was only about ten feet from the pinecone, but those last ten feet were precarious, as the pine tree was beginning to triangle. He climbed up another branch and tried grabbing the pinecone, but it was still out of reach. He adjusted himself and prepared to climb a little higher—one more branch and he was pretty sure he'd be high enough to get it. He looked down and saw Ginger looking up. She waved. The other guys were laughing. Russ made his move. He stepped up on the branch and shifted his weight onto that foot. At that moment, he heard a loud crack. He didn't even have time to scream as he lost his balance and thudded to the ground. Ginger put her hand over her mouth. The other guys looked over at him and laughed even harder. On the ground, Russ's whole body felt like it had been pumped full of air and was about to explode. He let out a moan and managed to say, "Oh, shit."

Chic Waldbeeser

■

August 1982

Chic got his first look at Russ's girlfriend, Ginger, through binoculars a few days after they arrived back in Middleville. The rumors around town said that Russ had gone off and broken almost every bone in his body, and that, like his father, he had found himself a woman from some faraway place and brought her back to Middleville. Chic spotted the two of them in the kitchen, where Ginger was hand-feeding Russ slices of apple dipped in peanut butter. The kitchen table was covered in flowers and get-well cards. Russ had broken both of his arms and his left leg. After each slice of apple, Ginger wiped Russ's mouth with a napkin. Chic wasn't sure what he had been expecting, but the girl looked just like any other girl.

Russ's fall had inspired Chic. After hearing the news, he had written three poems, after not having written one in nearly a decade. He mailed Russ a get-well card and included one of the poems. He'd come to the bridge with his binoculars to watch him open it. He imagined Russ and Ginger passing the card back and forth. He imagined them laughing. He imagined Russ hanging the card on the fridge. He imagined his brother and Lijy reading it. He imagined Erika reading it. He imagined them all smiling at its poignancy. He imagined the card hanging on the fridge for months and beginning to fade in the sun.

After eating an apple slice, Russ picked up a card from the table and read it. He smiled. Ginger took the card from him, read it, and smiled, too. Chic tried to zoom in on the card, to see if it was his, but there was no zooming, of course, with binoculars. He leaned over the railing of the bridge, trying to get closer. It had to be his card; it had to be his poem. His poetry was bringing people joy. His heart was pounding, and he felt connected to Russ and Ginger. Not connected like he was holding them or hugging them, but connected like jumper cables went from his heart to their hearts, from his brain to theirs, and even though he might not be happy, his words were making others happy. He leaned a little bit farther, then lost his balance and flipped over the railing. He caught himself, and was hanging by one hand, the water below him. He could hear the current rushing. He only had to let himself fall. He knew the water was deep enough. He would be all right. He would survive. He closed his eyes, held his breath, and let go.

Coming up out of the water, Chic gasped and flailed his arms. He felt like the biggest idiot in the world. He'd just fallen off a bridge while spying on his nephew and his new girlfriend. What kind of grown man does something like that? He swam to shore and climbed on the bank, using the weeds to pull himself out of the water. His clothes were soggy and heavy. His shoes squished with every step on the muddy bank. He slumped up the bank to the bridge. He hoped Russ and Ginger hadn't heard him. The bridge was over a hundred yards downriver, so they probably hadn't. He picked up the binoculars and looked through them. Ginger was feeding Russ another slice of apple. Neither of them were aware that outside of the kitchen, an entire world was spinning and churning and that people like Chic were falling off bridges. Not even Chic was aware of the outside world. He was aware only of himself, his wet shoes, his soggy clothes, the drips of water running down his cheeks like tears.

Fifteen

Diane Waldbeeser

■

January 1985

Each day, Diane prepared for Dr. Peale by toasting a Pop-Tart. When the Pop-Tart was ready, she smeared it with butter and carried it to the living room, where she clicked on the radio and snuggled into the couch. Each bite was heavenly. She would probably eat the whole box. And that was okay. She could listen to the *The Art of Living* and eat a box of Pop-Tarts, then go to the store and purchase more Pop-Tarts and come home and listen to Dr. Peale and eat more Pop-Tarts.

But, deep inside of her, something breathed its hot breath on her heart. That something told her to get on the Airdyne exercise bike. Remove the laundry hanging on the handlebars and lying across the seat. Get off the couch, and get on the bike. The same motivation that had made her join the bowling league now pushed her to get up, brush the Pop-Tart crumbs off the front of her nightgown, and click off the radio. She bounded up the stairs and, without taking off her nightgown, put on her sneakers, double-knotting the laces. Back down in the living room, the wall clock said it was almost four. She had a little over an hour before Chic got home from work. She threw off the laundry and opened the drapes. Sunlight washed into the living room. She was transfixed, staring at the exercise bicycle. Maybe this was how it would happen. She'd begin a new chapter. It wasn't too late. It was never too late. She could hear Dr. Peale's voice in her head.

She got on the bike and began to pedal. The front wheel fan came to life. She worked the handlebars back and forth. A bit of sweat beaded up on her forehead, and she wiped it with her left hand. She tasted it. It tasted awful, but it was her sweat, produced by her body. She was in motion. She was moving. She pedaled faster and moved her arms back and forth. Sweat trickled down the side of her face. The wheel fan whooshed. On the coffee table, the pages of the *TV Guide* fluttered, and the napkin she'd used during lunch blew onto the carpet.

After about five minutes, she couldn't keep going, and stopped. The room was silent, except for the buzz of activity inside of her, cells ping-ponging around her skull, reminding her that being alive had a palpable undercurrent that sounded like a dull drone of interstate traffic way off in the distance. She'd actually done something, and she was tired, actually tired. Her legs felt rubbery. She could feel her heart beat under her breast. She wiped the sweat from her forehead. She felt, maybe, a little bit better. She also felt hungry.

In the kitchen, she put the last two Pop-Tarts in the box into the toaster. Two minutes later, the Pop-Tarts shot up. She buttered them quickly and put the knife in the sink. On her way back to the couch, she spotted the napkin that had blown off the coffee table. She thought about picking it up, but left it on the floor. She plopped down on the couch and took a bite from one of her Pop-Tarts.

Mary & Green Geneseo

■

July 26, 1998

Carol Bowen-Smith, the activities director of We Care, kept stressing how well prepared the facility was to deal with stroke victims. "To We Care, you're an alive person. Very alive," she said, patting Green on the head. "And taking care of living people is something we strive to do well." She turned to Mary. "We take the residents to vote. And on Sundays, we organize church outings." Green didn't like Carol one bit—the way she patted him on the head, the way she smiled at him, the way she kept saying things to Mary like he wasn't sitting right in goddamn front of them. From his wheelchair, he looked up at Mary and shot her a scowl. Without taking her eyes off of Carol Bowen-Smith, Mary plopped her meaty, sweaty, adultery-committing hand on his shoulder, like a hand on the shoulder was supposed to soothe him when she wanted to stow him away in some old folks' home so that she could sashay about with her goddamn Cadillac-driving boyfriend. Well, she was going to see. Green Geneseo wasn't a guy who rolled over.

When they got to the indoor pool, Carol talked about the Saturday morning "Stroke Swimmers"—of which she was the coach—her awful voice echoing off the block walls and reverberating around the room as she raved about how We Care kept the pool water at a "balmy but refreshing" eighty degrees. Eighty degrees? Back in Las Vegas, Green used to keep the above-ground pool behind the trailer set at sixty-five, and during the dead of summer, that was about as refreshing as a warm puddle. Carol then told Mary about the monthly Hawaiian luau, where the residents gathered around the pool to listen to Lou's Luauers, a steel drum group made up of retired high school music teachers from Peoria. "We Care is so much more than a nursing home. It's a way of life," Carol said, pointing out a fake palm tree, which was leaning dangerously close to the pool. She smiled. "I like to think of us as a nursing resort. Nursing home sounds so . . . I don't know . . . boring." Mary just kept nodding like her damn head was on a spring. Suddenly, Green's attention was drawn to the door behind the wilting, fake palm tree, where an old man was cupping his face in the glass. Green tried to get a better look, but the guy ducked out of sight as soon as Carol turned around to lead them to the next destination on their tour.

Down a hallway, past an alcove with a pay phone and some vending machines, past a set of double doors that Carol pointed out was the cafeteria, past the nurses' station where a nurse, who

Carol didn't bother to introduce, played solitaire on a computer, they stopped in front of a closed door. Room 148. Carol pushed open the door and stepped aside so that Green and Mary could take it all in. To Green, the room looked like a regular hospital room, only a little larger. There were two beds with a nightstand separating them. The floor was covered in industrial tile and there were medical contraptions—blood-pressure cuff, oxygen noz-zle—on the wall behind the beds. A television was affixed to the wall opposite the beds. In the corner was a table with a bouquet of plastic flowers in a glass vase.

"Your roommate will be Leroy Midge," Carol said, pointing to an ancient man in the bed farthest from the door. He wore a flannel shirt and red suspenders and was reading a book. A can of soda with a straw sat on the nightstand beside him. "Leroy is deaf," Carol said. "It's an advantage to have a hearing impaired roommate. Although, Ms. Geneseo, mandatory quiet time is nine o'clock." Carol then walked over to the window and threw open the drapes, offering a view of a cornfield and a Dumpster over-flowing with garbage bags. "City garbage collectors come once a week," Carol said, quickly shutting the drapes.

Their final stop was the cafeteria. Mary pushed Green to a ta-ble, and then she and Carol got in line behind a cluster of nurses. It was only eleven in the morning, but the cafeteria was already full of fragile, zombie-like old people. At a table by the salad bar, a male nurse was feeding a resident cottage cheese. In the back corner, three residents, two in wheelchairs, drank mugs of coffee. The guy Green had seen spying on them at the pool was sitting at a table by himself. A green duffel bag was next to his tray. He was writing in a notebook. The guy glanced up and met Green's stare. His eyes were piercing, but Green couldn't look away. He was, for some reason, scared of this guy, even though he was thin and skeletal, like a tree without its leaves. He was wearing a stained v-neck undershirt, and deep lines of weariness were etched in his face. And, strangely, he was wearing a black beret.

Chic & Diane Waldbeeser

■

May 24, 1985

Chic was all set to do his business. The bathroom door was locked, and he'd just squirted a tablespoon of hand lotion into his palm. Diane was in the living room on the Airdyne bike—a recent and obsessive habit. She cranked up the volume on the radio so that she could hear Dr. Peale and spent half an hour at least, four times a day, perched on the bike's saddle, pedaling and sweating while eating Pop-Tarts or ice cream or whatever happened to be in the kitchen. He tried to block the noise out as he unbuckled his belt and slid his pants down to his ankles. He lifted up the toilet lid and focused on his fantasy: him and Diane in their honeymoon room at the Seashell Inn. Who cared if he didn't remember it correctly? This was the way he wanted it to go; the way it should have gone. If he ever got the chance again, he'd make sure it went this way. He'd tug off Diane's pants and lay her down on the bed. He'd kiss the bottoms of her feet. He'd kiss a trail up her calves and thighs.

For some reason, the fantasy wasn't working today. He squirted more lotion into his palm. He closed his eyes. His thoughts raced: he was a fifty-five-year-old man masturbating in the bathroom while his wife rode an exercise bike in the next room. He shook that thought out of his head and focused on Diane at the Seashell Inn, wearing nothing but a bra, lying on her back, him holding her leg as he kissed her inner thigh. This wasn't really doing it for him, either. He wanted Diane the girl who had just graduated from high school, not the overweight woman in the living room. More lotion. He closed his eyes, but had a difficult time ushering the young Diane into his imagination. To compensate, he focused on someone more readily available: the actress on *The Love Boat*, Lauren something or other. She was cute and young, with reddish hair and a high-pitched girlish giggle. They were on the Love Boat, in a cabin, and Lauren was on her back, and Chic was kissing a trail down her thigh. Actually, no, they were at the Seashell Inn. Then, from out in the living room, Chic heard a thud. He stopped rubbing his penis, and looked at the closed bathroom door. It sounded like something had fallen, or jumped. Maybe Diane had gotten off the exercise bike—the whooshing of the wheels had stopped. Maybe she was getting a glass of water. Actually, she might knock on the door. He'd been in the bathroom for nearly fifteen minutes. He had to hurry. He went for it. He was close . . . the top of his head tingled, and he ejaculated into the toilet. A wave of relief passed over him, and his right leg twitched. After a minute, he pulled up his pants, flushed the toilet, and washed his hands. He looked at himself in the mirror and adjusted the collar of his shirt. He unlocked the bathroom door.

Out in the living room, Diane was lying on the carpet, face-down. In one hand, she clutched a spoon; next to her hand was an overturned bowl of ice cream. At first, the scene didn't register. Then, he remembered the thud. Oh, my God. She's . . . Is she . . . He remembered Diane coming up the bleachers at the football game all those years ago. He kneeled down next to her and rolled her over. Her eyes were open, and she had chocolate ice cream smeared above her upper lip. He stared into her eyes. They were hollow and vacant. He remembered her at the bowling alley, standing at the mouth of the lane, holding her ball, her back to him and the group, and he remembered how, sometimes, when she stood there holding the ball and sizing up the pins, she sometimes, to make the group laugh, would wiggle her behind, and after she did that, while everyone snickered, she would glance over her shoulder, and when she glanced over her shoulder, it occurred to Chic, at that moment while he kneeled next to his dead wife, that she was looking at him to see if he was laughing at her joke. He put two fingers on her neck, but he knew he wasn't going to get a pulse. He slipped the spoon out of her hand and put it on the coffee table. There had been a half scoop of ice cream left in the bowl, and it was mounded on the carpet. He went to the kitchen to get a rag. He wiped the chocolate from her mouth and cleaned up the melting ice cream on the carpet. He took the bowl and rag to the kitchen. He rinsed the bowl and wrung out the rag. Then, he sat down on the couch and looked at his wife on the floor, her eyes open and staring at the ceiling. He had known this was going to happen someday, but here, right now, was that day. It was happening. It had happened. He looked up and noticed a crack in the ceiling, a long thin crack. He'd seen it before. He got up and tried to look more closely at it. It spanned the entire ceiling. He had no idea what had caused it. Then, he felt . . . he couldn't really explain it. He felt bad. Guilty, maybe. Ashamed might be better. He'd been in the bathroom masturbating when his wife died. He'd have to make up a story. He'd been in the garage. No, at the store. That was better. He had been at Stafford's and come into the house and there she was. What if she'd felt her chest tighten and called for him. Jesus, he hoped that wasn't the case. Imagine that. She was clutching her chest and trying to cry out for help, and he's in the bathroom, rubbing his penis. He kneeled down next to her and crossed her hands on her stomach. She looked peaceful; at least, she looked peaceful. He leaned over her, looking down on her face, into her vacant eyes. "If you called for me, and I didn't hear you, I'm sorry," he said. He knew he needed to say more. "If you can hear me, I love you. Or, I thought I loved you. I once loved you. There was love there, I think. I don't know what happened to it. You loved me, or you once did, or I think you did. Maybe you did. I don't know what to say. I'm sorry. If you called for me, and I didn't hear you, I'm sorry." He bent down and closed her eyes and kissed her forehead. Then he got up and stepped over the body and went into the kitchen and picked up the telephone.

Diane Waldbeeser, an epilogue

■

May 26, 1985

Along with her will, Diane had left two items in her safety deposit box at Middleville Community Bank. One was the copy of Chic's poetry chapbook that she had bought at Stafford's. In the margins, Diane had written things like: Interesting," "Good," and "I've felt this way, too." Chic wished she had said something to him about his poetry. Maybe if she had mentioned how much she liked his poems, he would have written a second chapbook. Or a third. Maybe he'd be teaching poetry classes at the library. Maybe he'd be reading poems to her right now, instead of sitting in the bank parking lot.

The second item was a sealed envelope with his name written across it. He ripped it open and found a letter inside. He opened the letter, and a photograph fell onto his lap. He ignored the photo, and started reading the letter.

Dear Chic,

I want to apologize for the last thirty years. I know I haven't been myself. Or, maybe I've been too much of myself. I'm not sure which. I know you like poems, so maybe I should use a metaphor. I feel like a rusted tea kettle. Actually, that's not a very good metaphor. I feel like a shirt worn backward. You were more the poet than I was, obviously. Anyway, all of this is to say, I'm normal but I'm not normal. Like things are right but not right. I guess what I'm trying to say is that I should have tried harder. Everyone says that, I know, but for me, it's true. When you wanted to have another child, I admit that I didn't really try. I just lay there. You knew I wasn't trying. I saw the way you looked at me. I'm sorry. I know you thought having another kid would have helped. But maybe it wouldn't have. Maybe it would have made things worse. I didn't want it to get any worse. I couldn't have taken worse. Worse would have been a hurricane during a blizzard. I don't even know if that's possible. If it is possible, it sounds horrible. I didn't want a hurricane blizzard, but maybe I should have risked the hurricane blizzard and everything would have worked out. Maybe that was my problem: I had a chance but didn't take it. Or, wanted to take a chance but couldn't make myself. I know it made you mad that we never took a chance. This, I think, was our major difference. You wanted to take a chance, and I didn't. What a pair we made. Anyway, I went through menopause prematurely, so maybe all of this doesn't matter. Oh well. Because these are my last words to you, I thought you should know that I felt my best the day we arrived home from the hospital with Lomax. What a day that was. Do you remember it? We carried that little baby into our house with these big grins on our faces. I was afraid if we had another baby, I wouldn't feel as good as I felt the first time. That scared me. I also felt pretty good in Florida, that night we made up, the night after I unlocked myself from the bathroom, that night after we went to dinner at that restaurant and ate crab legs. I wanted to have a baby more than anything and I seduced you, and afterward, after you fell asleep, I ate three chocolate bars and hoped and wished I was pregnant. The whole time I was eating those chocolate bars, you were snoring in the bed. I feel like that's a metaphor for our lives. We were both doing our own thing. Maybe that's what happens to everyone—you get so caught up you don't really notice the time passing. I'd go whole months without realizing that time was passing, and then, one day, I'd catch a glimpse of myself in the mirror or remember something from the past, and then all these emotions erupted and I couldn't do anything but lie in bed and stare at the ceiling. I cried all the time and hurt so much, and I didn't know what to do. I wanted Dr. Peale to help, but he couldn't. I think I needed something that didn't require effort. I just wanted to feel better. I didn't want to put in any work. I guess maybe I should have taken more chances. I don't know. Maybe this was my destiny, and there you were sitting in the bleachers of that football game and from that point on, it was your destiny too. It doesn't really matter now. I'm dead, and you're reading this letter. Anyway, don't remember me how I was when I died. You probably found a big blob of woman flat on her back. Fat is not healthy, but I couldn't help myself. I liked food so much. It was the only thing that really truly helped me feel better. I hope I died in bed. I hope it wasn't a car accident or, Jesus, worse: I hope I didn't fall down the stairs. I hope it didn't hurt, and I hope I didn't suffer. I hope it wasn't cancer. I hope it was quick and painless. I hope I was sleeping, and you tried to wake me up one morning, and I was gone. Anyway, don't remember me dead. Remember me like the photograph I enclosed in this letter. Again, I'm sorry. And, also, good luck. Keep trying. You have to keep trying. Take chances. Or not. Don't listen to me. I had no idea what I was doing. Just be yourself, I guess. Just keep living is what I'm trying to say. I hope you find what you're looking for. I hope things change for you.

Chic picked up the picture lying in his lap. In it, Diane stood in the kitchen and was lifting her shirt to reveal her swollen, pregnant belly. She was laughing. Chic remembered taking the picture. Diane was about eight months pregnant, and across her stomach he had written in black marker: OUR BABY LIVES HERE!

Diane Waldbeeser, an epilogue (continued)

■

May 27, 1985

Chic had no idea his wife's death would affect him so much. Until she was gone, he hadn't realized how much he depended on her, and not just for dinner or whatever, but for the little things, like hearing the creak of her footsteps upstairs as he watched television; feeling her weight in the bed next to him; the sound of her setting a knife in the sink after she buttered her Pop-Tarts. All these years, he had thought he was lonely. He wasn't lonely—she was always in the next room, in the kitchen, in the shower, listening to Dr. Peale on the radio. He had never really been alone.

At the Blessed Sacrament Church, Chic crept up to his wife's casket and looked at her dead body. A bouquet of red roses had been laid across her stomach. She wore a pillbox hat with a veil covering her eyes and looked uncomfortable squeezed into a small casket, but her makeup brought out the beauty of her face, a beauty that was still there, despite the years and the weight. He reached in and put his hand on her arm. "Diane," he whispered. Behind him, the pews were filling up with those who had come to pay their respects. Buddy and his family were sitting in the first row. His brother looked ridiculous in a white dhoti and now, a shaved head. Russ had pretty much healed from his fall, though he still needed to use a single crutch. Holding on to his arm was his girlfriend, Ginger. Erika had her hair in pigtails and wore white socks pulled up to her knees. Lijy had aged. She was not the beautiful woman Chic had lusted after but was now just a woman in her fifties wearing glasses. Chic turned back to his dead wife. He patted her forearm. "I'm sorry this was your destiny." He faced the congregation. "Now, it's just me. I'm a family of one," he announced.

"What?" Buddy said out loud. "He has us. And what about Russ?" Lijy nudged him, while Russ smiled sheepishly and put his hand on Ginger's knee.

Chic cleared his throat. "This is all I have to say." He then read one of his favorite poems, "I Know a Man" by Robert Creeley:

> As I sd to my
> friend, because I am
> always talking,—John, I
>
> sd, which was not his
> name, the darkness sur-
> rounds us, what
>
> can we do against
> it, or else, shall we &
> why not, buy a goddamn big car,
>
> drive, he sd, for
> christ's sake, look
> out where yr going.

After the funeral, everyone went to the Knights of Columbus Hall. While Buddy and Lijy prepared the food in the Hall's kitchen, Chic drank two glasses of red wine in quick succession and then slow danced to Bob Dylan's "You're Gonna Make Me Lonesome When You Go," with Ginger. It wasn't really a slow dancing kind of song, but they made do. After the song ended, Chic went to the jukebox and played it a second time. Then Buddy brought out the egg salad sandwiches. There weren't enough tables, so most people ate standing up. A couple of people patted Chic on the back and told him how sorry they were. Chic thanked them for coming. He hated the attention, though, and mostly stood off to the side, watching everyone eat. Watching people eat reminded him of Diane, so after a few minutes, he slipped out the kitchen door to the parking lot, where he found Russ sitting on the tailgate of his truck, his crutch resting next to him. He had loosened his tie and was smoking something that smelled like burning rope. When he inhaled, his eyes became narrow and his chest puffed out like he'd swallowed too much air.

"Hey, man, sorry about your loss," Russ said. "Truly. She seemed like a first-class woman. What I knew of her. Those pictures of her when she was young. Man . . ." Russ whistled.

Chic smiled. "Thank you, Russ. That's very kind."

Russ took another pull off the funny-smelling cigarette and held the smoke deep in his lungs. "Hey, man, I got your card. 'Reach, reach, way up.' Nice. It's a haiku, right? That's cool that you write those." Russ took another drag from the cigarette.

"Is that marijuana?"

"Don't tell anyone. My old man will give me an earful. He's so into being one with the moment and all that."

"Russ, I think I'm depressed. I haven't said that out loud to anyone ever. Not that there's anyone to say it to, but there it is. It's out there. I said it."

"Your wife just died, man. Your life partner. Depression is what you should be feeling. You're going to be fine. This will pass; it's a rough patch, man."

"It's a little more . . . I don't know if . . . it's hard to say. It's hard to admit, actually. I don't think I was a very good husband, I guess is what I'm trying to say."

"I think you're being too hard on yourself. Hey, man, you ever look at trees?"

"Trees?"

"Yeah, like a tree can't be perfect. It's perfect in here, like, you know, right here." Russ pointed to his head. "When I see a tree out here, in the world, it's never what's in my head. Like they don't match, man. Like the tree in your head and the tree in the world. Two different things. And that produces conflict, you know? That's where the depression comes from, the unacceptance of the two trees. Like you know what a tree is, but when you encounter one in the world, it's not the same as your idea of it."

"Interesting."

"I'll bet that Diane didn't match the idea you had of a wife, and you probably didn't match the idea she had of a husband."

"She was a good wife."

"Did she match the idea you had of a wife in your head? The wife that you wanted to have?"

"When you put it that way . . ."

"And that's the problem."

"What's your idea of a father—in your head? Does Buddy match that?"

"I know where you're going with this. They told me. We had the talk. I was a little kid. I get it. You're my father."

"I'm not your father, Russ."

"I get it. You're being humble," Russ said. "You don't want to, you know, creep in on Buddy's territory. It's cool. You're not. I dig it. I'm fine with this arrangement. Seriously. I'm not going to ask anything from you. I don't want to, you know, make some third act connection or anything. You're like, you're biology, and Buddy, man, he's my dad."

"I'm not biology."

"I didn't mean to sound harsh. Maybe you're not my dad, if that's what you're saying. If that's the case, then, whoa . . . that's . . . . I'm gonna need some time to process. I mean—why would they lie to me? I mean . . . Is that what you're saying? Are you saying you're not my father? Like, are you saying that this is just one big fiction?"

"That's not what I'm saying."

"Whew. That's cool, man. Because . . . man. That would be twisted."

"I'm sorry all of this happened like this, Russ."

"Don't be. People make mistakes. The trick is forgiving them. I forgive you, and forgive my mom."

"You've got a great dad. Buddy, I mean."

"I know, man. He's a good guy. He really is."

"I better get back in there."

"Good talk, man. I mean Dad. I mean . . . you know what I mean. Thanks for being humble by the way. I totally respect that."

Chic walked across the parking lot. Before going back inside the hall, he glanced over his shoulder. Russ was lying down in the bed of the truck. Chic couldn't see his face, only the sole of his shoe on one foot and his cast with his exposed toes. He exhaled some smoke into the air, and it looked like he was breathing out his cold breath, like he was behind his own barn, alone and surrounded by snow.

Mary & Green Geneseo

■

July 27, 1998

Mary shook Green awake and told him the van was on its way. What she said didn't register at first. He'd been dreaming about Jane sunbathing, about driving his '77 Oldsmobile Cutlass Supreme, about his co-workers throwing him a retirement party, about Jane using a pocket mirror to apply lipstick. Green tried to roll over. He didn't want to go. He wanted to stay in bed where it was warm. She could have her affair. He wouldn't ask questions or accuse her of lying anymore. He'd ignore it and let her do whatever she wanted. He just wanted to go back to his dreams.

Mary pulled the blankets down to the bottom of the bed, exposing his skinny body and knobby knees. He was wearing boxer shorts and a tank top undershirt.

"I'm not messing around, Green. Let's go. Get up."

He reached over for his pad of Post-it Notes on the night-

stand while Mary opened a dresser drawer and pulled out a handful of boxers and tossed them on the bed. "Where's your swimming suit?" she asked. Green wrote, *I love you*, but he wasn't sure
if that was true. He wanted to love her. Or, rather, he wanted to
be loved by her. He wanted it to be simple, but it wasn't simple. It
was complicated. He peeled off the note and crumpled it up. He
wrote another note and held it out to her. *Are you divorcing me?*

"I told you. This is short term. A month, two at the most,
then like I said, we'll move back to Vegas. I need to get some
things figured out." She'd explained all of this last night—stroke,
doctors, staff, blah, blah, blah.

He didn't believe her. She was going to stick him in We Care
and then blow out of town, leaving him to rot away with the
zombies.

From the closet, she pulled out a suit, the maroon one, the
one he wore the first time he visited the Brazen Bull, and laid it
on the bed. She held up a flashy black cowboy shirt with pearl
buttons and roses embroidered on each shoulder. "You wanna
pack this?"

He shook his head yes.

"Lots of people go to assisted living facilities for a short period of time. The people are nice. Your roommate is deaf. Carol
is nice. They have a pool and you like swimming. You can join
that morning club Carol talked about—the morning swimmers
or whatever it was called."

This had to be a big, cosmic joke. This wasn't happening; it
wasn't real. In a few minutes, he'd open his eyes and be back in
Vegas, floating on a raft in the above-ground pool, holding a can
of Budweiser, Jane sprawled out in a sun chair wearing ridicu-
lously large sunglasses. He'd be Green Geneseo again, with an
entire Saturday afternoon ahead of him, the mountains in the
distance, the hideously blue sky above him, maybe some Chinese
takeout on the agenda for dinner, the stereo speaker in the Airstream window blaring Billy Squier's "Lonely Is the Night."

"Are you listening to me?" She was holding two suits, each on hangers. "Do you want to take both of these?"

Yes, he nodded. He was taking everything with him. No guy was going to move into his bungalow and start wearing his suits and start pretending to be him. He, Green, was him, the only Green, the only him, the only guy who could wear his suits.

"I don't think I've ever seen you wear this one." Mary was now holding up a black pinstriped suit. "Sure you want to take it?"

Yes, he wrote. *I want to take it.*

Sixteen

Chic Waldbeeser

■

June–August 1985

In the weeks and months following her death, Chic settled into his new life without Diane. It wasn't a good life, not that his life with her had been the good life, but this was worse. He stopped combing his hair. He rarely showered. He didn't bother matching his socks. He wore threadbare v-neck t-shirts with stains under the armpits. Most nights, he would conk out on the couch while watching *The A-Team* or *Knight Rider* or some other action-oriented show he had little interest in, and wake up around midnight and head up to bed, where he would toss and turn, pulling at the sheets, rolling over on his right side, then his left, back to his right, his left, his right, onto his back, onto his stomach, his back again, until he would finally give up and open his eyes and stare at the ceiling, the same ceiling Diane had stared at while listening to *The Art of Living*. He thought about all the things he'd done wrong, and how he could have been a better husband, a better father, a better everything.

He rolled out of bed and went down to the kitchen for a glass of water. In the cabinet above the sink were nearly two dozen glasses, way too many for one man. He pulled open the silverware drawer. There were enough knives and forks and spoons for the goddamn Brady Bunch. In the living room, Diane's old issues of Dr. Peale's magazine, *Guideposts* were scattered about, on the coffee table, on the floor next to the couch. He went back upstairs and peeked into the nursery. The nightlight cast eerie shadows across the dolls' blank faces. They all wore the same expression: eyes wide and unblinking. He needed to get this stuff out of his sight, get it out of the house, get it out of his life.

He rented a storage space on the edge of town, out by the new soccer fields, and asked Russ and Ginger to come over the following Saturday. They started with the kitchen, wrapping the glasses and dishes in newspaper and carefully placing them in cardboard boxes, leaving behind two plates, two bowls, two glasses, and two settings of silverware. In the living room, they packed up the Airdyne bike, the couch, and the coffee table. In the bedroom, they emptied Diane's closet and her dresser drawers and pitched all of her makeup, except for the dry skin lotion. Chic told them he wanted to hold onto that. They took the clock radio from her side of the bed, the lamp, too. They loaded all of Dr. Peale books into cardboard boxes; Russ carried the issues of *Guideposts* to the garbage can outside next to the garage. Chic had made a list, and each time they finished a task, he crossed it off. In the nursery, they placed each doll in its own box, then took down the shelves where the dolls had sat for so many years. They also carried out the furniture—the crib, the changing table, the rocker, even the mobile that hung in the corner. When they were finished, the room was nothing more than an empty square with holes in the walls and indentations in the carpet where furniture had once rested.

Near the end of the day, Russ and Ginger came into the empty nursery to find Chic sitting on the floor with a green Middleville Junior High School duffel bag. He'd taken a box of keepsakes out of the closet and was rifling through it, stuffing pictures and memorabilia into the duffel bag. He was going to tell Russ about the lie. He'd been thinking about it all day, and he couldn't go on living it. It wasn't right.

"I think we got it all," Russ said.

"Unless you want us to take that lamp in the living room," Ginger added.

"All I want left in the house is a bed, the television, the dining room table with one chair, and my toothbrush."

Ginger looked at Russ. "We can get the lamp on the way out."

"You want us to take the duffel bag?" Russ asked.

"Duffel bag stays with me," Chic said. "The box, though, can go."

Ginger picked up the box. "You want to come with us? Take over the last load?"

"Actually, Russ, I want to talk to you about something." Then he noticed Ginger standing behind him, her hand on his shoulder. They looked—what was the word?—complete, that was the word, complete. Russ was a good-looking boy. He had darkish skin, like his mother, and dark hair that was shiny and inky, like someone had colored it with Magic Marker. Ginger was a lovely woman, maybe a little tomboyish, but she made eye contact when she talked and seemed understanding and sympathetic. She was the type of person who'd share an umbrella with you in the rain. She wouldn't hog the covers. She'd be a good mother one day. She'd clip coupons. And Russ, he had good teeth. Chic did not have good ones, especially lately. His dentist wanted to pull a molar on his right side. Russ would do the things that were necessary to avoid bad teeth, like flossing. Russ was smart, too, or at least, he said smart things, like that tree stuff. Russ would prepare himself for a time like this, a time like Chic was experiencing—this loneliness. After he told Russ the truth about his mother, after Russ asked him why he did it, what finally made him do it after all of these years, Chic would tell him he was getting whipped by his loneliness. It was a beast, a killer. It had fangs and claws. He didn't want to be the only one hurting, so he told him, to hurt him. And he was sorry. But why do that? Why make him hurt like he was hurting? There was no reason. Russ was young. He and Ginger had their lives spreading out in front of them, unfolding like a map. But, and here was the problem, their lives could go in two very different directions. Chic knew this . . . oh, did he know this. A life could bank and turn and end up in a grassy field full of wild flowers, the sun blazing down, the birds chirping overhead. Or a life could wash up on a beach after a storm, the waves crashing on the sand, the boat busted to hell. Maybe he should be like a lighthouse. Maybe that's why he should tell him. Lay all the hell out for him. Give it to him straight. Warn him. That was the fatherly thing to do. But he wasn't his father. He and Russ weren't even related by blood. So, what gave him the right? Telling him the truth would be a big glass of saltwater, and what was it really going to do but make him upset? He didn't want to see him upset, so he simply stared at him and said nothing, resigned, again, to say nothing, this time forever.

"What? What do you want to talk to me about?"

"It's nothing. Forget it."

"What, man? You can tell me. I'm not going to judge you."

"Thank you. I just wanted to tell you thank you. For today. I appreciate it."

"No problem, Dad."

"Don't call me Dad, please. Buddy is your father."

After they left, Chic went downstairs to the living room. The room seemed smaller now that it was mostly empty. He clicked on the television and sat down in the chair. He set the duffel bag on his lap and pulled out his hand drawing of the pool he had wanted to put in the backyard. He'd found it in the box of keepsakes. Diane must have kept it, although he didn't know why. How stupid he'd been. Like digging a pool was going to make things better. Not to mention the irony. What kind of person actually thought he could change things by doing something like putting a pool in the backyard? Maybe Diane had the right idea after all. Maybe there was nothing you could do. Just sit there and let things happen. Don't try to do anything. Let the sun rise and set. Don't move. Let the darkness surround you.

Mary & Green & Chic

■

July 27, 1998

Chic made it a point to be at the Pair-a-Dice the afternoon

Green moved in. It was bad enough that Mary was checking her husband into We Care, but Carol Bowen-Smith also did these elaborate welcome parties for new residents, plucking away on a guitar and making up lyrics about the person's life. Chic wanted no part of any of that. However, he mistimed his return trip from the Pair-a-Dice, taking the four o'clock bus back, thinking that the party had happened after lunch. When he arrived at the facility around four-thirty, Mary and Green and Carol Bowen-Smith were sitting together at a cafeteria table. Chic tried to do an about-face, but then he heard someone say his name.

"Mr. Waldbeeser," Carol called out, "you're just in time to welcome our new resident. Come say hi to Mr. Geneseo."

Chic smelled like cigarette smoke, and his shirt was wrinkled. He was also chewing gum, something Carol had disapproved of ever since Jack Kearns nearly bit his tongue off while chewing bubble gum a few years back. Chic took a napkin out of his pocket and spit out the gum. Mary, Green, and Carol stared at him. He felt like he was standing in the middle of a stage under a blinding spotlight. Carol asked him if he was all right, and he said that he must have drunk too much coffee at the Pair-a-Dice. She then introduced him to Green and Mary, which, of course, was awkward. When shaking his hand, Green held on for too long and gave him an up-and-down examination, like he was a dog sniffing another dog's backside. Chic wondered if he was onto him. Mary made a comment about his name, calling it "unique."

"It's a family name," Chic said. "It was my great great great grandfather's name." This was a lie. It wasn't a family name. It probably had significance, but he didn't know what it was. To him, it was just an odd name that followed him around like his sad life.

"Chic has been living with us for about what ... twelve years?" Carol Bowen-Smith said.

"Actually, thirteen. Lucky thirteen. But I'm planning a little break, a vacation if you will." Chic quickly excused himself and went over to the steam table and loaded up a tray of food: oven-fried chicken and instant mashed potatoes, along with a roll and a glass of milk. He sat down a few tables away from Mary and Green and did his absolute best not to stare, though he couldn't help himself. This was his competition—a guy in a wheelchair and lavender hospital pants. Wait a second, those weren't hospital pants. They were polyester suit pants. My God, who was this guy, some sort of Las Vegas pimp?

Carol Bowen-Smith stood up and clinked her fork against her water glass. "In fifteen minutes, we're meeting in the common room, folks. We have a new resident to introduce." Chic surveyed the other tables to gauge the other residents' interest. Janice Galbreath's head bobbed, a thin spider string of drool yo-yoing off her bottom lip. Leroy Midge, the deaf guy, was slouched in his chair sleeping, the food on his tray untouched, and Chic's roommate, Morris Potterbaum, dressed in his usual dinner outfit of shirt and tie, held up his water glass. "Cheers to the new guy. Bravo," he declared.

The nurses helped the residents dispose of their trays. Mary negotiated Green's wheelchair around some tables and out into the hallway. She gave a quick over-the-shoulder glance at Chic, but he averted his eyes, looking down at the floor.

"Join us, Mr. Waldbeeser? We're going to do the Name Song," Carol said.

"Yeah, quit being a sad sack, Waldbeeser," Morris called from the dessert cart. "Show some spirit."

In the common room, Green was parked in front of the television, facing the nurses and residents. Mary stood behind him, her hand on his shoulder, and Carol stood beside the couple, her acoustic guitar hanging from her neck. Several residents were squeezed onto the couch, and the ones who sat in wheelchairs were scattered around the room. Janice Galbreath was sitting in an old plaid chair, the same string of drool yo-yoing from her bottom lip. Morris stood against the back wall, eating from a container of yogurt.

"You folks wanna hear about Green Geneseo's life?" Carol asked, to no response. She then nodded at Mary, and all eyes in the room that were still open and awake turned to her. Mary didn't know what to say, as Green had never told her much about his past. She had tried to get him to talk, but he always gave her the bookie story, which she had her doubts about. One afternoon while he was out running errands, she'd snooped around the trailer and found a shoe box squirreled away in the bedroom closet. The box was wrapped shut with packing tape, but she managed to peel back a corner and weasel out a hand-twisted, tinfoil rose. She imagined the rose was something he'd given to the woman he'd previously shared the trailer with.

Mary cleared her throat and smiled nervously. "Green Geneseo," she began, "grew up in Las Vegas with a loving mother and father. Actually, that's not quite right. His parents weren't that loving." Green looked down at his lap. "He had a good childhood, though. He played peewee football and Little League baseball. His parents doted on him and called him Red Rider. They took him on vacations to the Grand Canyon and to California. He grew up fast and was a star athlete who lettered in two sports and got a football scholarship to the University of Nevada. He met his first wife, Kim, a cheerleader, during his freshman year. Her father owned a grocery store in her hometown of Dustin, Nevada. Love at first sight. They got married. He used to make her roses out of tinfoil and paper napkins, the Sunday comics. He was an accountant. She stayed at home and painted her fingernails. They lived in a trailer with a pool. They got older. They talked about retirement. Florida. Moving to Florida. Then, she died. Passed away is probably a better way to put it. Her heart. A heart attack. Forty-seven years of marriage or something like that. And then he met me, at a bowling alley. Two people in the right place at the right time, and you know what they say about love—you just know it when you feel it. And I've been the luckiest, happiest girl ever since. Or, at least, until he had a stroke a couple weeks ago."

She glanced over at Carol Bowen-Smith, who began strumming the chord progression to "Michael, Row Your Boat Ashore."

"Sing it with me, folks. Green, you've lived a long full life. Here we go now. Everyone. *Green, row your boat ashore . . . halleeelluuujjaaa.*" Mary joined in, her thick hand squeezing Green's shoulder. She leaned down and kissed him on top of the head.

As soon as the singing started, Janice Galbreath snapped alive and started clapping. Morris Potterbaum tapped a beat on the bottom of his empty yogurt container with a spoon. As part of the orientation ritual, Carol led a conga line of the residents around the common room and down the hall to the cafeteria where there was cake and ice cream. Mary pushed Green in his wheelchair, while the nurses pushed the other residents in wheelchairs. The rest, like Morris Potterbaum, walked, and the group headed down the hallway, everyone singing, *Green, row your boat ashore . . . halleeelluuujjaaa.*

Chic was pressed against the hallway wall as the group passed. He narrowed his eyes at Mary to let her know his utter disapproval, but she wouldn't look at him. She closed her eyes and sang. He noticed Green was staring at him, though. He had a pained look like he'd just been socked in the stomach. Chic turned his back on him and walked down the hallway to his room.

. . . *halleeelluuujjaaa.*

Seventeen

Chic & Buddy & Lijy & Russ & Ginger & Erika Waldbeeser

■

Christmas Eve, 1985

Chic sat on the chair with his coat on and the green duffel bag in his lap, waiting for Russ and Ginger to pick him up. He'd been waiting for over an hour, ever since Buddy had called to invite him to Christmas dinner—though Buddy had made it clear it wasn't really Christmas, but rather, just "a dinner." They didn't have a Christmas tree. And he shouldn't bring any gifts. (Not that Chic had any time to go to the store, anyway.)

In the truck, Russ and Ginger were both talking fast and finishing each other's sentences. They'd recently placed a down payment on a little farmhouse with a hundred acres and a pond outside of Farmington, about an hour's drive from Middleville. They told Chic they planned to grow white pines and Fraser First, and during the Christmas season, they'd hire high school kids to cut down the trees and tie them to the rooftops of cars. Ginger said that she remembered riding out to the country with her father and the two of them cutting down the family Christmas tree. Russ reached over Chic, who was sitting between the two of them, and patted Ginger's thigh.

Buddy greeted them all at the door, wearing a mint-green dhoti and sandals with black socks. He kissed Ginger on the cheek, then shook Chic's hand, noticing the duffel bag. In the open kitchen, Lijy and Erika were preparing the meal, which smelled spicy and a bit musky.

"What's with the green bag?" Buddy asked. "You planning on spending the night?"

"Memories," Chic said.

"He carries it everywhere," Russ said.

"I have something for you, Chic," Buddy said.

"I thought you said no gifts."

"It's not a gift. It's a loan. I want it back."

Erika brought over a salmon-colored, satin fabric that was folded into a perfect square.

"It's a dhoti."

"What's a dhoti?" Chic asked.

"It's like a robe. Like what I'm wearing. It's very comfortable. Put it on."

"I don't want to."

"Put it on."

Lijy turned around from the stove. "Don't make him put it on if he doesn't want to."

"Nonsense. He's putting it on. This," he said to Chic, patting the folded fabric, "will change your whole outlook." Buddy pointed him to the bathroom, which was down the hall.

After shutting and locking the bathroom door, Chic unfolded the dhoti. A piece of fabric was going to change his outlook? He stripped down to his underwear and caught a glimpse of himself in the mirror. He'd shaved that morning and nicked himself on the chin. He was skinnier than he should be. He could see his ribs. He wrapped the dhoti around himself. He wasn't really sure how it went on. Did he wrap it this way? That felt a little too airy. He unwrapped it and wrapped it a different way. He looked in the mirror. He felt ridiculous. This wasn't him. He took it off and put his clothes back on.

At the table, there was an open place for him next to Russ.

"Where's the dhoti?" Buddy asked.

"It wasn't really me."

"How is it not you?"

"No offense, Mr. Waldbeeser," Ginger said, "but it's kinda weird the first time you put one on."

"Well, we like them," Buddy said. He gave Lijy a look.

"He definitely likes them more than I do." Lijy said, dishing herself some aloo gobi and passing the serving bowl to Chic. Chic looked at the food, not quite sure what the yellowish, chunky, oily goop was. He smelled it. Musty. He took a spoonful and plopped it on his plate, then handed the dish to Russ and sampled a tiny bite.

"Do you like it?" Lijy asked.

"It's interesting," Chic answered. Actually, it was terrible—spicy and oily and strange. He'd never tasted anything like it. It made his tongue swell, and his eyes started to water. He wanted to spit it out, but he knew he couldn't do that. "Do you, by chance, have any white bread?" he asked.

"White bread?" Buddy said and pretty much clanged down his fork.

"Daddy doesn't allow white bread in the house," Erika said.

"Russ eats white bread sandwiches," Ginger said. "Lunch meat and yellow cheese, a little mayo."

"Mayonnaise? Lunch meat?" Buddy snapped.

Russ shrugged. "If I'm in a hurry."

"We have wheat bread," Lijy said. "Buddy baked it yesterday." She got up from the table and brought the loaf over. Chic took the heel and used it to scoop a potato out of the yellowish goop. Everyone watched as he bit into it, then spit it into his napkin.

"I guess I don't really like it," he said.

"Well, you don't have to pretend," Buddy said. "Eat whatever the hell you want. White bread and yellow cheese and mayonnaise sandwiches. That stuff will make you fat. It's terrible for you. But I don't care what you do. Gain weight. Get fat. Get obese and have a heart attack. Die a horrible death. I don't care. Who cares?"

"Daddy!" Erika said.

"What?"

"Diane didn't want to be fat," Chic said.

"I wasn't talking about Diane."

"It's okay. It's true."

"But that's not what I meant."

"Hey, you know, we have some news," Russ interrupted.

"Yeah, Russ. Tell Chic the news," Buddy said.

Russ put his hand on Ginger's leg. "You want to tell him or you want me to?"

"You tell him," Ginger said.

"Someone tell him!" Buddy said.

"We got married. A couple of weeks ago."

Ginger smiled. "At the courthouse."

"Married?" Chic looked around the table.

"We're having a little celebration. Just family. This spring, at the farm."

"Isn't it great?" Lijy said, looking at Chic.

Ginger put her arms around Russ and kissed him on the cheek.

Chic picked up his glass of water and took a drink. "That's really great."

"You don't seem excited," Buddy said.

"I'm excited."

"You don't seem it."

Chic held up his water glass and looked at Russ and Ginger. "Good luck."

"Good luck?" Buddy said.

"Look out where you're going," Chic added.

"Like the poem," Russ said.

"About that poem . . ." Buddy started.

"I thought it was a nice poem," Lijy said.

"I liked it," Russ said.

"Me too," Ginger said.

"Let's not talk about the poem. Congratulations, Russ and Ginger," Chic said. "Cheers, everyone."

They all held up their glasses.

After dinner, Russ and Ginger went for a walk, even though Buddy protested that it was too cold outside. They said they wanted to see the moon, which was full. Erika went to her room, and Buddy brewed Darjeeling tea and set a plate of cookies on the coffee table. Chic sat down on the couch.

"Have a cookie," Buddy said.

Chic picked one up and took a bite. He reached for a napkin. "Jesus," he said, spitting the cookie into the napkin. "That's the worst cookie I've ever had."

Buddy picked up one and dipped it in his tea. "No refined white sugar. No bleached flour. I even made the chocolate myself."

"When I want a cookie, I want a cookie."

"That's the problem," Buddy said.

"How is that a problem?"

"It's a problem. Trust me."

"I don't see how that's a problem."

"Okay, boys. Enough," Lijy interrupted. "Chic, we have something to tell you."

"Me, too."

"You first," Buddy said.

"No. Go ahead. You first."

"No, please, Chic," Lijy said.

"I just wanted to say," he looked at both of them, "that I thought you should know. Both of you. You should know . . ."

"Come out with it. What is it?"

"I'm lonely."

"Lonely?" Buddy said.

"Well, sure you are," Lijy said. "You live in that house by yourself."

"It's that . . . I'm lonely, lonely."

"Like you need a girlfriend?" Buddy said.

"No. Not that kind of lonely."

"You should get a dog," Buddy said.

"I think I've always been lonely. Even when Diane was alive. That's what I'm saying."

Lijy and Buddy exchanged puzzled glances.

"I've been spending a lot of time with Russ. That helps."

"That's good. You should do that," Lijy said. "That's important. You being his . . . you know. Isn't that good, Buddy?"

Buddy didn't say anything. He forced a smile.

"I don't want to be his father or anything. That's not what this is about. I'm happy for both of you. For all of you. The whole family." He gave Lijy a look, but she wouldn't meet his gaze. "I don't want to get in the middle of anything."

"I forgive you, Chic," Buddy said. "I should have said it years ago, but . . . well, I'm saying it now." Lijy grabbed Buddy's hand. Chic could feel his brother's forgiveness. He had a warm look in his eyes, and his eyes reached out to him. It seemed as if Buddy really had made peace with what had happened—or with what he thought had happened. Chic hadn't. He hadn't made peace with anything, and he didn't understand how his brother could have all this stuff, this warmness, this family, everything, and Chic had nothing. Absolutely nothing.

"I think I'm going to move into We Care. Sell the house," Chic said.

"The nursing home," Buddy said.

"Assisted living. I've been looking into it." He was bluffing, but he wanted Lijy and Buddy to feel sorry for him. He wanted them to do something for him. He was desperate. He didn't want to feel the way he was feeling, but he didn't know how to make it stop.

"You're only fifty-five years old," Lijy said.

"I'm lonely. I told you."

Lijy exchanged a glance with Buddy.

"So, we have some news for you," Buddy said.

"We're done talking about me?"

"We can come back to you in a second," Buddy said. "Tell him, Lijy."

"We're moving to Arizona."

Chic didn't say anything. He looked at his brother, then Lijy. "How is this helpful?"

"We're going to join a church," Buddy said.

"A church?"

"Not really a church, per se," Lijy said. "More a group of like-minded people."

"You're joining a cult?"

"No," Lijy said. "Not a cult."

"I wrote a book," Buddy interjected.

"When did you write a book?"

"It's like a cookbook type of thing, and I also included my thoughts on some things, and I sent it to this publishing company in Rock City, Arizona. The publishing company and the people, they're all in Rock City, Arizona."

"They invited us out there for a visit," Lijy added.

"We went out and stayed a week. And . . . we decided to move out there."

"Rock City, Arizona? You're leaving me? It's like Mom. It's like . . . I can't believe you're leaving. What about Erika?"

"She'll come with us."

"What the hell do either of you know about Arizona? You're from . . . Lijy, where are you from?"

"That doesn't matter," Buddy interrupted.

"There are rattlesnakes in Arizona." Chic said. "And cactuses. Have you ever seen a cactus? And not on television."

"And here's the thing," Buddy said. "We want you to come with us. So, you don't have to move into We Care. You won't have to be lonely. You'll be with us."

"Why can't we stay here? What's wrong with Middleville?"

"Middleville has changed. It's twice the size as when we were kids. Witzig's is gone. They're building new houses on the east side of town. There are a bunch of second-rate teenyboppers all over the place. You know this. You've seen it. It's not the Middleville we grew up in. I hear the teenagers talking. I see them.

The boys have long hair. They listen to loud music. I hear it coming from their cars. They're having sex."

"You should at least think about it, Chic," Lijy said.

"Rock City, Arizona. That doesn't even sound like a real town. It sounds made up. Are you making this up?"

"You just told us you're lonely."

"If I was going anywhere, I'd go to Florida."

"Florida? Like Mom. What the hell is in Florida?"

"I can't believe you're leaving me. My wife just died. You're leaving me, and my wife just died."

"Just think about it, will you?" Lijy asked.

"I thought about it." Chic picked up the wadded-up napkin containing the remnants of the cookie he had spit out. "By the way, if this is Arizona . . . this cookie . . . then I don't want it."

Mary Geneseo & Chic Waldbeeser

■

July 27, 1998

Mary knew Green was pissed after Carol's welcoming party. In his room, she tried to give him a little peck on the cheek, but he pulled the bed covers over his head. So, this was it. This was what she'd gotten herself into. "Come on, Green. Don't be like this. This is temporary. I told you. A few weeks, tops." Behind her, Green's roommate, whatever his name was, was snoring. In her wildest dreams, she never would have guessed she would be sitting in a nursing home trying to coax her "husband" into talking to her. Just go, the loud voice told her, let him be like this. You don't need this. You've already made up your mind. Just walk out the door.

Mary went out into the hallway. It felt like was four in the morning (it was twenty minutes after nine). The place was so quiet, except for the hum of the vending machines down the hall. It was after lights out, but since it was Green's first night, Carol had let Mary stay with him until he fell asleep. Chic's room was two doors down the hall. She stood in the hallway listening to the soft buzz of voices from the television in the common room. She wanted to go to Florida, but she didn't want to go, or rather she wanted to go more than she didn't want to go, or actually, she didn't want to go but wanted to go more than she wanted to stay. It was clear, but it wasn't. Nothing was clear. What was clear was that she couldn't stay, not in this town, not in Peoria. She wanted to go. That's what she wanted to do, and the loud voice agreed. You should go, it said. But the whisper voice didn't agree. She couldn't dump Green at a nursing home. People do it all the time, the loud voice said. You can't go, the whisper voice said. She couldn't help herself. She was pulled by some magnetic force, something larger than herself. She'd leave Chic too, someday. That was out there in her future, and she was speeding toward it. She knew, deep down, this wasn't going to work, none of this. She'd had a shot once at making something work, with Lyle, even though everyone who ever met him gave him a look that told her they thought he was an idiot. She saw the way they looked at him. But she ignored it. She loved him. She did. Or, thought she did. Or wanted to. Or, thought she should. And then . . . she opened that door. God, she felt that for a long time, the pain, like a mallet to her heart. She still felt it, actually, if she let herself think about it. Not that she wanted Lyle back. Jesus, no. She hoped he had gotten syphilis and gone mad and jumped off a bridge. But, holy shit, he had marked her, scarred her—whatever the hell you want to call it. Sometimes, at the strangest moments, she flashed back to that day, her keys jingling as she opened the apartment door, Journey's "Don't Stop Believing" on the stereo. When the memory snuck up on her, she had to sit down and choke it back, choke it the hell back. It was so much easier to think about it getting better. That's what she focused on. It was going to get better. It had to get better. It would get better. It was getting better. Chic had come into her life, and she was following the path his appearance had presented. She couldn't help that Green was going to get hurt as a result. She was only a blip in his life, something for him to see in his rearview mirror, like Lyle was something for her to see in her rearview mirror. She had to do what she was going to do. It was settled. She had to. She could. You can, the loud voice said. And you will. She tried the knob on Chic's door. It was unlocked. She peeked in. A slit of light from the parking lot squeezed through a part in the drapes. The room smelled of Vicks VapoRub. She slipped off her shoes and tiptoed across the tile floor. Chic's bed was the farthest from the door. She set her shoes in front of his nightstand and slid in behind him.

Chic was on his side, his back to the door. She nuzzled into him. "Hello, hello," she whispered.

He was spooned around the green duffel bag. He opened his eyes. "What are you doing here?"

"Shhhhh." She slid her hand down the front of his pajama bottoms.

"My roommate is in the next bed."

"Close your eyes."

"I don't want to close my eyes."

"This is Florida. Right now. We're in Florida." She blew her hot breath on the back of his neck. "Close your eyes and think about the beach, white sand, palm trees, blue sky."

He rolled over to face her. "Look, this is important to me. What are we doing? Please. Tell me."

She stared at him.

"Why'd you move your husband here?"

"I can't just leave him."

"So, you're choosing me?"

"What if, I was thinking, what if we went west—to Arizona? Your brother is in Arizona."

"Why does everyone want to go to Arizona?"

"Or Nevada? Or Utah? I'd even go to California."

"I want to go to Florida. That's the whole point."

She propped herself up on her elbow, and whisper sang: "Some will win, some will lose. Some were born to sing the blues. It goes on and on and on and on."

"What is that?"

"It's a song. By this band, Journey."

"Never heard of them."

Morris sat up in his bed. "Are you guys almost done yakking? I'm trying to sleep."

"Sorry Morris," Chic said.

"And don't think I don't know that you're the new guy's wife."

"I'm not the new guy's wife," Mary said.

"Very funny. I saw you come in. Now, please, shut the hell up so I can get some sleep."

Lijy & Chic

■

January 9, 1986

For the first time in over twenty-five years, Lijy told Buddy a lie. After dinner, he and Erika were watching television, and Lijy poked her head into the living room and said she had to run out to Stafford's to pick up some bananas. Outside, it had begun to snow lightly, little salt shakings falling to the ground. She knew she had about thirty minutes before Buddy would start pacing and looking out the window. A few days after Christmas, Russ had told her what Chic had said at Diane's funeral. He was curious. Was Chic really his father? He didn't seem anything like him, and why would Chic say he wasn't his father and then backtrack and try to smooth it over? Come to think of it, Russ had said, Chic hadn't ever come out and said that he was his father. The way Russ had looked at her that afternoon, like he wanted some answers, his eyes searching her eyes, trying to determine if she was lying to him, she had wanted to melt into a puddle and get the hell out of the conversation. She dodged the bullet by repeating over and over that Chic was his father and telling Russ that he was reading too much into what Chic had said, that he was probably just upset about his wife dying and not thinking straight. That seemed to do the trick. But she was worried. Could she trust Chic? She thought she could, but now ... Jesus ... she didn't know, and in a couple of months, she and Buddy were off to Arizona. As soon as they left, was Chic going to spill the goddamn beans? They'd been spending a whole lot of time together. Russ was always going over to his house. It was not his secret to tell—that's what really irked her. It was her mistake, and she was going to tell Russ. She had it all worked out in her head. She'd take him to dinner at some nice restaurant. Maybe she'd make him dinner. Or maybe they'd go for a drive. Anyway, she'd tell him—she hadn't decided on the time or venue and really those details didn't matter—and when she told him, she'd reach out and grab his forearm. This was how she imagined it. It would be spontaneous. She'd grab his forearm, and squeeze it, squeeze it so hard that Russ would look down at her hand and then up to her eyes, then down to her hand again. She'd probably be hurting him she'd be squeezing so hard. When he looked up to her face again, she'd come out with it. She'd start, of course, by telling him she was sorry. "Russ, I'm so sorry ..." But anyway, it was her truth to tell, and she wasn't going to let Chic Waldbeeser beat her to it. So she'd spent the better half of the afternoon locked in the bathroom writing Chic a letter, another letter, and the letter was tucked safely in her purse, and her plan was to put it in Chic's mailbox. However, there was a problem. Instead of a mailbox, Chic had a front door mail slot. She noticed this as soon as she got on his porch. She also noticed that the living room lamp was on, and she could hear the television, some sitcom with a laugh track. But she couldn't back out now. She had to get this letter to him, so she rummaged through her purse and got the letter out and ever so quietly, she began to slip the letter into the mail slot. She was careful not to go too quickly. She didn't want the metal flap to squeak. She kept sliding the letter slowly, slowly. She was breathing heavily, her heart thub-a-dub-dubbing in her chest. She worked the letter about halfway into the mail slot and stopped. That was good enough. He'd find it there. She stood up and quietly turned around, but before she could get down the first stair, the door burst open.

"Lijy?"

She looked at the mail slot. Chic looked there, too, and saw the letter hanging half in and half out of the slot. He snatched it. It was a white envelope with his name scratched across the front.

"It's not what you think. No lie this time. It's not like that."

"I don't care what it is. I'm not reading it. I refuse to read it. I won't let myself read it." He ripped it in half.

"Chic. No. Please."

He ripped it in half again. And again. And again. He ripped it until there was nothing left but tiny pieces. He threw the pieces at her, into the wind, which whisked them off the porch and into the winter night. "We both know what happened the last time you wrote me a letter."

"I talked to Russ. He told me. You made him suspicious."

"Do you know he has these ideas about trees in your head not matching the ones in the real world, or something like that? I don't know. It's not fair that he doesn't know the truth. I mean . . . he should know the truth."

"I'm going to tell him. When the time is right."

"He's married. He's twenty-five years old."

"The time isn't right."

"Suit yourself. Don't tell him. Do what you want. Is that all? Is that what your letter said? Don't tell him the truth. I can do that. I've done that for twenty-five years."

"Don't be like this, Chic."

"Be like what?"

"Like this."

"Like what?"

"Cruel."

"You dragged me into this. You concocted some elaborate secret that no one knows about but me, you, and my dead wife and son. And now you're moving to Arizona with my brother and leaving me here in Middleville."

"What's moving to Arizona have to do with anything?"

"Look, I get it. I'm not going to say anything."

"He likes you. And you two are starting to get close. I just want to make sure that you don't accidentally say something."

"I'm not going to tell him, but you know, if you wouldn't have gone off and did what you did, which was, I should point out, a very . . ."

"I know. You don't have to remind me. I know. Trust me. I know. And I'll tell him. I've been planning to tell him. And I will. I'll tell him. Just let me do it in my own time."

"I didn't want to be part of this in the first place."

"Actually, I think you did."

"I did not."

"Then why did you do it?"

"Why are we talking about this? Why does it matter? This happened so long ago, *so long ago*."

"You brought it up."

"I did not bring this up. You were on my porch. You came over here to give me a letter. I've made my peace with this, Lijy."

"You aren't over it. You're clearly not over it."

"I am too."

"I don't think you are."

"Let's drop it. This isn't going anywhere."

"I agree, but you should admit that you aren't over it."

"You should tell Russ, and you should tell him soon. That's what should happen. And while you're at it, you should tell my brother too."

"This bothers you, doesn't it, Chic? It *really* bothers you that I had an affair."

"I'm just looking out for my brother. That's who I feel sorry for here."

"Well, you're an awfully good brother."

"Thank you. Finally. Thank you. I've been waiting a long time for someone to tell me that."

"I'm going to tell him, Chic."

"No you won't."

"I will. I'm going to."

"For some reason, I don't believe you."

"I'm going to tell him the truth."

"No one tells the truth, Lijy. No one."

Chic & Buddy & Lijy & Russ & Ginger & Erika Waldbeeser

■

May 25, 1986

On the day that Buddy, Lijy, and Erika were leaving for Arizona, Russ and Ginger held their marriage celebration on the banks of the pond on their new farm. It was supposed to be just a quick afternoon picnic, but Buddy insisted on doing something more formal. After a minor argument beside the already packed station wagon, Russ agreed to let Buddy conduct a "ceremony." Russ set up some lawn chairs while Buddy picked a handful of black-eyed Susans for Ginger's bouquet. When he was done, Buddy ushered Russ up front and made Ginger stand behind the lawn chairs. Buddy then pushed play on a boom box, and *Canon in D* blared through the speakers. Ginger, wearing a tank top and shorts, slowly walked down the "aisle." When she reached Russ, who was wearing a mesh baseball cap, t-shirt, shorts, and sandals, she took his hand. Buddy then asked the two of them to turn and "face the congregation," which consisted of Chic, Lijy, Erika and a few cows about fifty yards away behind a barbed-wire fence.

Buddy first read a passage from his book. Chic tried to follow along, but Buddy mumbled the words. After a few minutes, he closed the book and went free form. He told Russ and Ginger that the greatest difficulty in life was finding something or someone to connect with. He hoped they'd found that connection in each other. He said he'd found connection with Lijy. He'd also found connection with what he called "spiritualism." At one time, he thought he had found a connection with coin collecting, but that had been an artificial connection, and artificial connections offered only the illusion of connection. He told Russ and Ginger to look out for artificial connections. "I'm connected to all of you," Buddy said in closing. "Me, Russ, Lijy, and Ginger, even Chic, all of us are connected to each other. We're family." He stood there and shuffled like he had more to say. "Do you mind if I'm honest?" He turned to Russ.

Russ shrugged. "Sure. Be honest."

"Ginger, it's your wedding day, and I don't want to ruin our connection."

She said it was okay for him to be honest.

"Honey, Lijy, do you mind if I'm honest?"

She looked over her shoulder at Chic, then looked back at Buddy. "Be honest."

"Erika?"

"Go ahead, Daddy."

"People can change," Buddy said. "People can change."

"Amen." Lijy clapped.

"As we all know, when I was a young man, I was full of rage. Chic, wasn't I full of rage?"

"You pulled me out of the living room window, if that's what you mean."

"That's an example. Yes. That's true. Erika, honey, I once pulled my brother out of a window, but luckily for all of us, people can change. I changed. Lijy, my beautiful wife, I have forgiven you, and you have forgiven me. Russ, you are my son. Ginger, you have the hands of a man, but the bosom of a woman. I want you to know that I'm not Russ's father, but you are my son's wife. You should know that."

"I knew that."

"Very good, then. Erika, my daughter, my light, my angel, my everything. My connection. You would not be with us without forgiveness and change."

Erika smiled at her father.

"And, Chic, my brother, my friend, my companion, my man, my dude—I learned that word from Russ. My dude, Chic, *my dude*."

"I'm not going to Arizona," Chic blurted out.

Lijy and Erika turned around.

"I know this is about me," Chic said. "That's what everyone wants. For me to go to Arizona. Well, it's not what I want."

"Chic, this isn't about you," Buddy said.

"Cut the crap, Buddy."

"This is about Russ—about family. About Ginger. About all of us."

"You have negative energy," Lijy said to Chic.

"I don't have negative energy."

"You do, Uncle Chic," Erika said.

"At one time, Chic," Buddy began, "I wished that your guts would rain down on your house and the crows would come in from the fields and roost in your trees. I'm sorry for the violent imagery, Erika. But, Chic, my brother, *my dude*, I forgave you. In the moment of my ultimate distress, in the parking lot of Roth Cemetery, when you were burying your son, I saw the ghost of our father, and all the rage I had, all of it, leaked out of me. Or, most of it. The point was that I felt relieved. I felt . . . better. You need to let it go, Chic. Let it go. Let it leak out of you. Let it be gone."

Chic just shook his head and glared at his brother. "I don't have negative energy."

After the ceremony, they all sat down at a wooden picnic table for the meal. Russ cooked black bean burgers on a grill, and there were baked beans and asparagus for sides. They drank lemonade from Styrofoam cups. Chic had brought a bottle of champagne, but Buddy wouldn't let him open it, so the bottle sat in the middle of the table next to Ginger's black-eyed Susans, which Buddy had put in a Styrofoam cup. They ate quickly because Buddy wanted to get on the road before dark. He was the first one done, and excused himself to take a walk around the pond. Chic watched as his brother stopped in front of a tree on the far side of the pond. Chic thought about his brother's sermon—or whatever you wanted to call it. He didn't give off negative energy. He was fine. A little sad, maybe. But negative? No way. Across the pond, his brother had his hands behind his back and was looking up into the canopy of the tree. Suddenly, about a dozen blackbirds flew out of the tree and into the sky.

After a few minutes, Buddy made his way back to the picnic table. Everyone was choking down the sugarless cake he'd made for dessert.

"How is it?" he asked.

"Tastes like dirt," Chic said.

"You need to get rid of that rage, dude."

Russ licked some frosting off his plastic spoon. "Well, it is a little dry."

"It's good for you and that's what's important."

"Did you really see a ghost, Dad?" Erika asked.

Chic laughed. "He didn't see anything. He saw his imagination."

"You don't have to believe me."

"At most, it was a metaphor. Erika, your father was using a literary device to make a point. But, still, his point was ridiculous. Does anyone really believe that crap he said?"

Lijy said she did, as did Erika. Ginger nodded her head. Even Russ, who Chic thought knew better.

"People can't change. Tell me you don't believe that, Russ," Chic asked.

"But Buddy changed," Lijy said. "He's living proof."

"Do you really think this is Buddy? Writing cookbooks and wearing pastel robes. This is Buddy? My brother?"

"It's me," Buddy said.

"This is not you."

"I'm standing right here, Chic. How is this not me?"

"It's a lie."

"I'm not lying. This is me."

"I think its crap. It's overdramatic. But then again, Buddy, you always were overdramatic. Look at you. You're wearing a robe and baking sugarless cakes. Well, I got news for you. We're all sitting behind our own barns, just like Dad. Sitting in the snow alone."

"Well, that's one man's opinion," Buddy said. He looked at Lijy. "I guess we better get going."

"Yeah, we should go," Lijy said.

"Wait a second," Chic said. "I'm not trying to run you off. I'm entitled to my opinion."

"You hurt my feelings," Buddy said.

"Settle down. Relax. Everyone just stay seated. No one's leaving without my surprise." Chic set his green duffel bag down on the picnic table and pulled out a box with a bow on it. "Someone get that champagne popped. Russ, please."

"We should get going," Buddy said.

"I listened to you."

Russ opened the bottle of champagne and poured everyone a little taste in their Styrofoam cups.

"None for me," Buddy said.

"Oh, come on," Chic said.

"I'm driving," Buddy said.

"Ginger, can you open the present?" Chic asked.

Ginger opened the box. Inside was a copy of *Onward Toward What We're Going Toward*. Chic had signed it, *Look out where you're going*. Ginger stared at the cover, a dot matrix printout of a single, large star.

"I want to propose a toast," Chic said.

"We really need to get going," Buddy said.

"He's right. We should get on the road," Lijy said. With that, she, Buddy, and Erika walked over to the station wagon. Russ and Ginger followed, leaving Chic alone. He was steaming; his brother got to sermonize about a bunch of bullshit, but he didn't get to read a poem and give a two-minute toast.

They all hugged in front of the car. Lijy and Erika called out good-byes to Chic, waving, but he didn't wave back. Buddy then slid behind the wheel, and Lijy got into the passenger seat. In the backseat, Erika put on Walkman headphones. Buddy maneuvered the station wagon around some sapling white pines. He honked twice when he got the car on the gravel road. Russ and Ginger watched and waved as the station wagon kicked up a cloud of dust and disappeared into the horizon.

"All right," Chic said when the two of them had walked back to the picnic table. "Grab a cup. Let me give my toast."

"Do you really think this is necessary?" Russ asked.

"We listened to Buddy. Now it's my turn."

Russ and Ginger each grabbed a Styrofoam cup.

"This is the first poem I ever wrote. I think it's appropriate."

"We're celebrating. No depressing poems," Russ said.

"What do you call what Buddy did? That was depressing as hell. Anyway, I won't read this poem." Chic flipped ahead a couple of pages. "Yes, this is a good one. And not depressing. I wrote it the afternoon after Diane's funeral. In the parking lot of the Knights of Columbus hall. You remember, Russ. We were talking. Here goes: *A life should be/ a voice that knows when to/ shut its big fat mouth.*"

Russ held up his cup. "Here, here."

"Put down your cup. I'll get to the toast. A few more poems, first." Chic stepped up onto one of the picnic table benches. He then read three more poems and downed his Styrofoam cup of champagne. He picked up the bottle and read two more poems. He took a pull off the bottle. He wound up reading the entire chapbook, taking a big sip of champagne each time he finished a poem.

"I think it's time to stop," Russ finally said. He grabbed Chic's sleeve to help him down from the bench.

"Be a man, Russ. That's what you need to do. That's my advice to you."

"Very good. Thank you for the advice."

"Be a man."

"I got it." He tried to take the champagne bottle away from him, but Chic wouldn't let him. He took another swig.

"Ghosts. Connection. Change. What-the-hell-ever. All of it. Bullshit. Arizona—bullshit. You know what family is?" Chic grabbed his groin. "That's it. Plain and simple."

"We're worried about you," Ginger said. "Are you all right?"

"I'm fine. I'm great. I'm the best I've ever been. Here, you know what. Both of you. Start your family. It's your wedding night. Start your family." Chic grabbed his groin again. "Make a family."

"Let's take you home," Russ said.

"I don't want to go home."

"I think it's time to go home."

"Who wants to go to Florida?"

"No one is going to Florida."

"We should get in that goddamn big truck of yours and drive. Go to Florida. It's your honeymoon. Start your family, Russ. Start it. You have to. It's where you're going. Why are you standing there looking at me? Don't look at me like that."

"You're drunk."

"One more poem."

"We've heard enough."

"One more drink, then." Chic tried to take another sip, but Russ snatched the bottle away.

Eighteen

Chic & Green, the beginning of the end

July 28, 1998

When Chic woke up the next morning, Mary was gone, and Morris Potterbaum was sitting at the end of his bed using a pocketknife to cut wedges from a Granny Smith apple. He told Chic he understood a man needed to "release steam," and he also understood that a man might want to release that steam with another man's wife, but he preferred—or actually "demanded"—Chic release his steam someplace other than their room, say the broom closet or a car in the parking lot.

"I'm sorry," Chic said. "It won't happen again."

"I hope not." Morris fed himself a slice of apple.

"You don't have to hope. It won't."

"Now that that is behind us, you owe me ten bucks, or I tell the new guy you're boning his wife."

"I'm not boning his wife."

"Aren't you planning a trip to, ah, Florida?"

"You're blackmailing me?"

"Yes. That's right."

Chic slid out of bed and put on his slippers. "I can't believe you're blackmailing me."

Morris shrugged. "There's a cost to all of this."

Chic got the money from his wallet and handed it to Morris.

"I'll see you in the cafeteria," Morris said.

Although his day had certainly started out poorly, Chic wasn't going to let Morris Potterbaum blow a storm cloud over the rest of it. He was going to Florida. To *Florida*. This was *goddamn it*. Finally. He was going to set himself, his life, everything, on the right path. He'd show his brother, show Lijy, Russ, Ginger, everyone, he'd show them all. He and . . . Mary . . . he and Mary were going to turn things around.

After a shower and a shave, he put on a pair of polyester slacks, a button-up shirt, and the alligator loafers Mary had given him. He had wanted to put on his poet clothes, but they were packed away in storage. He'd have to stop by the storage facility before he left because in Florida, he was going to be a full-fledged poet. He opened his notebook to the poem he was working on. *Around the corner is the end.* He sat on his bed and put the pen in his mouth and began to chew on it. He said, "Around the corner is the end." He smelled bacon from the cafeteria.

At a quarter to nine, fifteen minutes before breakfast ended, Chic waltzed into the cafeteria, strutting a little bit. The alligator loafers were too big, and with each step, his heel slipped and made a sound like someone walking in scuba flippers. Carol Bowen-Smith was drinking coffee at a table with a few nurses. At a table by the salad bar, Morris was spooning a grapefruit while reading a pamphlet about bone strength. In a far back corner, Green sat by himself, a bowl of soggy cereal set in front of him. Chic cut through the tables toward him.

"Hello, Mr. Geneseo. Good day."

Green wiped some milk drool from his chin. He wrote something on his Post-it Note pad.

"I enjoyed your introduction. It sounds like you've had a very eventful life. I'm sorry about your first wife—whatever her name was. I lost my wife, too. Thirteen years ago."

"Sit down Waldbeeser," Morris said from behind. "Leave the guy alone."

Chic turned to Morris. "I'm only making friends."

"The hell you are. You're messing with the poor guy. Leave him alone. Come sit with me."

"I don't think I'm in the mood to sit with you." Chic turned back to Green, who handed him a Post-It Note.

337

"The new guy would like to communicate." Chic read the note. "It says, 'spiff.' That's very interesting, Mr. Geneseo. Did you misspell a word?"

Green wrote, *I'm calling you a spiff.*

"He's calling me a spiff. And what is a spiff?"

You.

"Very funny, Mr. Geneseo. A real card you are. And why, may I ask, would you be calling me a spiff?"

Carol Bowen-Smith came over. "That's enough, Mr. Wald-beeser," she said sternly. Just then, Green pushed his whole bowl of cereal right onto the floor and all over Chic's shoes.

"Jesus Christ!"

Green, of course, recognized the shoes. He'd recognized them as soon as Chic had come slop-footing into the cafeteria. He'd bought them a few months before Jane's diagnosis. They'd spent the afternoon playing blackjack and eating shrimp cocktail at the Golden Gate San Francisco Casino. Jane spotted the shoes in a shop window and talked him into buying them.

"You like my shoes," Chic said. "They were a gift."

Green wrote *SPIFF* on a Post-it Note again.

"This again. Unfortunately, I don't have time for name calling."

"Mr. Waldbeeser, you'll need to clean up this mess," Carol Bowen-Smith said.

"I didn't make it."

"You instigated it."

"Do we instigate our messes? Or do messes just happen? This mess, I think, just happened."

"Very philosophical, Waldbeeser," Morris said.

Before Chic could turn around, Green wheeled over his foot.

"Jesus, watch out where you're going." Chic reached down and grabbed his left foot, and the loafer fell off into the pud-dle of milk. Green picked it up, and Chic grabbed it, but Green wouldn't let go. The two of them played tug-of-war until, finally, Chic pried it away.

"Boys," Carol Bowen-Smith said. "Control yourselves."

"What's your goddamn problem?" Chic asked.

Green turned his wheelchair around and headed toward the cafeteria door.

"Did everyone see that?"

"You weren't being very nice to him," Carol said.

"He dumped his bowl of cereal on my shoes. Then he ran over my feet. You saw him."

"Did you cause the mess, or did the mess just happen?" Morris said.

Green Geneseo

■

July 28, 1998

He'd made a terrible, terrible mistake. He'd trusted her. Actually, it was worse—he'd married her. He'd let his guard down. He should have known better, but he was desperate and lonely. God, was he lonely. He used to sit in the trailer in his boxers watching television in the dark. He ate Rice Krispies for dinner. He'd go get gas in the car, even if the car didn't need gas, just to do something. She'd totally taken advantage of him. He'd fallen for her, and now she was leaving him for what? Chic something . . . whatever his last name was. He lived at a nursing home. At least she could be leaving him for some guy who drove a convertible. There must be something wrong with him, some kind of health condition. She was leaving him for a guy with a health condition, a sick guy. What a goddamn joke. He'd been blinded by his loneliness. Now, he was in the middle of Illinois, sitting in a wheelchair in a godforsaken nursing home. He had to get out of here. He had to get in touch with Tim Lee. Tim would get on a plane and be here in a day or two and get him back to Vegas. He couldn't believe she'd given him his shoes. She was a snake. He should rip out every single one of her teeth with pliers. He should cut out her tongue so she couldn't lie to anyone ever again.

Morris Potterbaum came into the common room and sat down on the couch with a sigh. He picked up the television remote control. "You mind?" He motioned to the television.

Green glared at him.

"Look, don't worry about Waldbeeser. The guy is full of himself." He clicked on the television. "He thinks he's a poet."

Green wrote *Can I trust you?* on a Post-it Note and showed it to Morris.

Morris shrugged. "Sure, yeah."

Green shook the note for emphasis.

"You can trust me."

I need your help.

"This isn't about going to the bathroom or anything? There are nurses for that."

I think my wife is having an affair.

"Oh, that kind of help." Morris glanced over his shoulder to make sure no one else was around. "I think you should know something."

What?

"You have twenty bucks?"

What for?

"Give me twenty bucks. I think you'll want to hear this."

Green didn't have twenty bucks. He had a ten and four ones.

Morris counted the money. "This is fine. Look, I don't want to be the one to tell you this. Come a little closer. I don't want to talk too loud."

Chic Waldbeeser

■

July 28, 1998

"Listen to me," Chic said. "Listen. No, please, will you just listen."

On the other end of the phone, Russ was pleading with him. "Something could happen to you. Then what? What are you even doing this for?"

"Look, Russ. This is important to me. I need your help."

"I can't. Not today. I told you. I have to help Ginger with her pottery. She's kilning some coffee mugs."

"I just need you to pick up a couple boxes and bring them to me."

"No can do, man. Sorry. And I told you I don't think this is a good idea."

"You're really not going to help me?"

"Think about this. You're going to Florida with a woman you hardly even know."

"Look, when you get to be an old man and your wife dies and you've spent the last ten years of your life living in some assisted living place, you'll understand. Then you can give me your opinion. Until you've walked in my shoes . . ."

"What if this is a just a big scam and she's after your money or something. That happens, you know."

"What money? I don't have any money."

"You've only known her for—what—three weeks, four?"

"I gotta go. Thanks for your help." Chic hung up. Goddamn Russ. He stared at the phone. Russ was right. Chic didn't know this woman, and who knows, maybe she did this sort of thing all the time? Maybe he shouldn't be going. Wait a second . . . No. No. *No no no no no!* Goddamn Russ. Goddamn him. Why couldn't he just support him? What would be so wrong with saying, "*Hey man, great idea. I'm really for this. You need to do this. This is something you need to do. Let me help you do this.*" But, no, Russ had to plant some goddamn seed in his head.

Morris walked into the room. He was whistling. He went to his dresser, opened the top drawer, and took out his wallet and stuffed some money in it.

"You told Geneseo, didn't you?"

"I didn't say a thing—not a peep. Mum's the word. You paid me to keep my mouth shut. I kept my mouth shut." He stuck his wallet in his back pocket. "I'll be out for the day. Have a good afternoon." He pulled the door shut with a bang.

Chic could hear him walk away, jangling his keys. He got up and opened the door and peeked into the hallway. Morris was gone, but Green was wheeling toward his room. He screeched to a stop. The two men faced off. Green pointed to his eyes, then at Chic.

"Yeah, I'm watching you, too." Chic slammed the door. He stood there for a second listening as Green's wheelchair squeaked past. He had the urge to open the door and yell something at him, but he went back to his bed and took out his notebook. He had a knot in his stomach. He concentrated on the pain. He glanced down at his notebook and read the first line of the poem: *Around the corner is the end.* He felt kinda bad, actually, if he let himself think about it. Green was upset, and those shoes, those were his shoes. Chic glanced down at the loafers. Goddamn Russ. He had planted this seed, and now the thoughts were taking root. He wasn't going to let them. He needed to dig them out.

Mary & Green Geneseo

■

July 28, 1998

At a few minutes past five, Mary arrived at We Care and found Green in the common room, slumped over and sleeping. A Bugs Bunny cartoon was on the television. "Eh, what's up, doc?" The coffee table was littered with out-of-date issues of *Reader's Digest* and *Prevention*. Mary grabbed the remote and was about to click off the television and wake Green when she noticed how peaceful he seemed. She suddenly had the urge to touch his forearm and whisper a little bit of encouragement to him. How did we end up in each other's lives like this? How do we get to these places and why do we make these decisions to keep hurting each other like we hurt each other? You're a good person, the whisper voice said. Remember Christmas, 1970. It was your father's second marriage, or maybe his third. The woman had a daughter who was around seven. The little girl was having a hard time coping. You heard her crying one night. You stopped outside her door and listened. Her mother was in there, and was whispering, "It's going to be all right. This isn't like last time." You thought about your own mother doing the same thing to you—sitting in your bed, underneath the covers, combing her fingers through your hair while you cried. I'm sorry, Green. I really am. No, you're not, the loud voice said. She was, though. She was sorry. You're sorry, the whisper voice said. At least it's not you, the loud voice said. At least he's not watching you sleep and feeling sorry for you. Why couldn't these voices leave her alone? She just wanted to have a moment. Why couldn't she just have a moment? She reached out to touch Green's forehead to brush his hair back when he opened his eyes.

"Hi," she said. "Taking a nap?"

He reached violently to grab the remote from her. She handed it to him. Bugs Bunny said, "Of course you know this means war?" Green clicked off the television.

"I thought I'd take you to dinner." She hadn't noticed it before, but there were bags under his eyes.

He stared at her.

"Please don't be this way, Green. This is temporary. I told you. Please." She heard keys jingling in her memory. She was about to open the door. Lyle. She had to shake this out of her head. She couldn't break down now. Green would get over it. She'd gotten over it. Everyone eventually gets over it. You're a good person, the whisper voice said. Remember that little girl. You're being sentimental, the loud voice said. I'm just saying, the whisper voice said, it's not too late.

Chic Waldbeeser

■

July 28, 1998

Chic knew Mary and Green were in the cafeteria having their

"last supper," and she had been clear that she didn't want him there. But he was starving. The turkey sandwich with mayo at lunch just wasn't going the distance. Ten minutes ago, he had eaten a granola bar that Russ had given him. He hated granola bars. They reminded him of Buddy. Besides, they dried his mouth out, and they hurt his jaw—so much chewing. But, really, it was his brother.

It was 7:17 and the rendezvous time was set for nine. He had been in his room for the past two hours trying to resist looking at the clock, but he couldn't avoid sneaking a peek now and then, only to see that just a few minutes had elapsed. It was amazing how slowly time crawled when you were waiting for something. He tested the smell of his breath by breathing into his hand. Maybe he should brush his teeth. That would take some time. He went to the bathroom and got his toothbrush from the medicine cabinet. Russ popped into his mind. He was trying not to think about their phone call, but he was thinking about it, again. Maybe Russ was right. Maybe this was a bad idea. He didn't really know her, and what if she was after his money—not that he had any. But, still, maybe she was after something. Maybe this was just something she did. She'd been with Green only for a few months. He couldn't think this way. Why was he thinking this way? He needed to push these thoughts out of his mind. He looked at himself in the mirror. He spit into the sink. He rinsed his toothbrush. Russ was right—he hardly knew this woman. And what about Green? He had called him a spiff. He was stealing his wife. He'd never thought of himself as the other guy. Well, of course, his brother had spent a lifetime thinking he was the other guy, but now he was officially the other guy. He sat on the bed and glanced at the clock. 7:21. Jesus Christ. *Around the corner is the end.* Could he do this? Could he be the other guy? What did that even really mean—*other guy*? Okay, he knew what it meant, but what did it mean for him? When Lijy had asked him to help her, it had been . . . he'd never really thought about it like this, and besides it was Lijy and things were complicated. Not that he thought . . . okay, so he may have thought that Lijy maybe would have . . .

There was a knock on the door. Carol Bowen-Smith poked her head in. "Looks like you're all set to go." She looked at the suitcase at the end of the bed. "Now, where is it you're going again?"

"My nephew's."

Carol marked something on her clipboard.

"What time is he picking you up?"

"Nine."

"Well, have a good time. Tell your nephew hello." She closed the door behind her.

He looked at the clock. 7:22. He closed his eyes. Mary wasn't Lijy. She wasn't even Diane. What was Diane, actually? His wife, of course. His companion? The other person in the room? That sounded harsh. She was more than another person in the room. He used to wake up in the morning and feel her weight on the mattress, hear the whistle of her breath through her nose while she slept. He glanced at the clock again. Still 7:22. Outside, the sun was setting. He looked at Morris's bed; it was perfectly made, the comforter pulled taut. He wanted to rumple it up, pull the corners loose; he wanted to bury his head in Morris's pillow and scream. He wanted to be in bed next to Diane. He wanted to roll over behind her. That's all he wanted to do. Roll over behind her. What actually had happened, really? All of a sudden she was old, and he was old. They basically just sat on the couch and watched TV. Come to think about it, she was usually upstairs in the rocking chair or listening to Peale. He'd sit in the dark living room watching television by himself, and then it would occur to him that it was after midnight. He'd get into bed and she'd already be asleep. He never spooned up behind her. Or if he did, he didn't remember doing it. Or he didn't do it enough. Spoon up behind her and slide his arm around her. Fit his knees in the V of her knees. Close his eyes. Feel her. Listen to her breathing. And just be next to her. He should have done that more often. Why didn't he do that more often?

Mary Geneseo

■

July 28, 1998

Mary waited on Greenwood Street in the minivan. Greenwood Street—now that was ironic. You mean coincidence, the whisper voice said. Irony is when you say one thing but do another, the loud voice said. She knew what irony was. You just confused them, the whisper voice said. Okay, it was just a coincidence, but it was a weird coincidence. Did that make it ironic? No, the whisper voice said. But, by nature, coincidences are a little weird . . . She was not going to have this argument with herself. She knew what irony meant. The dashboard clock read 8:56. Four more minutes and Chic would be here. She had the window cracked. If she smoked, this would be the time to do it. She used to smoke, when she was with Lyle. They'd sit in the car, the windows down, the radio blaring, the ashtray mounded with mashed-out butts.

Headlights approached from behind. A Toyota Camry passed by, a soccer mom type behind the wheel. She wished she'd been a soccer mom, hauling her kids to practice, making dinner, stopping at their rooms on her way to bed to check on them. Her mother hadn't been a soccer mom, didn't have it in her. She hadn't had much of anything in her, actually, except for booze. And lies, which she called promises. Her mother always told her she was going to do better the next time. Why was she thinking about this right now? You always think about this when you get emotional, the whisper voice said. Don't think about this, the loud voice said. It's in the past. But it was true. Her mother was always going to do better the next time. After the divorce, they moved to

LA. "It's going to be better this time." Better? A one-room apartment, her mother unable to get out of bed some mornings she was so hung over. Why are you thinking this way, the loud voice asked. She's feeling sorry for herself, the whisper said. She's hurting someone. She doesn't like to hurt people. They'd had a terrible dinner. He might know. He doesn't know, the loud voice said. She thought about him waking up tomorrow morning and having to ask someone to help him into his wheelchair. How was he going to ask someone to help him? He can't goddamn talk, can't explain himself, can't share what's in his head, his thoughts, his ideas, his feelings, nothing. In his time of need, she was leaving him. She was ignoring his needs. He's ignoring your needs, the loud voice said. Don't forget about your needs, the loud voice said. He can't talk to you, and you can't talk to him. How is that a relationship? That's trying to communicate with someone who can only write Post-it Notes. That isn't a life. It's a life, the whisper voice said. It's not a good one, the loud voice said. It's not running on the beach and jumping into the surf, but it's a life. It's helping. Help yourself, the loud voice said. Chic needs help. You're helping him. He wants to go to Florida, and you're going with him. It probably isn't going to be running on the beach and jumping in the surf, but it is going to be better than washcloth baths and Post-it Notes. And besides, the loud voice said, he'll find someone to help him. A nurse will help him into his wheelchair. He's going to be fine. You were eventually fine. We are all eventually fine. The loud voice was right. She took a deep breath. A dog barked in the distance. She wasn't going to think about this anymore. She was doing what she needed to do. The dog kept barking, and she looked toward the sound, and there was Chic, carrying his suitcase, coming out of the darkness. He crossed the street, slid open the rear door, and stowed his suitcase in back, then climbed in the passenger seat.

"I was afraid you weren't going to be here," he said.

Mary started the minivan and put it in gear.

"I've got two stops before we get on the road. Take a right here at the stop sign."

She took a left instead.

"I said right."

"Sorry." Focus, the loud voice said. You need to focus.

Chic Waldbeeser & Mary Geneseo

■

The End, or maybe it's The Beginning

He'd said right, and she'd taken a left. He looked over at her. Every morning, in Florida, he'd be staring at her from across the table while she sipped her coffee, and he would he see this, this running away, in the dead of night, leaving her husband behind in a wheelchair. He was fooling himself. Nothing was going to change. He was who he was and that was who he was. For some reason, he started thinking about his brother. He'd made a life out of a lie, though he didn't know it was a lie. The one truth he did know was that Lijy had cheated on him. And that beat him over the head. He sold his house. He stopped collecting coins. He pulled him out a window. Then, somehow—*somehow*—he accepted it. He forgave her. And him. Somehow. His brother had forgiven him. Them. That was really something. He felt a little tingly. A rush of something moved through him. Tears sprang to his eyes.

"Stop," he whispered. They were headed farther into the cornfields, the minivan's headlights illuminating the two-lane road ahead.

"Stop," he said, more forcefully this time.

"Did you say something?"

"Turn around."

"Tell me you didn't forget something. We can't go back. I'm not going back."

"Pull over."

"But, we're going. I thought . . ."

"Stop!"

They came to a sudden stop in the middle of the road. Chic couldn't look at Mary, so he looked out the window over the cornfield, toward the lights of Middleville.

"This is a mistake," he said.

She didn't say anything.

He made himself look at her. "I can't do this."

She hadn't seen this coming. You should have seen this coming, the loud voice said. This is for the better, the whisper voice said. For the better? Are you kidding, the loud voice said. This is a goddamn dead end. What was she going to do now? She's going to keep going forward, the whisper voice said. But she liked Chic, the loud voice said. No way, the whisper voice said. She liked the idea of him. He was her excuse. This wasn't the end. Chic Waldbeeser was not the end. You were going to have the same thoughts about him that you had about Green. But she hoped, the loud voice said. You had hope. You have hope. You've never stopped hoping. Remember Green. The diner. You were playing footsie with him. That footsie was hope. Or Chic, that afternoon you slid onto his lap. Hope motivated that, too. And desperation, the whisper voice said. But where there's desperation, there's hope, the loud voice said. Dig deep enough and you'll find it. It's not going to get any better, the whisper voice said. You will always be the person trying to do better, but you'll never be able to do better. That scared the hell out of her. *It's not going to get any better.* She didn't want to think about that.

"Are you breaking up with me, Chic?"

"Oh geez. No. Don't say it like that. It sounds so . . . don't say it like that."

"It's okay," she said. "Really. It's fine. I'm not upset."

"Well, you don't have to be . . . I mean, you could be a little sad about it."

"This isn't coming out right. I'm sorry."

"I mean, you did kinda like me, right?"

"For a moment. I always do. There's always so much promise at first."

Chic reached out and put his hand on her leg. She put her hand on top of his.

"Can you give me a ride back?"

"Can you walk? It's only . . ." she looked over her shoulder, "maybe a mile, probably less. If I go back, then . . . I don't know what will happen. I'm already on my way. I've come this far."

He understood. She couldn't go back there. If she did, then she'd probably . . . she'd come this far, like she said.

He opened the door and stepped out of the minivan. He didn't know what to say. What did you say in moments like this? "I don't really know what to say," he said.

She smiled.

"Remember me."

"I will," she said. "Of course I will."

Chic Waldbeeser

Chic woke up, and Morris was sitting on the edge of his bed, his hand underneath the covers pinching Chic's leg.

"What are you doing? What time is it?" Chic found the clock on the nightstand: 5:00 a.m.

"I need twenty bucks."

Chic put his pillow over his head. "I'm not giving you any more money."

"In that case, don't get mad at me if the new guy finds out."

"I don't care if he finds out," Chic said from under the pillow.

"Look, I'm just trying to help the new guy. Can you give me twenty bucks or what?"

Chic removed the pillow. "What are you doing with the

new guy?"

Behind Morris, in the dull light of the hallway, he could see Green sitting there in his chair. When he saw Chic looking at him, he turned the wheelchair around so that his back was to him.

"There's twenty bucks in my wallet on the dresser."

"Thanks, Waldbeeser. You know, you're not such a bad guy after all. Hey, aren't you supposed to be . . ." Morris made a face, not wanting to finish the rest of his sentence.

"It didn't work out."

"Then, should I?" He motioned to Green in the hallway.

"You should go through with whatever you're doing."

"I got him a 7:00 a.m. flight to Vegas."

"Well, you better get going."

"All right, then. Thanks for the money."

Morris pulled the door quietly shut behind him.

The room was dark. Chic heard the squeak of Green's wheelchair, and then the whole place was quiet. He rolled over and closed his eyes. He thought about Mary out on the road, probably somewhere in Iowa, the dawn sky beginning to open up on the horizon behind her. His thoughts skipped to Lijy, that time in her kitchen, how he had tried to seduce her. He wished he could take that back. He thought about his wedding, Diane on the dance floor kicking her legs out wildly while a guy played an accordion. She looked so happy. Lomax. Poor Lomax. He'd be forty-eight now. Balding, with crow's feet around his eyes. Probably fluent in German. Maybe he'd be a high school German teacher. Maybe he'd be an architect. A poet. Something. He'd be something. His brother. Maybe people could change. Maybe that's what he had been missing all this time. Why hadn't he seen it? He had changed. Everything had changed. Everything. He hadn't let himself see everything changing. But it had

When Chic woke up a few hours later, the sunlight

streaked into the room. The cafeteria was closed, so he had to settle for a package of peanuts and an orange Gatorade from the vending machine in the hallway. Most of the residents were in their rooms taking their mid-morning naps.

Carol Bowen-Smith came out of the pool area in a hurry. She consulted her clipboard. She looked puzzled.

"I thought you were going to be somewhere."

"My nephew's."

"So, what are you doing here?"

"A change of heart."

She marked something on the clipboard. "Have you seen Mr. Geneseo? He's unaccounted for. And your roommate, too, Mr. Potterbaum."

Chic shook his head no. "Haven't seen either one of them. Morris's bed is made though. If that's any help."

"He's probably at the Pair-a-Dice. It's Mr. Geneseo I'm more worried about. Just vanished. Didn't even come to breakfast this morning."

Chic shrugged.

"If you see him, tell him his wife called."

"His wife?"

"About an hour ago. Left a message. Kinda cryptic. Said, 'It's not playing in Peoria.' I don't know. Maybe they were going to go to a movie."

He watched her walk down the hall. "I have poetry inside of me," he called after her. He didn't know why he had said it. Maybe he wanted to believe it. Actually, he did believe it, and he wanted someone else to believe it, too.

Carol stopped. She turned around slowly. "We all do, Mr. Waldbeeser. The trick is letting it out." She turned back around and pushed through the double doors into the cafeteria.

He stood in the hallway. The door next to him was ajar, and he could see a fully dressed man in slacks and a flannel shirt lying on top of his bedspread, his hands folded across his stomach. Down the hall, Janice Galbreath and her yo-yo string of saliva were nodding out in the common room. Around the corner is the end. Look out where you're going. As I said to my friend.

The trick is letting it out.

Acknowledgments

This book wouldn't be the book it ended up being if it wasn't for many people who pushed me to be a better writer and a better person, so I want to thank them all, starting with my editors Elizabeth Clementson and Robert Lasner. Thanks also goes out to my teachers along the way—both at Columbia and Iowa—Binnie Kirshenbaum, Ben Marcus, Alan Ziegler, Sam Lipsyte, Ellen Hildebrand, Amber Dermont, and Julie Orringer. Then, there are my friends, Eric Maxson, Ryan Effgen, Dave Reidy, Mike Harvkey, Johanna Lane, Mikey George, Nazgol Shifteh, Stephen Johnson, Farooq Ahmed, John O'Conner, Christopher Swetala, Claire Gutierrez, Alex Cussen, Mark Gindi, Jessica Roake, Dinaw Mengestu, E. Tyler Lindvall, Manuel Gonzales, Jonathan Blum, Josh Weil, Nic Brown, Cara Cannella, Bobby and Cara Finnegan, Mike Messier, and Brad Causey, who, even after I shoved my writing on them, still remained my friends. Of course, thank you to my mom and dad, and to my sister, Rachel. When I told you I wanted to be a writer, you began treating me like I already was one. Lastly, Rene—a long time ago, I sat across from you in a fiction workshop, and that has made all the difference.